Anna's Secret

Where failure, love, and romance collide

To my dear niece Larissa,
Thanks for being one of the first to support my writing — it means a lot. Hope you enjoy!
Love & Hugs
Auntie Blossom

Endorsements

From the very first sentence, I connected to Blossom Turner's book, *Anna's Secret*. When the single tear snaked its way down Anna's cheek, a tear ran down mine as well. I knew how she felt. I've been there. But whether readers personally identify, or they just fall into the story, they are sure to find *Anna's Secret* riveting, heart-wrenching, and too compelling to set aside.

—**Kay Marshall Strom**, author of the *Blessings in India* and *Grace in Africa* series as well as *Forgotten Girls.*

Blossom Turner takes us on a journey of true-to-life choices, the consequences of sin, and the redemption God offers. *Anna's Secret* is packed with raw emotion as we travel the twists and turns that ripple from one poor choice. Best of all, we see God's grace and feel compelled to respond to people in our lives with that same grace.

—**Shelley Pierce**, author of the *Crumberry Chronicles* and *Sweet Moments: Insight and Encouragement for the Pastor's Wife.*

Blossom Turner's book, *Anna's Secret*, is all about unconditional love, reconciliation and forgiveness. The characters are forced to deal with hurts from their past and failures marring the present, before realizing God's truth about themselves and their future. The author addresses tough questions prevalent in today's society without skirting the real issues. The book is a winner.

—**Claudette Renalds**, author of *By the Sea*

Anna's Secret

Where failure, love, and romance collide

Blossom Turner

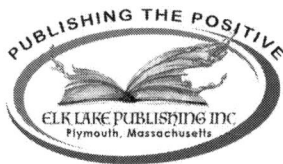

PUBLISHING THE POSITIVE

ELK LAKE PUBLISHING INC
Plymouth, Massachusetts

Cover and Interior Design: Derinda Babcock

Editor(s): Cristel Phelps

Author Represented by WordServe Media Services

PUBLISHED BY: Elk Lake Publishing, Inc., 35 Dogwood Dr., Plymouth, MA 02360, 2019

Library Cataloging Data

Names: Turner, Blossom (Blossom Turner

Anna's Secret / Blossom Turner

310 p. 23cm × 15cm (9in × 6 in.)

Description: Anna's husband has been ill a long time. When he dies, she is devastated, yet relieved. Matt, the doctor who cared for Steven, comes to call because he also cares for Anna, and a consoling hug turns into something more.

Identifiers: ISBN-13: 978-1-950051-33-5 (trade) | 978-1-950051-34-2 (POD) | 978-1-950051-35-9 (e-book.)

Key Words: Romance, forgiveness, grief, human failure, love, inspirational, grace

LCCN: 2019936898 Fiction

Dedication

For my dear husband, David, who has lovingly supported and encouraged my writing. God has blessed our love story through crushing storms and brought inspiration for this book out of the crucible of suffering and the power of forgiveness. Love and forgiveness—no friendship or relationship is possible unless these two principles walk hand in hand. I walk into forever with you—my best friend.

Acknowledgments

I'm thankful God brought my good friend and critique partner, Jennifer Sienes, into my life. Her willingness to help, to tighten, to give honest feedback of my writing has been invaluable. Thank you, Jennifer.

And to my beta readers whose input I could not have done without— Jan Hooper, Karen Moderow, Tisha Martin, Holly Varni, Kathryn Hughes, my sister Melody Thomson, mother-in-law Stephanie Turner, and mentor Ginny Yttrup. Thank you from my heart.

And last, but not least, to my forever friend, Suzie Zanewich, who prayed, pestered, and pushed me into a writing career. You know how much I love and appreciate you dear friend. Thank you.

Chapter One

Anna gazed down at her sleeping husband—the man she had once called lover, friend, soul mate. Somewhere along the way they had become no more than nurse and patient. Steven's sickness and remission had beaten a well-worn path to her door. Despite prayers for healing, this final diagnosis crushed all hope.

A single tear snaked its way down Anna's cheek. She brushed it off with a violent sweep of her hand, so tired of the pain.

Wake up, Steven. A deep desire to set things right before time ran out sent a shudder up her spine.

"Steven." She nudged him gently.

His eyes flickered open. He stared up at her with a drug-induced blankness.

"I need to talk to you."

He turned his head away and closed his eyes.

Anna understood. His response was nothing new.

She straightened his blanket and gently touched his upper forehead where dark thick hair used to spring beneath her fingertips. The smoothness brought back his words after he realized his hair would only grow back in scraggily patches.

"I got the nurse to shave it off."

"It looks good, Steven."

"Yeah, as good as a bowling ball after it hits the gutter. Worthless."

"Come on, Steven, we need to remain—"

"Don't give me your 'let's stay positive' speech. You're not the one lying in this bed completely useless. I wish you'd go, Anna."

"Steven—"

"No seriously. Find someone worthy. I'm nothing but a shell of the man you married, and this blasted disease doesn't let me live or die. I just hang here in limbo."

"Code yellow to unit ten. Code yellow."

Anna was grateful the intercom interrupted her thought patterns and brought her back to the present. She released one white-knuckled hand from her clutch on his blanket and smoothed out the twisted knot. She shook her head as if to dislodge that painful conversation from her mind.

Some memories are better left buried.

Dr. Matthew Carmichael had been notified by hospital staff that his morning run should include a look into Steven's room. They felt he was failing fast. One look at Steven confirmed their assessment.

He motioned the nurse over.

"This family needs our full attention until—"

She nodded. "I just started my shift and I'll stay nearby."

"Steven," he bent closer. "We're going to keep you as comfortable as possible."

Steven's eyes flickered open as Matt squeezed his hand and smoothed his brow.

Matt straightened and motioned Anna over to the far corner of the room. Every year he practiced medicine he assumed it would get easier, but at thirty-five he was granted no more wisdom, or strength, than the year previously.

He spoke the words that were always difficult to say to family members but especially hard to say to Anna, who had become a dear friend. "It won't be long now."

Anna collapsed against him. He steadied her and gave her shoulders a quick squeeze. When she looked up at him, her dark eyes brimmed with tears and a lump formed in his throat. He had to get away. The pit of his stomach tightened. He hurt because she hurt.

"You should phone your family."

"Yes. I will."

He held her a moment longer before signaling the nurse with a tilt of his head. She gently guided Anna to the nearest chair.

Anna had no idea what that simple condolence cost him as he battled a squall of emotion he knew he had no right to feel. He was free, but she certainly wasn't and wouldn't be for a long time to come. He was no fool. Grief needed time.

"Would you like me to phone your sister?"

Her large, soulful eyes shot upward. Anna's voice broke. "That would be wonderful, thank you. Please ask her to call the boys and the rest of the family."

"No problem, Anna. I'll handle it."

Matt's offer did not fall into his regular doctor/patient responsibilities, but Steven's illness had been a long, rocky road, and Matt had become a fixture in their family. Through it all, Anna had rarely complained. She had a beauty inside and out that intrigued him. The way she loved her husband unconditionally, despite his difficult tirades, showed a quiet strength that drew him.

He turned to leave.

"Matthew …"

His heart kicked against the walls of his chest. Was she aware she'd used his first name? Hearing his name touched something deep within him. He took a deep breath, squared his shoulders, and turned back toward her.

"Yes?"

"Thank you. You're a good friend."

Unable to speak, he nodded.

She smiled, and he read only innocence in her expression. Clearly, she had no idea the emotions she evoked in him.

Is it only friendship you desire?

A dart of guilt pierced him. He left the room before giving her the chance to read any emotion on his face.

Chapter Two

From the sanctuary of her bedroom, with her sister in charge of the growing crowd, Anna whispered a prayer for strength. "Oh, Lord, help me get through this." Even at her best, entering a room full of people was difficult. With one more glance in the mirror to make sure her riotous curls were snuggly fastened in a tight bun at the nape of her neck, she smoothed her hands over her skirt. The dull gray suited her mood. She opened the door, took a deep breath, and walked down the hall.

Her living room and kitchen teemed with all the people she knew and loved. One would think the funeral was hers, not Steven's. In the last few years, his reclusive ways and severe illness had thinned out his friends—all but a persistent few. She gazed over the group as they made eye contact. Support and pity jockeyed for position.

Small groups of people huddled in circles with plates of delicate finger sandwiches, fruit, and sweets piled high. Her stomach lurched at the thought of food, and she fought the urge to run for the bathroom.

Betty and George, Steven's parents, signaled her over to their corner of the room. Anna scanned the area to check if her sons, Mark and Jason, were okay before she joined them.

Only Betty could pull off a black pantsuit with such flare. She had obviously had a say in what George was wearing, because not a stitch was out of place, right down to the folded triangle handkerchief in his breast pocket. His new designer suit carefully hid his portly frame.

"Oh, Anna." Betty engulfed her in a warm hug. Her arms gave a tight squeeze before she pulled back and cradled Anna's face in her hands. Her bracelets jangled close to Anna's ear. "I'm sure you know this, but sometimes words need to be spoken. You're our daughter, with or without our son in the picture, and we love you."

Anna drew a weak smile. "I don't know how I would've done it without your love and support all these years."

"And nothing will change," George pitched in. "Until you find a job and get financially stable, we're going to continue to help out with the expenses."

Anna's gaze lowered and she shook her head. "I appreciate your offer, but I need to work this out somehow." She could tell from the pity in their eyes they had the same question she did. Where would a thirty-nine-year old widow who'd never been more than a housewife and mother find work that paid enough to survive?

"We're here for you," Betty insisted. "Do you remember the promise we made before you and Steven were engaged?"

Anna nodded. "—to fill the gap for the parents I lost."

"Yes. And George and I are not relinquishing that claim now."

Anna's eyes glistened with tears as she hugged them close. "I love you both so much."

"How are Mark and Jason? We were so glad they made it home from University in time to say goodbye to their father."

Anna gulped back a sob with a hand to her mouth.

"Oh, my dear, your grief must be unbearable," Betty said, as she pulled her into another hug.

A sliver of guilt jabbed in. Anna cried for her boys and the loss of their dad, but her relationship with Steven had been an emotional roller coaster for years. Why was relief at being off that ride a stronger pull than grief?

Pastor Harry and his wife, Eleanor, dressed appropriately in traditional black, stood on the periphery—waiting. Anna motioned them over as George and Betty moved aside.

"My dear, such a long, hard road." Eleanor said, shaking her head. Her voice caught in her throat.

"Anna, we've walked alongside you for years. And we're not about to stop now," Pastor Harry said. "You have to let us know how we can help— finances, yard clean up, your vehicle, whatever." His kind eyes sparkled with a sheen of unshed tears as he patted her arm.

Eleanor moved in for a long hug. She drew Anna into the folds of her chubby arms and squeezed so tight her glasses twisted to one side.

Over her shoulder, Anna noticed her eldest son Mark jerk his head to one side to get her attention. They had argued earlier about his choice of a bright lime golf shirt, so he had changed into a burnt orange one, not caring to bend to the social etiquette of traditional black. Anna had decided to say no more.

She pulled free of Eleanor's hug and waved him closer.

Anna noticed how he stiffened when both the pastor and his wife hugged him. At least, Mark nodded politely at their words of condolence. His hiked shoulders didn't relax until they moved on.

He lowered his voice so only she could hear. "Hey, Mom, is it okay if Jason and I leave now? This whole wake thing or celebration of life or whatever it's called, has me wigged out. I can't take another stranger hugging me."

Anna nodded. "I know it's uncomfortable, Mark, but it's a way for people to show they care."

He brushed off her comment with a shrug of his shoulders and rolled his eyes.

Everything about Mark—his tall frame, striking looks, and antics— reminded her of a young Steven, strong and capable, when life had seemed unshakable. A stab of pain spiked through her.

"You two go," she said. "My friends and Aunt Lana will help clean up, and they'll stay as long as I need company. Between the two of us," she said, squeezing him in a hug, "that was about two hours ago."

He exhaled with a deep sigh and whispered. "Glad I'm not the only one to feel this way. Most people don't understand," his voice cracked. "Dad's been gone a long time." He lifted his arm to quickly swipe away the tears with his shirtsleeve.

Anna couldn't believe her ears. Her son Jason was the one who readily expressed his feelings, but Mark so rarely did. His unusual moment of honesty brought tears to her eyes and she hugged him tight. "I'm so sorry Mark. You missed out on having a healthy dad, but I know how much he loved you."

His mask slipped back in place as he stepped back. "I'll live. Always have. Always will." He waved to Jason above the din and made a beeline for the door.

A steady stream of well wishes and awkward conversations continued until little by little, the crowd thinned and only a few helping hands remained. To her surprise, Dr. Carmichael was one of them.

"Where do you want all these folding chairs and extra tables?"

"You don't have to do this, Dr. Carmichael. My sons will look after that. They said they'd return them to the church tomorrow."

"I'm not your doctor, Anna. I'm your friend. Call me Matt. Okay?"

7

He didn't wait for a reply but grabbed a table, heaved it on its side and folded in the legs with a snap.

"I'll break down the tables and stack the chairs so you have room to move before I go. How about I take them to the porch?"

She forced a weak smile. "Thanks so much, Dr ... I mean, Matt."

His eyes lit up, and a grin split free. "That's better."

⁕

Matt was almost done with his morning rounds. He shut down the file on the computer. A sunset screensaver popped up with unmistakable cheer as he rolled the wheeled stand out of his patient's room. Pushed up against the wall, he kicked the brake lever on with his foot and slipped his stethoscope around his neck.

One look at his watch and he knew exactly where to head for his lunch hour. He waved at the pod of nurses and laughed at the way they sang out as if on cue, "Come again soon, Dr. Carmichael."

He turned and smiled, flashing his dimple in cheery response. "Oh, you can count on that."

Giggles and laughter followed. One said, "My, it's hot in here, and girl, I'm not talking about my hot flashes, either."

He caught himself humming a tune as he entered the elevator. *Why am I so happy these days?* Unwilling to unpack that question, he punched the button with a tad too much exuberance as the fourth and fifth button lit up simultaneously.

He smiled as the door opened one floor too soon. He stayed put and waited for the elevator to shut and open yet again. The cheery walls of painted flowers and gregarious animals welcomed him as he stepped out into the children's ward. With a beeline straight for room 4004, he succeeded in bypassing all interruptions.

"How's my favorite girl?"

Isabella gave him a lopsided grin and held out two arms for the taking. Matt moved in for the best part of his day. He never knew a child could tug at a person's heart the way Isabella did.

He lifted her frail body into a hug and could feel her tiny arms close around his neck as her head relaxed onto his shoulder.

"Do you think your mama will let me take you to see your good friend Joey at the end of the hall? He was asking about you."

The child lifted her head long enough to plead. "Please, mama."

"Of course, honey." She shifted her gaze to Matt. "But are you sure you have time in your busy schedule?"

Matt nodded. "Go get yourself something to eat, Nancy. I have an hour, and you need a break."

She turned to leave, then spun around.

"Dr. Carmichael …" She shifted from one foot to the other. "I don't know how to thank you. Without Isabella's dad in the picture, it's been a gift for her to have a father figure who cares."

He cupped the back of Isabella's smooth head in his hand where her natural blonde curls used to bounce freely.

"The pleasure's all mine, Nancy. If only her father knew what he was missing," Matt shook his head.

"Yeah, if only he knew." A wistful tone filled Nancy's voice.

Four days later, Anna hugged both her sons goodbye.

"Drive carefully," she reminded them for the umpteenth time. "And let me know when you get to Victoria safe and sound."

"Yes, Mom. We always do." They waved off her concern and jumped into the vehicle.

She closed the front door only after they drove out of sight, despite the chill in the air. The clouds fit her mood. Dark. Gloomy. Low.

"What now?" Her words echoed down the empty hall. Silence hemmed in around her, restrictive and depressing. She pulled the band from her hair and kneaded her scalp aching from the weighty ponytail. Determined to put on a good front for the kids so they would return to University without worrying, she had forced herself to rise each day, do her hair and makeup, and make a healthy breakfast. Glad the façade was over, she sank into the nearby couch and curled into the fetal position. She prayed she would fall asleep and never wake up.

A solid rap on the front door caused her to spring to her feet. She flipped the hair out of her eyes and smoothed a hand over the riotous mess before swinging the door open. A blast of winter air whipped in, but Anna froze.

"Dr. Carmichael. I mean Matt," she corrected. "What—?"

"I think I left my gloves here the other day."

"Come in. It's freezing out there." She closed the door behind him.

Matt rubbed his hands together. "Old man winter is grumpy today, and my hands feel like ice."

Anna's hands flew to her hair where she tried to smooth the waves that sprang free.

"I've never seen your hair down."

"I don't … well, it just isn't practical." She moved toward the couch, looking up and down for the band she had so carelessly discarded. Unable to find it, she smoothed her hands over the curls.

"I'm sorry, didn't mean to make you uncomfortable. I meant it as a compliment … you have beautiful hair."

A flush of heat worked its way from her neck to her hairline. It had been years since she'd heard a compliment, and she had no idea how to respond. "Um … your gloves. No, I don't think I found any."

"Hmmm, I must've left them elsewhere. But since I'm here, how about a coffee? I'll even make it." He didn't wait for an answer but walked to the kitchen and went straight to her coffee cupboard.

"How in the world do you know where I keep my coffee?" One brow arched skyward.

"Your sister gave me the task of making coffee the other day, and I don't forget much. You'd be surprised at the random paraphernalia that clutters my brain."

"Well, then, where are your gloves?"

He smiled broadly. "Okay, you got me. I had to make some excuse to drop by and check on you."

"Seriously?" With her hands on her hips, she gave a stern look before breaking into a smile.

"Forgive my white lie, but I was worried about you. It's what *friends* do." He scooped coffee into the maker, poured in the water, and pushed the button. Crossing the kitchen, he plopped down onto the stool.

He gestured at the seat opposite him. "Come, have coffee with me, and I'll be on my way. I promise not to be a bother."

"You're one bossy friend, Matthew Carmichael," she said as she slid onto the barstool.

"Well, at least I'm in the friend category." A twinkle sparkled in his eyes. "Things are looking up."

"Big surprise. I saw you more often than any of my other friends this past year."

"I know." His voice gentled as he shook his head, "Tough year … well, years actually."

Unable to go down the cancer road, she immediately changed the subject. "My boys headed back to University a few hours ago.

"UBC or UVIC"

"UVIC. It'll be a long day. They're hoping to catch the six o'clock ferry over to the Island. I hate them traveling over that highway this time of year. The weather can be so iffy."

"They'll be fine. They have each other." A reassuring smile spread across his face. "What year are they in?"

Does he worry about everyone like this …?

"Anna?"

She looked up, not sure what his last question had been. Her mind had definitely been elsewhere.

"Sorry. My concentration is gone these days."

Matt gave her a sympathetic smile. "What year are your sons in?"

"Mark's in his third year of Business, and Jason's in his first year. He wants to be a teacher."

"Oh, that's a great—"

"Why are you worried about me, Matt?" She interrupted, unable to manage small talk. "Are you always so concerned about your patients and their families?"

He placed an elbow on the granite island and rested his chin in his hand. Pressing a thumb to his lips, he was slow to answer. "Only those I consider close friends." He lifted his head and looked squarely into her eyes. A smile caused the dimple on his right cheek to sprout.

My, he's handsome. Why have I never noticed that dimple before? That strong jaw, and those eyes that smolder like blue flames … I'm staring like a schoolgirl with a crush. She rose, thankful for the diversion of gathering mugs, cream, and sugar.

Warmth knotted in her stomach as she caught his stare. His intense look drew her gaze, and a few unguarded seconds filled the silence. Something undefined simmered between them.

With effort, she turned back to the coffee. A slight tremor in her hand rattled the pot against the lip of the mug as she poured. She inhaled and slowly let the air flow free in effort to still the uptick of her heart. "Ahhh,

I do love that smell. Don't you?" Glad the roasted beans made for easy conversation, she averted his stare.

"Me too. It's that kick for many a long day."

Like the tendrils of steam lazily wafting into oblivion, she allowed the awkward moment to dissipate. Steven came to mind, and sadness permeated her again.

"Do you take cream and sugar?" Her voice dropped a notch as heaviness settled on her heart.

"Nope, straight up."

When she headed his way with two mugs, his expression held only warmth and friendship. Her stiff shoulders relaxed as she eased back onto the stool. A comfortable silence filled the room as she clutched the brew with both hands and lifted the cup to her lips. The rich, full-bodied taste did not disappoint.

"Anna, how are you really?" His voice grew soft and gentle.

She set her mug down with a thud. A splash of hot liquid landed on her hand, but she barely noticed.

"I hate that question, Matt. It's everyone's go-to question these days. How am I supposed to answer that?"

"Give me the truth."

Anna lifted her gaze. His eyes radiated genuine care. The door of her heart creaked open.

Matt wouldn't let go. "You must miss him a lot?"

She looked away, ashamed of the truth.

"Honestly, Matt … I hurt for so many years before his death. Now when it's time to receive sympathy as a grieving widow, I feel like a fraud."

He reached across the island and touched her hand, then immediately pulled back. "How so?"

"It's so hard to explain. As much as we loved each other, that illness drove a wedge between us. We became everything but husband and wife. Sadly, even our friendship waned as he slept hours and seemed far more content with the company of the television than me."

Matt nodded. "I've heard this happens. It doesn't mean you loved him less; it just means you loved differently. Long term care alters relationships."

She let out a sigh. "I grieve more for what should've been, than what I lost … that grief was done years ago. I feel guilty just thinking about it."

"Anna, you and Steven were one of the most loving examples I've ever witnessed, and over such an incredible long haul."

"But you don't know what I did to survive. The choice to feel nothing was safer than the perpetual emotional upheaval. I put up walls … I fulfilled my duty … I loved but from a safe distance. In the end, we were almost strangers." Her voice faded to a whisper. The heat of a blush worked its way from her throat to her hairline. *Why did I speak so freely?*

Matt remained quiet for a moment, then rose slowly. "As your friend, may I recommend a colleague of mine who comes highly recommended?" He reached in his pocket, pulled out a card and slid it across the counter. "It's one of the reasons I stopped by. I thought maybe you'd need someone to talk to. She is offering her services at no charge for as long as you need."

"What?" She stared at the card. "Why free?"

"Her sister was really sick, and I—it doesn't matter. We're friends, and all you need to know is that her name is Susan Jenkins and she's at the top of her profession. Grief counseling is her specialty."

Anna couldn't believe his kindness.

"I'll go now. But promise me you'll see Susan?" He slipped on his coat. "Promise."

She nodded.

"Oh, and I'll leave my cell number." He walked back to the counter, pulled a pen from his shirt pocket, and slipped the card from her fingers. In a bold scrawl, he penned out his name and number. "Just in case you need a friend. And I mean that." He held her gaze.

Anna could feel a palpable intensity. She glanced away to ease the sensation his piercing blue eyes created in the pit of her stomach. One look at the card and a smile broke through. "I see you live up to a doctor's standard. Your handwriting is atrocious."

He smiled, stamping that beautiful dimple back into place. "Yep and proud of it!" He sauntered to the door and closed it behind him.

Why am I noticing details … things I've never seen before … like the breadth of his wide shoulders? The sound of his rich baritone laughter … something this old house has not heard in a long time.

Anna walked to the window within the safety of the shadows, and watched him drive away. There was a part of her that was sad to see him go. She enjoyed his visit, maybe a little too much. The sound of his rich baritone voice echoed in her ears.

Thoughts of Steven pushed in, and guilt surged. *I shouldn't be thinking of Matt that way, I just buried my husband, for heaven's sake.*

———

Matt needed a wheel chair on the fifth floor and never waited for an orderly to do what he could do himself. He grabbed the extra one on floor two and made his way down the hall to the elevators. He felt the vibration of his phone yet again and slipped his hand into his pocket to pull it free. With a glance down, he almost ran into a colleague.

"Hey, Carmichael … no texting while you drive."

Matt looked up and laughed. "Sorry, buddy."

"You can buy me a cold one after work as an apology." They laughed in passing.

Not at all surprised to see yet another message from Tamara, he regretted the day he gave her his private number.

Why won't she take no for an answer? And when will my obvious lack of interest get through? Try as he might, he could never go back to the way things had been with her. It took no more than a fleeting thought of Anna to reinforce the difference of what had been to what he now longed for.

He hit the elevator button with a bang of his fist as an all too familiar hunger cut through.

Idiot. What kind of fool offers friendship when …? He refused to let his mind formulate words.

Anna's too fragile. She needs time to grieve and I need to stay away.

Besides, I've spent my life away from the entanglement of emotion. My parents cured me of that.

All his self-talk did little to convince his heart. An ache settled in.

Chapter Three

Anna flipped through a stack of funeral bills and slammed them down on the counter. They scattered and some fell to the floor. *How am I going to pay for these? I'm going to have to endure the embarrassment of asking Steven's parents yet again.* She sighed, stooped over and picked up the mail. She knew she should be thankful for their generosity but at the same time struggled with disappointment. Could thankfulness and anger toward God coexist?

Anna plunked herself down at the computer determined to draft up a résumé, but what did she have to offer? She snapped her laptop closed once again and stared off into space.

The only good thing she had accomplished in the past month was to visit the therapist Matt had suggested.

The thought of him brought a peculiar disappointment, one she dared not dissect. She slid the card with his phone number across the counter and picked it up yet again. She had not given into the urge to call, but his absence in the past weeks had unsettled her.

What a fool to buy into the notion of friendship. He has better things to do and was only being kind.

Anna tried to pray, determined to put the good-looking doctor and her worries to rest, but she felt like her words bounced off the ceiling right back to her. Giant tears rolled down her cheeks yet again.

The doorbell broke through her abysmal gloom. She brushed the wet from her cheeks and forced herself off the stool. If it was another casserole from the church ladies, she didn't know if she'd have the strength to nod her way through their platitudes and hear yet another, "God knows best," or "it's so good Steven's suffering is over."

What about her suffering? Macaroni and cheese casseroles did nothing to address that.

Or worse yet, it could be her twin sister, Lana. It was getting harder and harder to listen to her preach about the need to eat properly and return to the world instead of live in isolation. What did Lana and her charmed life know about misery anyway? How could she possibly relate with her high-paying job, perfect husband, and awesome kids?

Anna pasted on a cardboard smile and opened the door. "Matt! Oh, I'm so glad it's you. As nice as it is to have people care, I can only eat so many casseroles. I dreaded having to feign thankfulness for yet another one." She attempted a chuckle, but it fell flat.

"Can I come in?"

She waved him in. "Sorry, I've forgotten my manners. I've been less than hospitable lately."

"Your sister called me and is concerned about you." A frown puckered his brow. "You don't look like you've eaten any of those casseroles. Have you lost more weight?"

Anna bit at her lower lip. "It's all the jogging. Your friend, Dr. Jenkins, told me that people do more of what they always did to combat stress. For me, it's always been running. So, I run."

As he opened his mouth to speak, she cut him short. "And I don't need another lecture on exercising too much. Lana has already given me that one, just yesterday in fact." Both hands flew into the air. "And she has no right calling you, either.

"Besides, Dr. Jenkins assured me that I'd work my way through this phase and suggested I eat more … trouble is, I have no appetite." Her sentences ran together in rapid succession as she tried to make light of the situation. "Most of the ladies at church tell me they'd love to have my energy and not have to work off extra pounds. They call me the 'Energizer Bunny.'" Her forced laugh sounded phony even to her ears.

He didn't laugh, or even smile. Instead, concern deepened the furrows on his forehead.

"Have you had supper?"

"No, but I went for a run."

"Anna, your health is not something to joke about."

She turned from his intense stare.

"What does it matter? You don't have time to worry about every widow that comes your way." Embarrassed that her thoughts of the past month tumbled out, she turned and headed for the kitchen. She felt a headache press in. Her fingers massaged both temples.

She needed a diversion. "Would you like some coffee?"

"Anna, I've been a part of your family's life for years now." He put his hand on her shoulder and gently turned her back to face him. "That's why your sister thought to call me. She's worried about you."

"And you're right. I don't have the time I would like to spend with everyone. I wish I did. But with you … it's different. Right from the beginning, both you and Steven became more. His tone gentled. "I … I care. It's why I'm here."

His kind words drew her gaze from the floor. Genuine compassion flowed from his startling blue eyes.

He warmed her with a smile, which set the dimple on his cheek in place and accented his all too handsome features. Anna took in every detail. The strength of his six-foot-plus frame, the chisel of his well-defined facial features, the way his wide shoulders tapered—to perfection. Awareness coursed through the look that passed between them far outside the boundaries of friendship.

He touched her arm tenderly. Heat seared through straight to the bone. A current of raw emotion she hadn't felt in a very long time rippled up her spine. Her breath caught, and she forgot to breathe.

Their eyes locked. Unable to face the intensity, she blinked and stepped back. The dishcloth seized her focus as she wiped at an imaginary stain on the unused counter.

"Dr. Carmichael—" she sputtered, not sure how to respond to the emotion that danced between them.

"Back to Dr. Carmichael again? Do you call all your friends by their last name?"

"You've been Dr. Carmichael for—"

"Way too long. Now, what's it going to be? Italian? Thai? Steak? I'm taking you for supper, so it might as well be something you love."

Anna smoothed her hands over unruly curls and pulled at her oversized sweatshirt. She looked and felt like a day-old soda.

"I can't go out! Look at me. I didn't even shower after my run."

"Go take a shower. I'm not in a rush."

He walked back into her living room and plopped down on the couch. "Take your time."

Matt stretched out on the sofa and closed his eyes. He had won the battle, and she was going to eat. But fear of a whole different kind spiraled inside his head.

Friendship was a dangerous game to play. He had rationalized that he would concentrate on only being a friend, but could he?

In the past, she'd often brought up the subject of God when randomly talking about the challenges both she and Steven faced and believed he would give the strength she needed. But the way she looked today—like a scared waif that the wind could pick up and carry away—worried him. There was little wonder why her sister had called.

Though he had often reminded himself that emotions were for the weak and illogical, all it took was a thought of her sparkling black eyes and full red lips to run through his mind, and he was lost. Before he could stop, his imagination took him to where her thick, dark curls were given freedom from the clasp at the nape of her neck and his lips were lowered to hers.

It did not help to remind himself of the years spent on his education specializing in the love of his life—medicine—nor reflect upon the reputation he'd built as both a medical and surgical oncologist. He could daily tell himself, *Matt don't be a fool. Medicine you understand. Medicine you live for. Medicine is where you excel.* Then immediately slip back into daydreams of her far away from reason.

After watching his parent's tortured relationship, he vowed never to repeat that kind of insanity. Love and companionship came at too heavy a price. To prove his point, all he had to do was look into the lives of his colleagues. Far too many had their careers sidelined due to irrational affairs and domestic problems. He had never wanted, nor needed, the complication of love. *There was no such thing as fairytale romances or true love, was there?*

But try as he might to thwart all lack of reason, Anna had him thinking differently with a craving for something undefined. She had crept into his thoughts uninvited, and since Steven was gone, they had reached epidemic proportion. The safe and proper wall of friendship had crumbled, and his mind sprouted doors and windows that beckoned him into a world of much more. He had stayed away from her this past month with disciplined purpose and rued the fact her sister had called him.

Determined to eradicate thoughts of her and him, thoughts of them as a couple, thoughts of her in his arms, he came today to prove to himself that he could control such madness, but instead, faced the one word he never entertained when dealing with women. Failure.

Logic usually worked like a charm, so he reminded himself that she had just lost her husband and was a grieving widow. And if that was not enough, then the fact that she had two grown children and a belief structure he could not fathom should seal the deal. It did not.

Why did he feel the need to protect Anna? Why did the mere thought of her destroy that one thing he had always been able to control—his emotions? Why the startling surge, thrum, and kick of his sorry heart every time she came into view?

Thoughts of a snooze flew out the window. Agitation pushed in. Matt felt all too human for his liking. The sound of water splashed into his troubled thoughts as the shower turned on, and he instantly longed to join her. A colorful word slipped from his lips, one he knew she wouldn't approve of.

With a degree of willpower never before exercised, he squeezed his eyes shut and practiced deep breathing, with his mind focused on a difficult medical procedure he needed to perform the next day. Sleep thankfully followed.

Anna stayed extra-long in the shower. The steady heat of beaded water relaxed her shoulders. She smoothed her hands over the knot in the small of her back.

A rare flicker of something akin to excitement fluttered within as she contemplated a meal out with Matt. When was the last time she dined out? She'd had invitations, but she had rarely ventured far with Steven's illness.

She smiled ever so briefly into the mirror as she tried to calm the unruly curls that cascaded around her face and down her back. Unable to tame the riotous mane, she gave up on the blow-drying and fastened the still-damp hair with a decorative clasp. A few errant tendrils worked free. She sighed, deeply annoyed that they had a life of their own.

After putting on the scantest amount of makeup, she took one last glance into the bathroom mirror. The large dark circles that shadowed her eyes were far from attractive. She patted a light powder then shook her head. There was no makeup that could hide her life's recipe of late: hold the sleep, a sprinkle of nutrition, add a generous dollop of stress.

With a deep shrug, she headed down the hall.

"Matt?"

A gentle nudge of his shoulder and the whisper of her voice brought a sleepy smile to his face. *What was he thinking?*

He opened his eyes lazily, and an unguarded gaze of admiration swept over her before he successfully masked his expression.

A tender sensation tickled her senses and sent a warm flush to her cheeks.

"Man, I really crashed." He raked a hand through his hair and rose to his feet.

"That's my fault. You said to take my time, and that's exactly what I did. It's been over an hour."

"Well then, with that kind of time, you must've come up with an idea for supper."

"Honestly, I love Japanese take out. But that would defeat the purpose of getting ready to go out, now wouldn't it?"

He smoothed his hands over the five o'clock shadow on his chin. "With all that's gone on, you're probably weary to the bone. Let's go for a drive first and get you out of here for a change of scenery. Then I know an awesome place for the best Japanese take out. We can bring it back here to eat."

She clapped her hands as a genuine smile split across her face. "You read my mind. I'd love that."

"On one condition," he paused. "You have to promise to eat."

She crossed her heart. "I promise."

Chapter Four

"Irasshaimase." Anna bowed to him and waved her hand to the prepared area she had created in her living room. "That means welcome, please come in."

Matt's eyes widened, but he followed.

"Off with the shoes, Doctor." She forced a smile and with conscious effort curled the edges of her mouth up. For a moment in time she was determined to rise above her circumstances. She kicked her shoes free and plopped to the floor.

"Japanese food is meant to be consumed sitting on pillows around a low table in true Zashiki style, but this coffee table will have to do."

"I thought you told me you rarely traveled."

"My circumstances may have dictated lack of experience but trust me when I say I'm well read and have a vivid imagination. Now, when I attempt to eat with these chopsticks, you'll see firsthand what I mean."

She fumbled with the grip and sent a prawn flying his way. He laughed.

"I warned you."

"Two second rule." He picked the prawn off the table and popped it in his mouth.

The banter lasted a few more moments before her appetite waned, and she pushed the food around on her plate. Though she tried hard to focus on conversation, the edges of sadness folded in. She shifted to find comfort and propped a pillow behind her back. That all too familiar knot of tension twisted and settled into place.

She was annoyed at how he kept trying to bring the conversation back around to how she was doing, how she felt, if she was sleeping. Like a wagon train at night, she placed his questions outside the circle of safety and kept the conversation on—the weather, current events, his work—anything but her.

The minute he finished his meal, he jumped to his feet and removed the plates. "Relax." He waved her over to the couch as she rose to help. "I'll get these and be right back."

Rather than grab his coat as she had hoped, he seated himself beside her and turned her way.

"What's it like to work—"

Matt held up his hand. "Please. I don't want to talk about my work, myself, or anything else for that matter. I'm truly concerned about you."

She exhaled deeply. Defeated and distressed.

"I hope you feel comfortable enough with me by now to tell me how you're really doing?"

She turned from his intense stare.

"Every time I steer the conversation in your direction, you change the subject and ask about the weather or something equally irritating."

Unwanted tears pooled precariously on the edges of her lashes. All it took was for one to break free and roll down her cheek and the rush started.

He leaned toward her. She stilled him with an outstretched hand and rose swiftly to her feet. She headed to the kitchen island where she knew a box of tissues sat and grabbed a handful. She buried her head in a mountain of tissues as the stream of tears became a river.

"You want the truth? Fine." With an angry sweep, she brushed the continual flow of tears from her flushed cheeks.

"I'm a thirty-nine-year-old woman with no skill sets who needs to find a job. I can't rely on the generosity of my late husband's parents forever. The best years of my life were devoted to a sick husband and two growing boys, but now everything that gave me purpose is gone. Gone."

"What about your parents?"

She felt the blood siphon from her face. Her heart still tightened at the thought. "I lost them both in a car crash when I was twelve. Sadness and tragedy seem to find me."

She paced back and forth wringing the tissue into shreds. "And I'm tired of these blasted tears … they just keep falling. The quiet in this house closes in to the point I feel like it's choking me." She placed a hand to her throat. "To be honest, Matt, I've been lonely for a long, long time." She sank onto the bar stool and buried her head in her hands. "I'm so alone I could disappear for days and no one would notice."

Her cheeks grew hot at the thought of what her tirade had just divulged. *What was it about this man that made her spill her soul?*

She stiffened as she felt him place a hand on her shoulder and swivel the stool toward him.

"Please go. I don't know why I told you all of this. I didn't mean to dump my problems on you." Her eyes flickered up, then quickly down. "I guess it's because you're the first person who cared enough to demand an answer."

"Anna." His breath came out in a whisper as he bent toward her. "I do care." He pulled her to her feet and enveloped her in the warmth of a hug.

It had been a long time since she'd felt the strong protective strength of a man. Her head slowly relaxed upon his shoulder, and she soaked in the embrace. One hand gently cradled the back of her head as he whispered words of comfort.

"You're not alone. I'm here."

She closed her eyes and allowed the tears to subside. Raw awareness took over.

His hug became alive with movement as his other hand ran up and down her spine in a soothing motion. Her breath caught as he caressed his fingers through her long hair. Delightful. Delicious. Dangerous.

Warning bells rang out, but she willfully stilled their clamor. She was not about to let go.

The heat of his breath tickled her neck as her hair clip dropped to the floor. He buried his face in the thickness of her hair and then cut a path across her neck with his lips. A groan slipped from his throat as she bent her head back enjoying the sensation of warm lips against her skin. That sound triggered long forgotten pleasure, and before she realized what she was doing, her arms slipped around him, and she gave as much as she received.

He came to life in her arms with a vibrancy she had not felt beneath her fingertips in years.

"Anna," he whispered into her hair.

She pressed closer. A deep sigh of contentment slipped from her lips as she turned into his neck and began to nuzzle closer. The sharp intake of his breath caused excitement to spike.

A trail of kisses from her forehead down brought his lips dangerously close to hers. He pulled back, a question in his eyes.

She wound her hands tightly into his hair and pulled his mouth to meet hers. The sensation of his lips on hers created a hunger that one kiss was not about to satiate. She was lost in the loveliness.

Their breathing roughened. Kiss for kiss, she matched his intensity with a passion and need long since buried. She could feel his taut muscles shiver beneath the splay of her fingers up his spine. The sheer power of his reaction reawakened that which had been denied for way too long. She no longer felt like a mother, nursemaid, or housewife but a desirable woman who ached to be touched.

A tremble skittered down her backbone as his hands became hot, needy, and dangerously out of control. They were edging close to that place of no return. Her need for comfort had ignited into desire, and desire flared into an inferno about to consume.

"I can't, we can't—" His breathe ran ragged as his mouth tore from hers. "As much as I want to—"

"Matt—"

"God knows I want to Anna … but not now … not yet. I need to go."

Her words turned the blaze between them into a firestorm. "I need you," she whispered pressing hard against him. "Don't go!" she pleaded. "Stay with me."

He hesitated. Then swung her into his strong arms.

She rained kisses all over his neck and pointed to the bedroom at the end of the hall. They collapsed on the bed in a tangle of urgency. His mouth crushed against hers.

Everything but pleasure faded.

Chapter Five

The walk between floors and down sterile whitewashed halls from patient to patient gave Matt plenty of time to think. He was not sorry. The time they had shared had been one of most incredible nights of his entire life. Consumed with thoughts of her in bed next to him, he knew his attraction to her was beyond hope. She had no idea how he had refused to sleep, not wanting to waste a moment. He had pulled her onto his lap and sat up so he could drink in her loveliness as she slept. Their passionate night together was all he could think about.

He whistled a tune, as he pressed the elevator button for the fourth floor.

"Whatever you're on, I want some too," a colleague quipped as he hurried on by.

Matt tried to wash the grin off his face as he stepped into the elevator but couldn't. He loved her. That emotion he had mocked in others now enveloped his heart and left him feeling vulnerable but, oh, so alive. No other woman had come close to evoking the bittersweet torment of Anna. She was under his skin. In his blood. Stamped on his heart.

He stepped into the busy fray and scratched his head. *Where was I headed?*

The head nurse on the ward lost no time in refreshing him. "Dr. Carmichael, we need you in 303 stat."

Matt hurried in her direction.

A few hours later, he stepped outside for a break. The biting January air whipped down his coat collar, but he didn't care. He needed to clear his head. He fumbled in his pockets for his gloves and wrapped his scarf around his neck. Picking up speed, he headed in the direction of the lake. He had just enough time to walk the loop and enjoy a moment at the water's edge before heading back. He sucked the frigid air deep into his lungs. Clean air. Clear head. That was the way it had always worked. Not anymore.

Thoughts of Anna dominated his mind.

The only thing he regretted was his timing. Logic and reason had disintegrated in the heat of that fateful moment. A hunger for which no word existed had consumed him. For the first time in his life, he experienced what it meant to make love to a woman. It was so different than the mere physical reactions he had experienced in the past.

Though he had planned to give her time to heal, grieve, and nurture their friendship, common sense had failed him. Her reaction had caught him off guard and clouded his thinking. Falling in love had changed everything. He found that control was no longer a wand he could willfully wave.

He smiled into the crisp winter air and chuckled out loud. "Who knew it could be like this?"

Anna groaned. The memory of Matt and their time together brought a hot flush to her cheeks and sorrow to her soul. A contrast of emotions volleyed for attention. Pleasure. Pain.

The pleasure—the thought of warm, loving arms holding her. Sweet caresses. Soft whispers. Stolen kisses, captured long into the night. His attention and passion had been intoxicating after years of loneliness.

The pain—knowing they were incompatible. Her ill-timed fall from grace. The thought of what others would think if they knew. Failure. Shame.

How could she have been so needy, so vulnerable, with no regard for her faith or possible consequence? Yet she knew, in that deepest darkest place, she would succumb again to his charm given the opportunity.

Spread across her bed, Anna cried out, "God, please forgive me. I've failed miserably, but you understand how lonely my life has been. Not only recently, but through all the years Steven cut me off as his wife. Surely you know how many sacrifices I've made for the well-being of others? That must count for something? Please, make this go away. Make these feelings go away. I'll keep my distance from Matt, I promise."

Her cry for forgiveness felt incomplete, yet she rose from her bed and wiped the tears from her cheeks. She made her way to the kitchen fully aware she should eat but couldn't. Donning her running shoes, she slammed the door on the way out. She hit the pavement and powered down the street.

Beginning to feel like a stalker, Matt banged on her front door once again. "Come on Anna, I know you're home. We need to talk." He waited. Nothing.

He slid the box of chocolates onto her porch swing and made his way back to his Mercedes. The car shook as he slammed the door shut and turned the key. Adele's haunting voice filled the car with music.

With a smash of his fist on the dashboard, he flicked the radio off. The last thing he needed was to hear the crooning about unrequited love.

Tears stung behind his eyelids as a knot gathered in his throat. He cursed under his breath and backed out of her drive.

He headed to his office, thankful he had work to distract him.

His bang on the door made her heart jump and her skin tingle. She missed his dimpled smile, his conversation, friendship, but who was she kidding, she missed a whole lot more. The memory of his gentle touch thrummed. Hungry lips and soft caresses turned needy—her need.

She fanned the heat from her cheeks longing to swing the door wide open. It took every ounce of strength she had to stop that urge. Her body shook with visceral disappointment, and her hand trembled on the curtain she pulled slightly back. To feast her eyes on his slumped shoulders and bent head brought instant tears to her eyes.

Anna filled her days to capacity. She didn't try to analyze if it was a form of self-inflicted penance or the need to forget. She joined the choir at church, donated time at the soup kitchen, and volunteered at Pine Mountain Senior's Villa.

"Anna, come here." The head nurse, Sophia, waved her into the office. "We've been impressed with your knowledge base and the kind way you care for the elderly. What's your background in caregiving?"

"Well …" she stammered. "I've raised two boys and my husband was sick with cancer for many years. I guess I learned a lot taking care of him."

Sophia nodded. "Ahhh … the school of hard knocks." Her face softened. "You know Anna, we're always in need of compassionate and capable people. You should think about enrolling in the next nurse's aid program. Then we could pay you for your time."

Anna's heart did a leap. "Do you think I'd be good at it? I could really use the job."

"You're a natural. I guarantee it. In fact, we need help in the kitchen immediately, if you want to start there. And then when your training is done, we'll switch you over."

Anna couldn't believe it. She had a job. A smile of confidence split across her face.

As Anna wiped down the trays, one of her favorite residents waved her over. "I'll be right there, Rita. I just have to take these trays to the kitchen."

She struggled with a heavy stack to speed up the process, because she loved talking to Rita. Most of the residents wanted to be cheered up or doted on, but Rita was different. Instead of taking, she did the giving. They talked about Steven, the boys, or anything Anna cared to share. She found the gift of encouragement wrapped in this dear, old soul and naturally gravitated to her. Rita's kindness and wisdom helped Anna renew her belief in a God who cared about the details of life. She slid the precarious load on the counter and hurried to join her new friend.

Rita pointed to the bench across from her wheelchair. Anna settled in, expecting a good chat, but Rita scooted her wheel chair directly in front of her and reached out shaky fingers.

Anna bent forward so she could grasp Rita's outstretched hands and gently massaged the blue veins that traced their way under paper-thin skin. For a moment neither spoke.

"My dear."

Anna lifted her head to look squarely into Rita's faded blue eyes. Rita didn't sport her usual smile, instead a seriousness permeated her face. She briefly looked up and muttered, "Yes," before her gaze returned to Rita's hands.

"My dear, I have to ask. You wear a smile, but the Spirit reveals something more."

Anna shifted on the bench. Rita's words were as if God himself carried out an inquisition.

"Your sadness is more than just the passing of your husband, yes?"

Her heart began to pound. *Surely God doesn't expect me to reveal my secret.*

That still small voice spoke clearly. "*Yes, I do, because you carry guilt you aren't meant to carry.*"

I'm so ashamed Father. The way I've treated Matt when I was the one to encourage him.

Anna looked down, away from the set of kindly eyes that bore into her soul, as Rita waited in silence. The thrum of her heart picked up pace and began to beat an erratic rhythm, one she felt the whole room could hear.

"The Spirit of God laid a message on my heart," Rita said. "It makes no sense to me, but I know from years of experience, it'll make sense to you." She squeezed Anna's hands.

"God wants you to know you're forgiven, but you're not to make excuses before him!"

How can Rita know I had made excuses before God?

"Come closer, my child. I have a hug for you from God."

Anna rose from her bench and bent to hug the older woman. When she tried to pull apart, Rita hung on tight with a strength Anna knew she should not possess.

Rita whispered into her ear. "God has not left you Anna. The question is … will you leave him?"

Chapter Six

Anna drew in one breath after another, but air refused to fill her lungs. Buckled over with arms wrapped around her abdomen, she fought off another bout of nausea. Tears rolled down her cheeks and splashed onto the bathroom floor. The small room closed in on her and spun like she was whirling on a ride at the fair. She stumbled out and down the hall.

Cold, merciless fear gripped her and grew into full-blown terror. Anna slumped onto the nearby kitchen chair, her legs too weak to hold her.

Pregnant! "Oh, good Lord, no, no, no."

Although her last pregnancy had been nineteen years before, she had not forgotten the muzzy sensation and sharp pangs of nausea that ebbed and flowed. She had known in that deep part of her soul she was pregnant, yet denied it. The positive pink line on the home pregnancy test brought in a crushing reality.

How could she, an upstanding long-term member of the First Baptist Church, mother of two grown children, a woman so recently widowed, be pregnant? She could hear the dialogue of the gossip mongers circling in her head like vultures over fresh carnage. She would indeed deserve every unkind word.

Shaking, Anna buried her head in her hands. Like a rag doll, her elbows collapsed onto the kitchen table and her upper body followed in a heap.

Oh, God, what have I done? How could I have betrayed my own moral beliefs, the standard by which I raised my children, the building blocks of my Christian faith?

She lifted her head, and yanked the ponytail holder free. A curtain of hair fell over her face as if to cover the shame. *After all the years of careful living, of sacrifice, I've blown it. How? How? How?* That one word tumbled about in her head like a dryer cycle she couldn't shut off.

Anger snaked from the pit of her stomach up and out. She pulled to her feet in frustration and slammed the chair to the floor behind her. A guttural cry filled her lungs as she screamed into the heavens. "God, is this your answer? I live my whole life for you. I ask for mercy for one mistake, and this is what I get? What kind of God are you? I admit I messed up, but under the circumstances aren't my actions understandable? Don't I deserve at least one break?"

Silence filled the room.

In the days following, Anna nursed her acute disappointment in God. Like strands of a spider's web, Anna felt helplessly caught in its sticky filament. The more she struggled, the greater her entrapment grew.

How can I conceal the truth from Matt? How can I keep this secret from the church, my friends, my family? How can I wake up from this nightmare unscathed?

Abortion—the only option that allowed enough darkness in which to hide. Like a half-knit blanket, the core of Anna's belief structure began to unravel stitch by agonizing stitch.

She longed to pray and find comfort in the God she loved, as she had done through many struggles in her past, but Rita's words surfaced over and over … "God wants you to know you're forgiven, but you're not to make excuses before him."

Anger flared each time she thought of these words. "Oh, so caring for a sick husband for years, and the fact I raised my children without help from their father, not to mention the loneliness, counts for nothing? If you think I'm prepared to let my world fall apart because of one stupid mistake, you can think again."

In softer moments, she'd pray and plead. "God, please … I've stayed clear of Matt and all temptation. Surely, you don't want the world to know? My failure would only tarnish your name. What about my sons? They've been through enough."

Her anger and excuses were met with silence, and it infuriated her. "God, why are you silent?"

Will you listen? Your child and the father of your child have rights too.

She knew her behavior toward Matt was cruel, especially considering she was the one who had practically begged him to stay that night. Then when he succumbed to what most would consider a natural response, she spurned him. In truth, he displayed more character than she did. He made every effort to see her again. She was the one who couldn't face him after the way she had thrown herself at him. Though he kept trying to text and call, she remained a silent coward. The doorbell unanswered. Her front door locked.

Try as she might, she couldn't forget that night. They had connected in a way that went much deeper than a moment of pleasure, and the truth of that experience petrified her. In rare moments, snippets of honesty flooded in like dust mites dancing on a shaft of sunlight. She would promptly slam the door of her heart shut so the light could not reveal what lay in the shadows. Truth brought pain, brought accountability, and demanded action. With this new set of circumstances, shame knocked on her door, and she opened it wide.

Each day that passed, truth grew less urgent, less relevant. The solution and rationale of abortion grew sounder and stronger.

She'd been right to keep Matt at bay, and now she had more reason than ever to avoid him.

She heard that still small voice, *My child, this is not my way, it is yours.* An involuntary shudder worked up her spine.

How could she possibly reveal such truth to her sons, her sister and family, her church? And what would Steven's family say, especially after all the help they had given her? Even now, they were paying for her courses. No, she had too much to lose. Like leaves in the wind drifting in erratic directions, fear danced upon her troubled soul.

The ping of a message interrupted Anna's studies. She shut her textbook and searched for the phone beneath her papers. The last person she wanted to face popped up on the screen.

Drat, Lana! No, I don't want you to stop over. She dropped her phone in a huff. It scuttled across the table and dropped onto the kitchen floor. *Why do you always think you can barge in?*

Anna knew better than to dissuade her, because then she would truly suspect something was wrong and call Matt again.

Anna picked up her phone and read her sister's message.

"Worried about you, Sis. Popping over for a quick tea."

Memories flooded in. Lana, her fraternal twin—first into this world by a whole four minutes—had instinctively taken on the role of Anna's protector. When their parents died and two different aunts planned to separate them, Lana stepped in with fury and insisted they stay together. There was no way she was about to allow anyone or anything to come between them. They'd always been close, even though they were polar opposites. Where Anna was laidback and au natural, Lana was driven and well put together. Anna was quiet, tall, and willowy—Lana was the life of the party, short, and pleasantly plump. Where Anna loved to run, Lana would joke about hating all four-letter words that contained any type of activity such as walk, swim, bike, or hike.

As the phone screen faded black, Anna's mind returned to her present situation. There was no point in stewing. Lana never failed to hone in when Anna hurt. That sensory honing device was not about to stop now. She would have to pretend that life in her tormented world was okay.

Though they had shared everything over the years, this secret was different—it involved sin and failure. She knew her sister would be deeply disappointed, especially so soon after Steven's death.

No. I won't, I can't, reveal my shame to anyone.

She formulated a plan to use her grief card to get her sister in and out as quickly as possible.

Lana's rapid knock signaled her arrival. She entered on her own accord, as she usually did. The clip, clip, clip of high heels on the hardwood irritated the heck out of Anna. Why couldn't she take her shoes off like everyone else, but no, she had to wear those blasted heels 24/7. Anna couldn't remember the last time she saw her sister in bare feet or flip-flops.

"I'm here."

Anna shut her eyes and took a deep breath. "In the kitchen, Lana."

Perched on a bar stool at the kitchen island, she lifted her fork from a half-eaten plate of food. The last thing Anna wanted was another sermon on the need to eat more from a sister who loved food way too much. She hoped her strategically placed meal would still Lana's tongue.

"There you are, dear Sis. I thought maybe you'd gone into hiding." She gave a quick squeeze of her hand on Anna's shoulder and slid onto the stool across from her.

"So, you've actually made a decent meal for yourself and eaten half, or is this a set-up?"

Anna gulped her glass of water, as a piece of chicken got trapped in her throat. She hated her sister's perceptiveness.

Anna threw up her hands. "You got me there."

"Have I been that much of a nag that you've resorted to trickery?"

"Actually, yes. You give me the same sermon every time you visit."

Lana stood, crossing her arms in front of her chest. "It's only because I care. You've been through so much, and I feel helpless."

She plopped back on the stool. "My life's been a cakewalk compared to yours. I have a great job, a happy marriage, two wonderful kids, and, quite honestly, it makes me feel ... guilty. Like something happened in the womb that created this huge imbalance where I got the happy and you got the sad—"

"Ahh ... you just don't like the fact you can't control my destiny." Anna forced a laugh, trying to lighten the somber mood. "Remember, Sis, there is a God, and you're not him!"

Lana didn't even break a smile.

"Is there something you're not telling me?"

Anna dropped her eyes and pushed the food around on her plate.

"Do you need help financially?"

Anna shook her head.

"You know that Tom and I are here for you, don't you? Please, tell me what to do." She reached over and placed her beautifully manicured hand on Anna's arm.

Anna could barely resist the urge to open up. She pierced her lips tight and took a deep breath to get that impulse under control. She cleared her throat and marveled at the fact she could lie so valiantly. "Lana, I'm a grieving widow. What I need is time."

Her sister nodded in agreement. "Have all the time it takes, but I'm not going to stop reminding you that I care."

"I know you care, but you've got to stop smothering me. I need a little room to breathe, to cry when I need to ..." Anna's voice broke.

Lana covered the short distance between them and wrapped her arms around tight.

"You know that I'm not all that good at this affection thing ... that's your gig, but I really love you and I want to help."

Anna nodded. "I know, I know."

The lies and secrecy grew weightier.

With the sheets twisted around her, Anna punched the pillow down and flipped it over. A war of thoughts battled. Never in her wildest imaginings would she have thought she would consider abortion. But now, compassion welled up within her for every woman in her predicament, and she realized how logical terminating a pregnancy could seem.

In the next moment, she would imagine the feel of a newborn held protectively in her arms—one with Matt's gorgeous blue eyes and laughing dimple. An ache so deep would steal her breath away.

Back and forth. Back and forth. The two scenarios battled.

Rather than count sheep, she presented her case to God in logical one, two, threes.

"God, I'm an unmarried widow who has just started a new job and school. I don't have the means to support myself, much less a child.

"And … at my age, this pregnancy will be high-risk. Remember how I barely survived two very difficult births at a much younger age." She shuddered at the thought. Her fingers turned instantly cold. Some memories were impossible to forget.

"And it's not fair to Matt, God. He shouldn't be forced into responsibility when I threw myself at him. He's such a talented physician and has given his life to helping others, I can't take this freedom from him."

The same question surfaced each time she went through her list of excuses. *What are you really afraid of?*

All she had to do was ask herself what others would think, and her thoughts would circle around to one ready solution—abortion. The pro-choice slogans gave comfort. The more she entertained them, the bolder they grew. She was a woman of the 21st century in control of her body. The choice to have an abortion was her right. It's not a baby, just an inconvenient circumstance. She fell into a fitful sleep with the conclusion that abortion was a rational and sound decision, one she could no longer delay.

Awakened with a start, Anna bolted into a seated position. "What?" Had someone called her name? She heard the message. Crisp. Clear. Concise.

Will you obey Me?

Anna had been a Christian too long not to recognize the voice of the Spirit, but God was not the only one present.

A voice of darkness whispered into her thoughts. "*There's a simple way to hide your secret.*"

You're carrying a child, a baby, a living soul tucked safely in your womb, right where the child needs to stay until the time of birth. The Spirit of God thrummed a clear, powerful message.

"Nobody needs to know your shame. There's a way to cover this up."

You must tell someone of your pregnancy immediately. Make yourself accountable now.

"You may die, remember what it was like when you had the boys?"

I was your protector then, and I'll be your protector now.

"How well did that God of yours protect Steven?" Anna could feel the hatred hiss from that planted thought. A shiver ran up her spine.

Steven is with Me, he is pain free and full of joy. And I know the plans I have for you. Plans to prosper you and not to harm you. Plans to give you hope and a future.

"One small procedure, and your troubles will be over."

Trust me, Anna, and choose life.

Anna threw off her covers and stumbled to the bathroom. She splashed cold water on her face, as if to wash away the frightening thoughts. Anna knew she had to call Pastor Harry immediately. She didn't care that it was 2:00 a.m. She needed to set up an appointment now. If she waited until morning, she did not trust she would do the right thing.

Her rubber legs could no longer hold her. She nearly dropped the phone as she sank to the edge of bed. With a tremble in her hand she punched the number listed in her contacts.

"Hello," a groggy voice answered.

"Pastor Harry, it's Anna."

"Is everything okay?"

"Yes! I mean no! I guess, what I mean is that I have to talk to you tomorrow … first thing." Desperation oozed from her voice, but she didn't care.

"Of course. Can you come to my office in the morning around seven? My day is booked solid, but I'll come in early if you can make it."

"Yes, I can make seven … and thank you." Her voice wavered, and her hands shook as she placed her cell on the nightstand.

Anna sank into her bed. Every muscle and tendon clear to the bone relaxed. The heavy weight dissipated, and she knew her decision to obey had dispelled the darkness. A warmth, as if God himself enveloped her in a hug, flooded in as she basked in the joy of peace. She fell into a deep, restful sleep.

Chapter Seven

Though fear nibbled at the edge of her mind, Anna felt a peaceful freedom the next morning. Embarrassment was sure to come. The right decision had been made, but the truth came with the painful realization her Christian witness would be severely tarnished and others would be negatively impacted. God, however, didn't seem to care about that as much as he cared about the baby in her womb. Before she left, she took a few moments to open her Bible and read. The pages fell open to John 8:32 and the words jumped off the page. *And you shall know the truth and the truth shall make you free.*

God lovingly echoed his message from the night before and gave her the strength to press forward.

No wonder, I've been so tied in knots. I've been running from the truth right into the arms of darkness, and my secret has had the power to keep me there.

Anna stuffed a few soda crackers down to fight off the nausea and headed out the door with purpose.

She stopped for a moment to breathe in the crisp morning air. The trees were verdant with newborn leaves that spread open to the warmth of the sun. A gentle breeze kissed her face, as a sparrow darted directly in front of her and lifted its wings into the heavens. This small message from nature touched her soul. She was reminded of Scripture that said if God cared for the tiniest sparrow, she could rest in the fact he cared about every detail of her life. The gathering light of another day gave evidence of the sun just waiting to show off. For the first time in months, she felt a stir of hope. Her darkest secret was about to find its way into the light of day, and yet an unfathomable peace filled her soul.

She found herself humming to a tune on the radio as she drove to the church and realized how unnatural that small normalcy felt. She had not enjoyed music for months.

How long since she felt happy, truly happy? The answer to that question eluded her. She dared not open that door or visit that room.

Pastor Harry wore an expression of concern as she entered his office.

"Sit, sit, Anna," he said as he rose to usher her into a chair.

Rather than resume his chair behind the desk, he pulled up another one and sat across from her. He removed his reading glasses and rested them on the arm of the chair.

Without ceremony, he launched into prayer. As natural as breathing, he invited the Holy Spirit to join them and give wisdom. His prayer was short and heartfelt.

"Anna, how can I help?" He smoothed a hand through his thinning hair. "Eleanor and I talked in great length after your call this morning. We sincerely hope that the church hasn't let you down. Have we failed to help you in the ways you need? You've been through so much … for so long." He shook his head. "Too long." His kind eyes radiated warmth encouraging her to speak.

Anna didn't know where to begin. How did she tell her pastor she was pregnant only a few months after the death of her husband? Not a soul would believe the lonely existence they had shared together. Even if people could comprehend her loneliness, it was not an excuse she would use. She felt sorrow for those her mistake would hurt the most and prayed they would find it in their heart to forgive her.

"Anna," he coaxed. "What is it?"

She blurted out the truth. "Pastor, I'm pregnant!"

His eyebrows shot up, and she could see the shock her words brought. She knew she'd have to toughen up and get used to that look. It took him a moment to speak.

He shook his head and lifted a hand to smooth his scrunched-up brows.

"Well, well, well … the Lord surely works in mysterious ways doesn't he, Anna? He giveth, and then he taketh away, bless his name. But I guess in your case it's the other way around. He took Steven and gave you a baby."

Those were about the last words Anna had expected would roll off his tongue. A stunned and tongue-tied silence filled the room.

"Now remember, Anna, God wouldn't give you this child if he didn't think you were capable of raising the little one." He rose, walked over to his desk, and began jotting down notes.

"Let's see here. The prayer group will be notified and immediately begin to pray for an easy pregnancy, safe birth, and healthy baby. The women's ministry group will be put on a weekly schedule to give you any help or support needed."

Anna's surprise blossomed as her eyebrows knit together in confusion.

He glanced up over the brim of his glasses. "Now, don't even think of declining our help Anna, it's the least we can do in the circumstances.

"Oh, and what about your finances? The Lord clearly encourages us to take care of the widows and the fatherless. Sadly, in your case there will be both."

Anna remained speechless. She had always admired Pastor Harry's compassionate spirit but had not been sure what to expect. This was over the top. She'd anticipated, at the very least, he would pray for her sinful ways and would want to know who the father was so he could suggest counseling in hopes of it leading to marriage. But this was astonishing.

"I'm … I'm okay for now. I'll be able to carry on with my job for a number of months, so my finances will be adequate."

"Don't be afraid to let me know if you need extra help. Besides, you don't want to be exhausted because finances dictate you have to work right up to the end.

"Let's see?" A frown etched his brow as he thought for a moment. "You're what, at least four months along now? Although, my dear, you don't look it." He glanced at her midsection and shook his head. "It's all the stress you've been under, poor dear."

"Let's say you work another three months, and then we'll help you with your finances so you can have some rest before the baby is born." He jotted down another note. "I know that the church board will agree wholeheartedly, so you can consider it done. Then we'll continue to help you financially until you tell us otherwise. We're here for both you and your baby, Anna. You can rest assured."

He rose to full height and shook his head in wonder. "As hard as this may be to understand, dear Anna, God planned that you would have another legacy from the great man you lost. It truly is a miracle that you could conceive, with Steven being so sick and at your age. It's almost like a modern day Abraham and Sarah story, if you ask me."

Anna's head snapped up and she couldn't stop her eyes from bulging out of her head. The straightening of her spine nearly jerked her from the chair.

"What, Anna, you didn't seriously think we wouldn't support you in your time of need, did you?"

Anna shook her head. Her heart sunk to the bottom of her shoes. So, this was what he believed. It all made sense now. He thought the child was Steven's. Oh, it would be so simple to leave it there. If the child were born a month late who would suspect anything? Both her boys had been overdue and not a soul thought anything of it. The wheels of deceit began to turn and pick up traction.

Her relief lived but a second. As clear as if someone had audibly spoken the words, she heard the Holy Spirit speak into her soul, *The truth will set you free.*

She knew what God wanted her to do, but never had she been more tempted in her life to let a half-truth live. After all, she had not spoken one lie. Maybe this was God's form of mercy.

Again, the spirit spoke. *No, the truth will set you free.*

Just as she was about to tell the truth … a slight rap at the door interrupted and a head poked in.

"Come in, dear," Pastor Harry said, as he waved her into the room.

Anna had always loved the Pastor's wife, Eleanor, and it pained her beyond measure to have to tell the rest of the story with her present.

"Oh, my dear," she said bustling forward. Her arms squeezed Anna in a genuine hug before she prattled on. "We were so concerned. When you called, I almost got dressed and came over immediately. Had it not been for Harry fitting you in first thing, why I would've never lasted the night. I hope you don't mind me here. I just know that whatever you need, the Spirit of God has asked me to personally help you, and I would feel honored if you'd let me know what that looks like."

"Eleanor, dear—" Pastor Harry interrupted, "It's the most amazing and truly wonderful news. Anna is pregnant. God saw fit to send another little miracle our way—another addition to Steven's legacy."

Eleanor gasped in astonishment. "My dear, you never said a thing." Her eyes traveled down Anna's slim frame to rest upon her abdomen.

"Why, I look far more pregnant than you do." She laughed as she patted her round tummy.

Without a breath between she rattled on. "You're one of the strongest women I know. If only the rest of the church body knew how to take things to the Lord first, before running poor Harry ragged as if he was the Almighty himself." She clucked her tongue. "You've always been the rock-solid one. We could all take lessons from you. You help out at the retirement home, attend choir practice, and find peace in the midst of your grief by giving to others. Why, the other ladies and I just marvel at your strength of character and generous spirit."

Anna had never felt more the hypocrite than she did in that minute. Every word Eleanor spoke only served to drive the nails deeper into the coffin of lies that she now felt surrounded by. The four walls of this box squeezed in, the weight of her omission lowered her into darkness. The lid creaked shut and she felt suffocation take over.

Anna found herself surrounded in a circle of prayer with both the pastor and his wife praying up a storm. They pleaded with God for a safe delivery, prayed others would come around and give support, and that Anna would have health and strength in the months to come. They prayed, and prayed, and prayed, for everything except what she needed—the strength to tell the truth.

Chapter Eight

Before she could grasp the wherefore and the why, Anna was on her way home in complete and utter shock. She turned the radio off and felt annoyed by the cheerful sun. How had something she knew to be the right thing to do, turn out so wrong? In truth, the lie grew bigger and better than she herself could have concocted, and she had prayed … *so maybe, just maybe this is what they call divine intervention.*

The truth will set you free.

Anger surged as Anna entered the house. She slammed her purse down on the kitchen island and stomped to her room. She fell on the bed in a heap. "It's nobody's business who the father is. This child might as well have a beautiful legacy rather than sordid history. It's destined to grow up without a father anyway. Matt's way too busy. And God, I'm not aborting the baby, surely that's what matters the most? Besides, I raised my other two virtually alone, and I can do it again."

Relief poured over her. The more she thought things through, the better it got.

I won't have to tell my sons or in-laws. To remain quiet makes perfect sense— far better than the pain and shame the truth will bring to my family. And I won't lose the respect of others. Who in their right mind would argue with that? I'll get everyone's help rather than their gossip and scorn. She rolled over and spoke out loud. "Now, *that's* a blessing too good to pass up."

"And, God, I didn't tell one lie. Can it be that you understand and this is your hand of grace—after all my suffering, I'm finally getting a break?

Rationalization danced in her head. Deliverance lay spread before her until the thought of Matt bit into her consciousness. Like a ferocious attack from an angry Pitbull, a bite-size chunk ripped the comfort from her reasoning.

She'd have to deal with Matt. He was the only one who knew the truth. But their worlds never met, so this wouldn't be too hard. He lived, worked, and socialized in different circles, and he certainly didn't attend church, so the chance of keeping this from him seemed doable.

One caveat—she would have to do something about the way he kept showing up on her doorstep. This had to be dealt with immediately, *before* she was showing. No more skirting around the unavoidable. She had to squelch any hope he had of them becoming a couple.

A pang of regret flooded her soul. As much as she wanted to lie to herself about that night, she couldn't. They had connected in a way that went far beyond a mere indiscretion, but he could never know. He was a heartache waiting to happen anyhow. The heartache might as well begin now.

Anna, the truth will set you free.

She buried her head under her pillow and ignored the voice.

Chapter Nine

If only Matt had left her alone after that one night, life would be much easier. Instead, he'd sent flowers, dropped off chocolates, wrote a hauntingly beautiful letter, and left too many phone messages to count. He'd begged to see her, but she had ignored the plea. She knew she owed him an explanation but couldn't find the courage, all too aware of the attraction between them. Now, however, her hand was forced. His child grew within her, and she had to make sure he never found out.

The closer the hour drew to his arrival, the more miserable she felt. Pride and self-preservation held her firm and stilled her fingers from dialing the phone and cancelling their meeting.

Just beyond the curtain, she watched him jump out of his vehicle and climb the steps to her front door two at a time. He looked all too eager. Her legs began to shake. and she sank into a nearby chair. Could she really do this to him?

The doorbell chimed in rapid succession with a definite urgency. Anna clutched the sides of the chair in her hands. She longed to present a cool, collected front, but there she sat digging her nails into the leather. About as calm as a hummingbird in flight, she gathered her courage and rose.

With one last careful appraisal in the hallway mirror, she was thankful her tall frame and the choice of a loose-fitting blouse and flared black skirt carefully concealed the growing bulge. She had left her wavy hair flow free down her back knowing this would create a further distraction.

I wonder what he thinks about me agreeing to see him after three and a half months of silence?

There he stood, the outline of his wide shoulders and strong frame filtered through the misty glass in the front door. A flash of memory brought the feel of those muscular shoulders splayed beneath her fingertips alive. A hot flush spread over her body. She wanted to cower and once again ignore him but knew she must not. With the door handle grasped firmly in her hand, she opened it wide.

Matt's easy smile vanished and something intense took over. He didn't move or say a word as his eyes locked with hers. They stood silently staring, both tongue-tied, drinking in the sight of the other.

Anna's heart jumped into her throat. Blood began to thrum through her veins as she tried valiantly to still the raw emotion that flooded in. She didn't want to feel. She wanted to say goodbye with no heartache and had hoped it would be easy for the both of them. What a foolish notion.

"Doctor Carmic—Matt, come in." Her words sounded forced and fragile even to her.

She turned from his stare to break the awkward moment and walked into the kitchen, confident he would follow.

"Matt, would you like a drink, a soda, a wat—"

"No, Anna, all I would like is you."

An audible gasp slipped from her lips as she turned toward him, keeping the island safely between.

"So, this is how it's going to be, Matt, right to the point? No niceties, no small talk?" She tried to sound aloof and in control, but the fact her hands trembled didn't help the situation.

His eyes flitted from her hands to her flushed face in a way that told her he was fully aware she was affected by his presence. He had always been perceptive. She remembered how, as Steven's doctor, Matt had skillfully broken down the walls of her unspoken distress. He had taken the time to care not only about Steven but every family member who suffered alongside. With compassion and expertise, he had broken down the barriers. She had shared snippets of truth about her struggles that no one else knew. Many people commented on his exceptional bedside manner. Anna knew he was gifted. Today, that quality frightened her.

"Anna," he said softly as he wound his way around the island to stand before her. "I guess I could ask you to explain the silence. I could beg you to reconsider your decision." He reached out to touch her arm, and she flinched and backed away.

"I could even kiss you senseless, but then again what would tomorrow bring? Would it bring more regret? Would it stir your moral convictions and leave you a sinner?'

Her cheeks flushed with heat, and she brought her hands to her face to hide the obvious. His forthrightness cut deep.

"I never meant to hurt you or to go against your beliefs. And I swear I never meant for that evening to go beyond anything other than comfort. But I'm not in the least bit sorry. I won't lie, Anna, you mean a great deal to me, so don't ask me to regret something I found incredibly beautiful—" his words broke off in a whisper.

Anna felt control of the situation slip away. She placed one hand over the other to still the movement. Everything within her wanted to calmly confront him, but she couldn't even make eye contact. The tiles on her kitchen floor held her rapt attention. She was thankful he kept his distance.

"I've done some reading on what Christians believe and now understand that you have different convictions about premarital sex than I do. I also know this is not something you've ever done before. I don't make a practice of it either, but Anna you … consumed me. I've never felt anything before that came close to what we shared." He rubbed a hand around the back of his neck. "It's hard for me to be so honest."

Anna braved a quick look and knew he spoke the truth. His startling blue eyes held open emotion that pulled her in. Anna took a deep breath but forgot to exhale. This was not going as planned. She felt the spike and jolt of attraction course through her system.

Matt cleared his throat and swallowed hard. "I know you were in a vulnerable state that night, and for that I'm sorrier than words can say."

"No," Anna interjected finding her voice. "It was my fault. I shouldn't have—"

"Anna, let's not … try and figure out how to divvy up the blame. I'm having a difficult time regretting any of it, and I would rather not hear that you don't feel the same."

A longing soaked through his words, and he took a few steps closer. Instinct told her to back away. She was now up against the counter.

"Okay. Okay. I won't touch you, but where do we go from here?"

When she didn't immediately answer, he answered for her.

"We can start over. I'll give you time to grieve. I respect what you and Steven had. We can just nurture the friendship we've always shared. It's what I had meant to do in the first place. He lifted a hand up toward her face then dropped it. "You'll find me a patient man, but please give me a chance."

What could she say? How could she crush the heart of such a kind man? Her careful plan lay ripped apart by his gentleness. She had intended to do the talking but instead stood mute. Her short, pointed dismissal had turned into his sweet proposition. Where she planned to ask his forgiveness for her part and tell him that she was not ready for a relationship, he circumvented with his apology and respect enough for her beliefs to try and understand them. Her plan to communicate a need to be left alone instead became his offer—an antidote to a very lonely life ahead. What she hadn't counted on was how much his presence would make her feel—the spark of something deep inside her that wanted life, love, and happiness. Her heart skipped a beat as she gazed into his hopeful eyes.

"Matt, there's nothing I would love more. You're an amazing man …"

He stepped closer in anticipation, and she almost capitulated. It took all she had to shake her head. He stopped short.

"Matt, you don't understand. I just can't."

Brought back to reality, she remembered. There were a thousand solid reasons their relationship wouldn't work. First and foremost, he wasn't a believer, and secondly, they were worlds apart. His sheer good looks, position, intelligence, money and the fact he was younger, all screamed run. She had noticed the way the nurses on the cancer ward swooned every time he came around. She was no match for their constant charm. He would tire of her all too quickly, and then where would she be? They came from different worlds and different belief structures, and her decision was sound.

The support she had from Pastor Harry and Eleanor had been amazing. This baby needed the influence of a loving church that would stay the course. She didn't have it in her to cause shame and hurt to her sons and extended family by starting up a relationship that was doomed for failure.

A way out of her predicament had been handed to her gift wrapped and tied in a bow, and she planned to open it. However, if she didn't set Matt straight right here, right now, she would be tied to him forever.

The truth shall set you free.

She hadn't heard those words for a few weeks now, and she sure didn't want to hear them now. The one person she would have to directly lie to stood in front of her with soulful eyes and an intense determination. She needed strength to pull this off, not Bible verses flitting about in her head.

She turned away from his stare. "Matt, I'm sorry too. I'm not proud of what I did that night. I hope you can forgive me." When he tried to interject, she stopped him. "I listened to you, now please do the same for me."

He slid onto the bar stool beside the kitchen island. With deliberate care she positioned herself on the opposite side. She prayed he wouldn't notice the flush in her cheeks and hated the way she blushed when emotions ran hot. As she tucked a piece of hair behind her ear, the tremble in her hands came into full view. She lowered them to her lap and clutched them together.

"It … it just won't work. I'm still crippled with grief. I'm sorry for what I did, but I was lonely. It meant nothing more."

Matt stood abruptly to his feet and walked around the island removing the barrier between them. A ripple of fear skittered up her spine. She knew she couldn't hide the truth if he touched her. She would be lost.

"What are you so afraid of Anna? Is it possible that you're lying to me? What's going on? I don't fit into your perfect little Christian world, or you're embarrassed you have feelings for me so soon after your husband's death? Don't give me that shocked look, I know I'm very close to the truth. Your little speech rang far too hollow."

He reached for her and in one sweep pulled her close. Without giving her time to protest, he lowered his lips to hers.

Anna struggled not to respond, but after a second of hesitation all reason vanished and she melted in the warmth, the taste, the beautiful sensation of being kissed by a man who desired her.

Chapter Ten

Matt pulled his head up. "I'm sorry I had to do that, but I have my answer."

She caught his look of satisfaction and wrenched out of his embrace. Tears burnt hot. The desire to cry turned into anger. She lashed out. "Why did you do that? Can't you respect what I'm trying to say?"

"Anna, I can see you're angry, but you're lying to me and to yourself. You needed to know that."

The urge to hit him and finish that kiss collided.

Knots of anxiety twisted in her stomach and her forehead broke out in a cold sweat. She somehow had to make him believe her. Her whole future hung in the balance. The choice of truth or lies lay before her. She stepped into the fray. Once the lies started, they flowed like lava spewing from an erupted volcano.

"I … I'm truly sorry, Matt, but I don't feel anything for you. I was remembering Steven … both then and now." There was a catch in her voice, before she hammered the message home. "When we made love, I imagined Steven once again healthy and strong beside me. I'll love him until the day I die. There's no one who can take his place. Please, please … leave me alone."

Genuine tears flowed down her cheeks. She cried for Matt, for her lies, for their baby who would never know a father.

The crestfallen look on Matt's face spoke volumes. Her words had hit the mark.

"No wonder you responded so readily. You were making love to a memory, and I was the fool making love to you. What an idiot I am." He raked his hand through his hair and paced the kitchen. "You begged me to leave you alone these past three months, but no. I never imagined that you could respond the way you did and it not be *me* you wanted or needed. It all makes perfect sense now. What a fool I am." In a daze, he turned and walked to her front door.

"Goodbye, Anna." Though he paused, he didn't turn back. "I'm truly sorry, and I won't bother you again." The quiet click of the door was the last she heard before she fell in a heap to the floor. Agony roiled and twisted within her. She was sick to her stomach, and it had nothing to do with the pregnancy.

"I'm so sorry, Matt, so very, very sorry. You don't deserve this."

"Oh, God, what have I done?"

The agony and weight of her deceit crashed in damning her. Conviction pressed down. The depth of her cruelty to hide the truth stunned her.

Justification volleyed for attention. *I could hurt Matt, or I could hurt many others. What choice did I have?*

Truth, however, tugged at the edges of her mind. She liked the respect her good girl image had given. Perfected for far too many years, she couldn't bear the thought of a fall from grace. The destructive power of pride lay swaddled in the manger of her choice—deception.

Anna didn't need to question why God and his peace had become a distance friend. She had heard countless times that truth would set her free, and she had chosen lies.

Tears would not fix this mess, but they were all she had.

Anna scurried out the door to meet Steven's mom, Betty, for lunch. Matt had stayed clear, and now was the time to tell her family. Pastor Harry was waiting on her to make her pregnancy public so the church could lend a hand. She could not delay the inevitable. She had set the table of deceit, and now it was time to pull up a chair and eat the fruit.

Anna picked a spot she knew would put Betty at ease. Betty had a flare for the dramatic, loved good food and excellent service. The upscale Eldorado Hotel fit the bill perfectly and remained one of Betty's favorite places to "do" lunch.

Anna shifted nervously in the chair awaiting her arrival. Though spring still held crispness, the garden patio was open and afforded just the privacy she needed. Copious blooms spilled from the hanging baskets in a rainbow of cheery color and filled the air with a pungent fragrance. A cool breeze kicked up off the lake and made Anna second guess her decision until the patio heaters automatically turned on. They radiated a warmth she wished could reach the cold on the inside.

"Well, little one," she said as she smoothed a hand over the tiny protrusion beneath her fingers. It's time to tell your grandma all about you.

She's really not the child's grandma, is she? Matt's parents would be the grandparents.

Disturbing thoughts of truth cut into her train of thought. She hated the fact this often happened and pushed them away yet again.

"Yes, my baby, I'm so glad I can feel you now."

She had taken up the habit of talking to her little one ever since that first flutter of movement. Like butterfly wings gently taking flight, the tiny sensation caused excitement and brought relief. With the stress she was under, she had been worried about the development of her child. Though it had been difficult to face the pregnancy, she now realized how much she wanted this baby.

Matt would want this baby too. He has every right to know that you carry his child.

One daunting thought after another jabbed in until she felt like an over-used pincushion. With determination she redirected her thoughts to Betty.

Anna loved Betty. She had taken Anna in as a daughter-in-law and promptly removed the "in-law" thereafter. She helped Anna heal from the loss of her own mother by being a kind replacement.

With Betty and George always so good to her, Anna rationalized how it would hurt them to have the memory of their late son tainted by this pregnancy so soon after his death.

In quiet moments when truth prevailed, Anna admitted she craved their approval and didn't mind the fact they practically hero-worshipped her for all the years she had taken care of their son. She couldn't let one mistake wipe away twenty-three years of exceptional reputation.

Her lie gained power. Like the baby growing within, it had life. One lie bled into two, three, four, and many more. She now lived in a state of angst. Her life up to this point had not been one prone to deception.

Will I trip up on some detail? Will I forget to tell people that I'm a month farther along than I actually am? Will people believe that I'm not showing as much due to the stress and loss of weight incurred after Steven's death? Will I get used to the lies?

Anna's heart rate spiked each time a lie rolled off her tongue. The fringes of darkness crowded in.

She wanted to run when she saw Betty weave her way through the lunchtime crowd, but instead she waved her over with a well-practiced smile.

Betty hugged her and slipped gracefully into her chair. Her brightly colored sequined sweater and pencil slim skirt would have looked overdone on most people, but Betty could handle the look. With her trim, still youthfull figure, immaculate coiffure, manicured nails, and Louis Vuitton purse, Betty looked like she could have stepped out of the pages of a high-fashion magazine. Anna remembered being terrified of her at first. But Betty's genuine friendliness soon changed that. She had a flare for fashion, but beneath the surface lived and breathed a down-to-earth soul. Her bubbly personality soothed Anna's frayed nerves.

Betty placed a warm hand over Anna's ice-cold fingers and gently squeezed. "How you must miss our dear Steven. George and I think of you every day and wonder how you manage the grief."

She turned and waved the waitress over. "Could you bring me a Perrier, my dear?"

Anna was grateful that Betty would carry the conversation and flit from subject to subject invariably answering her own questions.

"How are Jason and Mark processing the grief? I suppose their studies help dilute the sadness. You said they both have girlfriends now?

"Oh, that just brings back such wonderful memories of when Steven first brought you home. You were so shy and incredibly lovely. He was smitten from the get-go."

Anna smiled and listened to Betty's chatter, it oddly gave her comfort.

The waitress had to wait a few minutes before she cleared her throat. "So sorry to intrude, but are you two ready to order."

"Oh, yes, my dear. Sorry. I didn't see you there. Now tell me all about your lunch special, does it have onions, I like them my dear, but they just don't like me." Before the girl could answer, Betty was gushing over the ring on her finger.

"Is that an engagement ring? Oh, how lovely. Why, your fiancé is a lucky man.

"Anna, look at the size of this ring and the beautiful bride-to-be. Don't you think her fiancé has impeccable taste?"

Anna nodded in agreement.

The young waitress beamed.

Anna sat and listened to a love story unfold as Betty genuinely wanted to hear how her fiancé had proposed.

Their lunch came and went, and Anna let Betty carry the conversation. They were currently on the latest kitchen renovation that Betty and George were undergoing. Anna nodded politely, answered where needed, but could barely concentrate. All she wanted to do was blurt out her news and be done with it.

She wished that things could be as they always had been, and she could have a peaceful luncheon with one of her favorite people in the world, without the guilt. Instead, peace had flown away that morning in Pastor Harry's office never to return. She was going to have to tell a boldface lie to this dear soul.

"My dear, did you hear me?" Betty patted her arm.

Anna's head snapped to attention as she forced herself to focus. She had no idea what Betty had just said.

"Are you okay, you look a little peaked?"

The opening that Anna needed fell into her lap.

"Well, actually, Mom, I have something to tell you. You're not going to believe this. I'm still in shock myself."

Betty was all ears. She leaned in closer and placed her hand over Anna's. "Go ahead, dear. You know that George and I will help you in any way we can."

The sincerity in her voice and eyes made Anna want to cry.

"I'm … I'm pregnant!

The astonishment on Betty's face could have registered a seismic wave of ten on the Richter scale. Her perfectly arched eyebrows shot up to the roof.

"What! How … can that be? Steven was so sick!

Anna nodded and used the same words Pastor Harry used. "I guess it's a modern-day Abraham and Sarah story."

"Oh, Anna, I'm both delighted and sad. This must be so difficult for you."

Genuine tears filled Anna's eyes as she nodded in agreement.

"We'll do anything, and I mean anything, to help. You just name it, and we'll be there." A troubled light stole into Betty's eyes.

Anna could no longer look directly at Betty and bent her head in shame. Remorse filled her soul, as tears broke free.

Warm arms enveloped hers as Betty pulled her chair close enough to hug her.

"Now, now dear, it'll be all right. How far along are you? You poor thing. You've looked so gaunt and malnourished, no one would guess." She looked directly at Anna's midsection and Anna breathed out trying to push the small mound to its fullest capacity.

"Five months now," she hiccuped between sobs, knowing full well it was only four.

"And you're only telling us now? Why haven't you said something sooner? You shouldn't have tried to deal with this alone. On top of being pregnant, you're dealing with grief, school, and work. How absolutely dreadful."

Anna had to think fast.

"It was the last thing I expected. I … I thought that I missed my cycle due to stress, and I had lost weight after Steven's death." She took in a deep breath, as a shudder ran through her. "I also became so distracted with starting a new job and school. I just wasn't paying attention."

One lie after another tumbled from her lips. Most of them were not complete untruths, but the message came through clear. Betty thought the baby was Steven's, and that lie lived and breathed and would be passed along as truth.

"There, there, my dear," Betty said as she patted Anna affectionately. "We're here for you. You just have to learn to lean on others more and not be so fiercely independent."

She pulled out a thick, soft tissue from her purse and handed it to Anna. "Promise me, my dear, that you'll let us help you."

Anna lay on her bed that night and trembled at the mess of her life.

Come to me, all you who are weary and burdened, and I will give you rest.

Another Bible verse filtered into Anna's troubled mind. She wished now she had not memorized so many Scriptures. They haunted her day and night. She knew if she came to God, he would give her rest but would also demand honesty. A mountain of embarrassment would follow. Honesty was off the table.

Betty had begged Anna to stop school and work, but Anna insisted they helped her fill her lonely days. She compromised and agreed to work only one day a week while she finished the six-month course she had started. Betty was only too happy to help out financially. Anna tried to refuse, but Betty insisted that Steven would have wanted both a restful pregnancy for Anna and a healthy baby. Anna had little recourse but to give in.

Guilt and sadness enveloped, and like a whirlpool she felt sucked into a vortex. Deep. Dark. Deadly. Who had she become? Where had that honest, dependable girl gone, the one who could sleep like a baby and had peace in her heart despite the hardships of life?

Anna tossed about and flipped restlessly from one side of the bed to the other.

The nights were the worst, and Steven wasn't the one in her bed or her head. Memories of Matt and the pleasure that followed haunted the hallways of her mind.

After punching down her pillow and rearranging her covers, she stared at the shadows cast from the street light through her window. She tried to distract her troubled spirit by counting the light beams streaming through the slats of her valance. When that didn't work she closed her eyes in hopes that counting imaginary sheep would help. Instead, another gnawing Bible verse came to mind.

My sheep listen to my voice; I know them, and they follow me.

Groaning into her pillow, Anna cried. Great wrenching sobs shuddered through her body as she curled into a tight ball.

"God," she whispered, "I didn't set out to live this lie, it found me."

I know my child, but it's still a lie. The truth will set you free.

Chapter Eleven

Somehow life went on for Anna, though she wanted to rage at the injustice or excuse the sin or turn the world off. Yet the sun rose in the east and set in the west. One day melted into the next, and her baby grew.

She had always loved late spring into the first blush of summer before the heat intensified. Cool mornings and evenings with sun-drenched afternoons made every living plant thrive. Flowers bloomed, birds fed their little ones, and life exuded hope, but not this year. Loneliness set in with a depression that skirted the edges of her mind.

Her sons hadn't come home in April when university finished. They stayed to work at summer jobs in Victoria. She missed their company but tried not to feel sorry for herself. Both of them had serious girlfriends, and they longed to be close to the ones they loved. She remembered that season of her life all too well, but it intensified her loneliness.

Time was up. She had to tell the boys about the baby, so she set out on a road trip for the Island to tell them in person. Normally, she would've prayed for a safe trip through the steep, windy mountains. She ignored that habit, feeling shame, hypocrisy, and distance—all of her own making. Although she expected to white knuckle it through the high elevations with a mixture of rain, sleet, and fog, the sun shone. Visibility remained bright and beautiful. When she reached the town of Hope, she breathed a sigh of relief. The worst stretch of highway, which dropped a full kilometer in elevation over a mere fifty miles, was behind her. Without thinking, she thanked God as she would have so many times before. Instant angst filled her heart. The easy relationship they had shared was gone.

When Anna got together with her sons and shared she was pregnant, they never questioned who the father was. Anna didn't have to voice the lie, she merely had to insinuate and perpetuate one. Somehow that didn't ease her unrest. A part of her wished that someone would question her, stretch her, make her face the truth—no one did. Her good-girl persona remained unchallenged.

Jason spoke first. "Would've never guessed this news in a million years. I'm shocked, but I'm coming home, that's for sure. I'm not leaving you alone at a time like this."

Anna had expected this kind of response from her gentle-spirited Jason.

"No, Jason. I've given this a lot of thought, and I don't want you boys to change a thing. Your life, your jobs, your girlfriends are all here and I'm busy with my course and my job. I keep my days full," she said with a firmness she never thought she could muster up.

"But, Mom—"

"No buts, Jason."

Jason turned to his brother for support. "Come on, Mark, help me out here. I know you can't leave Victoria, being you need the money for your last year of school, but I can take a year off and pick up where I left off later."

Mark frowned and rubbed his hand behind his neck.

Anna could tell that for her practical, level-headed son, an unplanned pregnancy would be unheard of. He kept his world perfectly ordered with a rigidness that screamed out the damage from his childhood. His dad's illness and death had been something he couldn't control but everything he could manage, he did down to the last jot and tittle.

"Mom, how can this be? Dad was so sick, and didn't you two ever do anything permanent to ensure that this wouldn't happen … with Dad's poor health, and all?"

Anna squirmed in her seat and felt heat swallow her face. She didn't lie, she merely told part of the truth.

"Your father and I were told years ago he couldn't have more children. That the drugs he used and the treatments he had made that impossible."

Mark shook his head. "I don't understand how God could let this happen to you now, when you have no help and are getting old … er." He rose to his feet abruptly. His hands tightened into fists, and he paced back and forth like a caged jaguar.

"Mark, don't blame God. Please. He hasn't failed me yet, and he won't now." Her words sounded weak, even to her ears. She knew them to be true, but she also knew that she wasn't exactly asking God for help.

"Ah, Mom, I can't bear to see you go through more." In a rare moment of tenderness, Mark broke down. His voice wavered as he struggled to hold onto control.

"I don't know how you keep on believing in God when he's done so little to make your life easy."

Disappointment and anger bled into his words. Anna could tell his walk of faith was struggling.

Thankfully, Jason came to the rescue. He stood up and gave his brother a quick hug but didn't linger, for Mark didn't accept hugs well.

"Come on, Bro, it's not that bad. We're family. If God's seen fit to add another little one, we need to find joy in that. I kinda like the idea of a little sister or brother ... don't you?"

Mark smiled despite himself. "Well, when you put it that way ... the kid will be spoiled rotten."

All the way home, Anna replayed their conversation. Her heart squeezed tight, and tears blurred her vision. She had to pull over to collect herself. The thought that Mark would blame God for her indiscretion felt like a thorn embedded in her flesh. Every conversation that fed the lie pricked her conscience, and the peace that had always been hers became a distant memory.

Anna's heart beat out of her chest, and knots as big as boulders weighted down her shoulders. Her sister was the hardest person to lie to.

"Why wait this long to tell me? Haven't I visited every week?" Lana's eyes grew large as she blinked back tears.

"Here I thought you were finally eating again and putting on some decent weight, only to find that you've got a lot more to deal with."

"I'm sorry, Lana. You can't imagine the pressure I've been under lately. I could barely comprehend what was going on in my body myself, much less talk about it. It's been forever since I was pregnant and believe me when I say pregnancy was the last thing on my mind. I thought I had the flu. And when I didn't get my cycle, I believed the effects of stress had finally got the best of me."

Tears filled Anna's eyes. She just wanted to be left alone. She hated the liar she had become.

"Sorry, Sis," Lana said. "I didn't mean for this to be about me." She fished in her purse for two tissues, one for each of them. "I'm just a little offended to be way down on your list of people to tell. But I'll get over it."

"What do you mean?"

"Don't worry about it. Eleanor came up to me the other day at church and quietly asked me if you had talked to me yet, like she was in on some secret. When I shook my head, she told me to pray for you. It felt weird to be left out of the loop. Why would you tell the pastor and his wife before me?"

Anna shook her head. No good lie came to mind. "I don't know. I'm not myself these days."

Lana graciously conceded. "I get that now more than ever, but I need to be sure that we're okay?"

"Yes. Of course." Anna quickly interjected.

"What I'm trying to ask is if I've done anything to change the trust and friendship we've always had? I get this distinct feeling that you don't tell me half the stuff you go through anymore, and I'm not sure why."

It was hard for Anna to answer. She knew it had nothing to do with her attentive sister and everything to do with the lie she was now living.

"Lana, please don't think it's your fault. It's … it's me. I haven't been a good friend to anyone since Steven died."

"You would tell me if there was more, wouldn't you, Sis? You seem so lost. I've never seen you like this, not even through the worst of it when Mom and Dad died, and then Steven. This scares me."

Anna longed to fill her perceptive sister in and ask her advice. She desperately needed someone to talk to, but knew that her fate was sealed, her choice made. For the first time in her life she would keep a secret from her twin—a horrible, deceitful one at that!

Chapter Twelve

"Yikes, Rita, your room is warm. I see you got those blinds wide open again. How do you sweet talk the staff into opening them for you when we all know we'll be cooked out of this place?"

Rita giggled like a schoolgirl. "I guess you're all scared of me."

Anna laughed. "Yeah, scared to disappoint the most loving soul in this place."

"Glad you don't want to disappoint me, Anna, dear, because I have something I want you to do for me. I know I've been bedridden for over a month now, but I need"—her voice became a whisper and Anna could not make out her words.

Anna walked closer and bent toward her.

"I want to go outside and feel the sun's warmth on this old face."

Anna smiled. "You're a plucky soul, because we both know this is going to cause you considerable pain to be moved and jostled about. Are you sure?"

Rita's eyes crinkled into lovely lines of laughter. "No pain, no gain," she said, "I aim to see the roses blooming at least one more time."

"Don't talk like that Rita, it makes me sad."

"Why ever so, my dear? We both know I'm going to a far better place. When I get there, I'll find your Steven and give him a big hug from you and tell him all about the baby."

Anna's eyes shifted down and she changed the subject back to Rita's request. "I'll check with the head nurse. If you're allowed on a field trip, consider it done."

The smile that radiated from that wrinkled, worn face lit up with the brilliance of a shooting star. She shouted after Anna, "See that the answer is yes, because I'm not taking no for an answer."

To rearrange Rita's schedule took some doing, and Rita had to forgo the rigor of her bath to have the energy for her trip outdoors. But the day was too perfect to pass up.

"The bath can wait. Because there's a chance that neither me nor that sunshine will be around tomorrow. I do believe the good Lord won't care a hoot whether I go to the grave without my last bath." She chuckled at her own humor, and Anna joined in.

With the help of the orderly, Anna dressed Rita and moved her from the bed into the wheelchair.

"I would like my purple sunhat, dear." Rita waved to her closet. "And that lovely colorful afghan for warmth around my legs."

Anna smiled and did her bidding.

"And I'm keeping my fuzzy yellows on. They keep the feet warm like nothing else. Don't care if they're slippers, won't be doing any walking anyhow." She chuckled.

As they rolled into the foyer, Rita caught a glimpse of herself in the hall mirror. Laughter rang out as she pointed at her reflection. "Why, Anna, look at that. If the good Lord can't see I'm in need of a new body soon, well, I'm just going to have to get stern with him. Every time I ask him to take me home, he tells me my work is not yet done."

"Tally-ho, my dear," she said as waved toward the door and broke into song. "Some glad morning when this life is over, I'll fly away." Anna joined in. "To that land where joy shall never end. Oh, I'll fly away."

Joy radiated from Rita's being, and her usual waxen complexion changed before Anna's eyes. Color burnished both cheeks, and her gray eyes grew bright with an unearthly sparkle. They sang their way out into the sunshine.

It was one of those rare summer days where a cool breeze rustled the leaves in the nearby maples and lifted the oppressive heat. The afternoon sun spread a buttercup yellow across the adjacent field and covered the waving grass in golden threads of splendor. Rita lifted her face into the warmth and breathed deeply.

"My dear, find me a rose. I need to feel, smell, and touch."

Anna cast her eyes around.

"Over there." Rita lifted her frail bony hand and pointed across the street to the wooded area. "I've been looking at those wild roses for a few days now, and there's nothing like the smell of a wild rose."

Anna was torn. Should she leave Rita unattended or disappoint her with a no?

"Go. I'll be fine." It was as if she read Anna's mind, and that thought unsettled her.

Anna hustled across the street. If not for her swollen abdomen that reminded her to be cautious, she would've broken into a full run.

It had been ages since Anna had gathered wild roses and stopped long enough to drink in the beauty or smell the woodsy perfume that floated up. She buried her nose into the bouquet as she headed back.

Rita gathered the sprigs in her fragile hands and gently rearranged the blossoms to her liking. She set them before her. "It's like having sunshine in my lap," she quipped.

A long moment passed as her gaze fixated on the flowers. "Did you know that summer has always been my favorite season?"

Anna shook her head. "No, why?"

Rita smiled. "Ah … because I love the sunshine and roses, especially the ones that grow wild." Her fingers touched the velvety petals, and she lifted one to her nose. She breathed in and exhaled slowly.

"How lovely. I may not be able to run or walk, but I can still smell."

She motioned toward Anna. "Can you push me through the park?" Anna slipped behind the chair and they moved along the walk.

"As believers, we want to be a pleasing fragrance like these wild roses, don't we?"

"Yes."

"I guess, then, the question remains, how do we lose that sweet aroma?"

Anna had no idea how to answer and turned the chair into the rose garden.

"Stop," Rita said. "Push me over to that rose bush, dear."

Anna felt glad that Rita's probing was distracted.

"Closer, please. I want to smell that beautiful yellow one right there." She pointed to a bush straight ahead. Anna wheeled her over and leaned in to bring the branch close to Rita's nose.

Rita breathed in deeply. "Hmmm, just what I thought. You smell it."

Anna bent down and took a good whiff. Nothing. She did it again. Still nothing.

"This rose has the appearance of the real thing, but isn't it disappointing when it has no scent?"

Anna stood up and moved back behind Rita's chair out of her view. She didn't answer.

"I ask. What is a rose without a beautiful smell?"

Anna's mind swirled in chaotic torment. As weird as Rita's questioning was, Anna knew exactly what she was asking.

Rita chose to answer her own question. "A rose without fragrance is like a Christian without forgiveness—it's just not natural."

Anna's heart began to pound within her chest.

"I am still here because of you, Anna. My work is not yet done, because you need prayer."

Shock radiated through Anna's being. Her eyes brimmed with unshed tears.

"You have a secret, my dear, that the good Lord doesn't want you to carry!"

Anna wanted to run from the conversation, but the wise old woman kept speaking.

"This secret goes against the will of God, doesn't it?"

Anna's eyes widened, and her hands began to shake. She gripped the wheelchair handles, glad that Rita could not see her.

"Don't be afraid. Our friendship is not a mere coincidence. You were placed in my life at this precise time, because God has ordered it. Do you believe that?"

Anna squeaked out a weak "Yes."

"God sees all and desires truth. He doesn't condemn you. He loves you. He longs to set you free and bring restoration to your soul."

Tears rolled down Anna's face. She tried to brush them away, but the steady flow made it impossible.

"Now, now, my dear, it's okay. Please push me over to that bench, and sit across from me." Anna could barely see through the tears, but she complied.

Rita reached out her hands. Anna leaned forward and took them in hers.

"Rest assured, God hasn't told me what your secret is, and I don't need to know the details to see that it's destroying you. So I stay, and I pray."

The elderly lady's eyes slid down to Anna's rounded stomach. That look gave Anna the distinct feeling that this spiritually gifted woman could make a well-educated assumption.

Anna had argued her case before God. She had justified the lies with the fact it wasn't her fault others had misread her situation. She had reminded

God how she had set out to tell the truth and had not concocted the story. But all the excuses in the world didn't bring back the peace she longed to have. He now used her dear friend Rita to bring home the truth—the one person she knew wouldn't judge or condemn her. A crack in the fortress door of her heart creaked open.

Rita waited patiently. The love that oozed from her eyes beckoned Anna to open her heart and give over her burden. Hope and shame volleyed for attention. Rather than unwrap the sordid details, Anna turned from Rita's gaze.

Rita nodded. She understood Anna's choice. "Please take me in. I'm exhausted."

Relieved, Anna scooted behind the chair, only too happy to leave that conversation behind.

Back in the room, Rita took one last inhale and handed the bouquet to Anna. "Choose the beautiful fragrance of forgiveness."

Anna's hand shook as she took the flowers from Rita's outstretched hands and set them on the dresser for a moment. She gathered the blanket around Rita's shoulders and tucked her into bed.

Rita whispered the strangest thing. "You know God loves you, don't you Anna?"

Anna nodded.

"Well then, my dear, since you can't find the strength to unload this burden, I'm going to pray that God brings about circumstances that force you to set this right." She closed her eyes and drifted off.

Anna's heart rate accelerated and pounded within her chest. She wanted to wake the now sleeping soul and beg her *not* to pray that prayer.

Chapter Thirteen

Matt tossed on his bed where sleep had eluded him for hours. He could not get comfortable.

Dreams of Anna flitted in and out of his consciousness and robbed his sleep. The longest eight months of his life had crawled by since their night together, and still his sorry heart beat that irregular rhythm at just the thought of her. Memories crept in at all hours of the day and night ensuring abject loneliness. A four-letter word slipped from his lips as he threw his covers aside and made his way to the kitchen.

With clenched fists he hammered the granite counter. *Maybe I should give into Tamara's invites. One quick call and I could have company.* Just the thought made his stomach heave. He had no appetite for anyone but Anna.

He ripped his hands through his hair and massaged the taut muscles at the back of his neck. He wanted to be angry at Anna for the way she had cut him out of her life but then remembered her tender care of Steven. *How can I blame her for loving so deeply when I want someone to love me that way?* A twist of envy tightened his gut. *No, not someone, I want Anna. But she has no clue how she broke down the walls of my guarded heart. No idea how my parent's incessant fighting turned me off marriage and how her example of love gradually wore away the stain.*

Nor does she have a clue how it took everything I had to keep proper boundaries. But once Steven died, yeah, I admit professionalism went out the window and possibility flew in. His heart picked up pace and his skin heated at the thought. *And then that night … wow!*

What a fool to let love grow just because she responded to me. And why can't I forget now that I know the truth? He paced back and forth. *It was just sex.*

Yeah, as if. I made love for the first time that night, and nothing in my past has ever come close to what we shared.

"Damn this hunger. Damn the pain." A string of unpleasant words filled the kitchen as he screamed into the silence.

It was one o'clock in the morning, yet the ping of a text came through. He picked up his cell. Tamara again.

"Hey, handsome, you available tonight? I have the wine and dance, all I need is you."

He hit the delete button. It sickened him to think of earlier days when that invitation would have been enough.

As he scrolled through the rest of his messages, his phone rang. The head nurse on the children's ward informed him that Isabella was failing.

"I'll be right there."

"Nancy, I'm so sorry." Matthew worked hard to choke back his tears. "Isabella was special to me too." It took all he had to press past the giant knot in his throat. A muscle jerked in his jaw as he struggled to hold himself together.

He put his arm around the sobbing Nancy as he guided her toward a nearby chair.

"Nurse Helen will stay with you until … you feel strong enough to drive home." He nodded at the nurse to take over.

Matt felt bad, but he didn't have the strength to stay one more moment. He hurried down the hall to a quiet staff room, glad it was three in the morning and few were about. He breathed easy to find the room empty and crossed to the window. The street light flickered on and off, on and off. Matt stood as if in a trance. Thoughts of sweet little Isabella brought a flow of tears. He had broken his own unspoken rule and allowed himself to care for that child way more than he should have.

What's wrong with me lately? First, I fall in love with a grieving widow. Then, I can't stomach my old lifestyle and choose to remain alone rather than have Tamara join me. I allow this sweet child I knew wasn't going to survive to work her way into my heart. And now I fall apart when a mother stricken with grief needs my professionalism the most.

A hollowness crept higher in his chest. His well-ordered life was spinning out of control. Years since the insecurity of his childhood and memories of his parent's volatile relationship had surfaced, tonight he felt he was back there … like that young unwanted, unsure little boy.

Why did Matt feel undone? Restless? And why the intense ache to see if Anna was okay, as if something was amiss?

A grocery store came into view, and he cranked the wheel into the parking lot. Not a store he normally frequented, but it would do. He needed a few things, and any distraction was better than his gnawing need.

With a basket in hand, he loaded up on vegetables and toiletries and headed for the check out.

"Hey, aren't you Doctor Carmichael?" the cashier asked.

Matt looked up from his task of emptying his grocery basket and recognized a face he had met at Steven's funeral. He rarely forgot a name. "Marcia, isn't it?"

She beamed. "I can't believe you remember me."

Matt smiled. "But of course, you sang at Steven's memorial service, didn't you?"

Marcia nodded. "We all go to the same church."

"How is Anna?" Matt asked nonchalantly, though his heartrate kicked up a notch.

"Oh, my gosh, like you will never believe it. What a miracle. But oh, how dreadfully sad all at the same time."

Matt didn't understand a word, but he was in the fast lane with a portly lady behind him clucking her tongue at their chit chat. It was time to tender his order, and knew he was holding up the line, but needed to know.

"What's sad?"

"Like the whole thing … Steven dying and now the fact she's—"

"Marcia, less socializing! Your lineup is out into the aisle and customers aren't happy."

Marcia rolled her eyes but snapped into action. She handed Matt his bag and receipt. "Nice to see you again, Doctor. I've got a solo part in the choir this Sunday, if you're interested." She smiled sweetly and turned her attention to the next customer.

Matt carried his bag to the car, more troubled than ever. *What had that conversation meant?*

Marcia had planted a seed. If he went to church on Sunday he would indeed see Anna for himself.

Chapter Fourteen

"God, I have no idea if you're up there or not, but since Anna seems to think you are … it would take a miracle to work out my schedule so I can get to church this Sunday. Can you help me?"

He had to sweet talk another doctor into working his Sunday shift with his coveted hockey tickets.

The whole time he prepared, he hoped good sense would prevail, and he would find the strength to talk himself out of such irrational behavior. Not this time. He needed to see her. His heart began to buck at the thought.

"What do I wear, Abby?" he mumbled to his cat that lay stretched on his neatly made bed. "What do you think the Sunday crowd wears these days?"

Abby slid her eyes closed.

Part of him wanted to look his best just in case a chance meeting happened, but above all he wanted to dispel the nonsense that something was wrong.

He dressed with care, glad he had picked up his favorite shirt and pants from the dry cleaners the day before. Not too dressy and yet not too casual. He slid a tie into his pocket, just in case and gave one last glance into the mirror. He picked a fleck of lint off his sleeve and slipped into his jacket. "Well, Abby, here goes."

Abby's eyes squinted open but only for a second.

He had done a little research online and found that the First Baptist Church was not one of those mega churches he had seen on TV. The congregation just big enough he wouldn't stand out, yet small enough he could find Anna.

He left early to allow ample time to get there but planned to wait until just before the service to enter. The surrounding area was quite different from his end of town, where million-dollar homes were perched on the side of a mountain. He rather liked the warmth of character that radiated from the small, older homes, where mature trees and trailing red roses draped over the white picket fences. Small front porches had the welcome of a bygone era when life had been less harried and neighbors took time to visit.

Situated in a part of town that typified the average income of a blue-collar worker, the church had an old-world charm with brick and a steeple. He began to relax as he climbed the steps of the church. Along one side, an addition had been built to house what looked like a gym or banquet hall, but the architect had tastefully kept the original building intact and added a brick foundation to tie it all together. The double wooden doors, open to the breeze, created an inviting entry. After a warm handshake at the entrance by a perfect stranger and hug from a little old lady standing in the wings, Matt slid into a seat at the back of the church. As planned, his timing was perfect. He blended into the gathering crowd without a hitch.

His heart sank when he couldn't find her. He tried to stretch above the congregation without bringing attention to himself. A dismal thought entered. What if he'd gone through all this trouble and she was absent? It hurt just to think of the possibility.

Then his eyes fell upon her. There she sat in the third row of the choir. A large man positioned himself in front of Matt creating a perfect set up. He could stay hidden, yet stare at her at leisure. He had to admit, she did look wonderful.

When they stood to sing, Matt could barely see her face peek out from the crowd. Thankfully, she'd put on some weight. That gaunt look was gone. He smiled.

The temptation to talk to her vanished. She was fine. He wished he could sneak out unnoticed. He had his answer. She was good, and he was losing it.

But why the angst? Why can't I let go? This obsession has to stop. He felt a bead of sweat trickle beneath the curls on his temple, and he brushed the drop away.

The choir rose and the singers filed out one by one. Matt stretched to see one more glance of her before he snuck out the back. A large mound protruded from her midsection, and it took a moment for his mind to catch up to his eyes. Anna was very pregnant. His heart slammed inside his chest and thoughts tumbled chaotically over each other. *Whose baby? Is it mine?*

Of course, the baby was his. Anna was not the kind of woman to sleep around. The fact she had ventured outside the boundaries of her beliefs even for one night had clearly upset her. He could not forget the guilt etched on her face the morning after and the way she could not look him in the eye. She had feigned a headache and whisked him out the door.

The choir filed out from a side door and made their way to their seats. Anna floated down the aisle toward him. He'd never seen anyone radiate such beauty, she had that natural glow pregnant women so often carry. Her dark hair bounced free over her shoulders and flowed down her back. Fire ripped through his heart at the memory of it tangled beneath his fingers, and he had to will himself back into the present as she slid into the seat halfway down the sanctuary.

She was far enough along. Every moment, every day, of the last eight months had been grueling, and he didn't have to do the math. Anna was carrying their baby. *His baby.* The thought jumped inside with a jolt of excitement … *a baby.* He was going to be a father. The gift this child would bring in connecting their lives together made his heart do back flips.

Had God allowed these circumstances in which to draw their lives together? He remembered his desperate prayer for an opportunity in which to win her love. *Why did I feel so compelled to see her? Was this a coincidence or an answer to that long-forgotten prayer?*

No, I can't dismiss the facts. God did hear. And not only did he hear, but he presented the perfect opportunity. Matt felt a stir of something undefined touch his heart. He shifted in his seat and stretched his neck from side to side.

But why would she keep a thing like that from me?

Ahh, yes. I always told her my life was wrapped up in medicine, and considering our last conversation where she admitted she still loved Steven, she wouldn't want to pressure me out of a sense of duty.

Matt's heart rate settled into a steady rhythm. He imagined his conversation with Anna. He would reassure her that she didn't have to raise their baby alone. Had he known, he would've been there all along. From experience, his last mistake reminded him to take it slow and respect whatever relationship she allowed.

With lots of time to think in the past eight months, Matt had concluded that when a spouse died, the surviving spouse couldn't, nor shouldn't, turn off years of memories and love. He somehow needed to convey that he had no desire to remove Anna's past, he just wanted to be part of her future. She could go on loving Steven for the rest of her life, as long as she could make room for the here and now.

Hope lit a candle in the pitch-black recesses of his soul and his heart. A world of possibilities flooded in.

Not a word of the sermon computed until the very end when the pastor called the congregation to pray. His ears perked. He wanted to know how to say a proper thank you to God for this huge miracle.

"Dear Lord Jesus, we come before you now and bring the sick and the needy."

"Our dear Rose is in the hospital just days from meeting you, Jesus. Hold her close, oh Lord, and be with her family. To say good-bye to this dear soul will be difficult."

"We also bring Emily and Bill's daughter Ruthie to you, Lord. You know, dear Father, how she has chosen to live far from your ways but how she is not far from your love. Please bring her home, dear Jesus, bring her home."

Scattered amens sprinkled from all corners of the church spilled out.

"And, oh Jesus, lest we forget dear Anna. We cry out to you, Lord, in the name of Jesus and ask for the healthy delivery of Anna and Steven's baby—"

Matt never heard a word after that. His blood ran cold, and a spike of anger rode his spine from top to bottom. A muscle in his jaw clenched, and he bit down so hard he could taste blood in his mouth. He rose from his seat and strode from the building in a rage. A blind fury made his world swim in darkness. He was not sure how he drove home, but there he sat in the garage unable to think straight. He slammed the dashboard with his fist.

How could she call herself a Christian and be so deceitful? There was not a chance in heaven or hell that the baby was Steven's. He clenched his teeth and bit back a blast of fury. They both knew that Steven was physically incapable. Anna's cover-up wouldn't work with him.

He cursed. He hated Anna. He loved Anna. No, he hated the fact he loved her.

Her betrayal cut deep. He had placed her on a pedestal, set her up as one to emulate, only to find that she was more fallible than he cared to admit. Pain clawed at his chest.

He slipped from the car and slammed both the car and house door and threw his car keys across the room.

He dropped his body to the couch and reminded himself to face this disappointment like all others—with logic and discipline—to act, not react.

Her world of pasted-on piety and people pleasing is about to end. And if she thinks for one moment I'm not going to be a dad to my child, she can think again.

Matt heard Isabella's laughter in his mind as he thought of being a daddy and he was back there. Her giggle permeated the hospital floor as he rounded the corner into her room. Her eyes popped big and bright as she noticed Matt. "Doctor Matt, come see what Mama bought me."

She held up a doll with big blue eyes just like hers. Matt could see that the hair had been cut back to show only a tuff of peach fuzz.

Isabella had a stethoscope around her neck and proceeded to go through the same motions Matt had done to her a million times.

"I'm a mama now. I have to be brave and strong to look after baby Destiny. She needs me."

Matt reached up and wiped the tears from his eyes. That memory reminded him of what Isabella had taught him—something he had not known about himself—he wanted to be a dad. There was something very special about the unconditional love of a child, and now that gift lay before him. Nothing could keep him away.

Chapter Fifteen

As much as Matt's initial reaction sent him reeling, he wasn't a man given to anger. He hurt more than he cared to admit, but there was a piece of him that understood the fear and shame Anna would have faced, and his responsibility in the situation.

A sheer determination to know and love his baby set in. At thirty-five, where he had once thought the prospect of fatherhood lost to him due to other priorities, excitement flooded in. Sweet Isabella had changed everything. The joy that child had given him lit a fire within.

Even if Anna had nothing to do with him, she would have to get used to the fact that he was the father to her child, and nothing was going to stop him from being a loving father.

Matt had little time to lose. Anna was due in a matter of weeks, and he wanted to be present when that baby was born. He planned to hold his child in the first moments of life and never let go.

He climbed the steps to her front porch, rang the doorbell, and waited.

The door swung open, and the blood drained from Anna's face. Her skin turned chalky white, yet her cheeks flamed red. Her lips parted but no words came out. He felt both sorry for her and vindicated all in one kaleidoscopic minute.

"Anna," he said firmly. "I do believe we have a pressing matter to discuss." Staring pointedly at her midsection, he entered without permission. He looked her squarely in the eyes, took the door from her white-knuckled hands and closed it. He moved across the foyer to the living room and took a seat.

She slowly followed and eased her body to the couch. Seated on the edge, rim rod straight, she clasped and unclasped her hands over her large abdomen.

He could see the sheen of sweat on her brow and the way she nibbled at her lower lip.

"Nice to see you again, Matt," she said, as she placed one hand over the other to still the shake that had taken over her fingers.

"Actually, I think you've gone out of your way to avoid seeing me."

"Why would you think that, Matt?"

"That's our child you carry, Anna, and what I'd like to know is—when were you going to tell me?"

For a split second, the anguish in her eyes appeared bottomless until she arched her brows questioningly and pasted on her fake smile.

"Our baby, Matt? No, you misunderstand. It's … it's Steven's."

"Don't lie to me, Anna. We both know only too well what condition Steven was in."

"You don't know anything." She rose, indignation on her face. "Miracles happen," she said pacing. "So, don't come in here assuming you know what went on in our private life."

He put his hand up. "Enough Anna."

She spun around, and stopped.

"I'm positive the child you're carrying is mine. I'd stake my life on it. There is, however, DNA testing if you want to carry on with this lie.

She turned and faced him. He could see the play of emotions flood across her face from anger—to fear—to a tired surrender.

A groan of despair slipped from her lips.

"Yes, Matt, the child is yours," she whispered. She turned away and back again. "I was so scared and felt so ashamed. Now all I've done is make matters worse." Her eyes stared blankly into the distance. Tears filled her eyes. One broke free and a stream followed.

"I don't expect you to forgive me, but I'm sorry … so very sorry." Her words subsided as great sobs racked her frame.

He stood, not sure what to do, and then threw caution to the wind and pulled her shaking form into his arms. They stood silently in the warmth of the other. He was careful not to draw her too close, and he could tell she was equally careful not to let him. The baby kicked. Matt felt the movement against his torso.

"Is that what I think it is?" He pulled back and looked down.

She nodded and reached out for his hand.

His heart slammed against his chest at the mere touch until she placed it firmly on her stomach. Movement danced beneath his splayed fingers. He laughed in delight.

"Wow, an active one."

Their eyes met.

A giant knot caught in his throat. "Why didn't you tell me, Anna? Didn't you believe that I would help you? Didn't you think I would care to know my own child?"

She shuddered, and moved apart.

"Oh Matt, it's not you, it's me! My life is so complicated. I … I never told the world that this baby was Steven's, everyone just assumed it was. I was wrong to let them believe that lie, but I knew the truth would hurt my sons, my in-laws—"

"It didn't matter that you hurt me?"

"Of course, it matters, but I thought you would never know. You … you have it all together. Your life is meaningful and career orientated. And you've shared countless times how much your work means to you. I … I didn't want to burden you with my mistake."

"Your mistake? First of all, there is no singular in this circumstance, *we* are responsible. Secondly, you may consider this pregnancy a mistake, but I do not. In fact, when I sat in your church on Sunday morning—" He was interrupted by her gasp.

"Yes, I was there, the fool that I am.

"Anyway, as I was saying—when I realized you were carrying our child, conceived in that one stolen night, I began to believe in your God. I actually thanked him for this miracle, until I heard the pastor pray for the safe delivery of Steven's baby. Your deceit and betrayal hurt deeper than you'll ever know." A jagged pain stabbed in. He decided to leave before saying something he'd regret.

Anna carefully lowered her heavy body onto the couch and placed her hands over her face. Soft sobs filled the room.

"I'm going now. I'll give you time to process. But I want you to know that I intend to be a father to our child, even if you don't want me in your life."

He walked toward the door. "This is not goodbye, Anna."

Chapter Sixteen

Matt's words had deservedly crushed Anna's heart. She was a phony and a fraud, and she was pained beyond measure that her Christian witness had damaged Matt. Regret washed over her like acid rain eating into her soul. How had she allowed one lie feed into a million more?

That conversation with Rita flooded in. Day after day Anna knew Rita had prayed for disclosure, for freedom, for a softened heart. Rita's work was done. Anna's world, now shaken and turned upside down by invisible hands, left little room for anything but the truth.

Anna gave into the sorrow. It grew from the pit of her stomach and flowered in her throat. Great wrenching sobs worked up and out, as she crumbled in a ball upon the couch. She wanted to lay down and never get up. Had it not been for a persistent kick in her side that reminded her there was a reason to live, she would have given room for her depressive thoughts.

What have I done? If I thought my initial sin was hard to confess, what is everyone going to think now, after months of half-truths and outright lies?

There was only one person in the world she could talk to about this. After a good cry, she picked herself up off the couch and headed to the nursing home. She didn't care if she arrived with blotchy makeup and red-rimmed eyes.

Huge tears rolled down Anna's face the minute she closed the door to Rita's room.

Rita motioned her over and hugged her close. "There, there, child, you'll be all right. Talk to me, my dear, and together we'll pray this through."

Anna tried to speak through sobs and hitches. Bit by bit she revealed the story from beginning to end. Not once did Rita cringe, cluck in dismay, or show any form of condemnation. She nodded and kept a hold of Anna's hand with an occasional squeeze.

When all was exposed, Rita bowed her head in prayer. "Lord, I ask only one thing, give Anna the courage she needs to do this your way."

"Now you pray, Anna." she encouraged.

Anna hadn't been able to pray for months. Her scattered version of "please, God don't let the world find out I'm a liar" had hit the ceiling and bounced right back to her.

"Oh, God, I'm sorry. I've messed up my life and hurt others by first my disobedience and then lies to cover my shame. Forgive me … forgive me, Father."

As she prayed, Anna felt weight roll off her shoulders. The concrete brick of sin crumbled. Laughter spilled from her lips with tears mingled in the mix.

"Oh, Rita, how am I going to make this right without hurting so many people?"

Rita pulled her close and hung on for a long moment. When she drew back she admitted. "Confession doesn't necessarily eliminate pain or hurt, but it's always God's way. Ask for forgiveness where forgiveness is needed, and leave the healing to the Lord.

"What you need to know is who you hurt the most, and work the list back from there. Do you understand what I'm encouraging?"

Anna thought for a moment. Different people flashed on the pages of her mind, her children, her sister, the pastor and his wife, her in-laws, the church body.

"The person you've wronged the most, dear child, is God! David said it best after his scandal with Bathsheba in Psalms 51:4. *Against you, you only, have I sinned and done what is evil in your sight.* And what he meant is that God was the most important relationship to set right, first and foremost. You've done that by your repentance today.

"Then secondly, the world would say you need to forgive yourself—"

"But, Rita, how can I ever forgive myself after what I've done?"

"My child, you can't—that's my point" Rita smoothed her weathered hand gently down Anna's face and rubbed a stream of tears away. "You don't and can't forgive yourself, that's God's job. Jesus died on the cross, so we know that work is finished. You have to accept God's forgiveness, and that's the hard part.

"You see, my dear, I know from experience. I, too, have a past that only God can forgive, and it took me years to let him. Don't make my mistake. Don't allow your soul to stay tied in knots because you somehow think you have to forgive yourself. If you don't accept his forgiveness, you'll never be able to accept his love. The two work together."

Rita's words rang true. Anna attempted a smile as she threw her arms around the old soul and hugged tight.

"I love you."

"There, there dear child … you're strangling me." She pulled back, and they both laughed.

Rita cupped both sides of Anna's face in her wrinkled hands. "I'll sum it up for you, my dear Anna, start with accepting God's forgiveness, and then ask forgiveness of Matt. After all, he's your baby's father, and a good relationship between parents is crucial for the child. The Lord will lead from there. Now let's pray."

Rita wore a smile as colorful as a rainbow after a storm. And when Anna gathered her purse and sweater and headed to the door, she was sure she heard Rita say, "Lord Jesus, am I done now, because I really want to see you?"

A few steps down the hall, Anna wheeled around and marched right back to Rita's room. She opened the door and said firmly, "God said no."

Rita's loud cackle echoed down the hall.

For the first time in months, Anna could both pray and pick up her Bible without guilt. She scanned through the stories of God's forgiveness wrapped from the beginning of time all through the sacred pages. The story of Adam and Eve unfolded in a new light. Their disobedience and then lies to cover the sin sounded much like her life in the past months. She read of David's adultery, murder, and lies to cover the truth, and Peter's lie of betrayal when Jesus was arrested. The stories had one reoccurring theme, sin, lies, forgiveness, and restoration.

But before she talked to others, she wanted to fully accept God's forgiveness and acknowledge all. This meant a trip back to that night. Where she had previously stifled all memory, the Holy Spirit guided her toward complete honesty.

"Oh, Jesus, I wallowed in a pit of fear concerning my future. Instead of turning toward you, I turned to self-pity.

"I allowed Steven to become a distant man, rather than fight for more in our relationship. In truth, I protected my heart. All those close calls over the years left me emotionally exhausted."

I know my child.

"By the time Steven passed away, I had cried so many tears for so many years, my grief was done. But oh, how I played the mournful wife card to perfection. Sympathy fed my soul until temptation brought something more powerful.

"I was angry, God, at the loss of Steven's health and the life I imagined we would have together. I was ripe for the picking. Agitated. Angry. Alone. A perfect set-up for the perfect storm. That's how Matt found me that night."

Yes, my daughter, let truth in.

Anna's hands fell over her face as a truth she had not previously allowed flooded through her mind.

"Oh, God, I opened my heart to Matt … before Steven died." This admission burned a hole in her heart, and she dropped to her knees in humility.

"I looked forward to Matt's attention like every other woman—attracted to his startling good looks—without a doubt.

"Though I never overtly gave free passage to these feelings, God, I opened the door to a friendship with a level of intimacy that should've been reserved for Steven. In truth, I had more connection with Matt most days than I did with Steven in a week."

Anna felt the tears course down her cheeks, but stayed on her knees. There was more … much more.

"God, when Matt arrived that evening sporting a virile masculinity with warmth and compassion, I ate it up. Flesh and blood rather than faded memories … Yes, I loved the delight of pleasure and sensation I felt in his arms. I initiated that first kiss. My hands were the first to creep under his T-shirt and bring flesh against flesh.

"When Matt suggested we stop, and I felt the kick of his heart beneath my wandering fingertips, I reveled in the power of that moment. I pressed my body closer, and moved against him in a message of encouragement older than time. In truth, God, I let pleasure rule though your Spirit screamed out otherwise."

Anna shuddered as a large piece of suppressed truth crashed in. Their time had not been just one passionate moment of unbridled passion. They had enjoyed a night together. The coupling of body, mind, and soul included words of endearment and sleep wrapped tight in each other's arms. Curled against him, they had slept until the first blush of dawn with morning kisses taking them away yet again. Anna's cheeks burnt hot at the recollection.

The memory she constantly referred to in her mind as one act of indiscretion, in reality had been a decision on her part to make the most of their night together. Not once in her selfishness had she given thought to how her behavior would affect Matt. Her need, her want, was all that mattered. She had drunk fully from the cup of passion.

"Oh, God, I finally understand how that choice now brings pain for all involved. I'm not the only one affected. The fingers of my failure fan out and pull in Matt, my family, my friends, the church, but most importantly … you, Jesus."

Anna could feel the sorrow sweep in like a thick wave. It picked her up and wrapped her in its folds. *Does redemption truly cover all?*

Yes, it does my child.

"Oh, God, you see all. You hear all. You know all. I openly confess to you what I couldn't face a week ago when I prayed with Rita. Please take every dark corner, expose each lie, and renew a right spirit within me. Purify my soul and take these lips that have dripped lies and fill them with truth. Give me courage, oh Lord, to stand in the heat of disclosure, no matter how difficult my life may get. Thank you for your sacrifice, Jesus, so I can stand pure and forgiven before you no matter what people may say. Amen."

Wrapped in a cocoon of peace, Anna rose from the floor and flopped onto her bed. She slept soundly that night for the first time in months.

Upon waking, one clear instruction from the Lord came to mind. She had to face Matt with the truth, admit her failure, and ask for his forgiveness. Every lie she told to him had to be revealed.

She was fully aware he might perceive the truth a gateway to relationship, but the Scripture clearly stated not to marry an unbeliever, and she was done with disobedience. Their two different worlds would not, and could not, mesh. She wouldn't lead him on.

In a matter of weeks, she would have a baby who needed her complete attention, and she planned to keep this child her focus.

Chapter Seventeen

Jason could not rid himself of the foreboding that nagged at his spirit. Something was not right with his mom. As much as she tried to put on a brave face, he knew he had to get home. He'd just started the September term, and to get away would be difficult. But when he talked it over with his girlfriend, Jennifer, they both agreed that a quick trip home to dispel some of Jason's unease would be worth the effort.

He left on Friday after his classes and caught the late ferry over to the mainland. After a night at a friend's place in Vancouver, he got an early start the next day.

Kelowna, the jewel of the Okanagan Valley, came into view. Jason was almost home. The entry to this beautiful city with its mountain backdrop against panoramic lake vistas usually gave him pause for appreciation, but today he felt only angst. He huffed at the aggravation the bottleneck on the bridge presented. The traffic crawled down bridge hill where it converged onto one of the world's longest floating bridges across the Okanagan Lake. Jason knew his hometown only too well. This meant worse congestion on the city side. His edginess increased. All he wanted to do was get home, not face another traffic jam.

Jason had deliberately not phoned his mom in advance. He wanted to surprise her and hopefully catch her without that plastic smile. He needed to see the real person behind the mask. In truth, he longed to see his old mom, the one without worry etched upon her face. He'd not seen that peaceful soul for far too long now. A new person had emerged after his dad's death, and he was worried.

He parked at curbside and entered the house quietly. Raised voices reached him.

"Drat," he muttered. "She has company." He glanced out onto the street but didn't recognize the vehicle. With no intention on eavesdropping, his mother's words stopped him short.

"Matt, you have to understand how sorry I am. I shouldn't have lied to you under any circumstances. There's no excuse. Please, forgive me."

His mom's voice wavered and Jason could tell she was crying.

"I do forgive you, Anna. I just don't understand the social pressure you Christians put on yourselves. I'll never believe that what we shared was anything but the most wonderful experience of my life … but all that aside, Anna, you have to realize with or without a relationship I want to be a father to my child. You can't deny me that."

Their voices hushed and fell to a whisper.

Jason was confused. Who was this Matt guy? Why was his mom crying about lying? She never lied. And what child were they talking about? Should he go back and enter with a loud knock, or should he walk into the kitchen? Like a wishbone, he felt pulled in two directions.

The moment of silence stretched into awkwardness. Had they gone out the patio door into the backyard? He didn't know where they were, but he knew if he didn't act soon they could come around the corner and find him standing there like an idiot, and so he entered the kitchen unannounced.

His very pregnant mother stood close to Dr. Carmichael, who pressed his hand intimately against her stomach as if it belonged there. With a tender look on her face, she watched Dr. Carmichael smile at the movement of the baby.

"Mom?"

Anna jolted at the sound of his voice. They jumped apart like they had each just touched a hot burner.

His mom clearly had been crying.

"Jason, my dear … why … when did you get here?" She moved quickly toward him, once again with that practiced expression he'd come to loath. "You should've called, I … I didn't know you were coming." Her voice wavered, and her hands shook as she pulled him close for a quick hug.

Jason had indeed interrupted much more than a casual conversation between them.

Matt moved forward and shook Jason's hand firmly. "Good to see you again, Jason." He turned toward the door and waved good-bye. "Anna, I'll talk to you later."

He was gone before either of them could respond.

Jason turned his attention toward his mom. "Are you all right?"

His mother shook her head. Tears brimmed and filled her bottom lashes. A few blinked free. "No Jason, I'm not all right and won't be until the truth is told." Jason placed an arm around her shoulders and guided her into the living room. "Let's sit down, Mom." They moved to the couch, and he helped her get comfortable with some pillows behind her back.

"Why are you here, Jason? I thought you were coming in a few weeks when junior here gives an appearance?"

"I can't explain it, Mom, but you've been on my mind and in my prayers, I just had to see you." It sounded lame. He could hear the echo of his brother's favorite way to tease him, "Mama's boy. Mama's boy."

Her words confused him more. "I wondered who God would send my way next. Rita, my friend at work, assured me God would guide me through this difficult process, and here you are, my gentle Jason.

"What did you hear today before you came into the kitchen?"

He felt heat rush to his face and knew there was no point in denying anything. "It made no sense, Mom. I heard you two talking about lies, forgiveness, and Dr. Carmichael's plea to be a father … I felt awkward hearing any of it. Are you two going out?"

His mom's face blanched at his words. Her guarded expression fell and pain painted a new expression. One look at her face had him wishing the fake smile was pasted back there.

"Jason, I need to ask your forgiveness, but this is really difficult for me to tell, so you'll have to let me finish before you ask questions."

Jason nodded in agreement.

"I've failed miserably."

Jason jumped up with a *no* on his lips, but she stilled him with the wave of her hand. "Sit, Jason. It's time for truth." She patted the sofa beside her.

"I let you, your brother, and the rest of the world believe a lie … because I wanted to cover up the truth. This baby has a different father than both you and your brother." She let the truth sink in.

"What? Mom, you can't be serious. Who's the father?"

A light dawned inside his head. "Dr. Carmichael?"

"Yes."

He felt like someone punched him in the stomach good and hard. "But … but, Mom, it would've had to have been …?"

93

Jason could tell by the flush of red to her cheeks she was embarrassed.

"Jason, I'm eight months pregnant. I became pregnant a month after your father's death. I was lonely and distressed, but … oh no, I don't want to cover my sin with excuses any longer. Please forgive me, Jason." She buried her face in her hands.

She sat beside him weeping softly, while he processed her shocking revelation. His mother was not a saint. She was a real person with failures, and she needed a hug. His arms encircled her, and they stayed that way for a long moment. Though disappointed, Jason thought of his mother as a woman. Compassion flooded his soul as he realized his mother's life had been filled with much more sorrow than happiness.

Anna drew back. "Jason, you're such a gift to me. The rest of the world will not be so kind, of that I'm sure. I can tell by that hug, you've somehow forgiven me already."

"Yeah, Mom … your life has been so tough—" He shook his head and ran a hand through his wiry hair that sprang back into place. "Life isn't fair, is it Mom? Some people get no breaks."

A few moments lapsed as they both sat in silence. Suddenly, Jason snorted.

"Oh, Mom, this one will go down big at church, and Mark is going to blow a gasket, not to mention Gramps and Gram Clarke." He whistled between his teeth. "There's a reason I felt compelled to visit you, Mom. I'll be praying up a storm."

"Are you trying to cheer me up, Jason? Because ice cream would work a lot better."

They both chuckled before Anna grew serious once again.

"Jason, I didn't set out to lie about this, but when everyone assumed the baby was your father's, all my shame was covered. A way of escape presented itself, and I chose a wrong path. I know that what I face ahead is considerably worse than had I spoken truth the moment Pastor Harry started rattling on about a modern-day miracle and Steven's baby."

Jason probed, "But, Mom, what made you decide to tell the truth now?"

"I wish I could say my good conscience kicked in, but truthfully it was Dr. Carmichael."

"Why did he let it go so long, before demanding you deal with it?"

His Mom broke out in a watery smile.

"What?"

She reached up and smoothed the lines from his brow.

"I'm doing my Grinch impersonation again, aren't I?"

"Jason, you're such a joy. I remember from the time you were two, you had us in stitches with your scrunched-up face, eyebrows knit together like two furry caterpillars doing a dance and furrows in your brow the size of an old man … not to mention the Grinch expression that still makes me smile."

"Well, if it makes you smile …" He deliberately made his best possible expression, and they laughed. "Happy to give a little comic relief considering—what's ahead."

"I don't look forward to it, but for the first time in months I feel at peace."

"How long has your relationship with the doctor been going on?"

She exhaled slowly. "Dr. Carmichael and I have had a friendship that goes way back, probably more of a friendship than I should've allowed. This made me vulnerable when he came calling a month after your dad's death. I cut off the relationship after that one night, other than to tell him what a mistake it had been, so he didn't know I was pregnant.

"But God wasn't happy with the fact that the world believed a lie, because lo and behold, Dr. Carmichael suddenly gets the urge to go to church. What a surprise I must've been with my stomach sticking out like a beach ball. Then when he heard the pastor pray for the safe delivery of your father's baby, he bolted from the church in absolute shock and fury, and I can't blame him."

She shook her head.

"Do you love him, Mom?"

Jason noticed the flush that immediately came to his mom's cheeks.

"Oh, Jason, I don't know what I feel. He's been a good friend over the years and part of that bled into that night. He was … is an attractive man, and it would be easy to make decisions based on infatuation, loneliness, or this baby." She smoothed a hand over her large tummy. "But those would be all the wrong reasons, not to mention the fact he's not a believer. I've done many things wrong in the past eight months, Jason, and I don't want to run ahead of God or outside his will ever again."

"And what I saw today—"

"Was no more than Matt feeling the baby's movement. He wants to be a father to this child … to his child, and I don't know what that looks like at the moment. He arrived unannounced today, just as you did, and I'm faced with decisions I have no answers for. I'm going to need a lot of wisdom, and I've had so little since your father died."

Jason squeezed her shoulders but remained quiet.

"Forgiveness is such a wonderful gift. I don't think I really understood that until now. I was always the good girl. I married young, took care of your father when the going got tough, and threw myself into being a mother."

"Mom, you were the best … and I'm not just saying that. I hear the abuse Jennifer went through as a child, and it makes me so sad. I was blessed to have you."

"Yeah. But, Jason, there was a certain pride I took in all of that. I often looked at others with superiority and a lack of compassion. I felt God owed me something for being such a great Christian. That attitude took away the true wonder of the cross." She dropped her head. "I've now been sufficiently humbled and have a much greater understanding of forgiveness. It's the one gift that has come out of this."

A sad look spread across her face as her eyes filled and glistened with unshed tears. "How easy it was for self-pity and self-righteousness to bring me down. I had everything on the outside looking good. People thought I was amazing, but in truth, I let the most important relationship with your father fade until we became nothing more than patient and caretaker. I regret that so much."

"Mom, you've made many sacrifices for the family, and no one can take that from you, but honestly, we've all put you up on some saintly platform when God is the only one who deserves to be up there. It's time to start taking care of yourself and this new baby and embrace your forgiveness. Who cares what people think?"

He rose to his feet. "Quite frankly, it's refreshing to see you as a real person. I can handle that way more than how you've been these last eight months—enough said. I can go back to school in peace, and I'll be back when my baby brother or sister is born."

"Now let's get some pizza, I'm starving." Jason smiled down on his mom and dropped a kiss on her cheek. "Let me help you and that baby up out of the couch." He reached out two hands.

"Okay, but only if we can get ice cream for dessert."

He laughed. "Mom, you and your ice cream."

Jason ruminated all the way back to Victoria. The one thing he could do to help his mom would be to talk to his brother on her behalf. He didn't dare suggest it, because he knew she'd say no. But he knew his brother. Mark would need time to digest the information. If it was sprung on him, he would make a colossal fool of himself and hurt their mom big time.

Jason would handle this one very important detail but not without prayer … lots and lots of prayer.

Chapter Eighteen

"You've got to be kidding me!" Mark slammed his fist down on the table. "Tell me this is your idea of a sick joke before I use my fist to send you into next week." Mark lifted from the chair with his body hunched forward over the table.

"Mark, I wouldn't joke about something like this."

Mark's face turned as red as a pickled beet. He rose to his feet crashing the chair to the floor behind him.

"Mom … our good, little Christian mother?" Unbelief and scorn bit crisp from his lips.

"Mark, our mom is not infallible. She has real weaknesses and failures, just like you and me."

"Weakness," he bellowed. "I find out my mother acted no better than a common hussy, and you call it weakness? Blast it, Jason, this mama's boy, bleeding-heart thing of yours has gone too far. Why didn't she tell me to my face?" His fists clenched and unclenched as he paced the floor.

Jason prayed for the right words. "I went to Kelowna last weekend unannounced. I kinda ran into the situation head on. Dr. Carmichael was at the house, and I heard some things … Mom doesn't know I'm telling you."

"So, we still wouldn't know if you hadn't gone there and caught them together? Mom was forced into telling and not by a bout of that spiritual guidance she so often preaches we need. And if I could get my hands on that Dr. Carmichael, I would bust his neck. How dare he take advantage of a grieving widow? What a swine."

"I don't think it's one-sided, Mark. Come on, you weren't born yesterday. We both know what loneliness feels like."

"Huh. Call it loneliness, but I see it for what it is … black-hearted sin."

"And you've never sinned?"

"Don't go there with me, Jason. Don't you dare play the devil's advocate. There's no excuse for what that rat Carmichael did. And as for Mom, as a Christian—there's nothing she can say to make this right. Nothing! She's disgraced this family and totally insulted Dad's memory."

"If Dad could speak from heaven, he'd have more understanding than you have, Mark. He knew how hard Mom's life has been."

Mark burst across the room and lifted Jason off the floor by the neck of his shirt. "Don't you dare tell me what Dad would say! That man deserves respect." He slammed Jason down on the nearby couch. "After all his suffering, the least Mom could've done was stay out of another man's pants longer than a month.

"And I'll tell you right now, I don't want anything to do with that bastard kid, and Mom can just forget about me coming down for that birth.

"I can't believe she would embarrass us like this. What am I going to tell Lori? It's bad enough that Mom is pregnant at forty, but this is … disgusting."

Jason stood to his feet and took a deep breath. "I knew it. We finally get to the heart of the matter, hey, Mark? It's all about you and your embarrassment."

Jason knew he took a risk to challenge his hot-headed brother, but somehow, he had to get through for his mom's sake.

He understood how hard Mark was trying to fit into Lori's affluent family—where God was allotted time only at Christmas and Easter—where money and prestige meant everything—where relationships were formed only if the Tomlinson's had something to gain. Mark's humble background didn't quite measure up. Their Grandma and Grandpa Clarke's money and acquaintance with Lori's parents was what had allowed Mark to be considered suitable for their daughter.

Mark closed in. He used his extra two inches in height and the older brother syndrome to intimidate. His chest puffed up and clenched each fist. The veins in his neck bulged, and the muscles in his forearms rippled.

Jason held his ground.

"I'm leaving, Jason. Count yourself lucky that I don't bust you through that wall like I feel like doing. It makes me sick that you're such a pushover, such a mama's boy who will let this ride."

"I'm not letting this ride, Mark. I'm choosing to forgive as I'm forgiven. Remember the Lord's prayer … you had it memorized at one time."

"Yeah, sugarcoat the truth, Jason. Call it what you will. You're just too weak to stand against obvious sin." He turned and lit for the door.

Jason had just enough time before it slammed shut to shout out. "It takes more strength to forgive than to condemn, Mark."

Jason knew his brother. He would rage. He would justify his anger and even believe his superiority. Jason's only prayer was that Mark had not become too hard in his spirit to allow the process of forgiveness.

Jason had accomplished what he set out to do. He had saved his mom from Mark's initial flare of anger and unkind words. He hoped by the time they had a chance to talk, Mark would've cooled down enough to think before he spoke.

Jason opened his clenched fingers and stilled his shaking hands. He hated conflict. He dropped to the couch and did the only thing left to do—pray.

Matt couldn't believe the incredible events of the past few weeks. He went from being an overworked doctor with no other reason to get up in the morning than to see his patients—to the excitement of becoming a father—the greatest high ever. The thought of a God in heaven who cared about him personally no longer seemed too farfetched. Anna carried their child, and he was shocked how much he wanted this baby.

His cell rang. He glanced down before he answered to make sure it was not Tamara. His pulse ran rapid when he realized the caller was Anna.

"Matt, it's Anna."

His heart bucked like a bronco … yeah, he knew who it was.

"Hi, there."

"Do you have time to get together? We need to talk about the future of our child."

Her voice sounded professional and businesslike.

"Sure." He knew he sounded too eager.

"I know you asked to be present when the baby is born, but … that won't be possible."

He bit his lip.

"My sister, Lana, has come to all the Lamaze classes, and she's my coach. I haven't had a chance to tell her the truth yet. I know it'll come as a shock, and she'll need some time to wrap her brain around all of this.

"But—"

"Matt, please. I'll get someone to call immediately, and you can be there to see the baby right after the birth."

His gut clenched tight as he held in his disappointment. He understood the dynamics. Had he wooed her slowly and worked hard at becoming a trusted family friend, things would be different.

"I hope you change your mind, Anna, but I will respect your decision.

"Where do you want to meet?"

She mentioned a small café, and they said good-bye.

All I want is for us to be a family, but take it slow, old boy. Fatherhood is an amazing start, and she used the word future. Matt's heart kicked up speed at the mere thought.

Chapter Nineteen

Matt couldn't imagine the amount of stress Anna had to process at the disclosure of this news to family and friends so late in the pregnancy. With this in mind, he prepared for their lunch determined to take a less selfish role. She needed to stay calm for the birth ahead. The least he could do was take it slow and respectful.

By the time he found the tiny cafe she suggested, the clock read five minutes late. He jumped out of the car in a rush but stopped short. Through the window, he caught a rare moment to enjoy her unobserved.

Her classic beauty and long wavy hair that framed high cheekbones took his breath away. A glow that people so often say pregnant women carry added the rosy color into her cheeks, while a set of hauntingly beautiful brown eyes stared toward the door. He marveled again at the fact this lovely woman, both on the inside and out, carried his child.

She dabbed the napkin to the corner of her eyes. That could only mean tears.

His stomach twisted into a knot. He felt responsible for her sorrow.

This one honest moment gave him pause.

What has my demand cost her? If I truly love her, shouldn't I choose what's best for her? But how? What?

The thought of forfeiting all rights to his child flooded in and pained him greatly, but seeing her vulnerable state had him so conflicted, he almost walked away.

Suddenly, she turned toward the window and caught him there. She waved and he waved back.

"Hello, Anna," he said, as he slid across from her into a booth that was reminiscent of the 1950s. The quaint roadside cafe made him feel like he had walked back in time. Not a place anyone in his circle of friends would suggest for lunch, the cafe exuded a comfortable charm and warmth that stilled his pounding heart.

She smiled that smile. The one he'd come to dread.

There was an awkward silence as they sat eyeing each other. In the past, conversation had never been a problem. Not so today. The tension grew palpable and could be cut with a knife.

Her obvious distress made things clear, he knew he had to gain the courage … to let go. Her happiness was more important than his. He would make the painful discussion quick, and then take a lifetime to heal. It was like he was ordering up a bitter sauce, rather than the lunch he had looked forward to.

"Anna."

"Matt."

They both started to speak at the same time.

Matt waved his hand. "Please … let me speak, and I think I'll set your mind at ease."

His throat tightened in an impossible ache, and he swallowed hard to release the knot. He forced himself to speak while he still had the nerve.

"I've done some thinking."

She didn't need to know that the thinking had been in the last few minutes viewing her emotion. Nor that the truth had hit him like the force of a loaded semi-truck rammed full speed into a brick wall.

He now felt crushed and mangled. He hated what he saw in himself. The selfishness. His demanding attitude. The lack of sacrifice for the one person in the world he loved more than life itself.

Silence, weighted and thick, hung between them. She sat across from him with a perplexed lift to her beautifully arched brows.

"I've been thinking about your friends, your family, your church … everything that is important to you, and I found something inside myself I don't like all that much. In my selfishness, I've demanded what may very well destroy you. I'm no longer willing to do that."

She stared at him with her dark brown eyes popped wide.

"I want to be a father to our child with all my heart, but I want you to be happy more. My demands will ensure the world knows our story and will cause you great embarrassment and shame. I can't in good conscience do that after all you've been through. I will help you financially, but that will be my only involvement."

"Matt, you'd do that for me?"

It pained him greatly to say yes, but he did.

A genuine smile flooded her face as she reached across the table to take his hands in both of hers. "Matt, you truly are a wonderful person. Your child is going to be so blessed to have a father like you."

He didn't know what to take from that remark, but it sure felt wonderful holding her hands and having her smile at him like she actually meant it.

Chapter Twenty

She pulled her hands from the table to her oversized lap. Matt watched Anna smooth the top of the mound in a gentle circular motion as she arched her back and shifted in her chair.

"Are you okay?"

"No worries, Matt. Sitting is hard these days, and junior here doesn't like the scrunched up feeling any more than I do. That's why I smooth my hands over my belly, it seems to calm him down."

"Him? You think it's a boy."

"Oh, yeah, this is a boy," she laughed. "The pregnancy has been exactly like the last two, same heartbeat, same positioning, everything."

"I think it's a girl." He shrugged. "I can't tell you why, I just do. But why haven't you found out? Most everyone does these days."

"What? And spoil one of the best surprises in life. Nope, I want to wait, so how about a little wager on it, Matt?"

"I thought you good Christians don't bet."

The pained look she shot him made him regret his playful banter.

"I guess we've established that I'm not always such a good Christian, am I?"

He could tell she was referring to their past. "Sorry, I didn't mean that."

"I know. And yes, we do have small fun bets, not like mortgaging the house or anything. When my boys still lived at home, we'd often debate a subject with the loser having to fulfill a favor or do a chore. Besides, it made them research the answer to prove their point. All in good fun."

"Okay, what do I want if the baby's a girl?" He brushed a hand through his curly mop. "I want to give our baby girl her middle name. I wouldn't suggest the first, but the second for sure."

Anna laughed. "I hope it's not Gertrude, Ethel, or Myrtle … because that wouldn't be considered a fun bet."

"I assure you, it's not any of those names. I've been thinking about Joy, because I've felt nothing but joy at the thought of being a father."

Anna's eyes glistened with tears, and a flutter of disquiet tugged at her heart. "You've already given serious thought to names?"

"Yeah, so how about our wager?"

"It's a deal."

"Hey, wait a minute. Before we shake on it, what do you want if you win?"

"I hope I don't win."

That made him smile.

"Let's go for a walk!" she suggested. "Baby and I will be a whole lot more comfortable." She fished some coins out of her purse for the glass of milk she had ordered and dropped them on the checkered tablecloth.

He followed her out of the restaurant wondering what else they'd have to discuss, since he would soon be out of her life, but decided he'd enjoy this last walk by her side.

He reached for her arm in protection as they crossed the street. Once he had touched her, it felt as natural as breathing to slide his hand down her arm and entwine his fingers into hers.

He could see out of the corner of his eye that she momentarily looked over in surprise but made no attempt to remove her hand. He kept his gaze straight ahead as if nothing was unusual. The sensation of her warm hands in his sent a shiver up his spine. Yes indeed, he'd enjoy this last walk. A smile tugged at the corners of his mouth.

They walked hand in hand in silence to a nearby park. He felt oddly at peace with his decision to give up his rights to the baby.

She interrupted his musings. "Matt, I'm glad you found me and forced the truth to surface."

He was shocked by her words.

"Living that lie chewed me up inside. And what I did to you was so wrong. For that I'll always be sorry."

"You've said you were sorry—"

She stepped in front of him to face him. "But sorry means setting it right. When you came along claiming the right to your child and a meaningful relationship with him—"

"Her."

A smile flooded her face, "Okay, her.

"Matt, it was the catalyst I needed to change. I've already told a number of people the truth. I have a long way to go yet, but as the Bible says, the truth will set me free. I haven't felt this good in months."

"Really?"

"Yes. You're this child's father, and if you desire to be a father then you deserve that right as much as I deserve the right to be a mother. Besides, our child needs you. I was cheating you and our baby, for the sake of my own pride."

Matt let her words wash over him. He was going to be a father, and the thought thrilled him to no end. Not to mention, having the opportunity to pop in regularly into this beautiful woman's life. His heart swelled in size.

Matt longed to drop a kiss on her sun-drenched cheek, or better yet on her glorious lips, but he remembered his decision to concentrate on the baby alone. They resumed their walk with his hand regretfully at his side, and he steered the conversation away from them. They talked, and even laughed about totally unrelated subjects. As they circled the park, Matt felt their easy friendship return and marveled at the gift of this awesome restart.

"But, Lana, you've got to believe me when I say that I'm sorry. This was not personal—"

"Not personal? Give me a break. You lie to me for months, and I'm not supposed to take this personally?"

Anna hung her head in shame. "I was wrong. Please forgive me?"

Lana shook her head. "I still can't believe this. You didn't trust me? The one person in the world that I thought I could always confide in didn't trust me with the truth."

Anna could feel the hurt oozing from her sister's words.

"Our families go to the same church, we see each other regularly, everyone always says we're as thick as thieves. People are going to think I was in on this lie, and I don't like that one bit."

"No, Lana, I'll go to the pastor myself. I'll tell them the truth, that you had nothing to do with this."

"As if I can believe you'll tell the truth."

Anna turned away. "I guess I deserve that, but I'll stand before the church and confess to everyone. I'm done with the lies."

"Oh, nice, then we'll all get to share in your public shame."

The click, click, click of Lana's heels reverberated off the hardwood as she paced back and forth.

"Anna, did you stop in your selfishness long enough to think how this situation would impact anyone besides yourself?"

"All I have to offer is my apology. Please forgive me."

"I'll have to think this through and talk to Tom. We'll decide how best to handle this. You've placed us all in a very awkward situation. I shudder at what to tell the kids. What a poor example you've been to them, especially now when they are in their teens and so susceptible to the ways of the world. Why, they may think that if good little Auntie Anna can have premarital sex, then so can they." The tone of her voice registered ten on the sarcasm scale.

"I should hope they'll see this as more of a deterrent than encouragement," Anna said, pointing at her stomach. "And grasp the pain sin causes others."

Lana lifted her nose in the air. "One can only hope." With that, she slipped out the door, always the consummate lady. She didn't stomp down the hall, nor slam the door. Her car rolled quietly out of the drive and gently picked up speed.

Anna wished Lana had screamed, yelled, and spun the car out of the driveway in which to release some of her anger, and then offer forgiveness. But that was not Lana's way. She simmered. She steeped. Then she cut people off and out of her life. The thought made Anna shiver. Surely, she wouldn't do that to her own flesh and blood?

The next day Anna received a short message left on her cell.

"Anna, Tom and I have talked and will endeavor to maintain a good Christian example. We've been sisters … well, more than sisters, friends for too long to jeopardize all that. We forgive you, but this hurts. You've let us down more than you can imagine. I, in particular, need time to heal. I don't think …" her voice wavered and silence filled the moment. "I don't think I can handle being there at the birth and supporting you in these circumstances. You'll have to make some other arrangement. Goodbye then." The message clicked off but not before Anna could hear her sister's sobbing.

Anna had considered the pain her untimely pregnancy would cost her family. It had been the reason she had allowed the lie. But having lived under the weight of such dishonesty, she knew it was not God's way. Sin had repercussions, but to hide the sin had even more.

She had to admit, the thought of Lana's refusal to coach her through the birth at this late date caused fear to spike. She remembered only too well how difficult the birthing process had been with both her sons, and she was a whole lot older now. To be left alone at this late hour was indeed a heavy price to pay. Her heart picked up speed and hammered in her chest. The baby kicked in retaliation.

"Oh, God," she cried, "Quiet my fear."

Chapter Twenty-One

Once the truth got rolling, it became easier to tell in one sense only—the more people Anna confessed to, the more freedom she felt. The rest remained difficult. She had a plan, the immediate family first, her pastor and his wife second, and then her friends and church.

Rita prayed up a storm daily. She assured Anna that each soul God laid on her heart, or brought her way, would be handled with prayer. Anna could feel the power and gave thanks to her wise friend and encouraging mentor.

A surprise visit thrust Anna into telling the pastor and his wife, Eleanor, before some family members. The doorbell sang out and Pastor Harry and Eleanor waltzed in. They carted a huge box, happily announcing a gift compliments of the church—a new crib for the baby.

"After I tell you what I need to, you'll more than likely want to cart that right back out," Anna confessed. "So, just leave it by the door." She ushered the stunned couple in and had them safely tucked into chairs before she started. She didn't want to have to catch them as they fell down in shock.

"There's no way to say this, other than say what I should've told you months ago. Steven is not my baby's father."

"Why, Anna dear, surely you can't mean that—" Eleanor sputtered and shook her head as if in a daze.

"Yes, my dear, that's exactly what she means." Pastor Harry reached out and patted his wife on the knee. Without words, he conveyed a message.

Eleanor gasped, and then pierced her lips tight as if to stem off a flow of words best left unsaid.

Chapter Twenty-Two

Pastor Harry shifted forward in his chair and took over. "Well, Anna, this does indeed put us in a predicament."

Anna nodded, as a tear snaked down her cheek. "I never meant for this to happen. I came that morning preparing to tell the truth and you—" She stopped herself. "Nope—no more excuses—I was wrong, and let's just leave it there."

A frown puckered Pastor Harry's forehead and then a lift of one eyebrow as truth dawned on him. "I kind of jumped in and made up a perfect story for you, didn't I?"

"Why, Harry, whatever do you mean?" Eleanor questioned.

Harry shook his head in sorrow. "Oh, Anna, it would've been so hard for you to face the music, and then I just went straight ahead and sang a song you liked a whole lot more, didn't I?"

"Harry, for heaven's sakes dear, quit talking in riddles." Eleanor huffed. "I'm so confused."

Anna spoke up. "Eleanor, when I told Pastor Harry that I was pregnant, he immediately assumed it was Steven's and started in about a modern-day miracle. Then you entered just as I was going to correct him, and between the two of you a perfect escape presented itself. Only it wasn't perfect ... to tell you the truth, it's been perfectly horrible." Tears flooded down her cheeks.

"My, oh my ... sweet Jesus, please help us muddle through this mess." Eleanor got up from her chair and pulled Anna into a hug. "There, there, child, no sin is too big for our Jesus to handle." She hugged Anna tight and wouldn't let go.

"Anna—"

Eleanor interrupted Harry, "Not now dear ... give us a moment. But don't just sit there. Pray. I'm not in the least bit worried about our Jesus forgiving this dear one. But I can't say the same for all of our fellowship. Some are going to need a miracle of muteness to shut them up."

Anna started to tremble, half laughing and half crying. She snorted so loud they all started howling.

"Well, now, that's just the comic relief we needed. Sometimes God works in mysterious ways.

"Harry, what's the plan?"

"I think your first suggestion was a solid plan, Eleanor. Let's pray for wisdom."

Eleanor drew a chair close to the couch where Harry was seated and escorted Anna over as if she was a fragile piece of pottery. "Sit, dear." She plunked her jolly girth close to her husband and grabbed all their hands together.

Five minutes turned into ten, and ten into twenty. A sweet communion of voices cried out to the heavenly Father, and peace descended in such a way that silence fell upon them. They basked in the presence of the surreal.

"Whew!" stated Harry. "That was beautiful, just beautiful." He pulled a rumpled tissue from his pocket and dabbed at one eye. "While we were praying, Anna, some clarity came to me."

"Normally I like to handle indiscretions of this nature between the couple at hand. Only in extreme cases, when it involves members of leadership who require more accountability, do I require a public apology. But when you let me believe it was Steven's baby, and that belief turned into a message from the pulpit that a miracle had happened among us, well it became a public affair. Then the whole church rallied around you in prayer and gave out of their generosity … do you see the situation this has put me in?"

Anna nodded in agreement. "I'll make a public apology."

"Yes, Anna. I can tell you are sincerely sorry, but I believe that it is necessary."

"We'll not expect you to do this until after the baby is born and you are home and rested. But I'll have to discuss this with the board directly. I can't guarantee their silence. Although I'll instruct them to keep it in strictest confidence, sometimes news of this magnitude slips to a spouse and then out into the community.

"Now about the funds—" Pastor Harry scratched his head. His brow knit together.

"I really didn't want to take the money, but once I let you believe that lie, I felt trapped, especially when you kept insisting it was what Steven would have wanted. The child's father has already offered to pay that back."

"Is the father in the picture?"

Anna nodded. "He is now. After that one night, I told Dr. Carmichael I couldn't see him again."

"Dr. Carmichael?" Pastor Harry said, scratching his head. "I don't believe we've met."

"No, he doesn't go to the church and isn't a believer. We met a few years ago when Steven needed surgery. And though we never did anything inappropriate when Steven was alive, we did forge a friendship. Apparently, it was a short trip from friendship to a whole lot more." Anna knew she was blushing by the heat rushing to her cheeks.

"Never you mind the details, dear," Eleanor piped in. "This is not an inquisition, we're just trying to understand what you need going forward. And to be clear, Anna, we don't advocate marriage for any reason other than love, and only to a believer, so please don't think we'll put any pressure on you in that way."

Anna nodded. "That makes good sense. Thank you."

"So how did Dr. Carmichael find out?" Pastor Harry asked.

"Though Matt tried to contact me, I never responded. Then just recently, I guess God had enough of my lies and sent him to our church. He said it was the first time in his life he had attended church when it wasn't a wedding or a funeral. I guess God meant business, because Matt took one look at me and instantly knew.

"When you started praying for the safe delivery of Anna and Steven's baby, he was understandably upset. A few days later, he came knocking."

Pastor Harry whistled through his teeth. "Anna, you sure have put yourself through the wringer, haven't you? Can't imagine the stress you've been under—"

"Matt wants to be a father and has offered to help with expenses, so please take the crib back."

Eleanor was not to be silenced. "The women's ministry held a bake sale and earned the money for the baby's crib, so I feel I can speak on their behalf. Anna, you've been a loyal member of the church for years. You've given of your time, your heart, and your money to anyone in need. Because you've made a mistake doesn't negate that it's your turn to have a little help. Last time I checked, you still have a little one coming into this world. Nothing's changed that."

Anna tried to hold back the tears, but they blinked free of her lashes and splashed down.

"This baby deserves all the love we can give, and the gift is for that precious child. So please, Anna, take it with our love. The message the ladies wanted me to convey when I dropped off this crib is that you are loved, and nothing changes that fact."

Anna felt like a watering pot. The tears now flowed freely.

"Harry dear, can you put that crib together. It stays!" Eleanor waved her hand in his direction. and he dutifully got up and pulled the box into the nearby nursery.

"Let's have some tea. Come." She waved Anna into the kitchen, as if it was her home, and began to fill the kettle with water. "Must be my British heritage, but there's nothing like a spot of tea to soothe the soul."

"One more thing, Anna …" Eleanor whirled around with the kettle still in her hand. "Whatever you hear down the road of a negative nature, let me know. I'll handle it. I expect the congregation to forgive wholeheartedly and no less. Jesus said clearly in his word that we've all sinned and fallen short of the glory of God. There's not a one of us who's perfect. Anyone who gossips and snips about will have to deal with me." She harrumphed as she pointed with a kettle in one hand and the other hand flying up and down as if she was conducting an orchestra.

"Anna, Harry and I do understand a lot more than meets the eye. We could see your loneliness and pain, and so did God. He grants you mercy and forgiveness, and so must we all, and that's that." She laughed as she slammed the kettle on the stove with a bang. "And my emphasis is on the word *all*."

Anna smiled at her antics and silently thanked the Lord for the love and true Christian leadership she had in her pastor and his dear, dear wife, Eleanor.

Betty and George sat in shock for a long moment. Anna could hear the tick, tick, tick, of the grandfather clock on the wall.

Betty was the first to speak, which was no surprise. In their relationship, she did the talking, and George nodded in agreement. In the past, Anna had often wondered what he thought, but that night he added his opinion.

"Not Steven's baby, oh my …" Betty shook her head in disbelief. "Well, my dear, although you should've told us, I can see how it would be easy to let sleeping dogs lie, as they say."

Anna waited for the indignation to surface. It usually took a few minutes for most people.

Betty folded and unfolded her hands. A frown knit her brow. "None of us exactly questioned you on the matter, did we, Anna? Although, had we given it some thought with Steven being so sick and all … we should've figured it out."

Here it comes! Anna braced herself.

George ran his hands through his thinning hair and broke the awkward silence. "Well, Anna, you were next thing to sainthood in my book—it's actually comforting to see you're human after all."

Betty smacked him on the arm. "George," she said, "this is no time to joke around."

"I'm not joking, Betty. After all the years she looked after Steven, and raised those boys primarily on her own—not to mention the loneliness that went along with that—I tell no lie when I say I thought she sported a halo."

"Come to think of it, Anna, it's true. George and I often commented how difficult life must be for you. We marveled at the amazing way in which you held your family together. All the while, we lived our life having fun. We socialized with our friends, went to movies, parties, and went on holidays, while you, dear thing, got so precious little of any of that. Not to mention the warmth of a body next to you at night. I know the last years had to have been … very lonely for the both of you." Betty's voice broke.

George took over. "Anna, we don't condemn you. Steven was gone, and I know you stayed faithful to him until the end. In fact, he was gone in a lot of ways long before he passed away, and still you remained at his side. We watched him check out on life before the cancer took his body, and the whole time we hurt not just for him but for you too."

They both rose from the couch and walked across the room. Anna rose to her feet and found herself wrapped in the hug of forgiveness.

"We still expect to be every bit the grandparents to this baby. Why, you wouldn't believe the shopping I've already done."

"Oh, I believe it. I've seen the Visa bill," George said with laughter in his voice.

Anna went home feeling blessed until a call from Mark wiped away the gift of grace like chalk wiped off a board in one swipe. He did not even say hello.

"Jason contacted me the other day. I heard the latest and just want you to know how disappointed I am. I feel you've dishonored the family name, and that Dad would be incredibly grieved you could jump into the sack so soon after he passed away. I want nothing to do with that slime ball, Carmichael. His type disgusts me. They prey on weak, foolish women."

Anna jolted and caught her breath. *He thinks I'm weak and foolish.*

"Mark, please—"

He continued to talk right over her. "That kid is not full blood, so don't expect me to come down like I had planned. And don't try to contact me, because I need time to work this through. You have no idea how hard it is to find out your mother is not who you believed her to be.

"I haven't a clue how I'm going to tell Lori. I know she'll be mortified. Thanks for thinking of no one but yourself, Mom."

Anna tried to respond, but the line went dead.

She hung her head and wept openly. A wave of hopelessness threatened to overwhelm her as she fought against the tsunami of heartache.

The baby had another idea. A sharp pain pressed in, and water splashed down her legs, pooling on the floor. Another pain twisted deep across her abdomen and into her lower back. There was no time for tears or sorrow.

Chapter Twenty-Three

Pain ripped through her body in waves. Anna knew she had to get to the hospital. She had no time to agonize over the fact her sister was not available and called the first person that came to mind.

"Matt, it's Anna. The baby's coming and I have no one."

"How far apart are your contractions? Can you wait for me to get there, or should I call an ambulance?"

"About ten to fifteen minutes apart, but my water broke."

"I'm on my way. Keep your cell beside you, and if the contractions speed up, call 911 immediately."

Anna sat waiting and was thankful she had packed her overnight bag the day before. This baby wasn't due for another couple weeks, but she guessed the little one didn't know that.

Between contractions, she had time to ponder her decision to call Matt. He'd been in the back of her mind from the point she heard her sister's message, and somehow, she knew God had this planned all along. Matt would be both knowledgeable and supportive. She needed that now.

The front door swung wide and slammed against the doorstop with force as Matt bolted in. His disheveled look gave Anna comic relief. Sprigs of curly hair sprang in every direction, and his T-shirt was inside out. His usual well-put-together-look was lost in his mad dash to her.

She laughingly teased. "Clearly you took your time grooming this morning."

"I was in emergency surgery all night. I was sleeping when you called. But never mind all that … let's get you in the car."

She smiled at the frantic way in which he grabbed her and almost lifted her off her feet.

"Matt, I can walk."

He stepped back. "Of course, you can … I'm just a little—"

"Undone?" Anna finished.

He ran a hand through his hair. "Yeah. Well, it's not every day a man becomes a father."

As she slid into the front seat, and he wrapped a blanket around her legs, she could see that his hands were shaking. "Matt, take a deep breath, calm yourself. I'm not dying. I'm having a baby. Besides, I'm with a competent doctor. Everything should be fiiiiinnnne … oohhhh, that one hurts." She quit talking and concentrated on her breathing. She could barely remember the ride to the hospital, she was so intent on controlling the pain. The contractions were coming fast and furious.

Wheeled directly into the maternity ward, they wasted no time. One look told the doctor on shift that this baby was waiting for no one. Her family doctor would never get there on time.

"I want an epidural," Anna cried out between contractions. "I was in labor so long with the other two, and I can't do that again." A feeling of panic welled up as another contraction stilled the words, and she buckled in pain.

Matt tried to explain. "Anna, they can't do an epidural, you're too far along."

She sobbed, "I can't do this Matt. I can't. I'm exhausted—so much has happened lately and I'm—ohhhhhh—"

Another contraction curled her body into a ball and sweat dripped down her temples. She heard a scream pierce through the air but didn't recognize it as her own. Pain sliced through her like it was splitting her in two.

Matt held her hand and smoothed a cool cloth over her brow. "You're doing good, Anna, things are moving along quickly. This won't take much longer."

Suddenly, panic filled the room. Words were flying around the room Anna couldn't comprehend.

"Too much bleeding. Code 5 stat! Let's get her into the surgery room now."

"Matt!" she screamed, when she couldn't see him. He immediately came into view, but his eyes were wide and wild looking. "I'm here, Anna, I'm here."

"Don't let her slip from us," the attending physician said. "Matt, keep talking to her. Make her understand she needs to fight."

"Anna, please push, my dear. This baby is right there, just one more push."

A contraction took over, but Anna's strength waned. Soft moans slipped from her lips. She tried hard to push, but dizziness pervaded and images blurred.

"We have to get this baby out now. The heart rate is falling. We're losing her—hemorrhaging—"

Words and phrases swirled around her as she closed her eyes. She could hear Matt praying for her and the baby, but Matt didn't pray.

"She's too far along for a C-section. We have to decide between baby and mother, Matt."

"Save Anna," was the last thing she heard.

He notified Anna's sister and sat by her side holding her limp, still hands within his. Matt didn't want to leave but knew upon their arrival he wouldn't be welcome.

"We'll take it from here, Dr. Carmichael." Lana said in voice as hard as stone. "Had it not been for you, she wouldn't be lying here now."

Her husband interrupted, "Lana, this is not the time nor the place."

Matt hung his head in regret and got up to leave. His weary legs carried him down the hall to the nursery. If he couldn't be with Anna, he would be with his baby girl, and no one could prevent that.

Taken with forceps, yet somehow not bruised, Matt gazed down at his perfect daughter. In awe, he smiled at the most incredible gift life had ever given him.

He donned a gown in preparation and signaled to the nurse he was ready. She brought the sleeping child and placed her gently in his arms. "Oh, she's so tiny."

The nurse nodded in agreement. "She's beautiful, Dr. Carmichael."

"That she is," he said, as a tired smile split his face.

He sat in the nearby rocker and soaked in her loveliness.

"We have to pray for your mama, little one. She has to come back to us." Giant tears coursed down his face, as he rocked back and forth. He would've never jeopardized Anna's life to have a baby, but holding this precious gift in his arms filled him with awe. In that moment, he knew without reservation that the beautiful baby in his arms was God's creation. Such perfection did not happen by chance.

Matt had never given in to emotion. In fact, he had prided himself on being a man of scientific thinking and rational behavior, but holding his newborn daughter changed everything. Pride flew out the window and faith flooded in. He understood how dangerously close he had come to losing them both and credited God where science and knowledge had failed.

Silent tears streamed. In humbleness, he thanked God for the life of his baby girl and begged God to save Anna's life for the sake of them both.

Without anyone to explain repentance, he suddenly understood what Anna had been trying to tell him. What they did that night had been of the flesh, undisciplined and selfish. He wanted, no, *needed* God to forgive him for that and a whole lot more. There in the nursery with his baby in his arms, he surrendered his life to Jesus. Peace like nothing he had ever experienced flooded in.

The little one squirmed, and a tiny hand stretched out. She was hungry and wet. Soft mewing sounds quickly escalated into a healthy scream. One of the nurses rushed to help, but he stayed close—he wanted to learn how to attend to her needs.

Anna's family, including both her sons, the pastor and his wife, and many friends, gathered to pray in the nearby waiting room. Only one person was allowed to be with her at a time. Matt would've loved to join in the prayer but didn't feel welcome. He ached to see her but dared not ask.

To the pastor's credit, he came in search of Matt. He found him gazing through the window at his sleeping child. "I see you have a healthy baby girl."

"Yes, she's an amazing gift." Matt's voice wavered and cracked. He stifled the tears and choked on his words. "But, of course, with a mother like hers …" a muscle jerked in his jaw and a groan slid out. "Her baby needs her, I need her."

The pastor's warm arm circled his shoulder. "We could pray about that together, Matt."

"I have been praying."

"Well, it never hurts to do it with a friend."

The genuine warmth of this man drew Matt. There in the hallway, Matt did something he'd never done before. He prayed out loud. He didn't care that his voice carried and echoed down the corridor, he cared only that Anna would be restored. Even if she never was his Anna, more than life itself, he wanted their baby to know her mother.

The pastor slipped away for a moment and returned with his wife. "We want you to take our turn and go in the room to visit Anna. We think she may respond to your voice, and I've talked to the family and have their consent."

Matt couldn't believe his ears. He was down the hall and in her room before they had time to second-guess their decision.

She stirred him beyond reason. His heart ached to see her frail and pallid complexion lost against the starkness of the white sheet.

"Anna, my love, we have a daughter. Please wake up. She's so beautiful, and remember, I get to give her the middle name Joy.

"What a miracle. Her life is an answer to prayer. Yes, the proud Dr. Carmichael cried out to God, and He answered, Anna. We almost lost her …" He could no longer speak through the knot in his throat. He smoothed his hand up and down her arm and ran his fingers tenderly down her cheek.

"Anna, come back to us. Your baby girl needs you. I need you—"

Anna could feel the pull of something much stronger than her. The light and peace that beckoned her forward faded. She could hear his voice and feel the agony of physical pain at the same time. She longed to run toward the light, but words tugged her in the opposite direction.

"Anna, come back to us. Your baby girl needs you."

"I need you—"

Try as she might she couldn't reach through the haze. Oblivion pulled her under.

Her sister's voice pounded in Anna's head.

"She's moving. She's waking up."

Anna struggled to lift her heavy eyelids, and when she finally succeeded, she awoke to a group of people gathered around. She wondered why. As bits and pieces of information returned she remembered … Her hands reached for her stomach, the large mound was gone. Terror ripped through as her heart began to beat wildly.

"My baby, where's my baby?"

Her sister patted her hand. "You have a healthy baby girl, but you sure gave us a fright."

"Where is she? I need to see her."

125

The doctor pushed his way through the crowd.

"You'll all have to leave. Go home, get some rest. You've been here a long time and need some sleep. Mrs. Clarke is safe now, but she needs time to recuperate before she can handle this many people." He spoke in a firm, deliberate tone that didn't allow room for argument.

He turned to Anna and said, "I'll send for your baby immediately."

One by one they kissed her, said a few words, and left the room. She felt exhausted.

The doctor stood like a sentinel on guard. He shuffled the last one out before he spoke.

"Anna, your baby is healthy and strong. She's a real fighter, just like her mom. We almost lost you. You hemorrhaged heavily and your little girl was stuck in the birth canal with the cord wrapped around her neck. Even with our modern-day technology, it was a miracle that you both survived."

"How long have I been unconscious?"

"Three days."

Anna was shocked. It felt like a couple hours.

"You had us worried, that's for sure.

"On another note, Anna, I have to ask you something more of a personal nature. Matt and I are friends, but you're my patient. He's told me a little of your story, but I have to ask, are you okay with him in here? It's apparent your family seems to think otherwise."

"Yes, doctor, Matt is welcome."

He smiled. "Good. Then I'll bring them in directly, but your visit must be short. Let's raise this bed and get you propped up a bit.

"I'm going to order some blood work, and we'll work hard at getting you home as soon as possible."

"Oh, and make sure that you don't try to hold the baby yourself just yet. Let Matt help you."

Anna nodded in agreement. "How long have you and Matt been friends?" she asked.

"Matt and I go way back. Congratulations to you both, by the way." He raised the bed while he chatted, and positioned the pillow behind her head. "I must say it's all a bit of a surprise. In fact, the whole hospital is buzzing with the news that Dr. Carmichael is a father." He laughed and then added, "It's quite comical to watch the single women literally wilt at the news. Everyone is quite curious about the mysterious woman who finally stole his heart.

"I'll go get them both. Matt hasn't slept in the last three days waiting for this moment."

Tears filled her eyes as Matt carried their child toward her. He looked haggard but somehow different. He lowered the baby in his arms so she could see her child for the first time.

"Oh, Matt, she's incredible."

"Incredible doesn't even come close to expressing how I feel," he said with conviction.

Anna looked at the two of them together with his smile fixated on their little one and marveled at the play of emotion she could see dance across his face.

"Are you okay if I sit beside you here?" he said, as he patted the bed. "I'll help you hold her?"

Anna nodded.

He draped one arm around her shoulder and the other cradled her arm that held their sleeping child. The heat from his arm penetrated into hers causing a warmth and comfort.

The two of them stared at their child in wonder.

"I had to come up with a name for the records, but given the circumstances you can readily change it."

She looked at him expectantly.

"I named her Melody Joy. I know this may sound corny to admit, but she makes me want to sing for joy, and she's only three days old. I can't believe how she has affected me, how much I love her already. I'll never be the same." His words drifted into a whisper as he stroked a finger softly across the baby's cheek.

Anna shifted enough to look directly into his warm blue eyes. He met hers full on. What she saw there scared her, and she lowered her gaze. "What a beautiful name, Matt. I love it! It'll bring special meaning to our daughter's life when she hears how her father named her. Little girls love those kinds of stories."

"What do you know about little girls?" He chuckled. "You had two boys."

"I was a little girl once upon a time."

"Right you are."

He smiled.

She smiled.

As if on cue, little Melody Joy opened her eyes. She yawned and stretched her tiny mouth open and then shut. Her scrunched up face sent a warning before she bellowed. The fact she was hungry was evident to the whole ward. Anna laughed and planted a kiss on her tiny cheeks.

The nurse bustled in. "Well, Mrs. Clarke, do you think you're up to trying to breast feed? The baby's been introduced to the bottle out of necessity, but if you're willing to try, we could see if little Melody makes a go of it."

Anna nodded in agreement, and Matt stood prepared to leave.

"You'll have to help her hold the baby. Anna is still too weak," he said to the nurse.

"No," she said with a point of her finger, "You'll have to help her. This is something that Anna will need help with in the next couple of days, and there's not always enough staff to accommodate. Besides, you've held that baby nonstop for the last few days, so this shouldn't be too difficult for you."

Heat rose from the neck of Anna's hospital gown to her hairline. There was no way that the nurse could understand their history. She most likely assumed they lived together like most of the world did these days and would think that things of an intimate nature were old news. Anna squirmed in discomfort.

The screaming child and the forceful nurse made the decision for them. She opened Anna's gown, and before Anna could blink, the child was placed at her breast and sucking madly. Anna could feel her milk come in and the baby relax into a rhythm.

"Ah, this one's not fussy, she'll be just fine." The nurse nodded with satisfaction. "Some little ones won't allow a change in nipple, but your little girl is a fighter. And with that kind of personality, she'll give you two a run for your money in the years to come." Chuckling, she made her way to the door.

"I'll leave you, Anna, in Dr. Carmichael's excellent care. He can bring the baby back to the nursery when you're finished." She exited with a march to her step.

"Well, Dr. Carmichael," Anna said, a smile tugging at the corners of her mouth, "we have a beautiful daughter and a very bossy nurse." Gazing down at baby, contentment filled her soul, and she felt an odd emotion she had not felt for a very long time. Happiness.

"Welcome, Melody Joy. Welcome, my love."

Matt chucked and asked, "Was that second endearment for me? Because I'll take it."

• • • • • • ▬ • • • • •

The only answer she gave him was a jab in his side with her elbow.

Chapter Twenty-Four

A small reprieve, a window of peace, and a sliver of joy fell between the pages of Anna's life before the daunting task of disclosure became necessary. Anna didn't want to show up at church with little Melody and have people fawn over the baby referring to Steven's child. Nor did she want the ladies to organize a baby shower without the truth. The final chapter had to be told, and she was in total agreement.

Pastor Harry and Eleanor entered the church office where they had agreed to meet and pray beforehand.

"Anna, if there was another way to handle this …" said Pastor Harry. A troubled light stole into his eyes.

"I know, Pastor Harry. I thank you for your consideration, but as you pointed out, this is a rather public affair. Besides, I want to be free from all lies, and this final admission of guilt will finish the deed."

Eleanor patted her shoulder. "You're a brave girl, my dear. May God grant you the strength."

Matt sat in the back of the church that Sunday morning. As the music played, his mind drifted to their conversation the night before. He had offered to stand beside her, but she would have none of it. A heated discussion had ensued.

"No, Matt, you didn't lie to these people."

"But without me, there wouldn't have been a reason to lie."

"Matt, you're not a believer. You don't have the accountability I have, especially after all the years I've been a part of these people's lives. I let them down, and I, alone, need to ask for forgiveness."

Matt longed to tell her that he had called out to God and become a believer that day in the hospital but held back. He didn't want her to think that the only reason he came to the Lord was to try and win her affection. He hoped and prayed his life would reveal a new Matthew Carmichael.

Pastor Harry cleared his throat and picked up his Bible.

"Congregation, today I want each and every one of you to pay special attention. How many of you brought your Bibles or have the Bible on your phone?

Hands went up all over the sanctuary.

"Good. Because I want everyone to turn to John 8:7-11, and we're going to read together. And no turning on any games …" The congregation laughed, and a rustling of pages and beeping of phones filled the sanctuary as he waited patiently.

"First, I'll set the stage and give the background of this short reading."

"A woman is brought to Jesus accused of adultery by a pack of angry men with rocks in hand eager to stone her. I always wonder where her partner in crime was? The men in that culture sure did get away with more than the women."

Matt squirmed in his seat.

"But let's read together how Jesus wisely responds to this dilemma."

"If any one of you is without sin, let him be the first to throw a stone at her." He stooped down and wrote on the ground.

At this, those who heard began to go away one at a time, the older ones first, until only Jesus was left, with the woman still standing there. Jesus straightened up and asked her, "Woman, where are they? Has no one condemned you?"

"No one, sir," she said.

"Then neither do I condemn you," Jesus declared. "Go and leave your life of sin."

He paused, took the Bible in his hand, and held it up. "We're going to have a little interaction today. Tell me, what is the key point of this passage?

"Come on now, I'm waiting. Give me your thoughts."

Short answers came from all over the sanctuary.

"Human failure."

"The sin of adultery."

"Forgiveness."

"The fact we all sin."

Pastor Harry encouraged. "Okay that's basic, but let's drill down. How do you think the woman felt? Give me some words that convey her possible feelings."

"Fear."

"Shame."

"Guilt."

"Embarrassment."

"Condemnation."

Pastor Harry nodded. "Good, good. And how do you think she felt after her accusers left and Jesus said He did not condemn her?"

Matt could tell the congregation was not used to this kind of message, but was catching on.

"Relieved."

"Free."

"Loved."

"Forgiven."

"Inspired to live a better life."

"Ah, beautiful answers, and I have one more question to ask. What do you think Jesus was writing in the dust with his finger while He waited for the mob to drop their stones and leave?"

Silence filled the room. No one had an answer.

He waited so long Matt thought it awkward. People began to shift in their seats.

Pastor Harry spoke with authority. "The answer to this question is worth dissecting, and I ask because the message can be summed up in its truth.

"Any ideas?"

Silence.

"Though it does not tell us, I believe Jesus was writing one sin after another. A secret sin in each of these men's life that they believed no one could possibly know. The fear of having their own sin exposed sent them running.

"The point here is not the sin of adultery, or any specific sin, it's the fact that we've all sinned. In other words, congregation, how would you like your worst sin made public? I want you to stop and actually think about that. What if I asked you, John, or you, Heather, or you, Linda," he pointed out into the congregation, "to come up here right now and confess a sin only God knows, which of course I will not—but how would you feel?"

Stillness filled the room. Matt looked around in astonishment. These people were visibly affected. Some squirmed, some shifted, while others had tears sliding down their cheeks. Most just looked down, making no eye contact with the pastor.

"We're all in need of our Savior daily. We've all failed. We'll never be free of sin until we walk into glory, but what we do have is enough. As Jesus said, 'go and sin no more,' with no condemnation, He lived out an example for us to emulate. We must offer forgiveness and encourage a sin-free life by being there for each other in times of weakness."

He paused with a catch in his voice. "I'm unwilling to allow this morning to be just another sermon and you tune me out. I need you to hear and follow with action."

"Love and forgiveness are two of the most important qualities we have as Christians to give to one another. The world will only be drawn to Jesus through our love. Can we do this family? Can we love unconditionally?"

"Let's end with the Lord's Prayer, but before we begin," he cautioned, "I want each of you to think through each word as you pray. Don't recite it by memory. Pray it with your heart. Pay special attention to the instruction on forgiveness."

Matt bit back the tremble to his lips but couldn't contain the tears that snaked their way to the cleft of his chin. Never had he heard anything so beautiful in all his life as those powerful words prayed in unison. The congregation filled the rafters with voices full of passion. He brushed the tears free as amens rose to the heavens in agreement.

Pastor Harry signaled Anna and his wife to come up. "Now, congregation, Anna has something to bring into the light. With help from the Spirit and support from both Eleanor and myself, she's going to face her darkest secret with courage and share it with you. My hope and prayer are that you'll put yourself in her shoes and think about what it would feel like to come up here and share your darkest deed. And then I want you to do as you just prayed— forgive as you have been forgiven."

Matt noticed how Pastor Harry protectively stood on one side and Eleanor on the other. They put their arms around her as she began.

Matt listened to her story, told with a humble brokenness and a plea for forgiveness in a way that broke his heart. Unbidden tears threatened to fall yet again.

He paid attention to the faces of those around him. There was genuine shock, but there was also a good number who bore the face of compassion.

He was glad to see people gather around her up front and hug her. However, it did not escape his notice that her sister sat in her seat with a fierce, unrelenting jut to her chin. He slipped from the pew and exited.

Lorena felt nothing but relief to hear about her Auntie Anna's failure. Her tortured soul found comfort in the fact that at least someone in her family was real. She was so tired of her stuffy parents and their friends who thought themselves perfect. In fact, Lorena felt repelled by their hypocrisy. How often she would hear her mom gossip about this one or that, or speak judgmentally as if she had no sin herself.

Her younger brother Todd fit right in. His mild-tempered personality that would do anything that Mommy or Daddy said irritated her to no end. He certainly didn't get the wilder side of sixteen-year-old Lorena, and she found his tattletale ways beyond annoying.

Lorena was angered by the public display the church had made of her Aunt Anna. She watched the faces of the people around her, their shocked expressions, as if they'd never sinned. As far as Lorena was concerned, it was none of their stinkin' business. She'd never understand why her Aunt allowed them to force her into such a degrading situation.

When she voiced her opinion on the way home from church, she was met with cold disapproval.

"Your Auntie Anna deserves every bit of the shame she felt today and more. How do you think we felt having to endure the public scrutiny of such disgrace within our family? I'm sure my friends think I knew about this all along, and it'll take some real talking to convince them otherwise."

Lorena watched her dad still the tirade with a hand upon her mom's knee and a knowing look.

"It's easier for you, Tom, she's not your twin." Her mother huffed and shifted her body toward the window to create a wall between them.

Lorena couldn't contain herself. "Why is it always about you, Mom? Can't you for one-minute think about what poor Aunt Anna is going through?"

Her mom's head swiveled around to the back seat, and her eyes bulged wide. It reminded Lorena of the screech owl they had studied in school. She smirked at the shocked, angry look her mother gave her.

"What did you say to me, young lady?"

Lorena hated that title, *young lady*. She was only called a young lady when punishment was doled out. The rest of the time she was treated like a child. If only they knew.

She could hear the intake of her brother's breath as he sat beside her. She knew he hated conflict but didn't care. Some things were worth fighting for and she was tired of the façade.

"I said, why—" She was about to repeat the words with an added measure of sarcasm, but they were cut short by her father's stern warning.

"Lorena! Don't you dare talk to your mother that way! You can see she's upset. Please, give her time to heal and don't make this worse."

She loved her father but hated the way he always gave in to her mother. Lorena muttered under her breath.

"What did you say?" Again, her mother turned. Her eyes flashed dark with anger.

"Leave it, Lana!" Tom demanded. "Neither of you are able to communicate right now."

"I will not leave it, Tom. Our daughter is insolent and rude, and you expect me to put up with that?"

"I want to know what you just said, Lorena, and I want to know now!" Her voice brooked no argument from any of them.

Lorena didn't care if it hurt her mother. "I said that you worry more about what your friends think than you do about loving your own sister."

"My sister's actions were disgraceful, from her promiscuous behavior to the truckload of lies she so easily spewed. Her behavior is appalling and disgraceful, and I don't even know who she is anymore."

"What about forgiveness, Mom?" Lorena couldn't control the desperation that laced her voiced. "Doesn't being a Christian mean that you love her enough to forgive?"

"Don't you dare lecture me on forgiveness."

Tom tried to intervene. "Lana, please, leave this for now."

"I don't need a mere child instructing me on how to forgive. She knows nothing about real life."

Lorena was glad when the car turned into the driveway. Everything within her cried out for escape from her mother's judgmental words. She couldn't in good conscience sit and listen to one more unkind remark, knowing that every word her mother spoke against Anna could as easily be directed her way. It hurt to know that her mother's love was so conditional. Joel was right, there was only one solution. With defiant determination, she decided what she must do.

Chapter Twenty-Five

Anna lay in bed after a busy day with Melody but couldn't sleep. She tossed and turned for a bit and then got up and made a cup of tea. Turning her computer on, she checked out Facebook until she felt the nudge of the Spirit.

"Okay, God, I hear you."

Liberated with forgiveness, Anna could feel her old joy return, along with her prayer life.

Pray for your family.

"Yeah, that one hurts, God. I thought my sister had forgiven me when she showed up at the hospital, and Mark too, but as soon as I was on the mend, they both disappeared. And since my public confession, God, Lana has treated me like the plague. She won't even sit with me in church anymore, insisting I use the pews designated for mothers with young children, And I haven't heard a peep from Mark.

"But you know all this. I lift them up to you, Father. I don't know what they need but you do. Help me forgive. Help me to stay soft so I don't get bitter.

"Oh, and God, thank you so much for Jason. The way he loves his little sister and is so affectionate with her, and the way he's forgiven me is truly a gift. Thank you, God, for mercies I do not deserve."

Hey, Auntie, I see you're still up.

A message pinged on her Facebook account.

Go ahead my child, this is a divine appointment.

"Yeah, God, she's been messaging me a lot lately, talking about Christians as if she is not one."

Anna shifted from prayer, took a sip of her tepid tea and answered.

You bet. How are you, Lorena?

Confused.

Anna figured a lot was said behind that one word and answered with question marks.

???

Is it okay for Christians to gossip and turn others against someone?

Lorena, I think you know the answer to that one.

Yeah, well, why then does my mom spend hours on the phone with Mark and others chatting not so nicely about you?

Oh, God, what do I say now? This hurts. But I'm not going to get into a discussion with Lorena about my son and sister, or I will be doing the same thing they are. I need wisdom.
The messages were coming one after another.

And what about forgiveness? Isn't this a basic Christian principle? They sure haven't forgiven you.

Yes, Lorena, but life isn't always figured out in a day. I was often judgmental of people too--having lived a good life for many years. It wasn't until I failed miserably that I fully understood the sacrifice of Jesus and what it meant to need forgiveness in a big way. I learned that lesson the hard way, so I know what your mom is going through. It hurts when people we count on let us down, and I let your mother down.

And she's not letting you down now?

Anna agonized over how to answer. *God, it would be dishonest to answer anything but yes to this question. Lorena is an astute young adult and I'm done with lies. So, what do I say?*
Anna smiled at the way God gave her the words to answer that would not disrespect her sister.

> People let us down, Lorena, but God never does.

> Isn't it supposed to be different with Christians? I find more love and acceptance from my non-Christian friends than I do at youth group or at home.

Anna could read the hurt between the lines. The conversation had switched from Anna's situation to Lorena's and had become personal.

> Tell me, Lorena, why do you feel that way?

No answer.

> Hey, Lorena, you still there?

Still no answer.
Anna now knew why the Spirit had her up this late, so she prayed.

A week later Anna received another message from Lorena.

> Can I come over and see you, Auntie? I could take the bus after school, but Mom can't know. If you feel you have to tell her then I'm not coming!

Anna knew from praying all week that Lorena needed her, and it was crucial she make herself available.

> No problem. Come anytime. 🖤

A sad waif of a girl showed up on Anna's doorstep the next day. Lorena looked like she carried the weight of the world on her two frail shoulders.

She avoided all eye contact. Her hair hung limp over rounded shoulders, and she kept her head down. Her once glossy auburn locks were dyed a dark black that stripped the hair of its natural shine. Her eyes were lined in a thick layer of black, her clothes predominantly black, and her fingernails painted a complimentary black. A deep concern to Anna was the dark circles that hung beneath Lorena's sad eyes and the weight she had lost on an already thin frame.

Anna felt scared to see her niece so depressed and dark. The heaviness Lorena carried resembled that all too familiar look Anna remembered in herself not that long ago.

"Come in, my dear," Anna opened the door wide.

"I tried to keep Melody awake so you can say hi. She's a little grumpy right now, but that's because it's nap time."

Lorena followed her into the nursery. Anna had just put Melody down, and already the baby's eyes were drooping, but not before she opened them one last time to give her mother a smile.

Giant tears rolled down Lorena's cheeks causing a stream of black makeup to follow. She swiped the tears away hard enough to take off a layer of skin.

Anna wanted to pull her into her arms and hug away the pain, but knew she had to take things slowly.

Anna lightly placed her arm around Lorena's shaking shoulders and ushered her out of the nursery. They made their way to the kitchen. "Sit." Anna waved to the barstool. "I have your favorites—my famous hot chocolate and some freshly baked sugar cookies." She slid a mug in front of Lorena and pushed the plate of warm cookies closer.

"Lorena, you can trust me, I'm here to help. What is it?"

It took a few minutes of silence before Lorena opened up.

Anna prayed.

"I just couldn't do it!" she cried. "Joel is calling me a coward and has broken up with me, and I don't know what to do."

Guttural sobs made it hard for Anna to make out what Lorena was trying to say. She came around the kitchen island and pulled Lorena into her arms.

"It's going to be okay, Lorena. Whatever the problem is, we can find a way through," Anna said reassuringly.

Lorena cried into her shoulder, and Anna held on tight, knowing that a hug could speak a thousand words.

Slowly the tears abated, and Anna could feel Lorena gain control.

"Mom will hate me." Her words came out in an agonizing tone. "She'll rant and rave how I disgrace and embarrass her and care only about what her self-righteous friends think. It'll be all about her, and I can't face that."

Her face twisted into a stormy scowl, and her voice grew edgy. "Mom is a hypocrite and a phony."

"Lorena, what is it? It can't be that bad. Honey, we'll work something out, I promise." Anna smoothed a hand back and forth across Lorena's shoulders in hopes of settling her frazzled state. "Talk to me."

Chapter Twenty-Six

"I'm pregnant," Lorena said, her eyes staring at the floor.

The words fell like lead raindrops. They battered the roof of Anna's heart. The room felt hollowed of air, as Anna contemplated the graveness of the situation.

Oh my gosh, Lana called this, and now that I'm involved helping Lorena. She'll really hate me.

Think only of Lorena. I have sent her to you, for good reason.

Anna could hear the words spoken into her Spirit as clear as if God spoke them audibly.

She pushed her shock into her pocket and ushered her niece into the living room. Once she was settled on the couch, Anna began to question.

"Lorena, when you said you couldn't do something, what was that?"

Lorena's eyes shifted around the room. Her head sunk lower as she mumbled, "I couldn't go through with the abortion. We were at the clinic and everything. Suddenly, I got freaked out." She placed her hands on her stomach and whispered. "I knew this was not just a blob as Joel said … I just couldn't—"

Anna couldn't contain her joy. She threw her arms around her niece. "Oh Lorena, you did the right thing. I'm so proud of you. I too contemplated abortion. I wrestled with the dark angels of hell on that one. I wanted to hide my sin from the world, but God wouldn't let me. You heard my story, Lorena. Trying to hide the truth never works … not with lies, nor with abortion. I speak from experience and truly understand your torment."

Large frightened eyes rose to meet Anna. "What do I do now? My boyfriend wants nothing to do with me or 'the blob' as he calls it, and my mom's going to kill me."

"Your dad—"

Lorena interrupted. "Dad never stands up to Mom. He rolls over like a wounded puppy every time they disagree. I can't count on him. He cares more about keeping the peace than standing up for what's right."

Her words spit out with conviction. "I also know everything she'll think of me, because I've heard the way she talks about you."

Anna tried to hide her hurt but wasn't successful. Lorena stopped. "I'm sorry, Auntie."

Anna gulped back the knot in her throat and turned to quickly stem the flow of tears that threatened to spill. This wasn't about her. She had to stay focused on her niece. If she was going to help Lorena, she couldn't get sidetracked with her own hurt.

"Lorena, you've done the right thing, first at the clinic and then in telling me. I have lots of room in this old house and care about you deeply. You'll always have a place to live, but I know that your mom and dad love you a lot. Please don't assume they'll respond the same way with you as they did with me.

"Lorena, honey, you're their daughter. And how many times have I heard your dad describe you as 'his baby girl, the joy of his world'? Way too many times to count."

Lorena sniffled and blew into the tissue Anna handed her. Both eyes now sported dark circles much like a raccoon as the makeup spread and blended.

"Lorena, they'll be disappointed, but our situations are different. You haven't lied to them."

"Yes, I have, Auntie, many times. How do you think I had time with my boyfriend? He would pick me up outside the church after they dropped me off for youth group, and he would get me back before the end, or I would say I was staying at a friend's house overnight but be at Joel's place. His parents didn't have any hang-ups about us sleeping together." Sighing heavily, she admitted. "Yeah, I lied a lot! I know only too well what my mother thinks of whores and liars!"

Anna grew strong. A protective spirit rose up within. "Well, she'll just have to learn that with God's grace, we're redeemed and forgiven too. Until she grasps that fully, we'll choose to forgive her. More importantly right now, you're going to get all the love and support you need and that's a promise.

"You let me handle your mom. All I want you to worry about right now is eating properly—enough for two—and getting some needed rest. If your parents aren't supportive, which I don't believe is how this will go, I'll help you with your doctor's appointments and anything else you need. You're not alone in this world, Lorena. Both God and I love you very much."

Lorena visibly relaxed. The woman-child sank deep into the cushions and closed her eyes. Anna lifted her legs onto the couch and covered her with a nearby blanket. "Sleep for a bit, Lorena." She smoothed the hair from Lorena's face and planted a soft kiss on her forehead. "Sleep."

Anna had never taken on her sister before. Lana was a force to be reckoned with, but in this case, not even the very gates of hell would stop her. Her sister could shun her, gossip about her, and call her whatever names she pleased, but Anna would support Lorena.

While Melody and Lorena slept, Anna prayed first and then set out to take on the giant. Her big sister by a whole few minutes had always played that role far too well, but Anna would no longer allow the usual intimidation. Lorena's future depended upon it.

"God, give me wisdom."

What she first thought would be a discussion with Lana, quickly changed to a new idea. Anna would talk to Tom. If there was to be harmony in their home and a safe landing for Lorena, Tom would have to be the one who stepped up. She dialed Tom's work number with steady determination.

His secretary placed the call through as Anna waited and prayed. How did one tell a brother-in-law such news about a daughter?

His deep voice resonated over the phone. "Hello, Anna, is everything okay?"

She couldn't remember the last time she dialed him directly. Little wonder he would ask if everything was okay.

"Hi, Tom. As a matter of fact, the answer to that question is no. Lorena is with me. She's fine for the moment, but I'd like you to stop by after work before heading home."

"Lorena? I knew that something was wrong, but I haven't been able to get her to talk," he admitted. "I've noticed huge changes in the past few months, but somehow neither Lana nor I can get through to her."

"Come and get her, Tom, she needs you ... she needs the both of you. But please pray before you come, and at this point don't bring Lana. See you then." She hung up the phone before she had to answer any questions. Lorena's situation was not something she wanted to discuss over the phone.

Melody's soft sounds filtered through on the baby monitor as she woke from sleep. Anna loved the coo and gurgle as her baby awakened. She waited a moment before heading down the hall.

"Come to mama, sweet pea." Anna was rewarded with a big smile. She picked up the baby and entered the living room.

"Wake up, Lorena. I have someone who wants to see you."

Lorena rubbed at her eyes and sat up. She held out her arms as Anna brought the tiny child close.

"Hold her a minute while I grab her diapers."

Anna came back to see Lorena smiling down at the infant, gently rocking her back and forth. Melody was wide-eyed and smiling back.

"Do you need to change her?" Lorena asked.

"In a moment, but first I have to tell you I called your dad. He's coming here after work."

Lorena sprang to her feet with Melody in her arms. "Take the baby, I'm leaving." She held Melody out to Anna.

Anna ignored her tirade. "Sit, Lorena, you're not going anywhere, and here's a diaper to change her. You'll need the practice."

A pair of flashing eyes were the only indication Lorena was not happy as she sat back down on the couch and unsnapped the baby's sleeper.

"I hope you believe I meant what I said. You'll never be left alone to handle this pregnancy, nor will you be left alone to raise this child. Can you trust me on that?"

Lorena turned from her task of putting on the fresh diaper to nod.

"I trust you, Auntie. That's why I came to you."

"Good. Now that we have that out of the way, the reason I want you to tell your dad first and then your mom is because we want to give them a chance to process and do this right. If they respond as I believe they will, with a whole lot more grace than they extended to me, then you'll have the best scenario. But rest assured, if they don't … I'll be that person for you, and my home is your home as long as you desire."

Melody started to whimper. By the time Anna got across the room, she had ramped it up to a full-out scream.

Anna laughed at Lorena's wide eyes and furrowed brow.

"What'd I do?"

"Relax, Lorena, she's just very vocal when she's hungry."

Anna took the baby and settled in the rocker. "Breastfeeding is the way to go, Lorena. It's a time to bond and no bottles to wash or formula to fuss with."

Lorena watched in astonishment as Melody instantly calmed. "Babies sure are amazing but scary."

"Yes, they're amazing, but you're the scary one," Anna teased. "You should see your face. Why don't you go wash up? I'm surprised Melody didn't start crying the minute she saw you."

She could hear Lorena groan as she reached the bathroom mirror. "Auntie, how did you keep a straight face looking at that? Yikes, I'm a freak show."

Anna's laughter floated down the hall.

Anna opened the door to a very concerned man. "Come in, Tom. Lorena is waiting to speak to you."

Anna guided him into the living room where Lorena perched herself on the edge of a lounger looking like a bird about to take flight. Tom moved toward her, but with one look at her stormy face, he chose to sit on the couch across from her. Neither said a word.

Anna felt out of place but necessary. Lorena's eyes darted her way as if to petition help. Anna had little choice but to forge ahead.

"Tom, Lorena has something to tell you. She desperately needs your love and support, and I've assured her of that."

"Why would you question that, Lorena? Why would you come to your aunt before coming to me?" A canyon of pain registered in his eyes.

"Because she's the only one who can possibly understand how I feel."

"Understand what?"

Her voice trembled as she dropped her gaze. "I'm pregnant."

A gasp slipped from Tom's lips as he jumped to his feet. He raked a hand through his hair and paced back and forth.

"I'm sorry, Daddy. I'm really sorry."

"Lorena, why didn't you tell us?"

Anna spoke up. "The reason she didn't want to tell you or her mom was because she heard all the negative things said about me. She thinks that she'll be considered unworthy of forgiveness and all the other things she heard. I assured her that it would be much different being that she's your daughter." A firm message burnt through Anna's words for which she made no apology.

149

"I haven't agreed with Lana." Tom said defensively.

Lorena's head snapped up and through the tears she cried, "But, Dad, you haven't disagreed either. You just sit there and listen to her. You let her dictate everything."

A sheen of tears glistened in his eyes. "It's true," he admitted. "Rather than fight with Lana, I keep the peace by saying way too little, way too often."

Anna nodded. "You don't have to tell me what a powerhouse my sister is. She's a strong woman, but even a strong woman can be a wrong woman at times."

He nodded. "Lorena, I've known that something was wrong for a while now. I've tried to talk to you, but you've shut me down."

"I know, Dad. It's just that you and Mom have been so busy with your careers and are hardly home. It's … it's hard to talk like we used to. I've been struggling with Christianity for quite a while now but didn't think I could question you and Mom about it. All my friends have walked away, and there's no one at the church I connect with. Then Joel came along and made me feel loved and needed. How wrong was that?" She hung her head in shame.

Tom stepped toward her, but she held up her hand. "Dad, I need to finish."

"I was pretty sure I was pregnant that day at church when the news came out about Auntie. I wanted to tell you both, but when I heard Mom talk with such disgust and anger, I didn't have the courage." A soft sob escaped as she admitted. "Dad, I almost got an abortion yesterday because of that—and the pressure from Joel. Then when I wouldn't do it, he broke up with me. He sure didn't love me much if he could kick me to the curb like that." Lorena's tears flowed down her face like a river, "Daddy, I'm terrified."

He held out his arms and she ran into them. He held on tight.

"Oh, Lorena, I've been so wrong. Please forgive me."

Lorena pulled back, her eyes widened in surprise.

"Yes, my baby girl, the joy of my world. I've been wrong. My lack of leadership in our home has almost destroyed you and the innocent life of my grandbaby, and I'm very sorry. And I owe a big apology to your aunt as well." He raised his head and looked across the room at Anna. She waved off his words and smiled.

He mouthed, "Thank you."

Anna slipped away with Melody in her arms but not before she heard Tom promise, "From this day forward, Lorena, things are going to change."

Chapter Twenty-Seven

"No way, Tom! I will not stand by and let Lorena dictate terms to us." Lana was practically screeching.

"Our daughter is not dictating terms, I am!" He could see Lana was visibly tense and was about to unleash that fiery temper. With everyone else, she was the perfect lady, but with him … she let the real Lana out.

Tom had done a lot of praying and knew that he could not bend. His daughter's well-being depended upon his strength.

"She would rather stay with my sister than us, and that's okay with you?"

"No, that's not okay. But if you can't assure me that you're going to put aside your pride, forgive her, and support her wholeheartedly, then I'll agree to her living at Anna's. And I won't have you talking behind her back like you have about your sister, either."

"My sister is *my* business."

"No, she's my family too. Remember that promise you made me give you before we married, that I would care for your sister as if she was my own. Well, I bought into that kind of love for Anna, and just because she made a mistake doesn't mean I have stopped loving her. My only mistake has been that I've been too weak to stand up to your bad behavior."

Her eyebrows lifted like a pair of startled crows and she gasped.

His tirade gave him strength, and when she opened her mouth to speak her mind, his hand went up. "You need to hear what I have to say, this is long overdue. You've been one of the least forgiving when Anna needed you the most. Lorena has picked up on that. There's little wonder she finds our ability to forgive too hard to trust."

Lana was done listening. "Well, I find it hard to trust her as well. Imagine her sneaking around. We didn't even know she had a boyfriend."

"Who's the adult here? Who's the mature Christian? Is it Lorena or us?"

Lana smacked her mug of tea on the counter, not caring that it splashed all over. "Lorena would not be in this situation if Anna had not been such a bad example," she spat.

"Lorena is three months pregnant, Lana, and has had this boyfriend for six months. This happened long before the news came out about Anna's indiscretion, so don't even go there. Besides, there's no one to blame for the choices our daughter made, except for her and our lack of parental guidance."

Lana sunk into the nearby couch and began sobbing. "Where did we go wrong? Why would she do this to us?"

"This is not about us, Lana. Sure, we're hurt and disappointed and will undoubtedly be embarrassed, but if we don't put our own pain aside, I fear we'll lose Lorena forever. She needs us now. She looks so fragile. If we're not a strong example of what Christ would do in this situation, her walk with God may be lost forever."

He dropped beside her on the couch and wrapped an arm around her shoulders. "Our daughter needs us, honey."

"I realize that, Tom, it's just so hard."

He held out the box of tissues. "Life is sometimes hard. We've had a fairly charmed run thus far, but we can't fail now when the going gets tough. Everything depends on doing it God's way at this point, and the first thing is to find it in your heart to forgive your sister. That'll speak more to Lorena than anything at this point. Then she'll believe and trust our love and forgiveness for her."

"And, Lana, that means a heart-felt apology, too, because your sin of unforgiveness and gossip hasn't been pretty."

A weak smile broke through the tears. "I'm not sure where you've put Tom, and I don't think I like this new guy much at the moment, but it is rather attractive having someone boss me around for a change."

He pulled her close and kissed her soundly. Then proceeded to kiss every tear away.

Anna felt the throb of a headache. She pressed her fingers to her temples and began to massage gently. *What a strange paradox I'm in. I want Matt, yet I know it can never be. Everything about him terrifies me. He's an amazing father, far too good looking, younger than me, educated, rich, and successful. I know I don't fit into his world, but his kind, gentle, persistence is wearing me down. And if I'm honest, I'd admit how much I look forward to our evenings together and the connection of something far deeper than friendship.*

She didn't have a clue how to stem the flow of her growing feelings. He weaved his way into her thoughts. He walked through her door every evening, eager to kiss his baby girl. He always wore a smile, brought a flower, or had a compliment for his two favorite girls. He was different. She couldn't quite put her finger on it, but there was a peace about him that grew madly appealing.

He remained careful, caring, and courteous. He never touched her, but at times she noticed how his eyes caressed her, and when he didn't think she noticed, they devoured her.

Just recently, he asked if she would mind if he attended church with them. He apparently had been going elsewhere but wanted to join her and Melody, if she agreed. She had hemmed and hawed, not wanting to hurt his feelings. She cared about his spirituality and wanted to encourage church, yet she was afraid of being seen as a couple when she didn't know what they were. Or worse yet, if he told her that he became a Christian, then she'd have to face the walls that she'd erected between them with the most important one demolished.

Matt was a patient man, but his patience wore thin. He wanted answers.

When is Anna going to notice the difference in me? When will she be as attracted to me as I am to her? When will she let those walls down? When? When? When?

They talked about a host of things, but the things he really wanted to discuss with her he could not. He wanted to ask her if she still mourned her husband. He wanted assurance that when she spent time with him, she wasn't wishing she was having a conversation with Steven.

He longed for the moment she would acknowledge a change in him so that he could give credit to God. He wanted her to see a different man, one that was not wrapped up in his own needs so much that he forgot what was proper and honorable. Did she have any idea how difficult it was to be in her presence and not succumb to the touch, the feel, the glory of the physical? If that was not a true example of power from on high, he wasn't sure what would be.

He had been praying for God's wisdom and opportunity to speak his mind. One evening her weird behavior triggered the timing.

He held Melody in the crook of his arm with her head cradled in the palm of his hand. As he tickled her tiny toes with kisses and made silly noises, he glanced up to find Anna staring at him with a very odd expression.

"What?" he asked.

She didn't answer, but looked stricken with fear. She averted her gaze as if trying to hide something.

"Okay, sweetie pie," he said to Melody. "Your mama has a secret that she doesn't want your daddy to know. But guess what. I'm going to rock you to sleep now and give her time to think. Then I'm going to demand an answer. What do you think about that?" Melody cooed in delight as if she understood every word. He watched Anna closely, her skin blanched white and she wouldn't make eye contact. *What was going on in that pretty head of hers?*

All while he rocked Melody in the nursery, he prayed. The sudden urge to push Anna for an answer to her unusual reaction grew powerful. He tucked the sleeping Melody in her crib, covered her with a light blanket, and crept out the door.

He found Anna sitting pretty in the middle of the swing on the back porch. Normally, he'd avoid joining her on a loveseat at all cost, but tonight it was as if God wanted him up close and personal. He boldly squeezed in beside her, and she made room. He placed his arm behind her shoulder on the back of the swing but didn't touch her.

Instead of his usual conversation on safe subjects like the weather, work, or her day, he got right to the point. "What's got you tied in knots tonight?" He shifted his body to better see her face.

"Now don't go looking shocked. You'd never make a good card player. Your expression is a dead giveaway."

Raw fear flickered in her eyes, and she began to fidget. Matt noticed how she scooted to the far corner of the swing to place distance between them. He wanted to put her at ease and tell her not to worry about whatever it was she didn't want to say, but felt compelled to sit silent. A long moment passed.

"It hit me tonight. Something I've not made right … and yet it terrifies me to do so."

Matt watched her curl her bare feet beneath her and crisscross her legs. She looked vulnerable, sweet, and beautiful all at the same time. It took all he had not to gather her in his arms that very second. Instead, he took a deep breath and asked. "Does this something involve me?"

"Yes, only you."

"Then that shouldn't be too hard. You know me. I'm easy to get along with."

"Matt, no joke, this is really difficult."

Matt watched as she clasped her hands together to still the shake that had taken over.

"Earlier when I watched you with Melody, I thought how right you two looked together. I got to thinking how much Melody would have missed if you hadn't found out the truth. That triggered a memory ... a lie I told to ensure you would stay away. I remembered some undone business, and I know God wants me to ask your forgiveness, but that means telling the truth. I'm not sure I'm ready, and yet ... the Spirit of God thinks I am."

Matt's heart hammered within his chest.

"I told you all those months ago, that when we were together ... that night we made love ..." She stammered over her words and buried her face in her hands.

He waited. Hope and dismay jockeyed for position.

She looked up and their gazes locked. "I told you that I was thinking of Steven both that night we were together and when you kissed me again that evening in the kitchen and I responded. In both cases ... I lied."

Her cheeks flamed red, and Matt could see her embarrassment.

"I'm sorry."

He stood quickly causing the swing to rock erratically and almost sent Anna flying, but he didn't notice. He stepped out onto the porch and leaned against the rail with his back to her. He slowly exhaled the air that had been caught in his lungs at her admission. A wide smile split across his face as he ran a hand through his hair.

The fact she lied to me means only one thing ... She's as affected by me as much as I am by her.

Hope and possibility made his heart slam against his chest.

"Matt?" Her voice sounded fragile. "Matt, do you forgive me?"

He wasn't sure how to respond. He desired to take her in his arms and kiss her openly just to feel the reaction it produced but what a dangerous an idea. He craved the sensation that would cause her to unravel, unglue, come undone. But he knew enough now to understand how unwise that decision would be. In fact, he was sure the pent-up passion he felt would probably overwhelm them both.

A soft hand touched his shoulder, and he felt the warmth of her presence behind him. "Matt, please talk to me."

He turned slowly. One look and he fell into the glow of her chocolate brown eyes. He ached to touch her, to feel her, to get lost in her love, but instead he distanced himself.

That one step back caused her expression to change. A troubled light soaked her eyes in pain.

"I understand." She turned abruptly and moved toward the door.

Instinct took over and he lurched forward to grab her. "No, you don't understand."

He eased her body around to face him and found the closeness intoxicating. Before he could stop himself, he wrapped her in his arms and rained kisses from her forehead to each closed eyelid, down her tiny nose to her waiting lips. With aching gentleness, he tasted the nectar that haunted him day and night. She opened to him like a tulip in the warmth of the sun. He touched and savored the joy of togetherness after months apart. His senses sprang awake, alive, aware. Passion thrummed through his limbs.

She sighed against his lips. Their kisses spoke words neither of them knew how to say. As breathing roughened and their bodies instinctively pressed closer, he felt the danger zone. A guttural groan escaped his lips as he tore apart. He took deep breaths to cool the hot blood racing through his veins with every cell screaming at the distance he placed between them.

"Oh my goodness, Matt, thank you."

"Don't thank me, thank God. Because there's nothing natural about walking out of your arms right now."

"What did you mean, thank God?"

"I mean … I wouldn't have been able to do that without his strength."

Her large brown eyes doubled in size. Shock flowered into a smile as large as a melon slice.

"Matt, are you telling me that you're a Christian? Because what you just did demonstrates the power of the Holy Spirit."

He nodded. "I've been a Christian since the day Melody was born. When you were lying so close to death on that hospital bed, I came to the end of myself. With all my knowledge and medical expertise and a team of doctors, only God could save you. I cried out, and he's been with me ever since."

"But that's over three months ago, and you never said a word?" Her eyebrows arched in question.

"I didn't want you to think I was making a spiritual commitment just to work my way into your life. I wanted you to see the changes."

"Oh, Matt, this is incredible news." She giggled like a schoolgirl.

"Please, tell me you've noticed some differences?" He found it charming how her eyes lit up in response.

"Yes, yes, I've seen changes but wouldn't let myself dare dream …"

"Ha—so you're holding out on me—you do dream of us."

He stopped as a guarded look spread across her beautiful face, and she turned and walked into the house."

He stood quiet for a moment and raked his hands through his waves. What was the problem? They shared an obvious attraction, a child, and the Christian faith. What in the world caused that reaction? He wasn't sure he wanted to know but knew he had to find out.

The slam of the screen door made her jump as she stood by the kitchen sink.

"What was all that about?" He asked as he moved close enough to read her eyes. He waited patiently for her to meet his gaze before he spoke. Unable to help himself, he smoothed an errant curl from her forehead and brushed a thumb under one eyelid to catch a giant tear.

"From happiness to tears, in less than a New York minute?"

"I'm so confused, Matt."

"Yeah, I think that makes two of us."

"I enjoy your company so much, and you're a great friend."

"Please, don't give me the let's be friends talk." A hint of frustration leaked into his voice.

"No, no, Matt, that's not it. I can't help but notice what a great father you are to Melody, and I'm moved beyond words. She needs you."

"But you don't."

"Matt, please, let me finish. As I've already admitted, I'm clearly attracted to you, but at the same time I'm afraid."

"Afraid?"

"Yes. I don't see how our lives can mesh."

"I think Melody has already done that, don't you agree?"

"On one level, yes, but there are so many other complexities."

"I thought the only reason you were holding back was because of how you felt about Steven and our different belief structures. But, you just admitted the first one is surmountable, though I'd never expect you to give up your wonderful memories, and the second reason no longer exists. So, what are you afraid of?"

"I … I …" She stepped back and turned away. He could tell she was clearly bothered.

"I have a problem with the fact that I didn't grieve my husband as I believe I should have. This pregnancy and all that has gone on in the past year has made me feel sad about that. I also think I need to respect where my boys are at and stay clear of any relationship, at least for a while."

Matt could feel her slipping away, and out of desperation he opened his heart to her. "Anna, I love you. I tried not to all those months we were apart, but I couldn't stop. I've never felt this way about anyone. I want you to be my wife. I want the three of us to be a family."

"But, but Matt—I don't know how I feel. I've not allowed myself to feel. Can you understand how difficult this is?"

He nodded but wouldn't relent. "That's understandable. I have no problem with you taking whatever time you need. I just want you to know my intentions."

"But … there's so much more."

"What do you mean?"

You're younger than me, and that's unsettling."

"That makes no sense, we live in the twenty-first century where age means nothing."

"I don't know why, but it seems out of order. I guess I'm old-fashioned that way. And that's small compared to the way women look at you."

He lifted his brows in question.

"Come on, Matt. You know how good-looking you are? Women … well I don't know … they savor you like a piece of rich chocolate, and I feel … I feel …"

He smiled. "Seriously? They savor me?"

"Yeah, I don't know a better word than that. They gaze at you with that hungry look, and you know exactly what I mean."

"Most people want an attractive spouse, and this is a problem for you?" He tried to make light of it. But she just kept on talking, and he realized how deep her uncertainties ran.

"Let's face it, the differences between us are monumental. You're affluent and educated, and I've been nothing more than a housewife. Your circle of friends, the huge house you live in, your cultured lifestyle with the theatre, opera, holidays all over the world, is all so completely foreign to me. I'm not a good fit for you. To start something that will only end in heartache for both Melody and me. It's just not wise."

"Seriously? When you said you were afraid, I never expected that you had a truck load of excuses piled in that pretty head of yours. For your information, I could've been married a hundred times before now, but I've never come close to wanting to ask anyone. Surely that dispels the threat of other women.

"Anna, you know you bring me joy in a thousand ways, not to mention you're the mother of our dear, sweet daughter who needs a family."

"But—"

He moved closer. "Please let me finish."

She dropped her head and placed her delicate hands over her face. "I'm so confused."

"Look at me," he said gently, as he lifted her chin and traced a soft caress across her cheek with the pad of his thumb.

"You're incredibly beautiful, and not just on the outside but on the inside. The sad thing is, you don't realize it."

Her eyes darted up to his face and back down.

"I could argue the point that we're never at a loss for good conversation, despite our educational differences, or that money and culture mean nothing without God and true love, but you know all that."

"I … I …"

He placed a finger against her lips. "No need to explain," he said gently. "I read 1 Corinthians Chapter 13 this morning, and it struck me what an incredible woman and wife you were to Steven. You loved your husband completely until the end, upholding all the qualities that chapter talked about. Although what we did was morally wrong, it wasn't a sin against your marriage, Anna. Steven was gone, and you did a lot of grieving before he passed away. But you'll have to let go of the guilt your son and your sister heap on your shoulders. I know God doesn't expect you to carry that load."

Tears clung to her thick bottom lashes, and he prayed his words would strike a chord.

"But the greater concern is that you don't love me the way I love you, or you wouldn't be filled with fear, insecurity, and a zillion excuses. I've never spent a moment giving thought to reasons why I should not step into a relationship with you.

"The opposite, however, is sadly your reality."

"I'm sorry—"

"No, Anna, I don't want your apologies. I want what you can't give me."

Giant tears coursed down her ashen face. He dropped a feather-light kiss on each cheek. He stayed with his forehead pressed into hers and his hands gently cupping the sides of her face for one last moment.

"It's okay, Anna. Love cannot be forced. It just either is or it isn't."

"Goodbye, my love."

He turned from her and walked out the door.

Chapter Twenty-Eight

Tears flowed down her cheeks. She could feel the finality in Matt's words. He hadn't said goodnight, or see you tomorrow, as was his usual. He said goodbye.

Anna didn't hear from Matt for four long days.

One glance at her call display with his number in view caused her to jump on it, which was telling in and of itself. She felt her heartbeat quicken at the thought of a conversation with him. She'd grown used to his company, and the last few days had been far too lonely.

"Anna." His clipped tone caused her to pause.

There was no hello or friendliness. Just Anna. He didn't wait for her to say hello before he launched into conversation.

"I feel it judicious to have Melody come stay overnight in my home with regularity. Based on our conversation a few nights ago, she'll need to get used to our different homes, and for her sake, sooner is better than later. Since you believe our lives cannot *mesh*—to use your words, then I want to set up a nursery and work out an amiable schedule for the both of us."

"But—" She could not get a word in edgewise as he kept right on talking.

"As you know, and most likely don't need me to reiterate, I intend to be a very active and loving father to Melody, so begin contemplating what kind of schedule will work for you. I'm sure we can affably work out the details without the court's involvement."

She couldn't believe it was Matt, he sounded like a lawyer spelling out an agreement.

"Please give it some thought, and I'll be in contact soon."

With not an ounce of warmth and all businesslike, he said, "Bye, for now."

The line disconnected. Anna held the phone to her ear in shock. A deep sense of regret flooded over her as tears sprung to her eyes. She deserved and understood his distance. It wasn't fair to enjoy his company when he desired so much more.

She would see to it that he had free access to Melody and work around his schedule until her maternity leave was finished. Melody was what they had in common and always would, and that thought oddly gave her a scrap of comfort.

Anna was nervous. Her sister had called and was popping over. It was their first conversation since the day Anna had talked to Tom. She had heard from Lorena and knew that things were tentatively working out at home, but she respectfully didn't push for more information.

In times past, Lana would've walked in, called out her presence, and made herself at home—but not today. Like the arrival of a distant relative, the chime of the doorbell signaled her arrival. Anna had to hurriedly finish the diaper change and scoop up Melody to answer the door.

She decided to treat her sister as she always had. "Come in, Lana, you know you can just walk in."

Lana moved in and stood just inside the door. She wrung her hands together but didn't speak.

Melody broke up the awkward moment. She began to gurgle and coo and gave her mother a huge smile. Anna nuzzled her close. "You're such a happy one, aren't you?"

"Lana, take Melody for a minute, while I make us tea." She thrust the child into her sister's arms, and led the way into the kitchen.

Melody smiled widely with pure innocent love, and Anna could see that Lana was overwhelmed with emotion.

"You haven't held her since the hospital, have you?"

Giant tears rolled down Lana's cheeks.

"Oh, Anna, can you forgive me?" her voice cracked as she spoke.

Anna put down the tea kettle and came around the island to hug her sister. The two of them cried with Melody sandwiched between them. She reminded them she was still there and none too pleased at being ignored. Her scrunched up face and squirmy body broke the two apart.

"Looks like your little girl has a mind of her own."

"Yes, she lets me know what she wants. But for the most part she's happy and content and fills my days with love. I feel blessed to have her."

"Anna, I've been so wrong to shun you and talk behind your back like I have. How self-righteous I was. I justified the gossip all under the guise of asking for prayer."

Anna knew not to interrupt. This would be hard for her sister.

"But the worst of it is, I talked negatively to Mark about you. I knew he was struggling, and I supported his bad behavior. I encouraged him to stay angry, and I fed his spirit of unforgiveness because it fed mine too. I wanted company in my bitterness."

"I know, Lana. It's no big secret how my son feels about me. He's never been one to hide his feelings, especially when he's not happy about something."

"But … but you helped us out when Lorena came to you, and I've done the opposite." She tried hard to blink back her tears to no avail. "It could've been the perfect opportunity for you to do exactly what I did to you, but you didn't."

As she rocked Melody in her arms with tears coursing down her face, Anna realized she had never seen her sister look more beautiful. The professional, got-it-together woman with smudges in her perfect makeup made her seem real and endearing.

"Lana, we've both failed each other. I know what I did really embarrassed the family and that it hasn't been easy for any of you. It's a good thing God's forgiveness covers all." Anna smiled and moved to give her sister a quick hug.

Melody lunged her body toward her mom with her arms reached out. "I'll put her down for her nap while you take a moment to freshen up, then we'll have some quality TTT and SSS."

Anna purposely used the code words they had created as teenagers to bring back their closeness. "Time, tea, and talk to share and spill secrets."

Lana smiled through her tears.

Walking back into the kitchen, Anna poured the tea and slid onto the stool across from her sister.

"I feel like such a failure as a mom." Lana confided. "I know that I've given more time to my career in the past few years than I have to my kids or husband. The real estate market has taken off, and my work as an agent has sky-rocketed. I've even had to hire an assistant. The money is pouring in. People love me. I thought all was going so well."

Lana flung her hands in the air. Her brightly painted purple gel nails with yellow sunflowers caused a momentary distraction for Anna.

163

"Then this hits and reality sinks in. I've been focused on the wrong things, and Lorena has slipped through the cracks."

"It's not too late. God is the author of second chances."

Anna lifted her teacup to make a toast like they did as youngsters. Lana smiled and joined in.

"Here's to a fresh start. You need to make some changes that will enable you to have time with your daughter, and Lorena will open up. I know she will. I witnessed some real tenderness underneath that crusty shell. It's all a ruse. Deep down she's frightened and really needs you."

"I pray you're right. All we've done is fight in the past few months. I've been easily riled by her saucy mouth and have retaliated in anger. But Tom is no longer putting up with any of that—neither disrespect from Lorena, nor anger from me. You'd never recognize him these days. He's really changed. He's taking this leadership role thing seriously, and he challenges my bad attitudes. I've had to back down numerous times."

Anna laughed, clapping her hands. "Now that I'd love to see—you backing down."

"It's actually a relief," Lana admitted. "Right now, I don't know how to reach Lorena, and it's going to take time to win back her trust. Tom on the other hand, has always been closer to her. He has a softer way about him which she responds to. It's actually comforting to take the back seat."

She snapped open the clasp on her purse and fished out a tissue to dab at the corners of her eyes. "There's some good changes going on, I just have to embrace them."

Anna got up and poured another cup of tea. She placed a piece of Lana's favorite chocolate cake in front of her. "Made it fresh today, just for you."

"Ah, Anna, you're so much nicer than I am. You didn't know how our meeting would go today, and yet you baked my favorite chocolate cake. What's with that?"

"I had hope. I believed we'd find our way back together."

"Speaking of "together," I've bared my soul, but what about your life. What's happening with you and Matt?"

"What do you mean?"

"Well, are you two together? It's been over a year, and you've had a baby. Obviously, there's a connection. I also heard he became a Christian."

"Yes, but where did you hear that?"

"Tom said Matt joined the Saturday morning men's Bible study. Pastor Harry is his mentor and has encouraged all the men to make him welcome. But it's weird, we don't see him on Sundays with you."

Anna shook her head. "That's my doing. I told him I wasn't comfortable with him at our church due to the way others were having difficulties with us being together."

"By others, you primarily mean me, right?"

Anna didn't want to answer. "It's not only you."

"It's okay. I deserve a smack upside the head. To think I've jeopardized Matt's spiritual growth because of my unforgiveness."

"God is faithful, Lana. Matt hasn't seen a great example from me either. Yet still the love of God found him."

"Tom and I were wondering if you two are talking marriage yet. You do love him, don't you?"

Anna felt a flush of heat and knew she was turning red. "I don't know what I feel. There's been a lot of guilt associated with how this all happened, and I want to give my family and friends time to work it through before I selfishly run ahead. We're actually not seeing each other at the moment, other than to drop off or pick up Melody."

"What! You're kidding, right? Doesn't God remove guilt? Because if he doesn't, then I'm in real trouble."

"Well, yes … but—"

"No *buts*, Sis, or we're all in a mess. I've done a lot of soul searching in the last number of weeks. I thought about the years of sadness and loneliness you endured during Steven's lengthy illness, and suddenly, I understood. It was as if God opened my eyes to the way he looked in on your pain. I'm ashamed of my behavior and lack of love. I felt if I forgave you too soon, others would think I was in on the lies and my reputation would be ruined." She shook her head. "I was more worried about what others thought than what God wanted me to do."

Anna smiled in acknowledgment, "Yeah, do I ever know and understand that sin. We must be twins."

They laughed together, both with the same inflection at the same time, which made them laugh all the more.

"I love you, Sis."

"Love you more," Anna said.

"Yeah, you probably do. I've been a royal pain these past months, but I know someone who loves you to the moon and back, so what's not to love? You look ten years younger than me, and you make chocolate cake in the face of tyranny." She popped a large piece in her mouth, smacking her lips in sheer enjoyment.

"Now, do tell. Come on, spill the beans."

Anna smiled at the thought of Matt. She knew what her sister was asking but didn't know what to say. She pushed her piece of cake around on her plate with a fork.

"I know Matt loves you. You should've seen him in the hospital when you almost died. I've never seen anyone look so tormented, and it made me angry. In my unrighteous indignation, I felt he had no respect showing that much emotion around the rest of us who had zero time to get used to the idea of him. But now I realize that when someone truly loves, they can't hide it."

Anna shook her head. "It's all so complicated. Everything is out of order, and you know me, I don't do chaos well. I like everything stable and sensible."

"Anna, I can't tell you what to do. But I can encourage you to stop basing your decisions on what others think, and ask God for wisdom. How about we commit this to prayer. We used to pray for each other way more than we do now."

Anna enveloped her sister in a warm hug. They stayed that way for a long moment.

Lana pulled back and they each dabbed at their eyes. "We've become watering pots in our old age."

"Hey, *you* may be getting old, Lana, but I'm much younger than you." Like school girls with a secret, giggles filled the room.

❧

"Hey, sweet pea, we're going to go see Grannie Rita." Anna lifted Melody from the crib. "It's perfect timing. You're bright-eyed, happy, and all napped out. But whew! I just got a whiff of something not too sweet. How can a such a pretty little thing smell like that?"

Melody answered with a big smile.

Anna pulled at the snaps on Melody's pink onesie to change her diaper. Then kissed the bottom of her feet. She squealed in delight.

"Come on, lovie, we have chocolates to deliver. It's almost Christmas, and I've bought Rita's favorites." She bundled Melody into her coat and adorable pint-sized boots and headed for the car.

A dust of snow covered the frozen ground with the promise of more. A few snowflakes drifted lazily down as Anna pulled into the Pine Mountain Senior's Villa. "We're not going to stay long, Melody. I don't want to get caught in a snowstorm." They bustled in doors.

Rita's smile split wide and she stretched out her arms for a hug. Her eyes lit up when she viewed the box of sweets in Anna's hand. "Oh, my dear, you didn't have to—" she chuckled, "but I'm sure glad you did. I can't tell you how much I've missed you since you been off on maternity leave, but my, don't you look beautiful. Motherhood really agrees with you."

Anna smiled. "I think it's forgiveness that agrees with me, Rita, but I love being a mother again too."

"Well, I would say both motherhood and forgiveness have you looking radiant, my dear. Now bring that wee one closer and help me hold her. I want to pray a blessing over her while I'm still this side of heaven."

With plumped up pillows in just the right spot and the bed raised so that she could sit, Rita held Melody in her frail arms. Anna gathered in close, perched on the edge of the bed to help. Melody instantly stopped squirming as if Rita had a calm button she switched on. Anna was amazed, because one thing her daughter didn't do easily was settle.

A soft prayer ensued, mumbled in words of the spirit that Anna couldn't understand. Snuggled in tight, Melody's eyes grew heavy and she batted her thick, long eyelashes a few times before succumbing to sleep.

Rita finished and handed the sleeping child back to Anna.

"How is the father to this dear, sweet child?"

Anna's heart started to hammer within.

"Why, he's fine Rita. He comes and takes Melody regularly and is a wonderful father."

"He has given his life to the Lord."

"Yes," Anna answered.

"I know the answer is yes, my dear, but what I don't know is why you deny this child her father?"

"But Rita, I don't deny him. He comes and takes her whenever he can. I try and make it as easy for him as possible."

"Anna, a father can't fully father a child unless he is in a family that lives together. It's too difficult to be part of Melody's life from a distance, a few days here and there. It's not God's way. It is the way of hard hearts and this crazy world. And it's certainly not in the best interest of our children today the way they get shifted back and forth like a ping-pong ball."

Anna felt the guilt of not having a family nucleus for Melody. She was good at guilt, but not so good at doing something about it. She hugged Melody close and avoided eye contact. She preferred to gaze upon her daughter's peaceful slumber rather than Rita's set of piercing gray eyes that could see their way into her troubled soul.

"You love him, Anna!"

Anna noticed how she stated the fact rather than ask the question.

"And you both need him, not just this dear child."

"But, Rita, I don't know what I feel."

"Yes, you do, Anna.

"A woman like you with Christian convictions and a tender heart doesn't just fall into bed with a stranger. That evening you had together was far more than the mere need for sex, and you know it."

Anna gasped at her bluntness.

"Has he told you he loves you?"

Anna could not lie and nodded her head.

"Anna, open your eyes into the window of your heart. You were friends, long before Steven died. You had established relationship, trust, and respect for one another. There's no sin in that. Then Steven died and all the barriers were taken down. There was affection, attraction, and yes, I wager to say … love.

"Just because you allowed things to evolve out of God's order when you failed as mere mortals often do, there is no need to carry on in guilt."

Clucking her tongue, she continued. "God isn't asking you to pay penance for your sin, Anna. He paid the price on the cross, as you well know. You've repented and no longer live that lie. Now the only lie you're living is not being honest with yourself."

Her gaze, full of wisdom, drifted over Anna like loving hands.

"Anna, I know you love this man. I hear the tenderness in your voice when you speak of him. I see the way the mere mention of his name brings color to your cheeks and a smile to your lips. I may be old, Anna, but I'm not yet blind."

Heat worked its way up in a hot rush from her neck to her hairline. Anna wanted to deny what the wise old woman was saying but couldn't. She longed to be anywhere but sitting across from the one person who was not afraid to challenge her.

"What am I supposed to do, Rita?"

"You're supposed to pray, Anna, and then do everything the Spirit of God tells you to do, whether you have all your ducks in a row or not."

"Well, that's rather vague, Rita."

Rita had the nerve to laugh. "Oh, my dear, you start praying, and I assure you it will not be vague."

Chapter Twenty-Nine

Matt felt at peace. For the first time in his life a calm engulfed his soul. He no longer carried the weight of human pride on his shoulders, thinking he had it in his power to heal everyone and then agonizing when he couldn't. An understanding that he was a mere instrument in the hands of God freed his tortured soul. His previous stress melted, and he slept like never before.

Though peaceful, Matt could not say he was happy. He concluded that happiness involved good happenings. Other than Melody, he had little in his day to bring cheer, yet he felt content. This conundrum baffled him. Could it be his previous quest for happiness was a deception and what he longed for was peace? What a revelation in the midst of turmoil, giving strength and joy despite the ache of loss. As natural as breathing, thankfulness flowed spontaneously to his Father.

Anna, however, continued to frustrate him. She remained his mountain to climb, his thorn in the flesh, his portion to surrender. He longed for her to come to her senses, so they could be a family, but he could do nothing except wait.

Perseverance developed his character in areas where he lacked depth, knowing it was because most everything in his life had come easily to him.

Anna changed everything. He couldn't be in her presence without needing her, loving her, longing for more. Yet, she seemed unaffected. Melody's visits ensured he faced that growth in perseverance most every day.

He thought his sorry heart would hurt less to have Melody in his home rather than spending time at Anna's. How wrong he was. The distance created an insatiable need. The time they had previously shared felt like crumbs when he desired so much more. But now that they had no time together, those crumbs felt like a loaf of bread. He had enjoyed the simple pleasure of friendship more than he understood. Those moments had brought life to their relationship. Now he was just the father to her child, a man she waved to in passing.

When he thought of her list of reasons not to enter into a relationship, he wanted to shake some sense into her, or kiss her senseless—both scenarios carried merit. Instead, he dropped to his knees and pleaded his case before God.

The weeks before Christmas carried a sadness Matt couldn't shake. The holiday season amplified a loneliness that had never surfaced before. He desperately wanted to push Anna for more in the relationship, yet he refused to run ahead of God. Try as he might, he found it difficult to decipher if his desire to spend Christmas together as a family was his will or from the Lord. He finally came to peace with the idea of asking her. For all he knew her sons could be coming home, and Mark, for sure, wouldn't welcome him.

On route to her house to pick up Melody, he prayed for guidance and by the time he pulled into her drive he felt ready.

They had a routine. He let himself in and called out her name so she didn't have to answer the door.

Her singsong voice called out. "I'm in the kitchen, Matt."

She was busy cleaning the kitchen which gave him a moment to stare. A ripple of delight ran up his spine, and he had to stuff down the desire to gather her in his arms and kiss her hello.

He took a deep breath to still the crazy slam of his heart against his chest. "We haven't discussed plans for Melody over the holidays yet. What's happening in your world?"

Her big brown eyes snapped up in his direction as she continued to wipe at an already clean counter. Without a word she hung the kitchen cloth neatly over the center between the double sinks, picked up the diaper bag, and headed to the baby's room. With a wave of her hand, he followed.

"Mark's not coming because he's still upset with me. Jason is visiting ahead of time for a day or two then plans to meet his girlfriend Jennifer and her family in Banff on the twenty-fourth for skiing. Betty and George are in Palm Springs, but I have an invite to Lana's house Christmas day. Did I tell you she's talking to me again?"

She stuffed the diaper bag with supplies but didn't look up.

"No, but that's great news." His insides dropped to the basement of his soul. *Fat chance I'll be invited to that party. Lana treats me like the plague.*

He moved quietly over to the crib and looked down at the only family he had. A sense of sadness threatened to overwhelm as an emptiness flooded in.

Their baby lay sprawled out in her crib, dead to the world. Chubby legs and arms kicked free of the blankets and a thumb in her mouth made her irresistible. He knew it was time for her to wake up from her afternoon nap and those cuddles when she first woke up were the best, but he needed a few more minutes with her mama.

"I would like to have Melody on Christmas day. It's been a long time since I haven't worked over the holidays. I always volunteered because I wasn't a family man, but this year is different. I booked it off months ago."

She whipped around, her expression pinched.

"Please don't ask me to give up Melody on her first Christmas," she begged. "Come, let's talk out in the living room."

He now had her full attention.

"Will your request be the same come her first birthday and every other special occasion?" he asked, as he followed her down the hall. He knew he was causing her distress, but they needed to come to an understanding or he'd remain on the sidelines of Melody's life.

She turned to him and reached out to touch his arm, then dropped it quickly as if she had placed her hand in the fire. She moved apart and sunk into a nearby chair.

"I have a solution. We could spend these special days together with Melody. I don't know if I'd be welcome at your sister's house, but—"

"Oh Matt, Lana and Tom have their own issues right now with Lorena's pregnancy."

"What? … Did you say Lorena's pregnant?"

"Yes, I don't talk about it because it's their business to tell. But please don't take it personally that I don't feel like I can press them for extra invites at the moment."

Matt flopped onto the couch and raked a hand through his curly mop in agitation. "I get what you're saying Anna, but Lana hasn't cared for me at the best of times."

"No, Matt, truly, Lana has come a long way, and I'm sure both she and Tom would welcome you. It's just the dynamics right now. In fact, I feel my invite is more out of obligation than anything. They're struggling to find joy in the midst of all that's going on. Lana confided she doesn't feel like doing Christmas this year at all but said for the sake of her family she'd have to muster up the ho ho somehow. It won't be the same carefree celebration that it's been in years past, that's for sure."

"How old is Lorena?"

"She's sixteen and her boyfriend moved on because she wouldn't get an abortion. It's a stressful time."

He nodded in agreement. "I can well imagine."

Anna paused and lifted her eyes to him. "I do rather like your idea of getting together Christmas day and sharing Melody rather than one of us missing out."

Matt's heartbeat kicked up a notch, and a surge of adrenaline pumped through. It took everything within him to calmly respond. "We could go to the Christmas Eve candlelight service together, and you could bring Melody over early Christmas morning to open gifts. I know she won't have any idea what we're doing, but quite frankly, I've spoiled that girl.

"Then if you want to go to your sister's later that day for the meal—"

"How about we reverse that? I'll talk to Lana about a visit on Christmas Eve after the service instead of on Christmas day. Honestly, I think she'll be relieved to have some privacy this year."

Matt's heart slammed against the walls of his chest. That meant they were going to share the whole day. "That's a great idea. We'll cook the Christmas meal together, and Melody will enjoy being spoiled by the both of us all day."

Anna gave him one of her rare, heart-stopping smiles and said. "Thanks, Matt, I can see you've given this some thought. What better way to spend the season than sharing our baby girl?"

He knew of one better way, but she wasn't ready to embrace sharing Melody with him every day. For the moment he was thankful. A glimmer of hope broke on the horizon, and he wondered if dawn was about to stretch its arms of light over the darkness.

Lana and Tom were worried sick. Lorena cried more each day, never in their presence, but they could hear her through the bedroom door. They had both tried to talk to her but she buttoned up tight. Once again sobs filtered down the hallway, and fear clenched Lana's heart.

"Lorena, may I come in?" She knocked lightly. Tom wasn't home, and Lana felt she had to at least offer to help.

The reply took a few seconds, and Lana could hear Lorena blow her nose.

"No, Mom, I'm fine."

That same disturbing answer.

"Honey, you're clearly not fine. Please let me help."

"Go away!" Her voice grew edgy.

"But, Lorena dear—"

"It's too late to help, Mom, way too late."

Lana's take-charge personality bit back the urge to bust down the door and shake her daughter into submission. She knew that response wouldn't help, but she didn't do well with doing nothing.

A whirlwind of questions caused a tornado in her mind. What if Lorena was suicidal? What if she did something to hurt herself and the baby? Lana felt powerless.

"Please, Lorena, come eat something—if not for yourself, then for your baby."

"Mom, food is your answer for everything, but it's not mine. Please—leave me alone."

Lana turned on her heels and marched to the kitchen. The fridge door was open before she realized what she was doing. She slammed it shut and flopped her body into the oversized rocker. Tears welled and ran down her cheeks in rivulets.

Thoughts swirled into a mountain of worry. Lorena was losing weight instead of gaining. The taut protruding mound looked alien against her skinny silhouette. Her usual rosy full cheeks were gaunt, tightly stretched skin over bone. Dark rings circled her eyes, and her pallid skin gave the impression of a convict who never saw the light of day.

Come to think of it, that's exactly what Lorena lived like, a prisoner too ashamed to come out of her bedroom. She had no interaction with friends and nothing to break up the day. Lana regretted she and Tom had allowed Lorena to finish her year of school at home. Now in light of the isolation, that choice didn't seem like a healthy option. Her daughter had climbed aboard a train hurtling toward derailment, and she couldn't stop the ride.

Lana had tried every angle to reach her depressed daughter. In the past, they had shared a love for the Christmas season, one of the few things they had in common. She had hoped to light a spark yesterday. She put on Christmas music, dragged out the tree decorations when she least felt like it, in hopes Lorena would join her. She had to finally insist that she come out of her bedroom, only to watch the wilted girl stare blankly out the window while Lana did the decorating.

As Lana sat in the chair with little hope left, she bowed her head to pray.

Not more than five minutes into her prayer she heard the whisper of an idea float on wings of wisdom into her mind.

She snapped up from the chair and grabbed her cell.

"Anna, I'm glad I caught you—"

Chapter Thirty

Matt pulled his collar up around his neck and slipped on his gloves before heading out in the cold.

"Hi, handsome." Tamara jumped out from a side door of the hospital that overlooked the parking lot.

Drat! She must've been waiting for me.

Matt said an immediate prayer.

"Tamara, I don't want to be rude, but you've got to stop this."

"Stop what?"

"You know exactly what I'm talking about—showing up at my office, harassing the nurses here at the hospital for information on my shifts, and texting me constantly."

"Baby, we go too far back … surely you miss me?" She grabbed his arm and squeezed in close. Her perfume assaulted his senses. "I can warm up these long winter nights, in fact I can make them hot."

Matt shrugged her off and stepped apart. "What's wrong, Tamara? You can have your pick of men. I'm just not one of them any longer."

She gave him a crestfallen look with her brightly painted lips pursed into a sensual pout. "We'll never be over, Matt. You know you'll get tired of that woman who saddled you with a child. You never stay with anyone for long before coming back to me."

"Tamara, it's different now—I'm a different man."

She blinked her fake eyelashes slowly. "I can work with different, spices things up."

"I'm a Christian."

She broke out in a raucous laugh while Matt turned and walked straight to his car.

She followed with the click, click, click of her four-inch stiletto boots tapping behind him and grabbed the door before he could swing it shut.

Her eyebrows raised and her head tilted in a practiced look of seduction. She purposely shrugged her fur coat open and bent toward him to ensure her low-cut dress gave him full advantage.

"You won't be the first Christian I made forget all about his God." She wiggled her bosom in confidence.

Matt pulled the door shut, but not before he heard her laugh. "Tootles, darling … God has never kept a bed warm, but I sure have."

⌇

"Come on, Lorena, for as long as I can remember, you've helped me pick out gifts for your family, and you can't let me down now," Anna said.

Lorena blew out a heavy sigh. "But Auntie—"

"No buts, I need your expertise and you're coming. Up you get!" Anna pulled her off the bed in playful banter.

Lorena groaned. "Okay, okay already. Give me a half hour to get ready. You should have called ahead." Her face scrunched into a sour look.

Anna smiled and ignored her. "Half an hour, and then I'll pick you up over my shoulder and cart you out of here."

"Yeah, yeah, as if."

"You'd be surprised what your old auntie can do when provoked." With a playful wink, Anna shut the bedroom door behind her.

With thumbs up to Lana, she entered the kitchen. "Just enough time for a tea, but let's start with prayer and bring this unhappy girl to the Lord. We need him to open up her heart and mouth so that we can reach her."

Lana nodded in agreement. "Funny how prayer is your first resort and somehow my last."

"Oh, please, don't put me on a pedestal, because if I start believing in my own goodness again I'm doomed. Trust me when I say, the crash off that platform is painful."

They prayed together for wisdom and guidance and peace flooded in. "Oh, I feel so much better," said Lana, "Not sure why it takes a crisis to get me motivated."

Anna laughed. "Because you're human. We mere mortals are a fickle bunch, but somehow God just keeps on loving us."

Forty-five minutes later, while on their second cup of tea, an unenthusiastic Lorena entered the kitchen with her head down and a scowl on her face. "Let's get this over with."

Anna refused to join her in that place of gloom and smiled wide. "This is going to be so much fun, Lorena. And if your ideas are great, I'll take you for ice cream."

"Like I'm six again?" Lorena asked with sarcasm.

"No, like you're sixteen and in need of some sweetening up." Anna placed an arm around Lorena's shoulders and gave a quick squeeze. "Besides, I'm forty and still love ice cream as much as I ever did. We'll stop at Purdy's in the mall and get those chocolate and nut covered bars. Yum. Yum. A perfect choice for the winter season, don't you agree?"

"Whatever."

Anna let the attitude slide and handed a coat to Lorena.

Lana mouthed "thank you" as Anna waved and closed the door behind them.

Once in the car, Lorena voiced her none-too-happy opinion yet again. "Just so you know, I'm not into this. I feel fat, clumsy, and embarrassed to be seen in public."

Anna ignored the tirade.

"Tell me, is there something in the air? Because Melody's been cranky too." Anna caught Lana's eye and gave her a playful wink. "I had to drop her off at her dad's so that I could have a few peaceful moments with you. Please don't tell me you're going to pick up where she left off? I don't think I could handle that in the same day."

Lorena threw an anemic smile Anna's direction.

"Now, where to first? Shall we look for a nice gift for you? I love the way you give me the perfect idea and then feign total surprise when you open it." Anna laughed. "To watch you unwrap your gift is a joy worth every penny."

Lorena glanced down at her bulging stomach and back at Anna. "Don't worry about me, Auntie. I can't fit into anything I like anyway." A flat, dejected tone filled the car.

Anna was determined not to leave her there. "Okay, let me get this straight. You're telling me the only gift idea for you is clothing? Come on, Lorena, that's never been the case in the past, and it's not gonna fly today."

Anna turned into the nearby Starbucks. "Let's get one of those scandalous, thousand-calorie Christmas creations, and discuss our list before we hit the mall. We'll think more creatively with a little festive help, don't you think?"

Lorena didn't respond, so Anna kept talking.

"Remember how we had one before and after last year's shopping spree? One for fortification and one to relax after a job well done."

Lorena looked out the side window as if lost in another world. Anna understood her sister's concern. Lorena had morphed into a solemn waif of a girl. The chatterbox of the past now barely spoke and only if prompted.

Seated at a low table in comfortable leather chairs, Anna prayed that somehow Lorena would open up.

"I know you're not okay, but can you talk to me … because I really care?" Those few words of encouragement opened up the floodgates.

"Auntie, how did you find the strength to go on when your whole world came crashing in? Surely you felt like giving up, especially when people gossiped and pointed fingers."

Her words brought back all the feelings of despair Anna had felt not so long before.

"Joel has a new girlfriend. Plastered her picture all over his Facebook page. He's telling everyone that I said I was on the pill, which is a bold-faced lie. I was the one worried about birth control, and he kept telling me to relax. I'm so humiliated." Her bottom lashes brimmed with unshed tears.

"Oh, honey, I do understand." She reached across the table and squeezed Lorena's hand. "In fact, I was so afraid of what others thought of me, I created a bigger problem by allowing a lie to live for months. I know what miserable feels like."

"How did you make yourself want to go on?" Her hands trembled as she raised the peppermint mocha to her lips.

"Lorena, I can't explain exactly how other than to say that the God of love is much greater than the one who wants to destroy our lives. He forgives our mistakes and we have to hang on to this truth, because we both have a baby who needs us."

Lorena sighed. "Truthfully, there's a part of me that wishes I hadn't been such a coward and had that abortion. It would all be over. Not a person would know, and I'd have my life back."

"You'd know, and I don't buy what you're saying. You would've been haunted by that decision for the rest of your life because you know the truth. I read that essay you wrote in tenth grade citing the American Pregnancy Association, "everything that is present in an adult human is present in the smallest embryo."

Lorena nodded her head as she swiped at the tears that coursed down her face.

Anna gathered up her purse and her gingerbread latte. "Come. Let's go sit in the car where we have some privacy."

Lorena slid into the front seat and slammed the car door in frustration. "What am I going to do, Auntie? I'm only sixteen. I'm not old enough to look after a baby. If only I had the answer, then maybe I wouldn't feel so tormented."

"Have you thought about adoption, Lorena? There're long waits for couples who can't have children."

"Yes, but the thought of never seeing my child again haunts me." Lorena began to sob. "I keep having this recurring nightmare where a little boy cries out for his mama, but I can't reach him." She was crying hysterically now.

Anna took both their cups and put them into the center cup holder. She reached over and placed her hand on Lorena's arm rubbing gently. They sat in silence for a few moments until the weeping subsided.

"Auntie, if I could just figure out what I'm supposed to do—I ask God, but I hear nothing."

"What do your parents suggest?"

"I can't talk to them about this. I overheard my mom and dad arguing. Mom said it wouldn't be fair for her to have to put her whole life on hold and look after my baby while I finish school. Dad didn't agree and said their grandchild was more important than a career. Then Mom began shouting that he felt this way because it wasn't his career on the line ... and the fight was on." Lorena sniffed loudly and rubbed her hand across her face.

Anna searched her purse for a tissue, to no avail, and came up with a napkin from the door pocket.

Lorena flipped the mirror down and swabbed at her face.

"Auntie, it's so weird. My parents fight more these days now that Dad has finally found his voice, but ... they seem closer than ever." Lorena shook her head. "I can't quite figure that one out.

"Well, my dear," Anna said, "conflict in relationship is inevitable, it's how we handle it that matters the most. Your parents are finally being real with each other where both have equal say—that's healthy."

Lorena nodded. "That makes sense, but what I overheard made me understand that I can't put this decision on them. You know how important Mom's career is to her. She would rather die than give that up."

Anna nodded unable to refute the truth. As sisters, they had always been polar opposites. She was all about family, nurturing and homemaking. Lana was more about education, career, and status. They both could've used a little of what the other had.

"Lorena, what if I raised your baby?" She was shocked at her own words, for she had not previously thought about or mulled over the possibility. In fact, it had not fully traveled to the brain when she blurted it out.

Lorena's face lit up like a Christmas tree with a thousand bulbs. She threw her arms around Anna and hugged so tightly she had to pry apart a bit just to breathe.

"Oh, Auntie, you would do that for me … for us?" She rubbed her hands over the growing bulge.

Anna couldn't retract her words, as crazy as they were, they felt right. "When your child's old enough to understand, we'll tell him about you and the sacrifice you made to bring him into the world. He'll know how much you love him.

"Oh my gosh, Auntie—I can't believe I'll get to see him grow and yet finish growing up myself. Just to know that he'll be safe and well taken care of." Her face brightened and a genuine smile split across her beautiful face.

"I was wondering why, if God was with me, that nothing seemed right, not abortion, not keeping the baby, not imposing the child on my parents, not giving the child up for adoption—nothing—until now."

"Lorena, this is just an idea. You must pray about it, and we must talk to your parents—they may have other ideas."

A hitch of fear bristled up her spine. What had she done? "Also, you may find as you pray that your thinking changes and that's fine."

Lorena's eyes grew wide and danced with fear. "You did mean what you just said, didn't you?"

"Of course, honey, but I want you to know that you have options."

Lorena's voice lifted in confidence. "Auntie, I've explored my options until my heart felt like it was bleeding out. This is the first bit of hope I've had in months. Thank you. Thank you."

Fully energized, Lorena literally bounced in her seat as if a load had been lifted from her tiny shoulders. "Come on, Auntie, we've got some serious shopping to do." Excitement was back in her voice.

Lorena flicked on the radio where strains of "Chestnuts Roasting on an Open Fire" filled the car. She began to do a tap dance with her feet as Anna pulled out of the parking lot.

In truth, Anna was flabbergasted. Her mind began to whirl and spin like a leaf in a windstorm. *Oh my gosh, what are Tom and Lana going to think? I should've discussed this with them first.*

The truth hit her full on. What just happened was not her idea at all—it had flowed as spontaneously as water runs downhill. She could not argue that God had planted, sprouted, and grown the idea in a split second.

Droplets of fear splashed upon the pages of her mind as one logical question after another surfaced. "God, don't I have enough on my plate? I'm a single mom. How am I going to raise two infants?"

You don't have to be a single mom.

Anna changed stations and turned the radio louder. She received an instant smile from her niece. She would grapple with the shadows some other time. For today, she dared not allow fear and doubt poke any more pinholes in her mind or Lorena would pick up on her angst.

Chapter Thirty-One

They pulled into the drive, and Anna squeezed Lorena's arm. "Let me talk to your parents first, okay? This idea may come as a bit of a shock. I think it's best coming from me."

"No problem, Auntie. I agree."

"Tell your mom I'll call her."

"Thanks, Auntie. I love you so much." They hugged and Anna watched her niece practically bounce into the house.

As soon as she got home she called her sister. "It went well, Lana, but I need to talk to you and Tom privately. Can you come over tomorrow night before you go home from work?"

"No problem, Sis, we'll make it happen."

Matt had to work hard to convince Anna to share Christmas in his home. Even after they agreed, she made numerous attempts to change the location back to her house. He was glad he had remained firm and argued that Melody needed to feel as comfortable in his home as hers. A friend of his who was an interior decorator was going to do him a last-minute favor and help bring some Christmas cheer. She was scheduled to arrive that afternoon.

Katrina threw up her hands in dismay. "A traditional Christmas feel, with warmth and welcome. Are you kidding me, Matt? How am I supposed to create warmth with futuristic style furniture, metal and steel accents, and these ghastly white walls? Everything you've created here, Matt, is the opposite of the classic traditional style. You've got modern style going on, if you can call it a style, and it's not my cup of tea, that's for sure."

Matt looked around with eyes wide open. The walls reminded him of the operating room and exuded a cold starkness. The furniture had never been to his liking but had been designed and custom built by one of the city's finest.

"What? The interior decorator I hired after the house was built recommended this style as the latest rage."

"But do you like it, Matt?"

He looked around thoughtfully and realized he far preferred Anna's home with its wonderful ambience of warmth and color.

"No. Change it," he said. "You have a week and an unlimited budget."

The shock on the designer's face registered fully, as her eyes popped open wide.

"Okay, let me get this straight. You want me to change the décor, not just decorate for Christmas."

"Yes," Matt nodded. "Yes, please."

"Well then," Katrina stated emphatically not about to argue, "let's not waste another moment. There's much to do. Matt, your house has beautiful bones, though unwisely appointed I might add, but not to worry … this will be so much fun." She clapped her hands in sheer excitement and opened her computer. "Come," she said. "You will not have another decorator choosing your style. Show me what you like."

***

Anna was barely out of bed when her cell rang.

"I don't know what you did, Anna, but we have our daughter back. I want to thank you from the bottom of my heart. I was so worried, but she's up already this morning and ate a full breakfast. For the first time in months, she's wearing a smile. I can't believe the change—she's her old chatty self again."

"Have you talked to her yet?"

There was a pause on the line. "Well, yes—of course we talked, but nothing specific. Should there be?"

Anna dreaded what was to follow. In her mind, she could see her sister flip a lid. The more time she had to think about it, the more fearful she had become. How had she been stupid enough to stick her nose into her sister's life in such a big way without consulting her first?

"Sorry, Lana, I intended to tell you and Tom tonight. In truth I've … I've needed time to pray."

"Okay, Anna, out with it! Surely it can't be anything too bad, because the transformation in Lorena is amazing."

"You've got to promise to let me finish and not interrupt until I'm done." Anna found it hard to be forceful with her sister but felt the situation merited a bit of grit.

"Yeah, yeah … now what is it?"

Anna explained the whole conversation she had with Lorena. When she was done, she waited to hear the lecture on why she had not been respectful enough to talk to them first. Instead, she heard soft sobs filter over the line.

"Lana, are you there?"

"Yes." She sniffled. "Give me a minute."

Anna heard the sound of a blowing nose, the click, click of heels, and a door shut before Lana whispered into the phone.

"Gosh, Anna, I should be the one offering to look after this child, not you. After all, it's our grandchild. But you know me, I was never great with babies. Tom and I have had some real good arguments about this lately. He wants me to be someone I'm not. I feel so selfish, but I don't want to commit to something I know I'll resent."

Anna didn't know what to say, she certainly didn't want to get between the two of them. "Lana, talk to Tom. We don't have to figure out all the details just yet. If this idea helps Lorena through a difficult time and gives her peace, then let's just leave it there. We'll all pray for the will of the Lord on this matter, and remember, we have months until the baby is born."

"You're right, Anna. The most important thing is Lorena's well-being. We'll have time to sort out the rest. Thanks, dear Sis. I'll call you after I talk to Tom."

"Oh, and Lana?"

"Yes?"

"God knows how he created you, and he knows how he created me. There's nothing wrong with either creation."

"Sis, you're the best."

Anna hung up the phone and exhaled deeply. She had fretted all night wondering how to tell her sister what she had done on impulse, only to find that the good Lord had everything in his control.

⁂

"Imagine a floor to ceiling fireplace without a mantle," she scoffed. "That's like having a pie without filling. We'll fix that in short order."

True to her word, a crew of masonry experts arrived and set to work. They tore down the colorless white marble and framed the fireplace with stones in rich, earth-tone colors, adding a complementary black slate hearth. A couple days later, a carpenter installed a meaty timber mantle that finished off the beautiful transformation. The room instantly became one of Matt's favorites.

A team of painters showed up and magically, warm, earth-tone colors sprang to life. An electrician worked around the painters replacing what Katrina referred to as the 'appalling light fixtures,' and the Salvation Army carted off the gaudy furniture.

With Matt's input, the transformation took on life. As per Katrina's only request, he kept in close contact with her in order to answer a myriad of questions.

About three days into the project, Matt received a frustrated text from Katrina. "I need photos, Matt, old and new. You have nothing personal out. Surely you have some old photo albums I can peek through, and what about some recent pictures of that beautiful baby you keep talking about?"

Katrina's no-nonsense, let's-get-it-done attitude, kept the ball rolling. After the painters were done, a team of women stormed the house. They cleaned, fussed, and carted in boxes and bags of endless décor items. Every day when Matt came in after work, he marveled at how his house was being transformed into a home.

Wide-open spaces were filled with a combination of new and antique furniture, creating a classic traditional feel. Warm Persian rugs that complimented the wall color were strategically placed on the hardwood floors to create a room within a room. The windows were covered in new, chic blinds and tasteful drapes. Beautiful paintings graced the walls, and his bookcases were filled with not only books but ornaments, candles, and pictures all carefully arranged. Flowers and plants spilled out of pots and vases. Every nook and cranny came alive with color and texture. Katrina was determined that he'd love his home when she was done. And love it he did.

On December 24th, the makeover complete, Katrina's team arrived to do what he'd originally hired her to do—decorate for Christmas.

Matt worked a half day then headed back. In those few morning hours, Katrina's team of elves brought Christmas into his home. A real tree rose from floor to ceiling permeating the house with a woodsy scent of pine. Garland, lights, and bows graced the balcony and stair banister. A smaller beautifully decorated tree draped with gold stars, angels, and red bows brought cheer to the living area just off the kitchen.

Matt especially loved the new swivel leather rocking chairs strategically placed where he could enjoy the stunning view of the city in one direction and his crackling fire in the other. Three stockings hung from the mantle, two filled to the brim with goodies for his girls. He glanced up at his favorite addition and smiled in delight. Twinkling lights woven into garland framed the photo he had enlarged and mounted. He couldn't be more pleased.

At his request, his recent purchase of a carved olive wood nativity scene received center stage on the mantle recreating the Christmas story. Poinsettias graced most every room in tasteful cheer. The whole effect was truly magical and hopelessly romantic.

"Katrina, you have outdone yourself. I can't say thank you enough." Matt handed her a check with a sizable tip.

Katrina looked down at the amount, and her eyes widened. "This project certainly challenged me in both the time allotted and the sheer magnitude of the job. But," she said holding up the check, "this soothed the tired right out of my bones."

Chapter Thirty-Two

Anna dressed with care for the candlelight service on Christmas Eve. An unexplained excitement jumped inside. She pulled the brush through her hair—a flash of the wedding ring still on her finger brought back thoughts of Steven.

He had died late November … so much had happened. The past year could be chalked up as her worst year ever except for the blessing of Melody and the redeeming love of God. Her Christianity had grown leaps and bounds out of the ashes.

She turned the single gold band around on her finger and shook off the cobwebs of the memories. With a smile into the mirror, she concentrated on the here and now. Her choice of a bright red sweater that hugged her curves and layered over a pencil slim black skirt that rode just above the knees gave her the pretty look she longed for. She dug her high heels from the back of the closet and was about to slip them on when she noticed a thick layer of dust. It made her realize how long since she had dressed up for an evening.

She focused on the full-length mirror in front of her and pirouetted for inspection. Her hair waved obediently down her back. She grinned at the fact she had actually tamed the frizzy sprigs that usually turned into uncontrollable fluff. Her makeup applied with intentional care provided the fresh natural look she desired.

One more glance gave her the inspiration for that last little touch. She rummaged through her dresser until she found the velvet box she had received after her mother's death. With care, she opened the precious gift. A matching set of pearl earrings and necklace stood out against the dark green velvet. They were just what she needed. The end result brought an instant smile to her face.

With the Christmas music cranked up loud, Anna waltzed into Melody's room. She had been awake from her nap for the past half hour. Anna had heard her sweet coos and babbles filter down the hall to her room.

A huge smile lit Melody's face as Anna came into view. "Come, my sweet baby. Let's get you looking pretty for Daddy too." Anna smiled. She had dressed with care for one person in mind, and there was no point in denying that truth.

Melody wiggled and reached with chubby fists toward Anna's hair that was usually pulled back. "No, no, little one. Mama just got that looking good." She pinned her hair behind each ear as she dressed Melody in a bright red dress with frilly white lace, a warm coat, and tiny moccasin boots. Melody cooed to the Christmas music in the car all the way to the church.

"Mama's angel, yes, you are." Anna whispered as she lifted her out of her car seat. The child smiled like a cherub.

Anna balanced the diaper bag, baby, and her purse. She should've accepted Matt's offer to pick them up, but she had wanted him to see her as a capable woman, especially in light of her recent offer to adopt Lorena's baby. She hadn't had the opportunity to share that possibility with Matt just yet.

Caught in one hug after another as she walked into the foyer, it amazed her how the majority of church people had forgiven and loved her. She felt truly blessed.

She waved as she caught a glimpse of Matt and moved toward him. She wondered if her hair survived the fact Melody had fistfuls in her mouth—one of the reasons Anna rarely wore it down.

"Beautiful," he whispered, leaning in.

She heard the word float her way and saw the way his eyes lit up.

Melody flung her tiny body toward her daddy. Anna stumbled and nearly landed in his arms.

He steadied her with one hand and reached for Melody with the other. They stood eyes locked on each other. Neither moved, neither breathed. Melody, however, made her presence known by batting Matt on the face. He kissed her tiny cheek but kept his eyes riveted on Anna. An unveiled moment of passion moved between them without a single touch.

A tingle started from the tip of Anna's toes straight up to the top of her head. She needed to get a grip.

"Here." She plunked the diaper bag in his hand and moved to the nearby rack to hang her winter coat. When she turned around, Matt was mere inches from her.

"Anna, you look amazing." His voice sounded breathy.

She smiled widely. "You don't look too shabby yourself, Doctor Carmichael, but enough of this mutual admiration. We'd better get a seat, it's filling up fast."

They entered the sanctuary looking every bit a family. Melody served up smiles all the way down the aisle as many waved and reached out to touch her. Matt beamed, and Anna stressed at the feelings crashing in.

Anna's mind was not on the candlelight service. Instead, the heat from Matt's shoulder seared its way into her consciousness. A craving to lean in and snuggle close bled into her thoughts. When they passed Melody between them, their hands touched and lingered just a tad too long. She was glad when Melody fussed, and he offered to take her to the back.

Her heart rate and mind settled but not on Christmas or the baby Jesus in a manger. Thoughts of Matt, their baby, and what it would be like as a family dominated. She wondered why God had not given clear direction. She had taken Rita's advice and spent time with God, asking over and over what she should do.

It's because you keep asking but not listening. The words exploded into her soul.

"I'm not listening?"

You embrace fear and fail to see the gift of love I've given you.

Anna felt the truth of those words.

I have not given you a spirit of fear, but a spirit of power, and love.

Anna fidgeted in her seat. Conviction ruled. She understood the message. She was not to fear relationship.

Matt slipped in beside her with a sleeping Melody in his arms. His smile radiated through her like a lighthouse beacon shining across black waters. She warmly returned his smile and marveled at how good Melody and he looked together, father and child.

Music played softly as the congregation rose to sing "It Came upon a Midnight Clear," and all became clear to Anna.

She understood the message, but the question remained … what would she do with her Christmas Eve revelation?

Chapter Thirty-Three

Anna touched Matt's arm. "How about coming over to my place, so we can get Melody settled and have a hot cup of my famous Christmas cider?"

His brows furrowed in question.

"Come on, the service started early, and the night's still young."

"What about going to Lana's?"

"Really? I didn't tell you?"

"Tell me what?"

"Tom and Lana decided at the last minute that a family getaway for Lorena was in order. Far away from prying eyes and nosy questions," Anna whispered. "Not that everyone is like that, but there're a few."

As if on cue, Myrtle Pinsmith beelined her way over to where they stood.

"Why, Anna, wherever is your sister and her family on this most important evening of worship?" She clucked her tongue and shook her head in contempt.

"They're out of town, Myrtle."

"Only heaven knows why anyone would travel on these winter roads? Why, that's just asking for trouble. Then, of course, they'd blame the good Lord if an accident happened."

"They flew to Mexico, so no driving necessary."

"Tsk, Tsk," the old bird fussed as she shook her head in disagreement and pointed her spotted finger in Anna's direction. "One would think with a pregnant daughter, they'd stay close to home."

Anna exhaled deeply. Matt picked up on her angst as he touched her arm with slight pressure and stepped in.

"Myrtle, is it?" He questioned. "We've never met." He extended his hand in greeting.

She whirled in his direction and ignored his outstretched hand. "Oh, I know who you are." Her nose lifted. "The least you could do is marry this girl now that you've gotten her into such a mess."

Anna could feel her eyes involuntarily widen as storm clouds billowed on the inside. "I would hardly call my daughter a mess, Myrtle, and neither would God. And though I know I'm far from innocent, I also know I'm forgiven."

Myrtle had to have the last word. "Maybe you don't think it's a mess, but I sure do. Seems your family needs a good dose of the Scripture and maybe all this fornicating will stop." She harrumphed and turned on her heels.

They stood with their mouths half open and watched her large caboose waddle away.

Matt started to laugh. "Well then, we've been told. Do you want to get married?"

Anna glared at him. "Matt, I don't find this funny at all. She's a self-righteous old biddy—"

Matt placed a finger on her fiery lips and stilled the tirade of not-so-pleasant words that begged to tumble forth.

"Come, my lovely. You look way too attractive when you're angry, and the church isn't the place to kiss that pout off your lips."

She slapped him on the arm. "You're incorrigible, Matt, and quit flirting with me." She turned and made for the door.

"I'll never stop, Anna. Never!"

Her heart picked up speed as anger flew out the window. With or without the likes of Myrtle Pinsmith, she planned on having a fantastic Christmas.

⁂

The two of them played with Melody for a bit before Anna tucked her into bed. She found Matt in the living room where he'd taken it upon himself to turn the Christmas tree lights on, the overhead lights off, and make a fire that crackled and glowed.

Anna felt a raw intimacy and began to babble as she fussed with a Christmas bulb on the tree.

"I'm glad that Lorena's getting away to enjoy some sun. They're at an all-inclusive resort in hopes Lorena eats a lot. She's way too thin.

"Oh, and did I tell you Todd is stoked … his words not mine. He got to bring a friend—"

"Anna." Matt interrupted. "Do you really think I'm interested in your nervous chatter about Mexico?"

Anna whirled around from the tree to catch a lazy smile play across his face. Her heart tripped a beat at him sprawled across her couch in total relaxation. Her breath hitched as she noticed a wayward curl that hung across his forehead. Her fingers itched to run through his curly locks and smooth that curl into place. Her eyes locked with his as she took a trip down memory lane to the passionate night they shared. Heat immediately rushed to her face.

He sat up straight and patted the spot beside him on the couch. "Come sit with me."

She made her way over and sat on the opposite end of the couch facing him.

"What, now I bite?" He asked lightheartedly as a crooked smile activated that crazy dimple on the right side of his cheek.

"Good thing you can laugh, Matt, because I'm so not comfortable here."

"Why? Are you afraid of allowing yourself to feel, Anna?"

He was so close to the truth that it hurt.

He slid closer and grabbed one hand and lifted it to his lips. Tenderly, he kissed each finger and then placed her hand over his heart.

She could feel the rapid movement beneath her finger tips through the weight of his sweater.

"That's what you do to me, Anna. I can't be in your presence without my heart racing like Street Sense in the Kentucky Derby." He laughed and dropped her hand but nudged closer.

"You should have seen that horse run. I was fortunate enough to be there. I'll have to take you to a race sometime so you'll know what I mean."

The low rumble of his voice relaxed Anna, and she sank into the cushions. When he slipped an arm around her shoulder, she allowed it to stay there. Warm. Welcome. Wonderful.

Christmas morning dawned bright and beautiful. Matt stood at his window with the view of the city and lake spread before him. His perch up on Dilworth Mountain was one of the best. There had been a time when his possessions and status mattered, but not anymore. He would sell his house in a flash and live with Anna in her quiet unassuming neighborhood far below, if only she'd have him. Just the thought set his pulse racing.

She had no idea of the torture she had placed him in the night before. Nor could she begin to understand the discipline it took to have her close and not succumb to the desire to kiss her or nuzzle her long graceful neck relaxed against him.

She couldn't know that he had prayed for a miracle as they sat side-by-side and begged God to heal her insecurities. All Anna would know is that they had a wonderful time. They laughed, talked, and enjoyed each other's company.

God, however, knew he prayed for so much more. The hope of a new day opened before him. A whole day to spend with his two favorite girls. He would make the most of it.

Covered beneath a dusting of fresh snow, the remnant of a few twinkling lights dotted the view. The world looked unspoiled and serene. He moved to his favorite chair with a hot cup of coffee in hand to watch the sun crest the eastern ridge. Like a million diamonds upon the surface of the earth, sunbeams spread and danced across the snow.

His cat, Abby, wound around his legs purring. He picked her up and stroked her back as he prayed.

"Thank you, God, for so many blessings. I surrender the difficult and believe you have all in your control.

"What a wonderful way to start both Christmas and my birthday. No one could've told me last Christmas, God, that in the span of the next year I'd have the gift of you, the gift of my beautiful baby, and the gift of a spirited, stubborn, but special woman in my life. My dreams never got that big. You have truly blessed me." Matt whispered an amen into the heavens.

He opened his Bible to read, but his mind drifted to the conversation he knew he had to have with Anna. If they were going to make it as a couple or raise Melody in harmony, Anna would have to accept the fact he had money and lots of it.

Pastor Harry had taught him how some people were given the gift of going to the ends of the earth to evangelize and others the need to support them financially and prayerfully. With an already philanthropic viewpoint, Matt found the idea of tithing and giving to missions exciting.

He could tell his possessions intimidated Anna. Born into money, he'd grown up in a privileged home where education and affluence were an everyday experience. Though he had worked hard, he'd been given every tool with which to succeed. He no longer felt the urge to hide his life in order to blend into hers. The truth was long overdue.

He was sure one of the reasons Anna may have felt less-than-pleased with his home had to do with the sprawling coldness. Hiring Katrina had been a gift.

He surveyed the transformation once again and his excitement grew. A sense of cozy welcome radiated from even the larger rooms, and he couldn't wait to see Anna's surprise. He hoped she would love the changes. When he'd first shown her his home, she hadn't been wowed by the opulence or fantastic view. She'd checked out Melody's nursery with little enthusiasm and sighed heavily when he insisted on a tour. Her politeness had sounded forced.

He hoped today would change all that. Rather than what was vogue or trendy, he wanted a cozy home for Melody, one that mirrored both his and Anna's taste. He prayed the effort would make Anna feel comfortable and treasured.

Chapter Thirty-Four

Anna awoke Christmas morning with a burst of joy in her heart. She spent the first moments of the day in prayer asking God for strength to do what she believed wisdom asked of her.

Anna could hear Melody babble over the monitor and smiled in wonder. What would her life be like without her baby girl? She couldn't bear the thought. Thankfulness flooded through her being. God had worked all for good, even her failure, with the added gift of Matt's love for the both of them. This blessing was way beyond what she ever expected to enjoy, especially after the way she had pushed him out of her life. All she had to do now was rise above their obvious differences and trust in this same incredible God who would not lead her astray.

Like a demon sitting on her shoulder with a bucket of ice water to douse the inner fire of faith the instant hope sparked, negative thoughts poured in.

What about when you married Steven ... look where love and trust in a good God got you there.

Anna brushed off the frustration and busied herself with a shower but couldn't wash away that nagging question. Where she wanted to focus on Christmas and all things bright and beautiful, instead she wrestled with darkness.

Why did Steven have to get sick and suffer for so long? Why the emotional roller coaster of sickness and remission? If I open my heart to love again, will this or something equally as devastating happen? A kaleidoscope of negative thoughts twisted and warped their way inside her head.

With Melody still happily in her crib, Anna took the time to kneel by her bed and pray.

"God, you hear my scattered thoughts. Just when I decide to move forward, doubt and questions pour in. I know what I'm really asking. It's that age-old question of why life brings suffering and how to avoid it."

The answer to that question remains a mystery only few discover.
"Will I discover it?"
You already have.

This puzzled Anna even more, so she silenced the barrage of questions and asked for wisdom. Like the light of dawn, darkness had no choice but to flee and give passage to understanding.

Her suffering had purpose. She wouldn't jump up and down and ask for more pain, but suffering was not to be feared or despised either. The pain had molded her into a kinder, more loving person, and had created a depth in her relationship with Christ she wouldn't otherwise know.

The one thing she now trusted without question was that God would never leave nor forsake her. He would help her find her way through. He had sent real people who cared to be his hands, who had gifted her with mercy, wisdom, and love. Each piece of the puzzle whether painful or joyful had a story, a color, a needed texture.

She had nothing to fear in walking into a relationship with Matt. All her feeble excuses melted in the fire of this truth. Trust in God beckoned, and all she had to do was answer that call.

She told the enemy of her soul that he could take his fear and twisted attack and move on out. Then she rose from her knees in confidence and headed to Melody's room.

Melody cooed sweetly and gave a dreamy smile. She stretched a tiny fist heavenward and opened her mouth in an adorable yawn.

"You're such a joy," Anna said nuzzling the soft baby curls. "Such a joy, indeed. Your daddy named you perfectly, didn't he?" Melody gurgled in delight.

Anna was anxious to get out the door and be on her way to Matt's, though the mere thought of his house had her wishing she'd been able to convince him otherwise.

She buckled Melody into her car seat as she squirmed in protest. "Yes, sweet pea, you need to be buckled in, like it or not."

Anna eased out of the driveway. A fresh blanket of snow caused the tires to slip and slide each time she applied the brake. She worried about the trip up the side of the mountain to Matt's and began to pray for safety. She had barely made it one block going at a snail's pace when she spotted Matt's vehicle coming the other direction and slowed to a stop.

"How are my two favorite girls today?"

Anna couldn't help but smile at his cheery disposition.

"The roads are not plowed or sanded up my way. I tried to call, but there was no answer."

"Oh, sorry, I must've been in the shower, and you know how bad I am with my cell. I forgot to plug it in last night."

"No worries. I'm your chauffer today so turn that car around, and I'll pick you up at your house."

He was out of his car and waiting. Before she could fully park the car in the garage, he had the back door open and little Melody in his arms. He opened her door like a gentleman and waited for her to get out. As she stood, he kissed her smack dab on the lips. "Merry Christmas, darling," he said, and chuckled at her obvious surprise.

That one kiss sent fire coursing through her veins and muddled her brain. She was going to suggest they stay at her house but couldn't think straight.

He didn't skip a beat. He buckled Melody in her car seat with major protests this time and hurried around to open her door. "I have the seat warmer on for you," he whispered in her ear, tickling her hair with his breath. His hand felt warm and sensuous as it lingered just a tad too long on the small of her back as he guided her in.

Matt proceeded to chat all the way to his house. He was in high spirits, which only heightened her excitement for the day.

He pulled into the drive instead of the garage, which puzzled Anna. "Don't you want to put these fancy wheels in your garage?" she asked. "The snow is starting to fall again."

"No, it's fine," he waved nonchalantly. "Come, let's get breakfast on, I'm starving."

With Melody tucked safely on one arm and the diaper bag hanging from the other, he handed her the house keys and asked her to unlock the front door.

Anna swung the door wide. Her eyes bulged at the huge Christmas tree filling the two-story entrance. Melody gurgled and lurched for the shiny bulbs that sparkled before her.

"Whoa there, little one, be careful," Matt chided as he held on tighter.

Anna whirled around in delight. "Why, Matt, what a gorgeous tree. Oh, and look at the stairs … the banister … it's all so beautiful."

"How—" her words trailed off as her mind began to compute the change in wall color and what lay beyond the tree. The entrance turned out to be merely the appetizer. Room after room she oohed and awed, mesmerized by the transformation. Somehow his large, rambling, ice castle had morphed into a home. She couldn't believe her eyes.

"Matt," she said, throwing up her arms. "This is fantastic. To be honest, I dreaded the thought of celebrating Christmas here—"

"I know, Anna. My house didn't thrill me much either."

She grabbed his arm in excitement and squeezed both Melody and him in a quick hug. A quick whirl showed her delight. "What a treat!"

She stopped dead when she spotted a photo she'd never seen before. There above his fireplace was a huge picture of her rocking Melody. Her long hair flipped to one side cascaded down the left side of the picture. Matt had taken the photo without her knowledge and caught a tender moment where she had brushed her mouth against the silky top of Melody's sleeping head.

"It's my favorite," he admitted.

She was moved beyond words. "Oh, Matt, it's all beyond incredible."

"The minute you said you would come for Christmas, I set this in motion."

"But … but how?" Shock flooded her face at the sheer magnitude of the job and the money spent.

"I knew you hated the house, and for that matter so did I. Long story short, your place felt more like home to me than mine did. I hired an interior decorator to decorate for Christmas, and well, it morphed into a home makeover. Do you like it?"

"Like it, Matt? What's not to like?"

Melody squirmed in Matt's arms and arched her back in a message to be put down. Her latest achievement was to roll around, and she loved being free to do just that. He laid her on his new Persian rug.

Anna grimaced. "Grab the play-pen, Matt, she could spit up."

He laughed at her concern but set it up anyway.

"Okay, now I feel better," Anna said. "That rug looks pricey."

"Really, Anna? A little bit of mess from Melody is the least of my problems, you're a far bigger one." He laughed and threw one of Melody's teddy bears at her.

She caught it and threw it back. "Oh, really Matthew, you think I'm a problem?" She moved closer. "Then why go through all this work just to impress me?"

"Yeah, well don't let it go to your pretty little head, or I'll have to—"

She grabbed him. "Or you'll have to do what?" And kissed him full on the mouth before pulling away and laughed at his shocked expression.

"What's good for the gander is good for the goose. Just getting you back for this morning."

He went to grab her, but she squealed and lit out in a run. He easily caught her and in one swift movement had her locked in his arms up against the wall. "Whatcha going to do now?" he challenged.

He brushed an errant curl from her face before his hands slowly slipped the elastic band from her hair and pulled it free. He dropped a kiss on her brow and slid his fingers gently through her hair.

She instinctively pressed closer, trembling at the intoxication of his nearness.

"Whoa, Nellie," he joked. "You'd better turn this stallion in a different direction or there'll be real trouble."

"So, you're a stallion now?" she teased. She could feel the crazy clip clop of his heart beat against her fingertips.

He laughed and dropped his arms from around her.

Chapter Thirty-Five

Matt worked on brunch while Anna got the turkey in the oven. The babble of Melody and soft strains of Christmas carols in the background covered the awkwardness between them. That surge of desire had them both tongue-tied.

They took pictures of Melody's first Christmas and shared in helping her unwrap her gifts, but the day felt weighted with unspoken tension. They ignored the undercurrents between them and engaged in small talk about weather patterns and the upcoming election.

Anna had a Christmas gift for Matt but held back hoping he would suggest their exchange. When he said nothing, she assumed he hadn't thought of a gift for her. The surprise of his beautiful home and all he'd done to make the day special was gift enough, but her gift was far more personal.

Matt jumped up the minute the Christmas meal was finished. He filled the dishwasher and washed the crystal wine glasses. Then, he immediately suggested he get them back in time for Melody's bedtime. A sad ache twisted in her stomach. She had envisioned time to sit in front of a fire and share her heart, but he seemed distant and eager to get her home.

The bang of the front door slammed shut her hope as he went out to start his car.

She sighed heavenward. "God, what am I supposed to do?" No sooner had the prayer been spoken than the front door opened again. Matt dusted large snowflakes from his coat and hair.

"There's no way I'm taking the risk of driving you two home tonight. The roads haven't been plowed or sanded, and it's snowed way more than I thought. We'll just have to put Melody to bed here. It's no big deal, she's used to her room."

Relief then fear flooded in. She'd have time to share her heart and a night—and a whole lot more.

"Surely it's not that bad, Matt."

"Yes, Anna, it is. I'm a confident driver, and even I don't feel comfortable going down that mountain. I'm not about to risk the two most important people in my life."

Anna nodded in agreement.

Together they bathed, changed, and put Melody to bed.

"You're so loved, my baby girl," Matt said, giving her one more hug. Melody burrowed into his arms and snuggled there.

"Why don't we go into the living room by the fire, and I'll rock her to sleep."

"Matt," Anna said, "she's got you wrapped around her little finger, and she's not even four months old yet."

"Did you hear what your mama just said, Melody?" Her head lifted and a big smile formed as if to prove she understood every word. They both laughed.

Matt settled in the rocking chair with Melody's favorite blanket and bottle in hand.

Anna watched the love between father and child, and her heart overflowed with joy. Everything was right about them together as a family, and she needed to set the record straight. She waited until Melody nodded off and Matt took her down the hall to her bedroom.

When he returned, she patted the seat beside her. "Come, sit."

His eyebrows lifted. He hesitated but moved from the chair he was about to sink into and joined Anna on the couch.

When she reached for his hand and pulled him down beside her, his eyes opened wide in surprise, but he didn't say a word. She let her head relax against his shoulder. Tentatively, he placed his arm around her as if waiting for her to protest.

They sat quietly, mesmerized by the dancing flames. The warmth of touch and the joy of togetherness filled her soul. When she could feel the tension relax within him and his body sink into the cushions, she knew the moment was perfect.

Chapter Thirty-Six

"I have something to ask you, Matt, but you need to open up your Christmas gift first." From behind her back she pulled a small box wrapped in sparkling gold paper with a matching bow.

He removed the bow with the quick precision of a doctor, tore the paper free and lifted the lid.

"What is this?"

"Read it, silly."

He pulled out the heart-shaped note and read out loud. "This coupon is good for one gold wedding band." His breath whistled between his teeth before he sucked a gulp of air into his lungs.

"Anna, does this mean what I think it means?"

"Yes, Matt. I love you more than words can say. Will you marry me and be my husband, my lover, my friend, and an everyday father to Melody?"

His arms enveloped her. He kissed her brow, her cheeks, the tip of her nose, whispering, "Yes, yes, yes. Anna, I thought this day would never come."

Anna's cheeks flushed hot.

His lips touched her in tender gentleness awaiting her response. A passion as old as time and as natural as breathing swept over her. Fire hungrily met fire. His kiss deepened and she responded in kind. His hands moved restlessly over her layers of clothing as taste, touch, and sensation took on a life of their own.

Melody's faint cry in the faraway distance brought Anna to her senses. She tugged away from Matt and popped up from the couch. One hand smoothed over her messy hair and the other pulled her shirt back into place. "I'm … I'm going to check on Melody."

Matt groaned and raked his hands through his hair in frustration.

A good half hour passed before Anna returned. It took only a moment to calm Melody and watch her nod off, but it took much longer for Anna to cool herself. Wow, did they have chemistry … it was going to be a long night, but she wanted to follow God's heart more than her own. That meant waiting for marriage despite their history.

When she returned she found Matt in the same spot, with his elbows on his knees and head in his hands. He looked up.

"Anna, I'm sorry. When it comes to you, I'm undone … undisciplined. If only I had an ounce of good sense, I wouldn't think I could play with fire—"

"This isn't your fault, Matt. It's mine."

"Come on, Anna, a Christian man should have a little self-control."

"You've had a lot of control, Matt, waiting for me. We should've been married months ago."

A smile split across his face. "No argument there. Let's not waste any more time."

"Whoa, whoa, Matt … I have something else I need to tell you, and what I'm about to ask may well turn your hair prematurely gray." She sat beside him and shifted her body so she could read his face.

He covered her trembling hands with his. "Anna, what is it?"

"How would you feel about being a dad to two little ones?"

"Two, Anna? Last time I checked, a good kiss doesn't create a baby … no matter how great it is." He grinned from ear to ear.

"I hope you're still smiling when I'm done telling you what I mean by two. I've offered to adopt Lorena's baby."

His eyes popped wide.

"It's not a done deal or anything, but there's a very real possibility Lorena may take me up on my offer. To put it bluntly, Matt, that would mean two babies a mere seven months apart. I'm not sure how I got myself into this other than to say the words were out of my mouth and Lorena pounced on the idea before I could think. It felt like a God thing. Still does. And Lorena's been doing a lot better, she's eating, interacting with the family, and Lana said she seems at peace. So, even if this turns out to be no more than the catalyst that helps her through to the birth, then it has served a good purpose."

"Really?" He ran a hand through his hair making it spring up beneath his fingers. "It wasn't all that long ago I thought I'd never be a father at all …"

He grabbed both her hands and squeezed tight. His eyes met her gaze directly. "I would've never risked your life having more, but the thought of enlarging our family … I'm thrilled." His smile lit up the room as he shook his head in disbelief.

He sunk back into the couch and folded both hands behind his head. "Two kids," he said, grinning. "I like the sound of that. I'm up for it if you are."

He pulled her into his side and threw an arm around her shoulder. She snuggled in. They sat in silence for a few minutes, mesmerized by the glowing embers, each lost in their own thoughts.

"Oh, yeah." He jumped to his feet and jolted Anna from a drowsy state.

"I can give you your Christmas gift now. I didn't feel right earlier—" He pulled out a large beautifully wrapped present from behind the tree. "Here you are."

With a smile that split across his face making his dimple dance into view, he placed the gift on the coffee table in front of her. He plopped on a chair across from her and leaned forward.

Anna took her time carefully removing the bow, the tape, and lastly the wrap. When she went to fold the paper before opening the cardboard, he threw up his hands.

"Oh, my goodness, Anna, don't tell me you're one of those. You're killing me here—open the box already."

She laughed at his impatience.

"It's part of the pleasure," she said, "To savor a gift, to respect the fact someone has taken time to choose, purchase, and wrap—"

He reached out. "I'll open it then."

She squealed and held on tight. "Okay, Okay." She slid her thumb through the tape, opened the end, and pulled. A lovely black and white painting cradled within an antique frame met her eyes. A sheen of tears misted her view. Words got stuck in her throat, and the best she could squeeze out was, "Matt, this is incredible."

She traced her fingers over each tiny face. There on the canvas were the three cherubim faces of her children, all at the three-month stage. The picture of Melody was one she had not seen before. The artist had masterfully blended three chubby faces into a collage.

"How?" She bubbled. "How did you manage to get the photos of the boys?

"From Lana. She said it was the least she could do."

"But, Matt, why did you hold off giving me this?"

"Well, when you were standoffish all day, I got a little insecure. Thought maybe our future was doubtful, and I shouldn't involve your boys."

Anna interrupted. "Standoffish? Is that how you took it? I knew I was going to tell you I was madly in love with you today, and after that kiss this morning, I didn't trust myself."

"Madly in love?" he teased. "I didn't hear that. Go ahead, Anna, tell me how madly in love you are, because I really like the sound of that."

"You're going to get a smack," she said with a tease in her voice.

"Anna, all kidding aside, I want you to know that all your children are important to me. Though I'll never be a father to the older two, they're an important part of my life, because they're an important part of yours."

Anna stood and bent across the coffee table to kiss his cheek. "Matt, thank you. This gift is beyond amazing."

"And we can always have a new one painted to add one more if Lorena's baby joins our family. I know the artist," Matt offered.

He stretched back in the chair, placed his hands behind his head, and closed his eyes. "This is the best Christmas and birthday ever," he said with a sigh.

"What?" she squealed. "It's your birthday too? You're a Christmas baby?"

He laughed. "Ha, I was going to pull the 'It's my birthday,' had you not wanted to spend Christmas with me, but when you agreed, it no longer seemed important. You've given me the best birthday gift possible, Anna. I'm truly the happiest man alive but—"

A shadow flashed across his face.

"What?"

"I haven't introduced you to my life, Anna. As much as I want to get married immediately, I need you to understand my work, my family, my past. If we're going to make this marriage a success, I don't want anything between us."

A slight chill of fear ran up Anna's spine. She liked the cocoon they had created within the boundaries of her life. The thought of entering his world held little appeal.

Chapter Thirty-Seven

What should've been the happiest time of Anna's life in many years was marred by the persistent demands of her eldest son. He felt she should respect and honor his father's memory by remaining single the rest of her life. He continually spouted off Scripture used out of context to suit his opinion. Anna felt exhausted. Only ten minutes into his weekend visit, and she wondered how she was going to get through.

"Don't you care how this looks?" he demanded. "Doesn't the Scripture say it's better for a widow to remain single? And I heard that doctor has women falling all over him and a not so stellar past."

Anna's heart skipped a beat. Fear niggled. "Mark, honey, is this about your concern for me or about you?"

Veins popped out on each side of his temples, and his brows knit together in an angry scowl. "Well, it's just plain embarrassing to have my mother marry a younger man. What am I going to say to the Tomlinsons? Can't you think of anyone but yourself, Mom?"

"I am thinking of someone other than myself, Mark," Anna said firmly. "What about your sister, Melody? Doesn't she have the right to a father in her home just as you had?

"Yeah, right," he huffed. "God saw fit to let me grow up with a father in a bed, so why should it be any different for … I'll never consider that bastard child my sister."

Anna gasped at his mean words. She bit her lip to stem the flow of an angry retort.

"I don't know why I bothered making this trip," Mark griped. "I thought maybe you'd finally see some sense, but instead, you tell me you're engaged." He spat the words out as if they were poison in his mouth, turned on his heels, and slammed out the door.

Anna had been looking forward to Mark's visit. She had hoped and prayed he would've softened and want to spend time and bond with Melody. Instead, his visit lasted less than fifteen minutes.

Anna dropped into the nearest chair. A deep sigh slipped from her lips. She glanced up on the wall above the fireplace and viewed her three babies, chubby, happy, and full of innocence. No scars, no pain, no failure to mar their tender hearts.

She felt for Mark. He'd taken on the brunt of responsibility far beyond his years. People used to say, "Mark, you're the man of the house now that your dad is sick, take good care of your mom and younger brother." Mark had always nodded in agreement, and then Anna had leaned into him after he graduated. She allowed him to take on the heavy role of arranging his father's funeral while she remained locked in grief and fear of her future.

She bent her head in despair. Tears blurred her vision.

"God, can I really marry Matt and sacrifice Mark?"

Anna's stomach churned. Matt was on his way over to pick her up and take her around the hospital and his office to introduce her to his world. She wilted at the thought—she hated the idea of being in the limelight.

She pulled a brush through her wayward curls and grumped at the way, today of all days, they refused to cooperate.

Melody, who normally loved her rocking swing, began to fuss. When Anna went to check on her, she noticed Melody had spit up all over the cute outfit Anna had chosen.

"Oh, Melody. Not today."

Melody Joy rewarded her grumbling with an easy grin.

Anna frowned in frustration and pulled her from the swing. "Let's get you changed, you little monkey. You're going to make me late." She scowled at the baby in an exaggerated face and kissed her brow. Melody giggled in reply.

"Now what am I going to put on you?" Anna stood frozen gazing into Melody's closet. She couldn't make a simple choice.

She heard Matt call out as he entered the house and groaned. She was nowhere near ready.

"We're in Melody's room."

He waltzed through the door of the nursery with a smile and bounce to his step. Today, even that annoyed her.

He planted a big smack on each of their cheeks, then stepped back in surprise as Anna blew out a deep breath and plunked Melody in his arms. "Matt, sorry, but I'm not ready. My hair is a disaster, and I don't know what to wear. I had Melody ready, but she spit up all over her pretty little dress, and now I don't know what to put on her."

"No worries, sweetheart. Take a deep breath, there's no rush or schedule today. I've got the whole day off, and I intend to take it slow and enjoy showing off my two girls."

"Go … take as much time as you need, but I think you already look gorgeous."

"Come, sweet pea. Daddy's going to find something nice for you to wear and give your mommy time to put on her sweet face … because this sour one doesn't work on a beautiful day like today." He winked and fixed another kiss right on Anna's lips.

"Now go!"

"Yes, doctor, anything you say, doctor," she teased and stuck her tongue out at him on the way out the door.

He laughed a loud boisterous laugh. "Love the maturity, Anna. Good thing to teach your daughter."

She swung her head back in the room and gave him another one.

He laughed all the more.

She marveled at how he had successfully removed her jitters and set the tone for a better day.

She wanted to jump in the shower and start over with her frizzy mop but knew it would take hours for her thick hair to dry, so she opted to pull it back into a French braid and be done with it. She knew Matt loved it loose, but that just wasn't an option today.

By the time she dressed and fussed with her makeup, Matt had Melody changed and ready to go. He was seated on the floor holding her on his lap while she played with an array of colorful toys spread around her. Everything went in her mouth. Anna enjoyed a couple of minutes just watching them. The joy of that simple pleasure calmed the nervous fluttering in the pit of her stomach.

The minute Matt saw her, he jumped up and placed Melody in her nearby playpen.

"I have a gift for you, my darling."

Her eyes widened in question.

"Christmas is over, and my birthday isn't until May?"

He moved close and shushed her words with his mouth.

Anna melted into his embrace.

He dragged his lips from hers and smiled. "Well … now that I have your attention." He pulled out a velvet box from his pocket and bent down on one knee. With a look that crackled with chemistry, he opened the box. A large diamond sparkled in vivid brilliance.

"Anna, love of my life, will you do me the honor of marrying me and exchange one ring for another."

Anna looked down at her hand and spotted the plain gold band that still encircled her finger.

"I can't exactly show you off without my ring on your finger," Matt stated. His startling blue eyes deepened and smoldered like blue flames in a fire.

"May I?"

She knew exactly what he was asking.

"Yes," she nodded. "It's time."

He gently slipped Steven's ring from her wedding finger and slid his in place.

"Do you like it?" An almost boyish quality rang from his voice as he rose to his feet, once again towering over her.

She brought the glittering ring closer and studied the intricacies. A large diamond dominated the center. Two hearts created with countless tiny diamonds hugged both sides of the shimmering stone and fed into a solid gold band.

Anna had never seen anything so beautiful.

"The two hearts represent my two girls—the heartbeat of my life."

Tears filled Anna's eyes and clung to her lashes. "Oh, Matt, I just finished my makeup, and you're going to make me cry. This is the most gorgeous ring I've ever seen."

He crushed her close, and kissed her deeply.

***

The hospital staff buzzed around them like bees to a honeycomb. They clamored to hold Melody and catch a glimpse of the woman who'd finally snagged the irresistible Doctor Carmichael. Anna felt like a monkey at the zoo swinging from floor to floor.

They moved through each ward, and Anna noticed how loved Matt was. They oohed and aahed over Melody and welcomed Anna with smiles and chatter. She wished she didn't feel so self-conscious but couldn't still the host of butterflies dancing in her stomach.

When they headed to his office, he confided that the girls there had been teasing him about this mysterious woman in his life who never called and never showed up.

"I use your cell, Matt."

"Yeah, but every other spouse or boyfriend phones the office at some time or another and pops in readily."

"But—"

"I know, I know … our relationship has been complicated and not public. But I'm just saying, they were most disappointed at the Christmas party when I showed up alone. How was I to explain that we weren't officially a couple?"

"Yeah, that would be my fault."

He patted her knee as they drove to the office. "No worries, Anna. Today is a great day to show you off, and we'll not fret over the convoluted path we took to get here. That's our business and no one else needs an explanation. I'm just thankful this day has finally come."

Once again on display, Anna entered his office to meet the ladies who Matt said kept him organized and on point.

Jasmine clapped her hands as she raced from behind the desk. Before Anna could think, Jasmine's sturdy round frame folded Anna in a motherly hug.

"Well now, isn't it a pleasure of all pleasures to finally meet the girl of Matthew's dreams. I've worked for Matthew for years, and I've never seen him so smitten. When he talks about you and baby Melody, why, his eyes light up like a Christmas tree." She tucked a chubby arm around Anna and propelled her forward. "Come meet the others." She giggled like a schoolgirl. "There's been a fair amount of curiosity about you, my dear."

Matt winked and smiled at Anna above Jasmine's head.

Anna lifted her eyebrows as if to employ help.

"Now, now Jasmine, don't overwhelm poor Anna or she'll never return."

Jasmine waved him off. "Don't you go spoiling all the fun, Matthew. It's only taken you a year to get this gorgeous thing here. We were thinking she had some warts on her face with hair growing out of them or something worse." She laughed. "Oh, and give me that precious one." She snagged Melody from Matt's arms and began to coo. Melody gifted her with a toothless grin.

"Oh my, how precious," she drew Melody close and inhaled. "Don't you just love the smell of babies? Until it's time to change them of course." Her laugh echoed down the hall.

"Come," she beckoned Anna on.

Anna glanced back toward Matt as she followed Jasmine. He threw his hands up in defeat, but the grin on his face clearly told her he was enjoying every minute.

"This is Rose—our accountant. Our office would be in shambles without her. She's the stickler for organization and keeps the rest of us in line."

Rose smiled and held out her hand.

Jasmine was out the door and hollering for them to follow. "She's a bit bossy, but we love her," Rose whispered.

"Here's Iris. She's our Jack of all trades … or shall we say Jill. Can't begin to tell you all the things this girl can do." Iris beamed, waved hello to Anna, and joined the group.

Jasmine marched ahead, rounded the corner to another office, but it was empty. "Maxine," she called, "where are you?" A chic, stylish woman came from a room further down the hall. Her uniform gave away the fact she was a nurse, but the sway of her hips, her updo and manicured nails looked out of place.

"Jasmine, can't a girl have a private moment in the washroom without your bellowing?" She snickered at Jasmine's crestfallen face. "Only kidding, Jas, chill!" She laughed with a brashness that irritated.

Her eyes travelled over Anna from top to bottom with a distinct coldness. "So, we finally get to meet the mystery girlfriend, Anna."

Anna bristled. Just the way Maxine said her name—grated. With a tad too much satisfaction, she corrected the woman. "Fiancée, actually." She held out the enormous rock on her finger for all to see.

The rest of the women gathered around for a close look and created quite the fuss. It did not escape Anna's notice that Maxine merely looked down her nose from a distance.

They pulled apart, and Jasmine, in her happy-go lucky way, started a story. "So Anna, you've met Rose, Iris, and myself, Jasmine, but—"

Maxine rolled her eyes. "Oh, here she goes again with her poor attempt at humor. She's going to point out they all have flower names and sing that silly little song, 'One of these things just doesn't belong here.' Jasmine, that is soooo old."

Jasmine's face dropped, and her cheeks blazed red.

"I'm sure all is said in the spirit of fun," Anna said. "Jasmine doesn't look the type to want to hurt anyone."

Maxine harrumphed, "Who said anything about being hurt. It's just so very juvenile, and I don't have time for such nonsense." With a flick of her head and a sway of her hips she sauntered away.

Iris raised her head with an expression of disgust. "She thinks she's the queen bee around here. Since Dr. Carmichael is so easy going, she literally thinks she can boss us around. She even said the other day that the only reason she stays is because the office would fall apart without her. As if! This office ran better before she came on board."

Rose piped in. "She's just mad that her good friend Tamara couldn't sink her hooks into Doctor Carmichael enough to get a diamond out of him."

"Yeah, but too bad Tamara had as much influence as she did. It's the only reason Maxine got hired, and now look what we have to put up with," said Iris.

"Now, now, ladies, we'll all try our best to rise above this kind of negativity." Jasmine said, putting an end to the discussion.

"Can't you see Matthew's eyes in this little one?" she said, skillfully turning the conversation elsewhere. "She's sure not afraid of strangers, either, the way she's let me hold her."

Iris and Rose took their turns with Melody, and she only too happily rewarded each of them with her winning grin.

"Ahhh, she has a dimple on the same side as Doctor Carmichael," Rose pointed out.

Anna stood by quietly watching, but her mind wandered elsewhere. *Who was this Tamara woman?*

Chapter Thirty-Eight

February turned into March, and they had not yet picked a wedding date. Matt remained determined Anna meet his family and friends first. He suggested they throw an engagement party, but Anna hated the idea. One-on-one proved difficult enough, but to meet all of them together horrified her, and so she committed to nothing.

Anna knew they were on different pages and needed to talk, so she set up a date for a walk in the park without Melody. Lorena had offered to babysit.

Anna took one look at Lorena and beamed. "You look fantastic, Lorena. What are you now, seven months along?"

Lorena nodded. "Yeah, I'm feeling great, and this little guy is super active, kicking all the time. Hope you're up to a lively one."

Anna smiled. "Whatever you decide, Lorena, is good with me, but you may well hold that baby in your arms and never let go."

Lorena's eyes filled with tears. "To be honest, Auntie, I think I'm more like my mom than I'd like to admit. The thought of caring for a baby 24/7 scares me to death, but the thought of a degree in microbiology thrills me to the core. Does that make me a bad person?"

Anna pulled Lorena into a hug. "Of course not, Lorena. You're young and smart and have dreams that are honorable. God uses people in all kinds of ways, and when you're ready to be a mom, you won't feel this way. I have to say, though, motherhood is the best job ever."

Lorena pulled apart and smiled. "That's exactly why I feel so at peace with my decision, Auntie."

Lorena had changed from a dark brooding teenager to a cheerful young woman. The transformation was like taking a trip from winter snow to summer sunshine. But the realization she would more than likely have two infants in a couple months hit Anna full on.

Matt arrived a few minutes later to pick her up, and they headed out the door. "See ya in a couple hours, Lorena. We're going to get a good power walk along the Greenway, and then we're heading to Moolicks for ice cream. You can reach us on the cell if need be."

Lorena giggled, "Oh Auntie, you and your ice cream. How come you're not three hundred pounds?"

Anna laughed, "Because I run it off."

"No running today, Anna. You did say walk? Lorena's my witness."

"Oh, Matt," she said, with a playful swat to his arm. "I know, I know. You hate running."

"Just checking, because if the word run is included, I'm really busy."

"Let's go. Time's a-wasting and we want every minute alone that we can get."

"Now you're talking."

She swung an arm around his waist and nudged him out the door.

Anna loved the first hint of spring as the leaves were just budding. She breathed in the scent and stopped short. "That smell, isn't it glorious?" Her eyes closed and her head lifted heavenward.

He inhaled deeply. "Why don't we do this more often? I love it out here."

Needles from the Ponderosa pine crunched beneath their feet as they followed a well-beaten trail through the evergreens. The angry chatter of a mouthy squirrel interrupted the song of birds overhead as they darted and dipped without a care in the world.

Anna stopped and bent low. She reached to pick a yellow flower on the side of the path. "Buttercups," she said. "My favorite. They're like finding gold dust." She stood and thrust the tiny flower his direction.

"Anna, if only you knew how beautiful you are this instant, you would know better than to look at me with those beguiling brown eyes of yours." He leaned into her waiting lips as she drew him close.

"Why, Doctor Carmichael, I have just the cure needed." The taste of his kiss took all the tease out of her.

He pulled apart still holding her close. A delicious but dangerous electricity filled the air, and she opened her mouth ever so slightly as he rubbed a thumb across her lower lip. Liquid heat flowed through her body, and she was all too aware of the longing between them.

He captured her face in his hands and groaned. "Anna, what you do to me—" He dropped his arms and turned. "We'd better keep walking."

"Okay, Matt, I don't get it. I was ready to marry you in December, and you said there was no argument on your part. Here we are in March, and we still haven't set a date. I feel you're hedging. And I don't like your idea of an engagement party. I want a wedding. Don't you feel the same?"

He whirled in front of her and came to an abrupt stop. She almost ran right into him.

"Of course, I feel the same. Surely you're not questioning that?"

"Then I don't understand."

"I want a wedding as much as you, but I need you to meet my world, my family ..." He paused. "... my past. And it's taken me this long just to get you to agree to an engagement party."

"What are you talking about?"

"Anna, I've met your friends, I know your family, your sister, your sons. And even if Mark doesn't like me, I know what I face walking into marriage. You know nothing about my life.

Anna threw up her arms. "Well, whose fault is that? You never talk about your family. I know nothing more than the fact your parents live in Toronto, and you're an only child. I've asked, Matt, but you remain vague."

She noticed an odd expression flit across his face before he turned to walk, but Anna stood her ground. "Please don't walk away."

He quickly turned back. "I'm not walking away, I'm trying to find the words to convey the world I grew up in." He brushed a hand through his hair in frustration.

"Let's walk. I can think better when you're not looking at me with those flashing black eyes like you're upset."

"I'm not upset ... I just don't understand your reservation. You knocked my door down. You pursued me. But since I said yes to marriage, I've felt like we're in limbo."

"You've got it so wrong." He whipped both hands through his hair, causing the waves to spring up and forward.

She ached to kiss the anxiety from his face and smooth the wayward curls from his brow, but this conversation was needed.

"How do I explain to the most loving mother in the world that my mother should never have been one? Thank God she only had me."

He paused.

"My so-called-mother openly accused me of wrecking her life, Anna. She told me I stole her freedom … but how that was true is beyond me. I had a full-time nanny who raised me.

"And she often went on about my father's affairs and how having me changed everything. I was only seven and didn't have a clue what that meant, but I felt her distance and her coldness. As I got older, I realized the fact she sat around all day with her friends eating and drinking had more to do with her extra pounds than having one child.

"Dad was not much better. He was never unkind to me like my mother, but neither was he a father. He cared only about making money and social status. He worked long days and socialized the rest. Went from one affair to another. When he and my mother were together, they fought incessantly."

"But, Matt, I don't understand. Your parents are still together, aren't they?"

"Because of the money. Dad came from a lot of money and Mom didn't. Mom signed a prenup. If she leaves him, the money stops. And so she stays. There is no love lost between them.

"The fact both of them were terrible parents scared me. I thought I would be the same way, coming from that gene pool. So, I poured my life into my work until you and Melody came along, and I realized I had a deep capacity for love."

Anna smiled up at him as he pulled her close, and they walked arm in arm.

"My relationship with Christ took me the rest of the way. I realized being a good father and husband has nothing to do with good or bad genes but everything to do with a relationship with Christ. He helped me set my priorities straight. It's why I booked off Christmas the moment Melody was born."

"We had a wonderful Christmas. You went all out and literally spoiled us both." She pulled him close to her waist, and he stopped long enough to plant a quick kiss on the top of her head.

"I have more." He grabbed her hand and continued walking.

"I left Toronto immediately after grade twelve and attended the University of BC. I wanted to be as far away from my parents as possible. I set out with only one goal—a need to prove my worth. My dad paid for my education because I performed. He made it clear if my grades dropped, the money would stop. He loved to control me and liked the fact he could brag to their friends about his son the doctor.

"But, I didn't do it for him. I did it for me. I sent every penny back once I became a physician. Then, I received a trust fund from my grandparents and I have more money than I could ever spend in a lifetime."

Anna gasped. Matt stopped and pulled her to face him. "Yes, Anna, you're marrying a very wealthy man. You'll never have to worry about money again. With no need for a budget, you'll enjoy vacations, clothes or, quite frankly, whatever your little heart desires."

"But, but … Matt, that's not good for anyone. I don't think I like the idea of that."

"It's the truth, Anna, I'm a millionaire many times over."

Anna blanched. "People will think that I'm a gold digger—"

"Anna, don't go there. We don't care what people think. Remember? That kind of thinking previously lead you down a wrong road."

Anna nodded. "You're right, Matt. I just wish I'd known … I mean I knew you lived comfortably, but I had no idea—"

"What? You wouldn't have fallen in love with me had you known?" His lopsided grin and dimple danced as he caught her close and planted a quick kiss on her lips.

"I hope you're good with giving a good portion of that loot away, Dr. Carmichael, because I for one do not want spoiled, overindulged children."

"I actually have some good ideas about that," he countered. "Nice to know we're on the same page, but that's a discussion for another day. Let's head back and I'll finish the saga … unfortunately there's more."

Just the way he said that made a nervous shudder work its way down Anna's spine.

"As for my parents, the only reason I'm inviting them to our engagement party is because I've talked to Pastor Harry, and he not only taught me as a Christian that I need to forgive them, but he encouraged I find a way to honor them. This is my first attempt."

"But why can't you just invite them to our wedding? Why do we need an engagement party?"

"The engagement party is not about my parents, although I do want you to meet them before the wedding. I don't want to give them the opportunity to ruin our special day. Trust me when I say my mom has a spiteful tongue, and she'll slice you open given the opportunity. You'll have a fighting chance to manage her on our wedding day if you know what to expect. Most people find her obnoxious and rude, and with my dad continually egging her on … well it's not pleasant. Their friends call them the Bickersons."

"It can't be that bad?" Anna questioned.

"You'll see."

Shaking his head, he said. "Enough about my parents. The engagement party is not about them but more about my friends. I care about them, and over time, I want to introduce them to the Lord. I want you by my side from the beginning. We need to establish relationships as a couple, so you'll feel comfortable having them over.

"They'll be a challenge as most are atheists, agnostics, or intellectual snobs." He laughed. "I know because I was one of them."

Anna sped up keeping a step or two ahead. She didn't want him to see evidence of the fear that gripped her. A quiver turned into a quake, and panic took hold.

"I want you to stand beside me and love them as God loves them. We'll be the only Christian example most of them see, and I don't want to abandon them."

"And you shouldn't, Matt." She tried to force assurance and confidence into her voice.

"Well, that's great to hear." He quickened his pace to come alongside her and wrapped his arm around her shoulders.

"And the only thing left to discuss is … my past. The stories you may hear from my friends are better heard from me." He paused. "You may have second thoughts."

"What, so it's okay that you forgive the fact I lived a lie and would've kept your daughter from you given the chance, but I can't forgive your past that has been forgiven by God? Are you kidding me?" She stopped and placed her hands on her hips.

"Do you really think I'm naïve enough to think that you don't have a history, Matt? We all have a story. Some things we're proud of, and some we're not. Now I won't hear another word about it."

Anna could see the vehicle in the distance. "Race you to the car."

"But … but I haven't told you about Tamara."

Anna shot away. His last set of buts … lost to the wind.

Chapter Thirty-Nine

Anna's gut twisted. In two short days, the engagement party would be hosted at Matt's home with arrangements made easy by a caterer and party planner, but the thought of a room full of strangers was what had her on edge. Matt had embraced her circle of friends as if they had known each other for years, but she could barely muster up a smile at the thought of this party.

"What is it?" Matt questioned. "Every time I bring up the party, you clam up."

"I don't know. I'm just not much of a social butterfly. And as for formal social gatherings ... well, my experience is limited. As in ... none."

"Ahhh, come on, Anna, you sell yourself short. You've nothing to worry about. I've watched you at church and your work, you don't come across as backwards or shy."

"Yeah, that's because it's familiar ... and I ease into things. Group settings are just not my thing."

His eyes twinkled, and he laughed. "Anna, you're bright, you're beautiful, and you're mine." He grabbed her in hug and whirled her around the kitchen floor.

"I just want to show off my beautiful bride-to-be. Is that too much to ask?" He did not wait for an answer but lowered his lips to hers.

"That's not fair," she giggled pulling back. "When you kiss me, I turn into a marshmallow and find myself agreeing to everything you want."

He laughed. "Oh, sweetheart, you never should've admitted that." His lips found hers in a searing kiss. "I'll just have to plant a lot of kisses on your beautiful lips during the party, and all will be well."

She playfully smacked him and tucked her fears in the back pocket of her heart for another day.

That day came all too quickly.

Anna grabbed her cell and answered Matt's call.

"Hi, honey, I'm on the way to the airport to pick up my parents. I hate to admit it, but there's nothing about their visit I'm looking forward to."

"Seriously, Matt. Take a deep breath. I've never heard you like this."

"Well, quite frankly, I regret inviting them. I swear, Anna, if my mom talks down to you—"

"Matt, relax. Honestly, your parents are the one part of this party that doesn't scare me. For whatever reason, I've prayed for them and feel peaceful."

Matt muttered. "I hope you can keep that peace when you meet her."

"It'll be fine."

"Don't say I didn't warn you if things go sideways. And not that I expect my mom's maternal instincts to kick in or that she'd actually want to hold a baby, but she was asking to meet Melody. Thankfully, Melody isn't fussy about meeting strangers. A crying baby would do my mom in."

"Matt, don't worry, we'll manage. Now put a smile on that grumpy-pants attitude of yours, and I'll do the same tonight." They both laughed and rang off.

"Anna, we're here."

Matt's voice carried down the hallway as Anna smoothed her hand over her curls one more time and excited her bedroom.

A short couple stood beside Matt. Matt's dad was a good foot shorter than he was, balder than a coffee bean, and sported a 70s-era pencil-thin mustache. His mom had to be five-foot-nothing. Her plump hourglass figure flared out to very large hips. Anna could tell by looking at her that she had been quite attractive at one time. Her thick curly waves pinned in a chic updo were clearly where Matt got his wonderful head of hair.

Anna towered over them both as she moved forward to meet them.

"Anna, this is my mom, Faye, and my dad, Darren."

"Mom, Dad, this is the love of my life, Anna."

Anna had prayed and asked God to lead her. So when she heard the Spirit whisper to give them both a hug, she did just that.

Faye stood stiffly in Anna's arms with her hands at her side, but Anna gave a good squeeze anyhow, and then turned to Matt's father and embraced him with a quick hug and a smile.

"I'm so happy to meet you, come in, come in." She waved them forward.

"Matt, I hear Melody, she's just waking up from her nap, will you go get her?" He nodded and disappeared down the hall.

Faye entered with a haughty jut to her chin. She looked around with a lifted brow at the humble abode before she sat gingerly on the edge of the sofa as if she was afraid of catching fleas. "How very … quaint," she said. "I bet you're looking forward to moving into Matt's lovely home."

Anna chose a smile. "We're thinking of selling his big home. He says he feels more at home here."

Faye harrumphed as if she did not believe a word.

Darren plunked himself in the chair across the room and leaned back. "Anna, I noticed you were surprised by us two shorties. I bet you're wondering where Matt gets his height and good looks from. I've been saying for years that the mailman must've been a tall good-looking dude.

"Oh, Darren, as if I was the first to have an affair. Back in that day, I actually thought you cared."

"Oh, don't start whining, Faye. You've more than made up for any indiscretions I had."

Anna felt awkward as the two glared at each other, clearly not caring who heard them. She prayed for wisdom.

"Are you looking forward to the party tonight?" Anna cut into the tension. "I'm not so good with crowds, but I'll do my best. Matt on the other hand is such an extrovert—the polar opposite of me. You know what they say, opposites attract." Anna knew she was babbling but didn't care. Babble was better than war.

Faye turned toward Anna. "Yes, but for how long, my dear? Now *that's* the question.

A muscle in Darren's jaw clenched, and his voice turned edgy. "Sour doesn't look good on anyone, Faye. I know you can't resist throwing a dig my way at every opportunity, but not everything is about you. Do you think you can manage a few happy moments for our only son's engagement party?"

A stormy scowl settled on Faye's expression, and she pursed her lips as if she had just tasted a bitter lemon. She pivoted away from her husband.

Turning toward Anna she said, "So, Matt tells me you're a widow? How long has your husband been gone?"

Anna blanched at the question but was not about to start lying again. "About fifteen months."

Faye raised her eyebrows. "Oh, I see the apple does not fall too far from the tree. Like father, like son."

"Now what exactly do you mean by that, Faye?" Darren huffed.

"Do the math, sweetie. Matt said their baby was six months old, that means they were dipping in the sunshine before her husband was cold in the grave! Obviously, they had a relationship while the poor man was on his death bed."

Anna looked toward the nursery and wondered why Matt was taking so long. What could she say? A defense would only strengthen the accusation.

"Aren't you religious?" Faye badgered. "Matt said something about going to your church and finding Jesus. Yup," she said, nodding her head, "it's always the religious ones you have to watch the most."

Anna felt heat swallow her face.

"I made a huge mistake, Faye, by not honoring my husband's memory as long as he deserved, but whether you believe me or not, I was not unfaithful to him." She sat up straight as if someone had put starch in her spine. "You're right, I didn't live according to my beliefs when I entered into a physical relationship with Matt before marriage. But I've asked God to forgive me and make no excuses for my failure. And this one thing I know" she said with a genuine gentleness. "Though I'm far from innocent, I know I'm forgiven."

A glint of respect flickered in Faye's eyes at Anna's honest answer.

"Now can I interest you in tea or coffee?" Anna stood and headed to the kitchen, glad the open concept design allowed them to stay put while she busied herself.

"Faye, Matt told me that your favorite cookie is shortbread. I just happen to have the best recipe ever, and I baked them just for you. Let me know what you think?"

Anna moved about the kitchen as if nothing unpleasant had just transpired.

"And Darren, not to forget you, I baked an apple pie. Matt wasn't sure if it was your favorite or not, but he knows you like pie."

Darren smiled in response. "Why, I don't know the last time I had a home-baked pie, and boy, do I like apple. He turned without thinking to his wife. "Faye, you used to make the best one ever."

He missed the look of shock on his wife's face at the compliment, as he asked. "Which way to the restroom?"

Anna pointed, "First room on the left. When you're done, check out the next room and see what's keeping Matt and Melody."

Faye turned to Anna and said. "Well, that's a first. Who knew I made the best apple pie ever?"

Anna chuckled. "I'm going to put salt under the crust of the piece I give him. Don't want you to lose that title."

Faye smiled her first genuine smile. Anna was surprised how that simple gesture transformed her face from plain into pretty.

A comfortable silence filled the room as Anna made the tea. Faye got up and slid onto a bar stool at the island.

"You really spent time baking our favorites? Who does that anymore?"

Anna nodded. "I love to bake and to run, both are therapy for me."

Faye chuckled, "Well I like to eat and to eat, and that's therapy for me."

They shared a laugh.

Matt entered the kitchen with Melody in his arms and his dad in tow. "Is that laughter I hear? What did I miss?"

Anna grinned. "Girl talk, Matt, just girl talk."

He looked from his mother to Anna and shook his head. "Okay, I'm not even going to ask, but Mom, come meet your granddaughter. Sorry it took so long to get her out here, but she made a big mess in her pants, and I had to give her a bath and change everything."

Melody gurgled and smacked her hands playfully against Matt's cheeks. He reached down and blew a big bubble on her tummy.

A tear slid down Faye's cheek. She brushed it off quickly and flushed red. Anna pretended not to notice.

Matt placed Melody in his mother's arms and stayed nearby. He had warned Anna that his mom would last but a second before the discomfort set in and she'd make some excuse to hand the baby back.

Melody cooed sweetly and gave Faye a winning smile.

"Oh, look, Darren, she has Matt's dimple and on the same side too." Darren closed the gap, and the two of them stared down in wonder at their granddaughter. They shared a smile before looking down again and began to engage in baby talk, each trying to make her smile.

Anna smiled at Matt with a knowing look as he mouthed the words. "I don't believe it."

All fell into place as planned. Matt took Melody over to Lorena's house before the party. They'd keep her overnight. And his parents were dropped off at his house for a short rest before the party. Anna expected Matt any moment, but she was far from ready.

Frantically trying on one outfit after another, she ripped the latest one over her head and threw it on the floor. The static caused by all the changing turned her hair to frizz. She groaned looking into the mirror. Her hair stood on end like a dandelion gone to seed. Tears blurred her vision.

The afternoon had turned out well in spite of the rocky start. Baby Melody and Anna's baking had saved the day. Somehow, that tiny act of kindness had calmed Matt's mom and delighted his dad. For the rest of the visit, they'd been civil to each other and to her.

Anna kept reminding herself that God had helped her with Matt's parents and would help her tonight, but still the party had her tied in knots. Uneasiness nibbled at the back of her mind like a mouse on a piece of cheese. A foreboding loomed large, and she couldn't shake the gloom.

Come on, Anna, this party is important to Matt. You can do this.

Anna shook off the doldrums and held up the sleek, black dress she had purchased for the night. Its simple, elegant flow perfectly suited her personality, yet she'd thrown it aside in search of something more fun. She slipped it back on, and turned before the mirror. Thin spaghetti straps covered in shimmering sequins with a single band of sparkle around the neckline were the only bit of glitz. The dress fit like a glove and showed off her slim, model-like figure. The length stopped just about the knee revealing long shapely legs. Her high heels with a splash of glimmer completed the look, giving a touch of class … but oh, how uncomfortable.

What a chore it will be to keep them on all night. She kicked them off in frustration. *The things women have to do to look attractive. They'll be the last thing I put on.*

She twisted the locks of unruly hair and pulled the sides into an elegant knot at the back of her crown. A glittering comb fit neatly into place. She smiled into the mirror and whispered a prayer of thanks. Miraculously she had tamed the mess and found a way to allow her long thick curls to flow free. Matt loved her hair down, and she wanted him to be proud of her tonight.

She heard the front door open and Matt call out as she finished her last touch of makeup.

"Are you ready, Anna dear?"

"No, I'll never be ready," she whispered into the mirror, "but here I go anyway."

"Be right there, Matt."

She slipped into her heels and headed down the hall.

With a confidence Anna didn't feel, she turned in a pirouette. "Will I do, Doctor Carmichael?"

He moved close and pulled her into his arms. His eyes darkened from blue to black. They smoldered in the shadow of desire. "Oh, Anna, you look absolutely gorgeous, and if I don't get you out of here, I won't be responsible for the consequences."

She smiled at the paradox, amazed at what a little bit of makeup and clothing could do to convey confidence when a frightened woman lived on the inside. She felt like a bird trapped in a thicket fluttering wildly to get free, but Matt didn't have a clue.

His dancing dimple and snapping blue eyes twinkled above a ready smile. How could she say no to a face like that?

Anna gathered her courage, locked her arm in the crook of his and declared. "Well, Dr. Carmichael, we have an engagement party to attend. Shall we?"

Chapter Forty

Anna followed Matt as they floated from group to group. She smiled until her face ached. Matt kept her close and introduced her to far too many people to remember. Her nerves settled to a tolerable level, but she wondered if anyone picked up on her discomfort?

Anna shuddered at the display of pomp and circumstance at a simple engagement party. From the tiny little canapés and hors d'oeuvres that did nothing to feed a crowd, to the bubbly in the punch bowl that made far too many tipsy and hard to converse with, to the loud music that made it hard to hear what people were saying—all of it felt like a scene from a Hollywood movie. Anna felt out of her element.

Memories tiptoed up the steps of her mind at all the ways Matt had embraced her world. She wondered how she would ever fit into this life. Despair crawled up her spine.

"Come, Anna, my buddy Justin is going to make our engagement announcement."

She whipped around to face Matt. "What?"

Matt gave her shoulders a squeeze. "It's okay, Anna, I'm right here." He kissed the side of her cheek.

Matt couldn't possibly understand how being in the limelight gripped her with fear. Surely everyone knew the reason for their celebration. Did their engagement have to be formally announced in front of everyone? She zipped her mouth shut and prayed for strength. This was Matt's world not hers, and she owed it to him to give her best. She pasted on a smile and gripped his strong arm. Her knuckles turned white.

"Ladies and gentlemen. Thanks for coming tonight and sharing in this never expected—didn't see it coming—altogether shocking turn of events. The greatly esteemed Doctor Carmichael—the heart throb of the hospital— bachelor-of-the-year for the past ten years has finally been—not only caught, but tamed by the gorgeous, mysterious Anna Clarke, soon to be Mrs. Carmichael."

Heat surged from Anna's neck to her hairline. She placed trembling cold palms against her burning cheeks, and prayed her embarrassment would subside.

A woman's voice loud and crass split across the din. "Matt finally unveils his little recluse, and she looks ready to run." A brittle laugh followed and the cackling of a small group of women at the back of the room caught the attention of everyone. Anna recognized one face—Maxine from Matt's office.

Matt promptly kissed her cheeks and laughed into the crowd. "Isn't she the most adorable woman in the world? No wonder I was a goner.

"Everyone, meet the love of my life, Anna. She hates crowds but is being a good sport. Her way to entertain is the best home-cooked meals you'll ever have the pleasure to enjoy, so be really nice to her and you may get an invite in the future." The crowd cheered and lifted their glasses in a toast. "To Anna."

"We're now going to go into the adjoining great room and have some fun. Anna and I will start the dance."

This Anna looked forward to. Her parents had been ballroom dancers, and from the time Anna and Lana were able to walk, they had been encouraged to dance. With no opportunity to dance for many years, Anna had wondered if what she had learned as a child had left her. When they practiced, though, it all came back to her.

"Come, my love," he whispered. "Let's set those gorgeous feet of yours to music and shock the socks off this crowd."

Confidence filled Anna's heart, and her smile blossomed into a genuine laugh.

"Share the joke," someone yelled.

Matt waved the crowd over.

The music started and he invited everyone to join, but the instant the two of them stepped into the music, the crowd made room and watched in awe.

Anna gazed lovingly into Matt's eyes imagining there was no one in the room but the two of them. Chemistry crackled between them as they wove effortlessly in and out of each other's arms in perfect rhythm and timing. Anna's hair followed like a curtain of silk as Matt twirled and pulled her intimately close. Their footwork blended as if they were one, and they stole a quick kiss. Thunderous clapping erupted from all over the room as the music drew to an end.

Justin grabbed the microphone. "Didn't they look amazing, folks?" The crowd whistled and clapped. "That, my friends, was a front-row view into what real love looks like. And when I find a girl who looks at me like that … well, I'll be walking down the aisle too."

Matt laughed and shouted back. "What else would you like to see? Give us a song, any song."

Anna's eyes danced with laughter. "Matt, are you sure you can keep up with me?" the crowd hooted and hollered to see the shy Anna come to life.

"How about the cha cha."

"Perfect," Anna whispered, "The cha cha is my favorite, do you know it?"

Matt laughed, "Not well, but I'm game. All eyes will be on you anyway."

Matt snapped his fingers. "Justin, find us some Latin music. We're going to do the cha cha.

Everyone laughed and clapped in anticipation.

Anna grabbed his left hand in her right and held it up in prep. She placed her right hand lightly on his shoulder while he put his around her waist. She whispered, "Okay, so it's three side steps, cha, cha, cha and forward rock and then repeat in the other direction and backward rock … got it? I'll tell you when to let me twirl.

"Two, three, cha cha cha."

Anna laughed her way through the song, not in the least bit affected by the fact Matt was clearly not as well versed in the steps as she was. Her instructions helped him lead with the basics, and it surprised her when at the end he twirled her close and whispered. "Let's end with a backward bend."

Her eyes sparkled. "Don't drop me now, Matt."

She swirled in a final spin, and he skillfully pulled her close and bent her over his arm. The crowd whistled and roared as he brought her up and planted a kiss directly on her full lips.

Someone yelled, "Get a room," before they came back to earth. Matt waved the crowd onto the dance floor. "Come dance, because I'm busy." He lowered his lips to Anna's once again.

She giggled beneath his lips and pulled apart. "Matt, your manners."

He grabbed her close. "We have to get married soon."

A ripple of delight ran up her spine. "That's what I've been trying to tell you."

The next hour slipped by in sheer enjoyment. Whatever music the DJ played, Anna could dance to. Jasmine, Rose, and Iris from the office started a ladies' group when their guys didn't want to dance. Anna joined in enjoying the camaraderie, missteps, and laughter.

Anna's feet were killing her. She needed a break from the high heels and the exertion of a couple hours of dancing. She slipped from the group and stretched her head above the crowd looking for Matt but couldn't see him.

Anna made a beeline to the bathroom and sighed in relief as she locked the door behind her. Her heels went flying as she shook them free. She blotted the drips of sweat that beaded along her hairline and held up the heavy mass to cool the nape of her neck. Relief filled her. The night was almost over, and she'd actually had some fun.

Someone knocked on the door and she knew her reprieve was over. With her heels in hand, she headed out. Matt's den across the hall beckoned. The thought of a few more minutes of peace felt too tempting to resist. She slipped into the room and sank into a nearby chair. Relaxation hit her for the first time that day, and she closed her eyes.

"Well, well, well, if it's not the little dancing queen."

The sound of a sarcastic drawl popped Anna's eyes open. She sighed and rose gracefully to her feet. "Well, as you can see I dance better than I do crowds."

Anna faced a tall willowy woman. A shocking amount of cleavage spilled from her skin-tight dress. Her wild mass of hair shimmered with every shade from cinnamon to russet and bounced above her shoulders in a saucy look. Her beauty was undeniable. Flawless porcelain skin. High cheekbones. Bewitching hazel green eyes flashed with a glint of anger Anna could not understand, and she held her chin at a haughty angle looking down on Anna.

Anna's height rarely had women towering over her, and she didn't like the way this woman was trying to use it as a form of superiority. Anna straightened her spine and lifted her head with confidence.

The woman moved closer. "I'm Tamara," she said. "I suppose Matt has told you all about me?"

Anna searched her memory for a story, but none came to mind. "I'm not entirely sure. What's the connection?"

"Well, that's one way of putting it, darling. I guess you could call it a connection."

Chapter Forty-One

A shudder rode Anna's spine as Tamara's raucous laughter filled the room. Anna recognized the condescending tone as the same voice who had tried to embarrass her in front of the party crowd.

"Oh, yes, I remember your name now. Not from Matt but from the girls at the office. They said something about a girl named Tamara recommending Maxine for the job there. I assume that's you?"

Tamara huffed. "Do you mean to tell me that Matt has not mentioned my name to you at all?

"Nope," Anna said, "not a peep."

Tamara arched one brow and smirked. "Ask yourself this little question, how do you think I had the influence to get my friend Maxine that job?"

Anna felt the hair prickle at the back of her neck. There was something about this woman that rattled her, but she had no intention of carrying on a conversation without talking to Matt. She refused to answer and sat back down. She took her time putting her heels on in hopes Tamara would disappear and then rose to her feet eye to eye with Tamara's stormy glare.

"I'm sorry, Tamara, I barely know any of Matt's friends. Now, if you'll excuse me, please?" Anna stepped to the side to go around Tamara and out the door.

"Not so fast, lady." Tamara blocked her path. "I've no idea how you managed to seduce Matt into not using precaution, but your type always tries to trap a man anyway they can. I'll have you know, I'm not some mere blast from his past you can swat away like a pesky fly. Matt and I go way back. Our history and relationship span decades … friends with benefits, if you get my drift?"

Anna felt her eyes widen and her brows rise like a flock of startled birds. She didn't want to give this woman any reaction, but those words bit hard.

"Oh, I see I finally have your attention." A smug look spread across Tamara's face.

"So, you were more than friends?" Anna said matter-of-factly, stilling her racing heart. The last thing she wanted to do was to give this woman an edge. "Do you really think I'm naïve enough to think an attractive man like Matt hasn't had a few relationships in the past? However, the operative words here are *in the past*." Anna said the words clearly and precisely, so there was no mistaking the line drawn in the sand.

A charged silence hung between them as Anna stared her down. She was not about to draw back.

"Oh, you think?" Tamara snorted. "Do you consider last week, the past?"

Anna's world began to swim in a black fog. Her mind raced in all direction. *Surely Matt wouldn't ...*

"I can see your shock. You actually think a man as hot-blooded as Matt can go months without his needs being met?"

Anna bit back a sob.

"He told me about your silly Christian standards and how you don't want sex until marriage, which I find utterly ridiculous after having a baby together ... but as I said, everyone knows and talks about how you did that just to trap him. You're probably frigid."

Anna felt the sting of tears press against her eyes.

"What's a man to do other than marry you? Especially a good man like Matt who wants to do the right thing.

"I'm not complaining, mind you. Your arrangement suits me fine. Hope you don't mind sharing, because I sure don't. Matt is a fantastic lover, and I have no problem filling in when needed. He told me this would be just until you're married, but something tells me one does not forget the heady taste of the wine when boring grape juice will be all you'll offer up."

Anna gasped, and the tears she had been fighting to suppress, welled and glistened.

"Not to mention ... I'm a girl who loves diamonds, and the extra benefits are not too shabby either." She fingered a large diamond hanging from a pendant around her neck.

Matt's mom, Faye, pushed the door open. "There you are, Anna! Matt is looking for you, and Darren and I are getting a hotel for the night so we can get some sleep. We wanted to say goodbye."

Anna turned from Tamara, desperately trying to regain calm and not show her mounting fear.

Faye rattled on without understanding what she'd interrupted. "I want to thank you for letting us visit Melody. Will we be able to see her again tomorrow? We leave for home the following day—"

"Excuse me, but we're talking here," Tamara said. "And tell Matt that Tamara said he can wait a few minutes." She flicked her hand toward the door as if to dismiss Faye.

Faye stopped and took a close look at Anna who blinked a tear free. She turned and gave Tamara a once over. A look of knowing flashed in her eyes. "I'm Matt's mother, and I think it's *you* who can get out."

"You're the so-called excuse for a mother Matt told me about, the shrew that can't get along with anyone. Go figure. It seems like the two of you have bonded. No surprise there, you're both gold diggers going after a man for his money." Tamara spit her words out.

Faye instantly pulled back her shoulders and glared. "And you are?"

"I'm Matt's girlfriend, Tamara." She let the words slip from her lips implying the statement was still current and true.

"Oh, that explains everything. You're the jealous wench who couldn't land him. Ain't it a pity?" Faye slipped her arm into Anna's. "At least Anna and I have what it takes to get a ring on our finger. You obviously don't."

Faye's words were like throwing oil on a banked fire.

Tamara's knuckles turned white as she clenched her hands into tight fists and her lips formed a tight ashen line. "How dare you—"

"Oh, I dare," Faye cut her short.

Tamara's cheeks turned red and her nose flared.

"Now who has the unattractive blotchy skin? At least Anna looks adorable when she blushes. You look like you have an outbreak of some ghastly infection," Faye taunted. "Serves you right for trying to embarrass my dear Anna earlier. I can tell by the sound of your voice, those rude words were from you."

Anna could not believe her ears. *Matt's mom was not only defending her but calling her 'my dear Anna.'*

"And furthermore," Faye said, lifting her arm to wag her finger in Tamara's face. "You would do well to stay away from Matt and his family, or you'll have me to deal with." Fire danced in her eyes. "Trust me when I say I have more than one way to bury anyone that messes with my family. And if you think I make false threats, I'll give you the names of some tarts that dared to trespass on my marriage. You should see them now—pitiful creatures, no money, no friends, no connections.

Tamara blanched.

"Yeah, you take me seriously or this little social network you have hobnobbing with the doctors, the rich and the upper crust of this city, will be over."

With that, she literally dragged Anna from the room.

Anna was visibly shaken, not used to that kind of bold confrontation, yet she inwardly rejoiced at the fact Faye had stumbled upon them.

Faye hugged her close. "Come, Anna, I'm going to take you directly to Matt, and you're not to leave his side again for the rest of the evening until that witch departs. I know her type, and they spew nothing but venomous lies. Promise me you won't believe a word she said."

Chapter Forty-Two

Two weeks had passed since their engagement party and Anna stayed quiet. She wanted to talk to Matt about her conversation with Tamara, but the moment never felt right.

Matt's mom had reiterated to disregard anything that Tamara said as lies, but Anna was not so sure. A faint memory from the day they walked in the park tapped on the door of her mind. Matt had desperately wanted to discuss his past, and she had refused to open that door.

A wave of fear picked up Anna and swept her in its folds. Question after question rolled over her, and she felt like she was drowning. One question stood out above all the rest. What was Matt's interpretation of the word past?

Had Matt been with that woman after Anna came into his life? Could she blame him? For months, they had not been a couple. Worse yet, had Matt been with her since he became a Christian?

Anna felt trapped in an impossible nightmare. If she questioned Matt and Tamara had been lying, he would be devastated that she didn't trust him. Yet to have her mind troubled with unanswered questions did not set a good foundation for marriage.

"Come on, Anna, now you're hedging." Matt said. "We need to set a date for our wedding. Lorena's baby is due in early May and if she decides to give her baby up, then I want to be there from the start, not only to bond with the child but to help you with the responsibility."

Anna stared off into space. "Okay, Matt. I'll talk to the family and see what works best." She could barely concentrate on what he was saying. That conversation in the park skirted the edges of her mind. The few words she remembered gave pause for angst. *Anna you may have second thoughts.*

Her head grappled with shadows. Knots of anxiety twisted in Anna's stomach and peace eluded her. Rita was just the person she needed to talk to. Anna was confident she would help her view the circumstances through the eyes of God.

⁓

Rita tented her wrinkled hands over the soft pouch of her tummy and paid careful attention. Her head rested on a stack of fluffy pillows, and she nodded encouragingly to Anna but did not interrupt. Anna unfolded the story of Tamara and her many questions.

Rita motioned her close and hugged her tight before placing her weathered hands over Anna's. "Well, my dear, you have only one option, and it's not complicated. You have to talk to Matt."

Anna let out a deep breath. "I was afraid you'd say that."

Rita smiled. "Take this bit of advice and carry it with you long after I'm gone. Conversation with the one you love about every detail that concerns you is wisdom. And trust me, my dear, there will be many more things to be troubled about before your watch is done." She smiled a toothless grin and laughed.

"Rita, do you want your dentures?"

"Not on your life. Since they changed them, they do nothing but hurt my gums. I ask the Lord to take me home where I won't need such paraphernalia, but so far he has not complied."

"Rita, you mustn't talk like that? It makes me sad."

"Anna, you have to promise you'll rejoice for me. You know I'll be in a far better place."

Anna nodded. "I know. I'm being selfish, but I'll miss you. Since I quit working here, I don't get to see you enough."

"Not to worry, dear girl. Soon you'll have another baby and life goes on. It's a natural progression and not something to feel guilty about.

"By the way, how are things between you and Mark? Has he accepted the fact you will be married soon?"

Anna smiled at the way Rita successfully turned the conversation to the hot spots.

"No, he breaks my heart, Rita. There's been no softening. He won't even answer the phone when I call. I leave messages, but he never calls back. I get a bit of information on his life through Jason but not much. He's still with Lori. This April, he'll finish up his education with a degree in accounting, but Jason told me that Lori is pushing him to go another two years for his master's degree. Not sure how he intends to finance that, as Steven and I only had enough saved for four years of studies, but I guess we'll have to see if he even talks to me about it. Matt, bless his soul, has offered to pay for it."

Rita clucked her tongue and shook her head. "You know the story, Anna, of how I lost my youngest son, Eddie, in a motorcycle accident. But there is something tougher than death. I lost my other son, John, to bitterness over decisions I made—some right, some wrong. John, who is still alive today, I never see. That grieves my heart way more than the son I have no chance to see until we meet in heaven.

A smile filled Rita's face with joy as her mind clearly switched to memories of Eddie. "Yes, Eddie is up there waiting for me. He was such a gentle boy with a zest for life and adventure. Oh, how he loved Jesus. Did I ever tell you, Anna, how Eddie introduced me to the Lord?"

Anna knew the story well. Rita loved to retell the way her son Eddie brought Jesus into their troubled home.

"Rita, that story gives me such hope, do tell me again."

The canted afternoon light split through the western window and spilled on the bed. Rita turned her face into it. A faraway look spread across her face as she began the story as if for the first time.

Anna's eyes pooled with unshed tears gazing at Rita. Her once plump cheeks were sunken and hollow, her voice whispered through empty gums, and her fair skin was leathered and seamed with endless lines, but a joy radiated there. Anna had never seen anyone more beautiful.

***

Matt could tell something was wrong. Since their engagement party, Anna held him at a careful distance.

He couldn't put his finger on anything that went wrong, for though she had been nervous, she had skillfully conversed with everyone. The fact she was well-read on current events and delightfully unassuming won over even his staunchest of colleagues. She had a way of turning the conversation around to ask about their life. Most of his friends loved to talk about their latest and greatest discoveries, and Anna listened well with genuine interest.

Then on the dance floor, his quiet fiancée became elegance wrapped in beauty. The crowd was mesmerized by her grace and incredible ability to glide like an angel around the room.

His colleagues teased him unmercifully, wondering how he had landed such a classy woman and had shown genuine interest and acceptance. Even Tamara had given him thumbs up from across the dance floor while they were doing the cha cha, and he now hoped she got it. Anna was the love of his life.

He had not invited Tamara but knew her curiosity would propel her to break etiquette and attend uninvited. He had expected trouble, or at the very least a snide remark or two, but she had been on her best behavior.

That one remark about Anna wanting to run away made by Tamara's group was about the worst of the evening. For the life of him, he couldn't tell what the problem was.

Anna had even won the hearts of his mom and dad, which blew him away. His mom and Anna had giggled like teenagers and whispered like old friends. He had teased Anna saying, "Who knew a good shortbread recipe would have that kind of power?" She had wrinkled her nose at him and laughed. "As if. Why are men so clueless?"

He hadn't understood that comment then and still didn't now. But what he did understand is that his Anna was missing, and the troubled woman of his past had returned. He needed to find out why.

That Saturday afternoon he prepped for the evening meal. They would enjoy barbecued steak, baked potato, and a tossed salad. He had insisted Anna rest while Melody had her nap and assured her he could handle the details. He had every intention of getting to the bottom of her angst and didn't want her exhausted.

A disheveled Anna with Melody in hand appeared on the patio a good two hours later.

"Can't believe I crashed like that. I didn't hear a thing until Melody woke up."

Matt looked at his adorable girls, both with sleepy eyes and hair sticking up in every direction. He kissed them both on the cheeks.

"Got the lawn cut while my two angels rested," he said. "And supper is well underway. I've phoned Lorena, and we're going to drop Melody off at her house so we can have the evening to ourselves."

He glanced at his watch. That gives us five hours alone before we'll have to pick her up and get her to bed. Times-a-wasting—let's get going."

Anna smiled in delight. "Melody, did you hear that? I get to eat steak without you bothering me twenty times." She snuggled Melody close and then whirled her around. Melody giggled in pleasure.

Dinner passed slowly—a wonderful treat where they both took the uninterrupted time to enjoy every bite.

"Goodness, I'm sooo full." Anna placed her hands on her stomach and rubbed. "I'm going to have to undo the top button on my jeans, and you're going to have to be a gentleman and not say a word."

"I warned you, Anna, three pieces of sour dough bread before a steak is never a good idea."

She scrambled around the table and placed her finger on his mouth. "I told you, not a word."

He rose from the table and grabbed her close. "Well, I know how to make that happen," he said. With a gleam in his eyes, his head drifted slowly down to her laughing lips.

The heat from her body radiated like the afternoon sun as shivers skimmed along his flesh. She reached up and circled the muscled column of his neck. Her fingers lightly combed their way through the ends of his hair. A hunger coursed through his body. His mouth left hers with a tearing slowness as he stepped out of the danger zone and back into reality.

"What? The grape juice doesn't taste good after having the wine?" She muttered under her breath.

"What did you say?" He couldn't keep the shock from his voice.

She moved aside and picked up the dishes from the patio table. "Nothing."

For a couple of hours Anna had returned to him, but now the guarded Anna was back, the one who perplexed him to no end.

He marched over and took the dishes from her hands and placed them heavily back down on the table. "Come," he said. "We have to talk."

He captured her hand in his and pulled her to the porch swing where they sat together. Not once did he break his stare. He needed to know what was going on inside that pretty little head of hers.

He waited.

She waited.

They both started talking at the same time.

"So, what is—"

"I'm sorry, Matt—"

"Ladies first." He said. One hand gallantly rolled in the air.

"Matt, I'm sorry, I don't know how to even have this conversation."

His hands turned instantly clammy, and his heart hammered in his ears. "What is it?"

"What I just said is something Tamara said to me the night of our party. She was the wine and I was the grape juice."

Matt's eyes fell to his lap. "I wondered if she would try and corner you. I didn't invite her, by the way—she just showed up. But when you didn't mention her, I thought maybe she had enough class to let things be." He read hurt in Anna's eyes.

"Anna, I tried to tell you about her that day we went for a walk in the park. I wanted you to know about my past, but you said you didn't need to know. Remember?"

He paused. "I have no problem sharing my life with you—all of it, the good, the bad, and the ugly."

A disturbed look flickered in her soulful brown eyes. "I have only one question, Matt."

He inched closer taking both of her hands in his. His thumbs traced up and down her wrists, but his eyes never left her face. "Ask me whatever you want."

"How long ago was it over between the two of you? Because she was talking about a current thing."

He did not hesitate. "Not a chance, Anna. I haven't been with Tamara since you came back into my life."

"Matt," she said falling forward into his arms. The swing jostled wildly and she laughed against his lips. "I love you, Matthew Carmichael, so much."

Anna's peace of mind lasted exactly two weeks. Long enough to set the wedding date for April thirtieth and meet with Carla the wedding planner. Matt had hired her to help pull off a wedding in six weeks—and no more.

Anna had been thrilled that God arranged the opportunity to talk to Matt and that one question had quelled all the others. She concluded that Tamara was exactly who Faye pegged her to be—a brilliant liar.

Then Matt's cell phone dinged, and a text appeared. Anna didn't mean to be nosy, but Matt had left the phone on the counter and gone to the washroom. Enough of the message was visible to send her heart crashing to the floor.

"Hey, Matt, are we meeting at seven tomorrow night or eight? Can't wait." The contact name clearly said Tamara Stanton.

She waited for him to return, and watched him grab his phone and quickly slide it into his pocket, but not before he glanced at the message. He held his face poker straight, with not a hint of emotion.

"Okay, dear," he said with a smile, "I'll head home now, got surgeries scheduled early first thing and I need to get some shut eye.

"Oh, and don't forget I have a long workday tomorrow and won't be over in the evening. Instead, I scheduled Carla to come over for some girl talk to sort out all the arrangements for the wedding. Stuff I know nothing about— like decorations, flowers, color themes, and a host of other things she was all in a dither about." He kissed her full on the lips in a hurried embrace and headed out the door.

Questions boiled and bubbled. *Why is Matt meeting that woman? Why did he make excuses about working late? Why didn't I jump up and down and demand an explanation immediately?*

Explanations threw ice cubes into the boiling pot of angst and cooled the worry.

I trust Matt. He'll have a good reason. As Rita suggested—all I have to do is ask.

She headed to bed with the decision to take the time to digest and pray rather than instantly call him. A fitful sleep ensued. She tossed and turned and dreamed of gorgeous Tamara hanging possessively onto to Matt. Numerous times she woke up in a cold sweat.

The gathering light of sunrise filtered through the cracks in the blind. Anna was thankful she could finally get up. The long night had brought clarity. She would choose to trust God and Matt. This meant she would allow the day to progress as planned and have a conversation that following evening. She would not be one of those women driven by suspicion, who tracked him down or texted nonstop. Anna knew if she started down the road of distrust she'd never be free of that kind of fear, and over time, that would kill their relationship.

That day peace settled in, and Anna thoroughly enjoyed her evening with Carla planning fun ideas for the wedding. She slept like a baby and entered the new day with joy in her soul.

Mid-morning her cell rang. She looked at the number but didn't recognize the caller.

251

"Hello?"

"Anna. I hope you enjoy sharing your fiancé." A voice of mockery dripped over the line. "We had a fabulous time of it last night. A wonderful meal at Toberta's, you know that high-class steak house which is just the rave and then …" She paused for effect. "Honey, use your imagination. Just like the good old times, only much hotter … guess you haven't been keeping him satisfied!"

Anna hit the end button. She couldn't listen to another word. Her legs buckled beneath her, and she crumpled in a heap on the couch.

The reality of the situation rolled over her like a tsunami. Matt had lied to her. Tamara remained in his life and they'd had a rendezvous the previous evening while she foolishly trusted him. Another wave hit and she felt the world, as she knew it, float away.

Chapter Forty-Three

Anna was about to be a mother of two infants. She had quit her job because Matt had insisted they had more money than they could spend in a lifetime. She had placed all her eggs in the Matt Carmichael basket only to find Tamara had been correct the whole time, and she was the one so easily duped.

Anna stifled another yawn. She had not slept the past two nights. The terror of her situation virtually rendered her useless. When Matt called, she made excuses that she was too busy to see him. In reality, she needed the time to process and steel her heart with enough determination to make a clean break.

Anna had a baby to look after and could not stay in the doldrums though everything within her screamed to curl up in a ball and die. Tentacles of fury reached inside as if to strangle the life right out of her. Anger surged—at Matt—at the all too beautiful Tamara—but mostly at herself for being such a fool to trust so fully. The only smidgeon of good came from the realization she had not yet walked down that aisle. For that small mercy, she was thankful.

His happy-go-lucky voice sang out as he entered the house without knocking. "Anna, I'm here, where are you?"

Anna came in from the back porch and sighed heavily. She had never been good at confrontation, but this turn of events demanded action.

Matt took one look at her face and was instantly at her side. "Anna, what's wrong?" He placed his hand on her shoulder and tried to pull her close. Anna spun out of this reach.

"Matt." A tremble shook her lips. "Did you, or did you not see Tamara on Thursday night?"

The blood drained out of his face, and he grew deathly white. "Yes, I did, Anna, but I can explain."

"Explain? No! I don't want explanations. I want—no, I need to trust you. You'd better go."

"Anna, you can't be serious."

Her words bit back, laced with anger and sadness. "Matt, I've had enough sorrow to last a lifetime, and I'm not signing up for more. The wedding is off, and as for that brash, immoral woman—" Her lips trembled, but her voice turned edgy. "As for that despicable woman, she may be inclined to share you, but I'm not."

"You spoke to Tamara?"

"Why, Matt, worried your past—that is clearly not your past—will catch up with you? Well, rest assured it has, and I'm not a player in a game of three."

A muscle in his jaw clenched. "So, our relationship means so little to you that you're going to write me off without an explanation?" He ground his teeth and ran a hand around the back of his neck.

She fought the sting of tears. She didn't want to break down in front of him. Sorrow grew out of the pit of her stomach and flowered in her throat as she choked out, "You shouldn't have been with her for any reason, and worse yet, you shouldn't have hidden it from me. I saw your phone the other night, and the way you read her message and stuffed it in your pocket right in front of me. Tamara gave me all the explanation I need. I'll be in touch through a lawyer to set up joint custody of Melody. Please don't call me."

Through a curtain of tears, she walked to the front door and held it open. A canyon of pain registered in his eyes, which she could barely see through the misty veil of her own.

Pain rose like a banshee cry on the winds as deep guttural sobs worked their way up and out. A groan from his throat unlike any sound he had ever uttered filled his car as tears came in torrents. He drove having to continually swipe at his eyes to clear his blurred vision and arrived home not sure how he got there.

He fell on his bed and punched his pillow. A spike of anger rode his spine. How could he have been so stupid as to meet with Tamara without telling Anna? Why hadn't he insisted Anna at least listen to his side of the story?

A sad truth drove that decision. She didn't trust him or love him the way he loved her, and it bit like a venomous snake whose poison leaked slowly into his brain. There was no other excuse for the way she had so easily dismissed him.

In a fit of rage, he lurched his body off the bed and slammed the front door behind him on the way back to his car. He was done waiting … the police had better have an update on the Tamara situation, or he was going to come unglued. She had successfully damaged his most treasured relationship, and it had to end.

His hands turned white as he gripped the steering wheel in outrage. All the prayer Pastor Harry had suggested he do had done little good, and disappointment ran through to the bone. The more he thought about the situation, the angrier he became. His tires squealed around the corner, which didn't change a thing, but it sure felt good. Adrenaline roared through his veins as the needle on the speedometer soared.

Anna didn't have the energy to call the wedding planner—she assumed since Carla was a friend of Matt's that he would make the call.

The next day, Anna opened the door to find Carla sweep in with her arms loaded with bags and a bolt of sheer fabric.

"Anna, look at this chiffon I found to decorate the head table and hang between the pillars and ceiling."

Her voice so chipper and light mocked the sorrow Anna felt.

Carla dropped the bags on the counter and held up the material with triumph. "What a find. These tiny rosettes are divine and woven right into the—" One look at Anna, with tears streaming down her cheeks, stopped the conversation dead.

"The wedding's off, Carla," Anna gulped between sobs. "I'm sorry, I thought Matt would've called you."

Carla's eyes bulged large beneath arched brows. Her mouth flew open forming a perfect circle. "Oh my, no. That can't be. Why ever would you two break off the engagement? I've known Matt since we were kids, and I've never seen him so happy or in love."

Anna's chin quivered but she held onto control enough to say one word. "Tamara—"

Carla dropped everything and wound her arms around Anna in a warm hug. She pulled back and concealed her expression behind a mask of professionalism but not before Anna caught the pity pooled there.

She gathered up the shopping bags over her arms. "Tamara's a real piece of work. I've known that witch for years now, and all she does is create havoc wherever she goes."

Anna blanched at her words.

"I'm going to hold onto your goods and all the arrangements for a bit. I have a feeling you two will work out whatever happened here."

Anna shook her head.

"Now don't you shake your head, Anna. I've noticed the way Matt looks at you, and I've never seen any man look at his bride that way. You two have something special. Trust me when I say, I do a lot of weddings and I know what I'm talking about.

"And heed my words, Anna. Tamara has been trying to get her hooks into Matt for years to no avail. If this is due to anything she told you, don't believe a word."

A shaft of pain pierced into Anna's heart like the blade from a twisted knife. *If only Carla knew.*

No sooner did Anna have Carla out the door when her cell rang.

"Anna, it's Faye, Matt's mom."

Anna didn't want to be rude, but Faye was the last person she had energy for at the moment.

"I got your number from Matt when we visited but haven't had the nerve to call you. I want to thank you for being so kind to me in spite of my bad behavior, and well, I'm curious. I've noticed such a big change in Matt … Oh, excuse me—"

Faye sounded like she was next to tears. Anna could hear a sniffle and Faye clear her throat.

"Anna. I can't believe Matt calls me regularly and he's so kind. He's told me he forgives me—"

Between sobs she admitted. "I was a terrible mother, Anna, not like you at all. I resented poor Matt for disrupting my selfish life, and I paid others to raise him." A soft wail slipped from her lips.

Anna didn't know what to say, but she remembered how cathartic it felt to have Rita just listen and show empathy.

"Faye, I'm sure Matt truly does forgive you."

"Yeah, but I can't forgive myself."

Anna remembered that battle all too clearly. "Faye, I know all about that. You can't forgive yourself, that's not your job, it's God's."

"I guess that's my point, Anna. We haven't been a family of faith. I don't know anyone in our circle of friends I can talk to about this, and some things are just too personal to talk to Matt about. I haven't a clue how to get this forgiveness you're talking about."

Anna couldn't comprehend God's timing. Why would God send Faye her way now with their engagement off and Matt out of her life? How could she on one hand lead Faye to the Lord and on the other hand tell her that the son she thinks has changed so much is two-timing with Tamara? God was asking too much.

Anna cleared the giant knot formed in her throat and made one decision—to obey. The minute she opened her mouth, wisdom poured forth and the Holy Spirit took over.

"Faye, God's son, Jesus, paid the price for our mistakes when he died on the cross. All we need to do is ask him in faith to forgive our sins and come into our life. He removes them as far as the east is from the west."

"But, Anna, you have no idea—I've done unspeakable things in the wake of my hurt. I was so angry with Darren when I found out he cheated on me that I did even worse. Can I really be forgiven?"

Anna assured her. "Yes, Faye, there's no record of wrongs once we hand them over to Jesus."

"But, Anna, I honestly don't know anything about this Jesus other than to hear people use his name when they're angry, me included."

Anna's heart lurched in genuine excitement. "Oh, I could spend hours sharing, but in a nutshell, Jesus, the Son of God, came to earth in the form of a tiny baby born in a humble manger. You know—the Christmas story."

Faye laughed. "Yes, that one I know. But the baby Jesus story always …" She hesitated. "… it makes me uncomfortable, as if this tiny baby somehow expects something from me. Santa is a more comfortable option."

Anna agreed. "Yes, every celebration which would turn us toward God, Satan has presented a counterfeit to distract, but that's a subject for another day. Let's stick to the Jesus story for now.

"Many miracles occurred during Jesus's ministry on earth, but the most incredible miracle of all was the fact he subjected himself to a horrible death on the cross in order to pay the price for our sins."

"I've heard of this," Faye admitted, "but the circle of friends I hang with, laugh and joke about a so-called powerful one who would allow mankind to kill him. We questioned that if he was so powerful, why didn't he come down from the cross and destroy them all?"

Faye's words held a whisper of regret. "But now I think I understand. He had a purpose for dying … me."

"Oh, Faye, you *do* understand." Anna said with conviction. "But Jesus didn't remain in the grave they put him in. He rose on the third day like he said he would, so that death was defeated. We celebrate this at Easter.

"You mean Easter isn't about the Easter Bunny? Another distraction, right?"

"Faye, you learn fast."

Faye laughed through her tears causing a snort to cut loose over the line.

Anna couldn't contain her laughter. They both started to howl.

"Oh my gosh, I'm sorry," Faye bubbled. "That was so unladylike."

Anna was surprised to hear the sound of her own laughter. Somehow out of the ashes, joy found a window and streamed in. Anna felt a power from on high and carried on with the conversation as if she didn't have a care in the world.

"Okay, I'm going to finish up so I don't overwhelm you."

"No, no, Anna, I've got this. Jesus came to earth. He died for my sins. He rose from the dead."

"Faye, I can see where Matt gets his smarts from."

"I know, right? That's what I've been saying for years." She giggled over the line. "But how was death defeated? We all still die."

Anna had to shake her head clear. Just the name of Matt brought instant tears.

"Yes, we die physically but have the privilege of living forever with Jesus in a place where there will be no more sadness or sorrow."

Faye cut in. "Oh, I like the sound of that. This old world has been much too painful."

Anna smiled into the phone. "I know. The thought of heaven brings me a lot of comfort too. But it's not just about the eternal, it's also about the here and now. When we believe in Jesus, he sends the Holy Spirit to help us live a better life. It's why you've seen a big change in your son."

As Anna voiced the words, a single bead of perspiration worked its way down her spine and thoughts began racing through her head like gusts of wind dancing through an open field.

If Matt is a changed man, then why didn't I let him explain?

The spirit of God instantly answered her question.

Fear. You're afraid of facing his past, but you will need to in order to embrace the future.

Faye's voice snapped Anna into the present. "Anna you've given me a lot to think about. I'll certainly need some help to sort out my messy life."

"Yes, it can be convoluted." Anna agreed, but she was thinking about her own dilemma.

"I've got it, Anna, I know just what to do. I'll be on the next plane out," Faye declared. "I've so much to learn, and the fact my son loves me when I don't deserve it proves to me there is a God. I already believe."

"And, Anna, I'm so thankful you came into his life and brought this Jesus with you. It's just what our family needs."

Anna gulped back a cry.

"I can't wait to see you and Matt and hear about Jesus—and learn even more. Oh, I have so much to arrange."

"I'll text you with details of my flight. And if it's okay, I'd like to stay with you and Melody. That little girl just melts my heart. I know Matt visits daily, so I'll get to see you all this way. I'm so excited, Anna, I can't thank you enough. This is the best day ever."

Anna didn't know what to say. She paused but then heard nothing.

"Faye? Faye?" The line was dead.

A groan of despair wrenched deep from within and found its voice as Anna cried out, "God, what now?"

Chapter Forty-Four

The steel gray sky with low heavy clouds suited Anna's disposition. She donned her spring raincoat, new running shoes, and her watch, which tracked her time and distance. She planned to run off the doldrums, even if it killed her, and sort out how to handle Faye's ill-timed visit.

Melody arched and squirmed in protest as Anna placed her in the stroller and then let out an angry squeal when Anna zipped up the rain cover.

"Come on, baby girl, your mama has to run, or you're not going to like me at all."

Melody screamed all the louder.

A blustery wind howled through the neighborhood and the clouds opened. *Let it rain, I don't care.* A steady pattern beat against Anna's cheeks in rhythm to the slap of her feet on the wet pavement.

Melody quieted at the feel of the motion, and Anna picked up her pace. She lifted her face to the warm April showers and ran like an athlete in training. The hill ahead demanded a level of exertion she didn't have, yet she dug deeper. All else faded as she concentrated on her breathing and the length of her stride. At the top of the hill, the road snaked down and up again. Her lungs burned and her joints ached but onward she ran. Cathartic. Cleansing. Clarifying.

A good hour later, she rounded the corner to her house and slowed to a walk for the cool down. The run had successfully diminished the strain of her tightly wound nerves and cleared the depression that nipped at her mind. She wiped drops of sweat that inched their way down her brow and temples.

Melody started to howl, clearly not impressed with her mother. Anna pushed the large wheeled stroller carefully past her car in the garage and unzipped the cover. "Come, come my little Melody, that's not a very nice sound." She lifted the baby and received instant quiet and a big grin. "Oh, you little faker," Anna said. "Stirring up a fuss for no good reason. Let's get you fed and down for your nap."

Melody reached for her face and smacked wildly.

Anna grabbed her chubby hands and blew kisses all over her tummy.

Melody giggled in delight.

"You betcha, little girl. To beddy-bye you go. Mama needs some alone time and prayer to think straight."

Anna had done nothing but ruminate for the past couple weeks. Deep down, she knew something wasn't right with what Tamara said and longed for Matt to fight for their relationship, but he did not. He respected her request and had stayed distant. He phoned ahead and asked Anna to bring Melody out to his car each time he picked her up. He remained polite, aloof, and conversed only about Melody's schedule, then immediately departed. No questions. No explanation. No conversation. Nothing. And that was far scarier to Anna than she dared admit.

Matt's countenance was like a black hole where nothing could be retrieved. But then again, she had told him to go, what did she expect?

A conflict of emotion raged within. She could not turn off the taps of love instantly, and her heart had not caught up to her reality. Three was too many in any relationship, so why then did her sorry heart pick up pace each day he arrived, and not settle until long after he left?

She had tried to drag him into conversation on how best to tell the world their engagement was off, and he had grunted.

"If you want to tell them go ahead. I have no stomach for it."

Oddly, she had not told anyone but Carla.

As she complained to God in prayer and felt sorry for herself that life had turned so difficult, she felt the nudge to pick up her Bible. She randomly opened to the gospel of John and the words of Jesus jumped up off the page. *Do not let your heart be troubled. Trust in God; trust also in me.*

Anna grimaced at how simple trust should be but wondered how to fully implement it when life was falling apart?

"God, I need you. I trust your care and love, not only for me but for Matt and Faye, who is arriving in two short days … Now, please, tell me what to do."

Silence filled the room. Anna read all the Scriptures surrounding the initial verse that had popped off the page, but nothing spoke into her spirit other than to trust. She wanted more information, yet God remained silent.

Broken and humbled she cried out, "God help me trust you. Increase my faith. Help my unbelief."

Tranquility filled her soul from the inside out. Like a cool spray of water misted over the body on a hot summer's day, relief permeated. Peace pushed back the worry though nothing had changed. Anna rested. She believed she would understand what to do when God's timing was right.

That moment came sooner than she anticipated. The ring of her cell phone shocked her out of a much-needed afternoon nap.

Matt's voice, no longer flat and despondent, lashed out. "Why didn't you tell me my mom was coming?"

Anna shook the cobwebs from her head and sat up on the couch. "Matt, this only transpired yesterday, and she sent me a text this morning giving me her travel plans. I intended to talk to you today when you picked up Melody."

"What's going on? She rattled on how she came to Jesus and how excited she is to share this experience with the both of us? The least you could have done is give me a heads up." His voice sounded as bristly as a hedgehog.

"Matt, I had hoped she wouldn't call you so soon and I would have a chance—"

"A chance to spread your tall tale version about what a two-timing son she has and why you had to break off our engagement? I can't believe she still wants to come!" His voice rang with sarcasm. "She has no use for anyone that—"

"Matt!" Anna's voice cut in with a level of indignation. "No, I didn't tell her. She raved about how much her son had changed and how kind you've been to her. Then she asked me how she could believe in this same Jesus. What was I to say?"

"The fact remains, Anna, whatever you would've told her concerning our relationship would've been far from the truth, because you didn't even give me the courtesy of an explanation."

The phone clicked dead, and Anna stared at her cell in utter shock.

No wonder she felt ill at ease in telling anyone about what brewed between them. A piece of this puzzle was missing.

"Oh, God," she cried, "What have I done?"

Do not let your heart be troubled, trust in me. Matt needs healing from his past, and you need to embrace his story. This is all part of my plan.

Twice in one day, an assurance that God had their circumstances in his trustworthy hands enveloped her like a warm blanket on a cold winter's day. She laid her head back down and drifted off to sleep.

The anguish of the past couple weeks bled into trembling rage, bubbling up, boiling over. Matt smashed his fists down on the coffee table and jarred the glass of water, so it tipped and splashed all over his computer. A curse slipped easily from his lips as his brooding flashed into sudden anger. He had not entertained that kind of language for months now. Where was this coming from?

The call from his mother sent him in a tailspin. He knew that she loathed anyone who cheated in a relationship, though she had stooped as low many a time. He had assumed Anna would tell his mom her version of their story. Why hadn't she? That fact remained more of a puzzle to him than anything.

The more he thought about the situation, the more confused he became. A spike of anger rode his spine, and he bit back the pain. One part of him wanted to run to Anna and beg her to listen, but another part hung back in hurt and anger that she would believe the worst of him. He wondered how they could begin a marriage with so little trust. But worse yet, he felt that same pain of abandonment he had felt as a child. And he had promised himself he would never allow that again.

He should have stuck to his original plan and kept relationships on the superficial level. No pain that way.

Melody suddenly danced in his head. Her playful gurgle and baby laughter filled the lonely crevices of his mind, and turmoil vanished. She brought instant joy.

He glanced up to see the picture of Anna tenderly gazing down at Melody and a flood of love swept over him. His breathing quickened and his pulse rate accelerated. After what she had believed, his mind objected with vigor, yet he could not force his sorry heart to say goodbye.

Life had been so much easier before God's love swooped down in the forms of Anna and Melody. He could no longer live without them, even if hurt and disappointment reigned. And now to complicate matters, his mom was scheduled to arrive the next day, which forced him to talk to Anna and bridge the canyon that cut between them.

••••••• ■ ••••

Anna fussed with her hair, changed her clothes from her sweats and T-shirt to a blouse and a pair of jeans that showed off her trim figure, and applied a light dusting of make-up. As nervous as a cat on a shaky limb, she needed a boost in confidence. The glance in the mirror did not disappoint. Matt was due to pick up Melody any moment, and she was not about to let him escape.

The cell rang as it had the last few weeks. Matt announced his arrival then immediately hung up.

The rain had not let up all day. Anna slipped on her raincoat and ran out.

He rolled down his window with his eyebrows arched in question. "Where's Melody?"

"She's playing in her playpen. Come in for a moment." When he did not immediately respond, she pleaded, "Matt, with your mom about to arrive, you know we need to talk."

A band of sunshine split between the storm clouds and lit the world around them. Anna lifted her head. "Oh," she gasped. "I just love it when it's raining and yet the sun decides to shine." Sunbeams danced on rain droplets and the trouble between them took backseat to the display of God's nature all around them. Color caught her eye, "Oh, Matt, look at the incredible rainbow and these clouds with the sun breaking through … it's like God has us in his spotlight."

"I'll grab Melody and we can drive up the hill toward your place where we'll be able to see the show." She didn't wait for his reply.

As if nothing brewed between them, Anna had Melody in her car seat and jumped in beside him. A comfortable silence filled the car other than the occasional coo from Melody. The rainbow intensified in color and brilliance and Matt stopped along the side of the road as soon as they had a view of the city. Anna jumped out to snap a few photos and waved at Matt. "Bring Melody."

She motioned to him to stand with Melody against the backdrop of the rainbow filled sky and snapped a photo with Melody's chubby hand pointed heavenward and Matt smiling down at her.

She brought the cell over and showed him. "Daddy and his Melody."

He smiled but still did not say a word.

"Shall we continue to your place?"

He nodded.

With Melody settled quietly in the playpen just inside the French doors where Anna could keep an eye on her, she made her way out to the deck. She stood by the rail and gazed over the valley below. Matt came up beside her. Shadows lengthened and gave way to evening light. Clouds splashed with colors of red, orange and purple burnished the ever-darkening sky.

"It's so beautiful," she said.

"Yes, most beautiful."

She looked sideways to find him staring at her rather than the sunset. Their eyes locked and his gaze crackled with heat.

Silence hung in the balance, but Anna could feel currents move frenetically between them. Undertows. Riptides. Dangerous forces that could so easily sweep them up in a sea of emotion hovered within her reach.

Matt suddenly hauled her up against him. In a desperate kiss, hunger fed hunger. Pent up emotions exploded between them. A heat thrummed through Anna's limbs as breathing roughened and their bodies pressed closer yet. Matt dug his fingers into her hair and kissed a line from her throat, to her earlobe.

"Anna, what have you done to me?" he groaned against her lips before he claimed them yet again.

A ripple of delight ran up her spine, and a warm knot settled in her stomach. *He loves me, of that I'm sure, but how does Tamara fit into the picture?*

Nothing made sense. When he was touching her like he was, she couldn't think.

His mouth left hers with a deliberate slowness as he pulled her head to rest on his chest. She heard the buck of his heart against her ear as he gently rubbed his hands up and down her spine. A delicious but dangerous electricity danced between them.

His thumb slid up her jaw to brush lightly over her lips before he touched hers with the lightest of kisses. An aching gentleness replaced the previous fervor.

When he stepped out of her reach, she felt undone like she was part of him, the way salt is part of the sea. She longed to draw him back into her embrace and never let go. Her emotions vacillated wildly. One moment she was in heaven and the next, she was stone-cold terrified. He had the power in which to hurt her like none other.

"Matt?"

"Give me a moment," he said, as he turned and walked indoors.

Anna followed Matt back inside and scooped up Melody from the playpen. She grabbed the diaper bag and pulled out a jar of baby food. Melody gurgled in delight. She stretched out dimpled hands determined to help herself.

Anna busied herself feeding the baby while Matt sat silently on the kitchen barstool gazing into thin air. She decided to wait for him to speak.

Matt stood and began pacing. "I can't tell you how difficult these past few weeks have been. I've had every emotion in the book, from wanting to kiss you into submission, to wanting to hurt you like you've hurt me.

"Matt, I—"

"Please, let me finish."

Anna nodded.

"Disillusionment and disappointment don't sum it up. Desperation comes close … and anger—oh, man!" He shook his head in disbelief. "I possessed anger I never thought I was capable of. The fact you didn't trust me enough to allow an explanation crushed me. The one thing I thought came easy besides our obvious attraction for each other is the fact we were best friends and could talk about anything. What happened there?"

Anna looked away as guilt flooded in. "I was angry and hurt too," she admitted.

She filled another scoop of food for Melody and tried to feed her. Melody decided it was playtime and grabbed the spoon. She sent it flying with a giggle.

Matt jumped to the rescue and pulled the sticky Melody from the highchair. He grabbed the kitchen cloth to wipe her down and offered, "How about we see if Lorena can watch this monkey, and we'll go for supper? I think neutral ground where I don't feel like making love to you on the spot may be more conducive to conversation." Matt's eyes held a familiar twinkle.

Hope, albeit small, trickled across Anna's soul like a stream in a drought. The words of the Lord echoed in her mind. *Do not let your heart be troubled, trust in me.*

She offered him a shaky smile and nodded her head in agreement. "Sure."

Chapter Forty-Five

"Hey, do you want to try that new steak house, Toberta's," Matt asked, as they wheeled away from her sister's house?

Anna couldn't believe her ears. He was really going to take her to the same place he had just taken Tamara?

"Not a chance!" Her words sounded clipped and uptight even to her ears.

"Why do you answer like that?" Matt asked. "No problem if you don't want steak, there's Italian too—"

"Tamara told me you took her to dinner there."

"I see you bought into everything she said, but you'll have to believe me when I say, I didn't take her to Toberta's. I've heard the restaurant is great, but I've never been there."

Anna's stomach dropped like she was on a flight with severe turbulence. *What other lies had Tamara told her?*

"In fact, Anna, we're going to go there, because I know the owner and you can ask him to order up what I had last time, just to see his reaction. I'll stay with you the whole time to remove any doubt of me having a conversation with him ahead of time." He fished in his pocket, pulled out his phone and lobbed it into her lap. "You can have that, too, just so there's no question in your mind about me texting him, because obviously you don't trust me."

Anna could feel the heat rush to her cheeks at the sting of that truth. "Matt, I'm sorry … we don't have to go to that restaurant."

"Yes, Anna, I think we do, because if nothing else, I need you to trust the rest of what I have to tell you." A muscle in his jaw clenched.

An uncomfortable tension permeated the silence that filled the car. Anna was relieved to see the restaurant straight ahead.

A skip of hope leaped within her when Matt parked the car and turned to her and said, "Come, my lovely. This conversation is long overdue." A warm smile kicked his dimple into full glory and eased the palpable strain between them. He hopped out and was around to her side before she could gather her purse and slip his phone into the side pocket.

He opened the door with chivalry and extended his arm to help her out. He pushed the door closed, hit the lock button, and pivoted in the direction of the restaurant without letting go of her arm. His hand slid intimately down her forearm to clasp her hand in his. A spike of sensation ran up Anna's arm at the mere touch.

They were barely through the door when a large man caught sight of Matt and came running. He swallowed them both in a giant bear hug. His beefy arms held tight. When he pulled back, he dramatically bowed as if greeting royalty. "Welcome."

Matt smiled. "Tony—"

"Ahh, Matt, I see you finally made it to our new restaurant and brought your lovely lady with you." He turned directly to Anna, "Roberta and I have been badgering him to take an evening off work and bring you along."

He stood back with careful appraisal and inspected Anna like she was one of his scrumptious desserts. "Matt, I see your wait paid off," he said, as he slapped him on the back. "You held out all these years for the cream of the crop, the icing on the cake, and for that cherry on top—you got it all." With a hearty laugh, his voice boomed throughout the restaurant.

Anna smiled, as he cracked up at his own brand of clever.

"How can you tell I love food?" He rubbed his well-pronounced girth with one hand and raised his fingertips to his lips with the other. He smacked out a loud kiss before his hand flew into the air. "Ahh … but the culinary arts, that glorious creation of exquisite dishes is truly my love—second love, of course."

Matt shook his head. "Anna, this is the owner, Tony. He has a flare for the dramatics, but I put up with him because he has the best food in town." Matt laughed as Tony's eyes bulged in feigned offense at the teasing.

"Tony and his wife, Roberta, have had an Italian restaurant for years, but this is their newest venture—Tony's love for steak and Roberta's love for everything Italian—hence, the name Toberta's."

"Yeah, I only get two letters, and she has the rest." Tony's chubby jowls jiggled as his head bounced up and down in amusement, and his eyes twinkled with laughter. "Notice I said food is my second love. Roberta reminds me daily that she's my first, and I dare not disagree."

He threw his arm around Matt's shoulder and chuckled. "Soon you'll understand, young man.

"Now are you going to properly introduce me to this lovely woman or not?"

Matt rolled his eyes. "Well, if I could get a word in edgewise. Tony, this is my fiancée, Anna."

Anna's heart leaped at the declaration. In Matt's mind, they were still engaged. The thought brought a smile to her soul.

Anna reached out to extend a handshake. Tony bowed gallantly and raised her fingers to lightly plant a kiss on the back of her hand.

"Tony, are you flirting with the pretty girls again?" A short, round woman with beautiful chocolate brown eyes far too large for her face came into view.

"Roberta darling," he placed an arm affectionately around her shoulders and drew her close. "There is no other as lovely as you, but come meet Matt's fiancée, Anna."

Roberta squealed in delight, and the next thing Anna knew she was engulfed in a warm hug.

With a snap of her fingers, Roberta had the head maître d' at her side. "That table with the view in the corner?"

"Reserved," he said.

"Un-reserve it," she said, "and bring me a bottle of our best Cabernet Sauvignon, please."

The maître d' moved swiftly away.

"Come, you love birds, we've just the spot for a romantic dinner."

As if they were dignitaries, Anna and Matt were ushered into a secluded corner table that faced the lake. Roberta clucked and fussed until they were nicely settled with menus in hand, water in their glasses, the candle on the table lit and glowing romantically. She waved to a nearby bus boy who intuitively knew what that meant. A hot basket of fresh bread and flavored butters were placed on the table without a word being spoken.

"Now, we'll leave you two to enjoy." She giggled like a schoolgirl with a starry look in her eyes. "Ahh, I still remember the days when Tony and I were engaged. You sure don't need my company or anyone's for that matter." She bustled off with a wave and a smile.

If only she knew, Anna thought. She turned toward the view. City lights shimmered off the lake and wisps of clouds scuttled across a full moon. She snuck a peek across the table at Matt. He, too, silently drank in the beauty.

She assumed he felt the same as she did, neither of them wanted to ruin a perfect setting with difficult dialogue.

Anna felt Matt's hand cover hers and her heart skipped a beat. The warmth of his thumb rhythmically traced a pattern back and forth on the inside of her wrist.

"I see you're still wearing your engagement ring."

Anna nodded. "No questions that way."

His face dropped. A crestfallen look entered his eyes and he pulled his hand away. "Is that the only reason?"

"No, Matt." She quickly admitted, "I thought we should talk, or better yet, I thought I should listen before breaking up with my best friend."

Anna looked down at her ring and fiddled with it, unable to make eye contact.

"Matt, I can tell by the fact both Tony and Roberta were overjoyed to finally see you in their new restaurant that you haven't been here before, and I know I didn't handle that evening well. For that, I'm truly sorry. But there's so much that doesn't make sense. And when you hid the fact you were meeting Tamara, and then she called to spew her poison, I was ripe for the picking. Why would you keep that from me? And why were you seeing her?" Anna blinked back the bite of tears that threatened to surface.

Matt cleared his throat, as if to swallow a large lump. "Anna, I'm the one who should be sorry. I should've told you about Tamara long ago, the history and the current situation. I thought I could handle the problem without it getting out of hand."

"What problem?"

"That day in the park when I shared my history, I wanted to tell you about Tamara, but you made it too easy for me. You said that you forgave my past and didn't need to know more. At the time, that suited me fine." His iridescent blue eyes darkened with a troubled look.

"But, Anna, it's not fine, and I need to tell you."

She nodded, resisting the urge to look away. There was something about his intensity that made it important to face this head on.

"I'm not proud of the fact that in the past I used Tamara for the physical. More accurately, you could say we used each other. Now with my biblical understanding of how precious the gift of marriage and physical union is, I wish I could go back and change that decision, but I can't."

Anna felt a twist in her gut. The thought of them together made the green goblin of envy bubble and stew.

Anna dared not waste the opportunity. She didn't want unanswered questions causing suspicion and mistrust any longer. "Then, back to the same question I asked you before—how far back is the past to you? And why are you currently seeing Tamara?"

Matt slumped back in his chair and shifted his eyes away. "This is where it gets complicated."

Anna's heart dropped to the basement of her soul. She took a long pull of air into her lungs and breathed out slowly. It took all she had to remain calm and collected in order to encourage the truth. "Go on."

Matt fidgeted in his chair. "We'd better order first." He waived the waiter over.

They made their selections, and Anna smiled after the waiter left. "One last moment of reprieve seems to be just what the doctor ordered."

"Yes, I needed that." Matt smiled a watery smile. "Another moment to figure out how to tell you something I'm not proud of."

Anna blinked twice in an effort to hold back the sting of tears just below the surface.

"Anna, I truly fell in love with you that first night we were together. In my past, I'd been with Tamara and other women, and yet I'd never felt any of what you stirred in my heart, my soul—" His voice cracked, and she could see him swallow hard.

She reached across the table to momentarily squeeze his hand.

"Man, this is difficult." He exhaled deeply and raked both his hands through his hair. "After our first night together, and then the fact you wouldn't see me, I truly thought our relationship was over before it began. Tamara came knocking, and I weakened. That night, I felt the shame and the weight of my sinfulness like never before. You know the part of every person that nags at them—that knowledge of right from wrong before they're even a Christian?"

Anna nodded.

"Well, that ate me up inside. My conscience demanded an answer. How could I love you and yet be with someone else? The hypocrisy disgusted me.

"I remember getting up from the bed and immediately taking a hot shower, as if to wash off the guilt, which didn't work. Then, I asked Tamara to leave and told her we could remain friends, but the physical was done.

"She interrupted and smirked, confident enough to declare that we were a forever thing and I would never get her out of my blood. I admitted that I already had and that I'd fallen in love—real love—for the first time in my life. I apologized for our evening and admitted that sex without love pales in comparison, which really irritated her. Then I told her there would never be a repeat. And there hasn't been, Anna. I swear I haven't been with her since. But—"

Anna held his gaze. "But what?"

"But I should've paid more attention to her obsessive behavior. She was livid. Told me she hadn't waited all these years just to let me go and pointed out how I loved someone else but spent the night with her. Then she said to go ahead and dabble with love until I got bored and in the meantime, she'd be quite willing to share."

Anna gasped, "That's what she said to me both times—at our engagement party and when she recently called."

Matt turned white. "She talked to you about this at our engagement party?"

"Yes, but I asked you point-blank about your relationship with her, and you told me there was nothing current. I believed you. I didn't feel I had to go into the sordid details of her tirade, nor dig into your past."

"Anna, I'm so sorry. That last night I spent with her haunted me. The fact I could clearly love you and yet appease the physical made me realize the depth of my human darkness.

"Once I became a believer, I told Tamara I was a Christian. She laughed at me and kept sending me texts asking me if I was bored to death with my church mouse yet. She clearly didn't believe a word I said. And although she kept trying, I never looked back, Anna, no matter what lies she told you."

He reached forward and took both her hands in his. "I know I'm forgiven by God, but I have to ask … Anna, will you forgive me?"

Anna squeezed his hands tight before relaxing back into her chair. "Of course, I forgive you, Matt. I was the one who confused the situation, and you weren't even a Christian at the time. However, don't get me wrong, I don't like that woman in your past, but I believe you when you say the physical is in the past.

"What concerns me more is what's going on now. Why is she still leaving intimate messages on your phone, and why are you sneaking off to see her?"

The waiter smiled in their direction as he moved toward them. He carried a tray above his head in one hand and a stand in another. With the skill of a professional, he flicked the stand open and placed the tray on top. Steaming hot Basil Chicken Carbonara appeared in front of Anna, and a large steak topped with crab slid in front of Matt.

They smiled and offered their thanks.

Matt pointed at her dish. "You eat while I'll try and explain. Hope you don't mind my talking through the occasional mouthful." His easy smile was back.

"I eat, you talk. Sounds like a great deal to me." She picked up her fork.

"What started out as an annoyance, where Tamara wouldn't leave me alone, soon turned obsessive and ugly. She began stalking me. She showed up on my doorstep, at the hospital at all hours, in my office, and she even dared to crash our engagement party uninvited. Up until our engagement was official, I felt I could control the situation. But after that night she went into crazy mode. The problem exacerbated to the point I needed to involve the police. They told me they couldn't do anything without a restraining order and so I jumped on that.

Anna's breath caught in her throat. "Why didn't you tell me, Matt?"

"I didn't want to scare you, and the police advised the same. Apparently, she has never harmed anyone, just made their life miserable and used extortion for financial gain. The police wanted to get enough information to charge her. They asked me to set up that meeting you saw on my phone and gave me a device that looks like a pen to record our conversation. I swear that is the one and only time I initiated a visit. I'll give you the name of the officer I worked with if you want more clarification.

"Of course, Tamara assumed that our meeting meant we would resume the relationship. Instead, when I served her with a restraining order, she did exactly what the police thought she would do. She threatened to kill you, threatened to steal our baby. She rambled on how Melody would be the child the two of us never had."

Anna dropped her fork. "Matt, does she know where I live?" Her voice carried a tremor.

"No. I don't think so, or I'm sure you would've seen her on your doorstep by now. I fired Maxine when I found out she gave out your cell number. Thankfully, I didn't have your address anywhere on the records at work.

Jasmine was the only one who had your cell number—in case of an emergency. Maxine snooped around until she found it and gave it to Tamara."

"But what if she followed you to my place?"

"After the party when she began to get really strange and the police became involved, I paid careful attention to my rearview mirror and made sure no one followed me. I also hired a private detective to follow her and inform me of her every move.

"Anna, I honestly don't think we have anything more to worry about. When I got up to leave Tamara that evening, it was like a switch flipped. Her ugly threats turned all business. That's when I knew her threats were a ruse to incite fear. What she wanted more than anything was money. She demanded a lump sum in order to leave us alone. In a calculated confidence that could only come from practice, she named an outrageous amount as if making a reasonable business deal. The police view her actions as a premeditated ploy in which to exhort money. They have enough information now to charge her, and that's been done. She will go to jail."

A faraway look entered Matt's eyes. "I've known Tamara for years, and I was one of the many men that used her. For that I'll always be sorry.

"I always wondered where she got her money. She'd disappear for months but always come back. Now I understand. She is a predator. The police have a network of complaints from different cities, as she targeted wealthy, married men on the internet. The police said she set up profiles on various websites and drew them in, then demanded hush money.

"Then why you, Matt? You weren't married." Anna questioned.

"I've given that some thought," he said, pausing to take a bite of his steak. "The way she turned possessive after she heard about you, I believe, in her mind, she thought that one day we'd be a couple. I was her ace in the hole. But in this last year when I refused to see her at all and ended social contact completely, she became desperate. She tried to create a wedge between you and me with her lies. Little does she know how close she came to succeeding."

Anna pushed the last bit of Carbonara around on her dish unable to make eye contact. A wave of guilt surged. "I'm so sorry, I should've listened before I leapt to any conclusions."

"Do you know what made me furious, Anna? The reason I walked out your door without insisting you hear the truth?"

She shook her head. "No, that actually bothered me. After all was said and done, I wished that you had fought for us and made me listen. But it was like you had nothing to say."

"Oh, I had lots to say, but I was feeling too sorry for myself. You hurt my pride. And it took my mother's pending arrival to finally get me on my knees and pray about our relationship. God hit me over the head with my pride.

"I realized I came unhinged because I couldn't control the situation. I've been a man with few setbacks and live in a world where no one tells me what to do. I manage my own practice. I have employees, nurses, technicians, you name it, at my beck and call. I'm a specialist in my field and very good at what I do. I have money, position, and the intellectual advantage in most circumstances. There hasn't been much to humble me until you came along. First you took your sweet time falling for me, and then you call off the wedding. I was flabbergasted. Proud. Angry."

Anna's eyes widened in shock. "But, Matt—"

He waved his hand. "It's okay, I needed a good dose of reality to help me understand how to depend on God and not Matthew Carmichael. It was God that allowed the situation with Tamara to become uncontrollable. Then he permitted you to rise up and show me the door. These past few weeks of disobedience have been sheer hell, because I knew God wanted me to humble myself and tell you the truth. My pride at being rejected held me in its ugly grip. It felt like the old days when my mom would send me packing."

"Oh, Matt, I'm—"

"No, this was all in God's divine timing. Remember on Sunday, the sermon about the need to ask God for healing from past wounds? That was for me. God was turning up the heat and showing me just how much I needed him.

"I also didn't like the fact God asked me if he was enough. I had to honestly look at my relationship with him and know, that even if you and I never got back together, I would still love God and live the Christian life. Though I begged him for a second chance with you, I had to first surrender my will. Those words in the Lord's Prayer, 'thy will be done' had to become mine. That was a tough one for my stubborn heart.

"So, I came to your house today expecting nothing, totally surrendered to God, knowing I needed him more than life itself. But I had asked him to give me a small sign of hope if we had anything left. When you came to the car all covered in raindrops and sunshine wanting to talk, I knew I was putty in your hands."

Matt reached over and placed one hand over hers. "All I asked from God was a small touch of encouragement, but in his extravagance, he split the heavens open and poured out sunshine, a rainbow, and smiles from you, my dear sweet Anna. How could my ugly pride live amongst such beauty?"

Anna could not contain her happiness. She giggled like a teenager with a secret. "Oh, Matt, I've been so miserable without you, but don't let that go to your head."

They both laughed. He reached across the table and trailed his other hand down the side of her face. "Let's get out of here, my love," he whispered.

She nodded in agreement.

He cupped her chin in his hand and leaned forward to place a gentle kiss on her waiting lips before he pushed his steak aside and waved the waiter over.

"Two Tiramisus to go and the bill." He winked at Anna. "Can't ever leave without having Roberta's famous dessert. We'll pick up Melody and get her settled, then enjoy dessert at your place." A smile as broad as a watermelon slice split across his face, and his dimple danced in delight.

Anna's heart soared at the lightness in Matt's voice. Hope filtered in like the steam from a hot cup of tea and curled its warmth around her soul. God had been working and His plan had been so much bigger than she could have ever imagined.

Chapter Forty-Six

"Oh my, Matt, this is divine. Best Tiramisu I've ever had." Anna scraped her plate to get the last morsel and licked her fork for good measure.

Matt rose from his barstool and held out his hand to Anna. She swiveled on hers and slipped effortlessly into his embrace. On the sofa, Anna snuggled up against Matt and dropped her head to his shoulder. His arm came instantly around her.

"Here's the plan, Anna Clarke. I want to be married by month's end if you're agreeable. I'm tired of this cat and mouse game we play."

Anna's heart fluttered. The thought that she would not have to say goodbye each evening and have the freedom to express her love without restriction, to know him body, mind, and soul thrilled her. "Yes," she breathed. "I wholeheartedly agree."

They melted into each other. Their brief touch sent shivers from tip to toe before Anna jumped to her feet.

"Okay, Matt. Scat!"

Her abruptness caused a grin as Matt rose and grabbed her tight. "What, Anna? You can't stand the heat." He laughed. "Now you know how I've felt for months."

His breath fanned hot against her face and the tips of his fingers sent flames dancing up her spine. She shivered in delight barely able to breathe. Every detail came alive—the strength of his muscles in the column of his neck, the beating of his heart beneath her fingertips, the scent of woodsy aftershave. An avalanche of emotions shuddered up from the soles of her feet and a wash of heat.

Love radiated from his intense blue eyes. Anna felt drawn into his vortex. He gently grazed the back of his hand up the side of her cheek and pushed an errant curl from her brow. Both hands got lost in her luxurious waves.

All teasing faded as their lips collided in a passionate ragged pull of need and desire. A rush of taste and tremor exploded between them. Hands began to frantically pull at the barrier of clothing.

He literally groaned in agony, as he pulled apart. "Sorry, Anna. I thought I could tease in fun, but there's no middle ground with us."

Anna smoothed down her rumpled tee shirt and repeated her earlier words. "Matt. Like I said. Scat. Go. Vamoose!"

He laughed his way out the door. "Two weeks, Anna, you got two weeks to pull our wedding off."

"But that's not enough time to get invitations out."

"Email, text, shout out the invites from the mountain top. I don't care how you do it, or what it costs, but in two weeks I'm making you my bride." With a wink, he shut the door behind him with a decided bang.

Faye Carmichael arrived with a happy Darren in tow. "Don't know what you did with the old Faye," he teased, "but I have my girl back—the happy one I married all those years ago."

Matt smiled at Anna then struck up a conversation with his dad about the trip out.

Faye whispered to Anna. "Darren doesn't know it yet, but he's got a way better version than he's ever had. Jesus is really changing me, and Darren is feeling loved by me for the first time in years."

"Have you told him, Faye?"

"No, this is all too new, and I want to be sure I understand the basics before I start spouting off. I've been through New Age, Buddhism, Eastern Meditation, and numerous other strange quests in order to find peace, and I don't want him thinking I'm on just another kick. Besides, none of those other attempts changed me from the inside out, but this truly is different. I felt it best to show him first, rather than tell him."

Anna nodded in agreement. "That sounds like wisdom, Faye, I'm so glad you're here. Can you stay the next two weeks and help me pull off this wedding?"

"Oh, Anna, I'd be delighted and honored to help you."

The girls fell together. As they hugged and laughed, tears mingled in the mix. Anna took one look at Matt and Darren who stood with questioning looks. "Don't ask."

Faye laughed all the more. "Oh, Anna, I love you," she said as she hugged her again."

Anna slipped out to the back porch with an early morning coffee and her Bible in hand. She wanted to start her wedding day with her heavenly Father before the whirlwind of celebration began.

Dawn's pearl-gray sky gave way to gathering light. The sun poked its head above the eastern ridge. Anna breathed in the wonder of a new day as the cloudless sky opened to depths of gentle blue. Warm lemony sunlight shimmered over the valley in a glow of dancing sunbeams that promised a glorious day.

Anna raised her heart in a prayer of thanks before her mind turned to her son Mark. He was the only one who refused to come to the wedding. His negative reply came swiftly via email with the excuse he was too busy at work and couldn't in good faith support their union.

Anna loved her son. His decision caused deep pain, but she chose to pray and trust that in time, their relationship would once again be restored. Anna's instinct was to fuss, fret, and fix. God's wisdom was to love unconditionally and not allow bitterness. Leave the rest to him.

Peace flooded over her as she once again prayed for her son and soaked up God's joy.

When Anna reached the Lakeside Resort, she breathed easy. Carla had seen to every detail and shooed her off to the dressing room to get ready. Her nails and hair were already done. She fiddled with a sprig of fresh flowers pinned just above one ear. Her waves flowed long and free down her back, just as the doctor ordered. It was Matt's one and only request for the day.

Anna slipped on her wedding dress with confidence. The ivory gown of flowing tulle ran asymmetrically to the floor showing off a peek of her legs in the front at knee length then cutting diagonally down to brush the floor in the back. She swished in front of the full-length mirror loving the fact the dress was glamorous but not overdone. She had chosen it for its classic A-line simplicity with a splash of elegance. The petal sleeves with three overlapping panels of lace resembled a tulip in bloom, and the sweetheart V in both the front and back permitted a touch of sexy.

She groaned as she slipped on the dreaded high heels but knew they were a must to finish the look.

Lana barged in with a hand-tied bouquet of spring blossoms and Faye close behind.

"Oh my, Anna, don't you look absolutely stunning." Faye gushed in delight.

Anna smiled and kicked up one heel. "Lana how do you wear these things all the time? They are sooo uncomfortable."

Lana laughed. "A girl has to do what a girl has to do. But I'm glad you don't look this good every day, Anna, or they'd really think me the ugly stepsister."

Anna swatted at her sister and then gave her a hug. "Let's go, Sis. Since birth you've been my shadow and I yours." She looped their arms together. "Come, walk me down the aisle."

Rows of chairs covered in satin and bows led the way toward a flower-encased archway where Jason stood proudly beside Matt. Melody in Matt's arms entertained the crowd with her loud squeals and happy waves.

The path of rose petals scattered upon the grass and gorgeous lake background blurred in Anna's view. She had eyes for only one. He stood before her with a smile as wide as the sea and his dimple planted securely in place.

Epilogue

A ringing phone woke Anna and Matt from a deep sleep. Anna rolled out of Matt's arms and fumbled to answer her cell.

"Anna, come quick." Her twin sister's pitch was a few octaves higher than normal. "Lorena's in labor and wants you there. We're on our way to the hospital. Things are going quickly."

Anna jumped into gear and pulled on the set of clothes she had ready for this very moment.

Matt got up and kissed her lips. "Keep me updated. I'll be there the moment the sitter gets here. I know I'm not supposed to be too excited just in case Lorena decides to keep the baby, but just the thought of being a dad for the second time thrills me."

Anna grunted in return, annoyed that Matt woke up anytime, anywhere, and instantly functioned with a penchant for chatter. She on the other hand, woke up slow and steady, in need of quiet.

She pressed her finger to his lips. "Shhhhh."

He laughed. "Oh, yeah, I forgot my princess doesn't arrive until after an early morning run or a cup of coffee, whichever comes first."

Anna dropped a kiss on his smiling mouth and scooted out the door, glad for the silence.

Lorena was already in the final stages of pushing by the time Anna arrived, and her healthy baby boy entered the world with a boisterous howl. She held her baby for a few minutes and then tearfully handed him to Anna.

"Right now, the greatest expression of love I can offer my son, Auntie, is to give him to you. I know I'm not ready for such a huge responsibility. But, oh, it's hard." Lana and Tom folded Lorena in a hug and wept with their daughter.

Anna gathered the beautiful infant snug in her arms and began to sway back and forth. "You're so loved, little one. There's so much love in this room, you have no idea how blessed you are." A giant tear coursed down Anna's face as she felt an instant affection and love bloom within her heart for the sleeping child.

***

Matt entered the room and hurried over to Anna. He embraced them both in the circle of his arms. "Matt, meet your beautiful baby, chosen of God to be your son." Large tears pooled in his eyes as he gingerly took the tiny infant into his arms and kissed the baby's brow. "He's so perfect, Anna, so incredibly perfect."

They walked over to Lorena, who now sat peacefully watching the exchange between them. "Lorena, we'd like to call him Jesse if that's okay with you. The name means *gift.*"

Lorena smiled through a curtain of tears and nodded readily. "Yes, I like that. I like that a lot."

Matt looked up to see Lana and Tom wistfully looking on. Intuitively, he knew what the Spirit wanted him to do. He walked around the bed to where they stood and carefully transferred the baby into Lana's waiting arms. "It's time Jesse meets his grandma and grandpa." Anna nodded in agreement and mouthed, "You're the best."

Lorena caught the exchange. "I've made a wise decision today, haven't I?"

Matt leaned in and gave Lorena the biggest hug and whispered a few words. Lorena smiled and hugged him again.

Anna moved closer, placing her arm around Matt. He drew her to his side as she looked down at Lorena and reassured her, "Although we'll legally adopt Jesse and love him as our treasured son, you'll always be his birth mother. When you're ready to let him know, we'll stand beside you. We don't want this to be a big secret. We'll all join in raising him in an environment with so much love he'll feel special and chosen rather than adopted. He'll know, Lorena, that you gave the greatest gift of all. You gave him life, and you should be very proud of yourself."

Lorena's eyes lit up and a tired smile spread across her face.

***

Anna just had to know. "Hey, what did you say to Lorena when you hugged her at the hospital?"

Matt laughed. "That'll cost you a kiss, Mrs. Carmichael."

"But that's too easy," she giggled, planting a smooch right on his lips.

He grabbed her close and held on tight encouraging two, three, four and a whole lot more. Lying in the crook of his arm an hour later, she finally got her answer.

""I told Lorena I would never again risk losing you but that I secretly wanted another child. I thanked her for the incredible gift she gave me in that little boy, and how thrilled I am to be his daddy."

Anna snuggled close and threw an arm around his chest in a bear hug.

"I find it so fascinating how God works. What you and Lorena felt was your most devastating failure, he turned into good—a beautiful gift of life. All because you both chose to do it his way. Could you imagine life without little Melody and now, baby Jesse?"

Anna shook her head. "Matt, I've thought about that many times. Melody brings me so much joy, and my heart bursts with love for Jesse. What I would've missed—"

Matt rolled over and held his face just above Anna's.

"And what I would have missed." Matt planted a kiss on Anna's brow. "Sweet Melody for one." He planted another kiss on her left cheek. "And her stubborn but beautiful mama." He dropped a kiss on the other cheek. "Who would've kept dodging me." He kissed the tip of her nose. "Had that little girl not brought me to her doorstep over and over again." A rain of kisses found their way to her lips.

Anna laughed up at him. "Ahhh, Doctor Carmichael, you truly are too good to be true. How did I ever get so blessed?"

Matt rolled back beside her and lifted her hand to his lips.

"I feel the same about you, my dear lady. God is so good."

"Yes, Matt, he truly is."

Their words of faith ascended into the heavens, and a gift from the invisible realm descended and perfumed the room with a surreal presence of peace.

"Do you feel that?" Matt whispered.

Anna nodded, unable to speak, and squeezed his hand.

About the Author

Blossom Turner is a freelance writer published in Chicken Soup and Kernels of Hope anthologies, former newspaper columnist on health and fitness, and an avid blogger. She lives in British Columbia, Canada, with her husband, David, of thirty-six years. A former business woman, personal trainer, and mother of two grown children she is now pursuing her lifelong dream of writing full-time.

A hopeless romantic at heart, she believes all story should give the reader significant entertainment value. However, her writing embodies the struggles of real life. She infuses the reality of suffering with the hope of Christ to give a healthy dose of relatable encouragement to her reader. Her desire is to leave the reader with a yearning to live for Christ on a deeper level, or at the very least, create a hunger to seek for more.

She is an avid blogger who has contributed to the Mount Hermon Blog, Christian Devotions blog, and writes a weekly devotional blog on the names of God. Read more at blossomturner.com.

Her authenticity comes from the crucible of suffering. Through understanding the restorative power of God's forgiveness when humanity fails, she could write *Anna's Secret* in a way that grips the reader on a profound level. A strong thread of hope is woven through this compelling novel where failure, love and romance collide.

Watch for Blossom's next novel, *Katherine's Arrangement*, a historical romance about an arranged marriage, set in the Shenandoah Valley—post-Civil War. The prologue and first chapter follow.

KATHERINE'S ARRANGEMENT

Shenandoah Brides Series Book One

PROLOGUE

Civil War—October 1864, Rockingham County, Shenandoah Valley

"Katherine. They're coming." Pa swung his rifle over his shoulder and grimaced, the gun slipped to the floor. With jerky movements, he retrieved the weapon.

"Pa, your shoulder."

Go, girl, and do exactly as we planned."

Through the window, the smoke from the neighbor's farm caught Katie's eye—a cloud of ominous black splashed across the distant horizon. She glanced back. Her heart leapt into her throat as he fumbled with his rifle. She froze.

"Katherine!" Pa shouted. "Get moving. I'll be on the porch."

His shout broke her inaction, and she shot forward. She stumbled on the hem of her dress as she ran toward the kitchen. "Ma, we gotta go."

Ma stuffed a pillow case with food. A loaf of bread fell through her trembling hands and tumbled to the floor. Katie's sisters huddled close with wide eyes and tears streaming down their faces.

"Ma, come on." Katie picked up three-year old Gracie, put an arm around her ma's shoulders and steered them toward the door. Her other three sisters followed close behind.

Gracie squirmed, fighting to get down.

"Beckie. I need Beckie." Gracie howled.

"There's no time," Ma said.

Katie thrust Gracie into her ma's arms. "She carts that doll around constantly. If I don't find it, she'll keep screaming and that could be dangerous."

Katie placed her hands on both sides of Gracie's small round face and leaned in. "I'll get your doll if you promise to obey Ma and do everything she says. Understand?"

Gracie whimpered. Her thumb went into her mouth.

"Ma, take the girls, I'll find the doll."

Katie raced from room to room. Bile rose in her throat and she swallowed hard against fear. *Where is that doll? God if you're up there, please ...*

No sooner had she voiced that prayer than she spotted the arm of the doll poking out from underneath her sister's small bed. She swooped it up.

The smoke in the distance had increased and billowed into a thick black cloud. Katie picked up her skirt and ran. The Yankees were closing in.

She headed for the hedge that lined a small section of the dusty drive. The boxwoods, her mother's priced token of her childhood in Richmond, would serve them well today. A thick blackberry bramble sprawled directly behind preventing any rider from coming up from the rear.

Her Ma and sisters huddled in their makeshift shelter in the ground. Five sets of frightened eyes looked up at Katie as she approached.

She tossed the doll to Gracie and nodded to her ma. "I'm not leaving Pa alone," she said, as she kneeled down and grasped the wood cover beside her.

"What about you?" fourteen-year-old Amelia cried out, her dark eyes saucer wide and brimming with tears.

"I'll join you as soon as I can."

"But, Ma ... stop her." Amelia protested.

Ma looked away. Her silence spoke volumes.

The leaf and twig covered board wobbled in Katie's hands as she pulled the cover into place. A quick glance back assured their hideaway looked like the surrounding area and the pipe buried for an air supply was carefully hidden in the brambles.

She moved further down the hedge away from the hiding spot and settled into the perfect ambush site. Laying low with her Springfield rifle held in one shaky hand, she nestled the ammunition close to her side. She felt for a small six-shot revolver pocketed in her dress, the one she'd removed from a dead Yankee earlier that year. The cold from the metal bit into her fingers as she pulled the gun free, but the steel was not as cold as her heart. Those Yankees had killed her two brothers. A surge of hatred flared.

Her heart pounded so loud she feared it was audible. With a deep breath slowly in and out, she worked to calm the thumping. The revolver lay loaded and ready as a backup. Katie fit the rifle onto her shoulder and shifted to find comfort on the uneven ground.

Her teeth clenched tight as her mind darted in and out of the past few years. The fear of mean-spirited soldiers and deserters roaming the valley had kept her tense and alert. She stayed close to home and kept her gun at her side when tending the animals. Her pa had warned the war would get uglier before it was over. He was right.

Their beautiful valley had been hit hard with battle after battle, and the Yankees repeatedly confiscated whatever they wanted. But this was different. Homes had previously been spared but not today.

Sheridan's troops were systematically eliminating the Shenandoah Valley as a source of grain and livestock for General Lee's army—one field and one house at a time. The neighbor's place, devoured by flames, now looked like a beast from hell had feasted.

Her vision blurred, and she brushed away tears with an angry swipe.

She tensed as she spied movement on the road. Her adrenaline spiked as she peered through the sight on her gun. A Yankee. The soldier boldly turned into the drive. Hatred washed hot, and then she froze. The young officer reminded her of her twin brothers—the same wispy hair, angular cheek bones, and deep-set eyes. The urge to rise up from her hiding spot lifted her torso until the blue of his uniform caught her eye. She sank back shaking, until hate once again gave her courage.

A swarm of soldiers followed the young officer to the front porch.

"State your business," Pa said. The Enfield he held loosely at his side looked more like a toy than a weapon. They immediately trained their muskets upon him. Still mounted on his horse, the officer spoke. "Surrender your gun, and we'll spare your life."

A belligerent soldier stormed the few steps and knocked the rifle out of Pa's hand and laughed into his face. "Come on, old man, got any fight left in you? 'Cause I'm itching for some action."

A flush of heat washed over Katie as she set her sight on the pig-headed soldier. Her finger itched to pull the trigger.

"Take whatever you want. Just please don't burn the house."

The officer hesitated. "Sorry, old man, but an order is an order. You'd better get your family out of the cellar."

"Hope you got a pretty one for me," another said. He licked his lips slowly with his long snake-like tongue. Even from the distance, Katie saw the lust smoldering in his evil eyes. She knew only too well what that look meant. She clamped her lips tight to still the scream of rage clawing at her throat.

Pa shook his head in confusion. "What did you say?"

A group of them laughed. "This crazy old buzzard's gone mad."

"Can't understand simple instructions," another scoffed.

Katie wanted to blast them off the porch. How dare they make fun of her pa when one of their Yankee shells was what destroyed most of his hearing. Turmoil roiled in her stomach and she fought the nausea down.

"Leave him be," the officer snapped. "When we start burning, he'll understand."

He barked out a few short orders, and the soldiers jumped into action, scurrying about like dungeon rats. He dismounted and went into the house with a few of his men.

Pa collapsed into the chair on the porch. His head fell into his hands.

They piled straw around the barn and drove Bessie, their milk cow, and old Sam, the mule, inside. The doors were shut, and their torches lit. Katie watched in surreal horror as the flames danced into action. She lowered her gun and shoved her fist into her mouth. She bit down hard to stifle a cry as the Sam's bellow reached her ears. Next, the small hay field they had worked so hard to plant was set ablaze. Their last few chickens were thrown into a sack and the little bit of cured meat left in the smokehouse taken.

Katie looked toward the house as the screen door slammed, and the officer and his soldiers carried out provisions. "Come on, old man, off the porch." The officer grabbed her pa's arm and lifted him from the chair. He propelled Pa down the steps and into the yard. The house was lit. They stayed just long enough to ensure the damage would be complete. The whole episode took less than fifteen minutes before they turned and rode out of sight. They had been amazingly swift and thorough.

Pa sank to his knees in the dust.

Katie stood on shaky legs and watched the flames lick their way into a towering inferno. The fury inside her heart equaled the intense heat. Black smoke filled her lungs as she ran to her pa. She crumpled beside him and fell into his arms.

Giant tears coursed down his soot-covered face. "Gone. Katherine, everything's gone. I couldn't—"

"Shhh, Pa," she said. "It's not your fault. There's nothing anyone could have done."

Chapter One

Katherine glanced up from her work and squinted into the afternoon sun. Dust billowed behind a lone rider. Was that really who she thought it was?

Five years since she had last laid eyes upon the man she would never forget. A tremor took to her hands.

What did he want?

She rued her untimely escape from the stifling heat indoors to sit on her aunt's front porch and stitch up a frayed hem on her day dress. The urge to dart back inside welled up.

No such luck, his eyes were pinned upon her. She forced herself to stay put but wove the needle into the fabric so she would not prick her finger. Thankfully, a slight breeze lifted the hair on the nape of her neck to cool the heated flush. She had to get over her embarrassment of what happened in the past at some time, and today was as good a day as any. With a show of confidence, she forced a jut to her chin. The only things moving were her hands that nervously threaded material through her fingers.

A tiny bead of sweat trickled down her spine as she reminded herself to smile and stay calm.

He swung from his horse and tethered the reins to the porch rail.

She took in a cleansing breath.

I'm a lady now—a civilized young woman, no longer traipsing unchaperoned about the countryside.

He climbed the steps confidently and made his way toward her. An irregular beat thumped inside her chest. He moved with strength and assurance despite a slight limp to one knee.

She willed the telltale blush of pink away, but with the burn in her cheeks, she knew she'd lost that battle.

He removed the hat from his head and nodded. A wavy, russet-brown curl fell across his brow. The flattened hair sprang to life as his fingers raked through the thickness. Peppered gray tinged his side burns.

"Good afternoon, Miss Williams." His eyes crinkled with friendly warmth.

She mumbled an obligatory hello and dropped her eyes to her lap hoping to look demure and hide the tell-tale heat.

"I'm here to have a conversation with your father and hope that my request will meet with your approval."

Her head snapped up.

He flashed an easy smile.

Katie's mouth went dry. *What did he mean, I hope my request will meet with your approval?* She chose not to speak.

He slipped his hat back on his head and took a step as if to leave, then stopped.

She gathered the strength to meet his gaze square on.

His smile softened. "We'll talk soon enough, Katherine." A light danced in the depths of his steel-gray eyes.

Apprehension nipped at the back of her neck. "What do you want to talk to my Pa about?" Katherine blurted out the words before her head had time to catch up to her mouth. "If it's about that incident before the war—"

"Goodness no, Katherine. I told you that would remain between us." A flicker of disappointment shot across his face.

She shifted in the rocking chair as his intense stare bore down.

Why was he looking at her like that?

She jumped to her feet and inadvertently brushed against him. A quick step back set the rocker swaying, and she stumbled forward as it hit her in back of the legs. He reached out to steady her and held on.

She breathed in a woodsy mixture of pine and leather. A tingling sensation worked its way up her arms, as the warmth from his large but gentle hands penetrated through the thin cotton sleeves of her well-worn dress.

Abruptly turning, she distanced herself. "If you'll excuse me, Mr. Richardson, I will fetch Pa. I mean—Father for you."

***

She was thankful the men settled on the front porch away from her. Katie was glad to stay hidden in the background helping in the kitchen.

Ma fussed about as if the king had come for tea. She pulled out the best dishes, Aunt May's serving tray and good cutlery. Her constant prattle set Katie's nerves on edge.

"How embarrassing we don't have tea. That blasted war is not over, even when it's over. Her grumbles grew louder. "When will we be able to get decent supplies that don't cost an arm and a leg?"

"Katie," Ma said, "set the Sassafras to steep on the stove and, Amelia, fetch me a few springs of mint from the garden."

"May, do we have any of your tea biscuits left, or did the kids eat them all?"

Her Aunt May threw a gentle arm around Ma's shoulder and smiled. "Yes, there's plenty. Now take a deep breath, Doris."

Katie wished yet again she had that kind of relationship with her ma.

Aunt May gave a squeeze to Doris's shoulder and moved to the counter. She lifted the checkered cloth that covered the tea biscuits and placed the plate onto the tray. "Why don't you go sit with them, and I'll bring everything out when the tea is ready?"

"No, I won't meddle in men talk, but Jeb asked specifically that Katherine serve the tea.

Aunt May swung around. Her eyes widened when Ma gave a slight nod.

Something was up. Katherine wasn't sure what.

"Katherine, go tidy yourself up and fix your bun, you look unkempt."

"But, Ma, when have you ever cared what I look like—"

"For heaven's sakes, Katherine, is there ever a moment when you do as I say and don't argue with me?" She threw up her hands. "Go."

Aunt May stood behind her ma and shook her head, motioning to Katherine to not engage. Katie huffed out a deep breath.

"And change out of that old work dress. Put on your Sunday—"

Katherine spun around. "Mr. Richardson has already seen me out on the porch when he arrived, and if my dress was good enough then, its good enough now." She slipped into the bedroom before Ma could say another word.

When she reentered the kitchen, both Ma and Aunt May stood side-by-side at the sink snapping off the ends of fresh beans from the garden. Their chatter filled the room.

"We can't live here much longer. We've imposed upon your family enough. This house barely squeezed in the four of you without adding the seven of us, and now with another young'un on the way—"

"God will provide, Doris. Maybe, just maybe, salvation sits on our front porch as we speak."

"And just what does that mean?" Katie asked.

They jumped apart and whirled around.

Aunt May recovered quickly. She masked the odd light of hope in her eyes. "Oh, Katie girl, you scared us sneaking up like that." Her laughter filled the room. "You always did have the stealth of an Indian brave." She motioned toward the table. "The tray is ready to go. Would you be a dear and take that out?"

Katie frowned but did their bidding. She swung open the screen with a tad too much frustration. The door swung wide and crashed against the house before slamming shut.

Good one—so much for making myself invisible.

Both Pa and Mr. Richardson stopped talking. Katie felt their eyes upon her though she refused to look up. She set the tray gingerly on the small table between them with a quick escape in mind.

Mr. Richardson caught and held her gaze. "Thank you, Katherine." A row of straight white teeth widened into a full smile as he boldly captured her attention.

Propriety demanded she answer. "You are mo-most welcome, Mr. Richardson." She forced a slight upward curve to her lips and hated the fact she stammered.

"Can you pour us each a cup, Katie girl?" Pa asked.

Her hands trembled as she lifted the pot, and she spilled a bit of the first pour onto the saucer. She gave that one to Pa hoping Mr. Richardson had not noticed. One sideward glance told her his eyes were still pinned on her. Determination held her steady as she poured and handed the second cup. Their hands brushed against each other, his rough, hers soft. She pulled away as if she had touched hot coals and beelined for the door.

"Katherine, come sit with us for a few minutes," Pa said.

She kept walking. "I have to help Ma with supper preparations. You know how she is when I shirk my work." She disappeared inside before he could protest.

· · · · · · · ■ · · · ·

The safety of the kitchen never felt so good. She blew out a deep breath as the door slammed on its hinges behind her. There was something about Mr. Richardson's familiarity that unnerved her. Not to mention the breadth of his wide shoulders over a thick, barrel chest. He was tall. And big. Too big.

Ma and Aunt May were huddled together in the far corner of the kitchen as close as an apple to its skin. They stopped their chatter as she reappeared. Aunt May moved toward her.

"I think you have an admirer, Katherine," Aunt May teased, with a twinkle in her eyes.

Katie's mouth dropped open and her eyes widened. "You can't be serious. He's almost as old as Pa."

"Don't look so surprised, girl," Ma said. "Why with your comely looks, what man wouldn't be interested?"

The all too familiar disapproving tone and set of her ma's chin told Katie she was in for a fight.

"Ma," she pleaded. "This is ludicrous. I'm too young for him. What about Widow Laurie up the road? Why, she would jump at the chance of marriage with her brood of children and no husband to run the farm."

Ma's lips formed a tight ashen line and her eyes narrowed into a glare. She moved in close, her voice hushed but stern. "You'd do well to remember that is a very influential man sitting on our humble porch. I will not have you embarrassing us with your haughty ways. All I know at this point is the conversation out there concerns you, and you will show nothing but respect. Do you hear me?" She clenched her teeth together and wagged her finger so close to Katie's face she could feel the fan of a breeze.

Ma's countenance held no room for argument.

***

Katie would rather run down the streets of Lacy Springs naked than marry old man Richardson. She couldn't believe her Pa. Was he out of his mind? Could another twist of fate far crueler than what had already happened be her lot in life?

"Oh, so that's why he showed up out of the blue last week all friendly and sure of himself. I wondered what brought the high and mighty Mr. Richardson to our humble door." She intentionally flashed her pa a stormy scowl. "Apparently, I was the bait."

He dropped his eyes to the floor.

Made in the USA
Middletown, DE
22 April 2019